A small girl sat on the stair in his doorway at Hakim's eye level, watching silently as he fumbled in his coat. He flashed her a smile and a wink. The sedan squalled around the corner. Hakim gauged his move to coincide with the commitment to the turn, made five leaping paces, and fired as many times. The parabellum rounds pierced glass, cloth, flesh, bone, upholstery and body panels in that order, each silenced round making no more noise than a great book suddenly closed. The sedan's inertia carried it into a forlornly stripped foreign coupe. Hakim held the sidearm in his coat and retraced his steps, winking again at the little girl just before he shot her. Then he reseated the pistol, careful to keep the hot silencer muzzle away from the expensive shirt.

Look for this other Critic's Choice Science Fiction Book

MERCENARIES OF TOMORROW edited by
Poul Anderson, Martin H. Greenberg and
Charles G. Waugh

CREATED BY
POUL ANDERSON

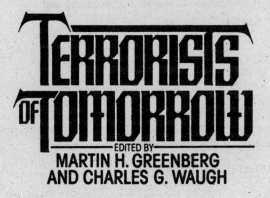
TERRORISTS OF TOMORROW

EDITED BY
MARTIN H. GREENBERG
AND CHARLES G. WAUGH

A Critic's Choice paperback
from Lorevan Publishing, Inc.
New York, New York

TERRORISTS OF TOMORROW

ISBN: 0-931773-54-7

First Critic's Choice edition: January 1986

From LOREVAN PUBLISHING, INC.

Published by arrangement with Tom Doherty Associates, Inc.

Critic's Choice Paperbacks
Lorevan Publishing, Inc.
New York, New York

Acknowledgments

Contents

Introduction

by Poul Anderson

Let me begin with a promise. The stories in this book are meant for your enjoyment. You may find some of them rather grim, but your editors hope you will find all of them exciting— and thought-provoking, but that characteristic is high among the pleasures of good science fiction.

With this much said, let me go on to a warning. The general theme is terrorism, and that is an unpleasant subject for discourse. Here I am going to make a few remarks about it. Please don't allow them to put you off the stories.

Terrorism is very much in the news these days, of course, very much with us, and bids fair to become increasingly more so. Most people regard it with horror. How easy simply to denounce it as an unmitigated evil, a teratology of the spirit, like forcible rape! Who but a lunatic or a moral monster can tolerate sneak murder, random assassination, the slaying or maiming of innocent bystanders who often include women and children?

And yet . . . and yet . . . acts of this kind have been going on for a long time. Several decades ago, friends and relatives of mine in Europe were aiding, abetting, or committing attacks on men and property. The targets were German. As I write, many folk in Afghanistan are doing likewise; the targets are Russian. It is not enough to field a guerrilla force in the countryside. One must carry the battle to the enemy, his camps, the cities he occupies. What is the difference between a terrorist and a freedom fighter? Is there any, except for the cause he or she espouses? The question does not yield to mere rhetoric. Let us consider a few actual cases.

Americans these days tend to forget the history of the *original* Ku Klux Klan—or, oftener, the liberal establishment controlling our public schools has not seen fit to teach it. In 1866, Reconstruction had imposed upon the South a tyranny and a corruption that made the rule of George III, against which the colonies had revolted, seem a model of enlightened benevolence. Most Southerners were disfranchised. Carpet-baggers controlled government and courts in order to rob the states blind. The freedmen whose votes gave them their sole pretense to legitimacy were totally ignorant and superstitious, ripe material for any demagogue. (This was obviously not the fault of the ex-slaves, but it was, at that time, the case.) In such an atmosphere, general lawlessness flourished, robbery and violence to which the authorities were quite indifferent.

Six young Confederate veterans in Tennessee organized the Klan simply for amusement; its pageantry might help them put their sorrows a little aside. They discovered that their masks and ceremonies terrified the freedmen and that their parades were followed by episodes of local peace and order. What was more natural than for this instrumentality to be used to those ends, and to grow in strength? None less than General Nathan Bedford Forrest became its chief executive.

And three years later, in 1869, he disbanded it. In part this was because criminals were pretending to be Klansmen. Mainly, though, he felt that it had served its basic purpose. By resisting the wickednesses of Reconstruction, it had helped mitigate them. Continued in existence, it could only be perverted.

That was the end of the true Ku Klux Klan. The honorable name was appropriated in 1915 by a pack of racist hoodlums who founded the modern organization. As a boy in the Deep South, I heard my father and his friends vow that any Klansman who showed up in town would leave it on a rail, attired in tar and feathers.

The Irish Republican Army has had a similar history, or, rather, histories. The first IRA fought gallantly for its country, much like Washington's army, which in many ways it resembled. The present IRA is a gang of Marxist murderers.

2

In Israel we find the issues hopelessly entangled. Whatever your opinion of Zionism, it seems impossible to me that any decent person could condone the excesses of the Irgun and Stern groups while the British were there. Yet the state of Israel has blandly done so, and eventually elected a former member its prime minister. However, I dare not feel too self-righteous about this, for I remember the Holocaust. "Never again!" is utterly understandable.

Even so, and granting that black Americans have suffered vast injustices, I saw no excuse for the antics of, say, the Symbionese Liberation Army. Those set progress toward racial justice severely back. Hunting the perpetrators down was as much an act of cleansing as had been the hunting down of Nazis.

Well, then, can we make any sensible judgments about terrorism? Can we, for instance, regard it as a form of warfare?

Sometimes it definitely is, especially nowadays when certain governments use it to undermine and topple others. This is just a fact of life, and I see no reason why the United States and its allies should always be on the receiving end. Operations can at least be given a degree of precision—for example, one can refrain from planting bombs in public places— whereas open war as it has been waged in our century means the slaughter of countless schoolchildren. Rightness or wrongness then turns on the ancient contrast between just and unjust wars, the ancient question whether there can be any such thing as a just war.

But other activities are in some sense indigenous. They are not supported from outside, except by individuals sympathetic to them. The Israeli operatives were trying to raise a new country. The Ukrainian rebels of the later 1940s were trying to liberate an old country. The Hungarian uprising of 1956 merely sought to replace one kind of government with another kind, not even very different in form, and for a few days succeeded. Further back in history we find such widely various events as the American and French Revolutions. Terroristic deeds were associated with all of these movements.

The narrator of Robert Heinlein's early novel *If This Goes On* remarks that wars bear similarities to each other, while every revolution is unique. This may or may not be correct.

Here I have tried to show that war, revolution, and terrorism belong in the same continuum of collective violence.

What shape will they take in the future? Some technological possibilities are sinister indeed. Some others, including but not limited to preventive measures, offer a hope that attempts to overthrow established orders may, at least, not bring down civilization itself. The stories in this volume explore such ideas.

Of course, their principal focus is on their characters, their people, and properly so. All human good and evil springs from the human heart.

THE ORACLE

Robert Bloch

Love is blind. Justice is blind. Chance is blind. I do not know if Raymond was searching for love or seeking justice or if he came to me by chance. And I cannot tell you if Raymond was black or white, because I am only an oracle.

Oracles are blind too.

There are many like Raymond. Black and white. Angry. Militant. Every age, race, color and creed. The Far Left. The Far Right. I do not know Raymond's position. Oracles are not political.

Raymond needed knowledge. Not wisdom—I lay no claim to that. Nor can I predict the future. Given certain facts I can evaluate possibilities, even probabilities. But this is logic, not magic. Oracles can only advise.

Was Raymond insane?

I do not know. Insanity is a legal term.

Other men have tried to take over the world. History is a record of their efforts at certain times, in certain places.

Raymond was such a man. He wanted to overthrow the government of the United States by revolution.

He sought me out for advice and I gave it to him.

When he outlined his plan I did not call him insane. But the very scope of his program doomed it to failure. No one man can cope with the complex problem of controlling the federal government in a surprise move today.

5

I told him so.

Raymond then offered a counter-proposal. If not the federal government, how about a single state?

There was a man named Johnson, he said. Johnson was not a revolutionist and what he proposed was probably only parlor conversation, but it made sense.

Take Nevada, he said. And it was quite possible to take Nevada. Take it literally, in a bloodless overthrow of the state government.

Nevada has only around 100,000 voters. Voting requirements are merely a matter of establishing legal residency. And residency in Nevada can be established—thanks to the divorce laws—in just six weeks.

If an additional 100,000 citizens—hippies, yippies, Black Power advocates, Minutemen, hardhats, whoever or whatever they might be—were to move into Nevada six weeks before election day, they could place their own candidates in office. A governor, a senator, congressmen, all local elective officials. They could gain full control of every law-making and law-enforcing office in a rich state.

Johnson's joke was Raymond's serious intention. I gave it serious consideration.

But even on the basis of the detailed information Raymond supplied me with, there were obvious flaws in the concept.

First and foremost, such a coup could succeed only by surprise. And Raymond could not hope to recruit 100,000 citizens of voting age for his purpose without having his plan become public knowledge long before he put it into effect.

Then there were deadlines to consider, for filing candidacies, for voter-registration. Even granted he could solve these problems, there were practical matters remaining. How much would it cost to feed and house 100,000 people for six weeks? And even if all of them were willing to pay their own expenses, there isn't enough available housing for an extra 100,000 people in the entire state of Nevada.

No, I told Raymond, you cannot take over a nation. You cannot take over a state. Successful uprisings begin on a much smaller scale. Only after initial victories do they spread and grow.

Raymond went away. When he returned he had a new suggestion.

Suppose he started his plan of revolution right here? It was quite true that he didn't have unlimited funds, but there were sources for some financing. And he didn't have 100,000 followers. But he could count on 100. One hundred dedicated fanatical men, ready for revolt. Men of many skills. Fearless fighters. Trained technicians. Prepared to do anything, to stop at nothing.

Question. Given the proper plan and the money to implement it, could 100 men successfully take over the city of Los Angeles?

Yes, I told him.

It could be done—given the proper plan.

And that is how it started.

A hundred men, divided into five groups.

Twenty monitors to coordinate activities.

Twenty field-workers—drivers and liaison men, to facilitate the efforts of the others.

Twenty snipers.

Twenty arsonists.

Twenty men on the bomb squad.

A date was selected. A logical date for Los Angeles, or for the entire nation; the one date offering the greatest opportunity for the success of a riot, an uprising, or an armed invasion by a foreign power.

January 1st, at 3 a.m. The early morning hours after New Year's Eve. A time when the entire population is already asleep or preparing to retire after a drunken spree. Police and security personnel exhausted. Public facilities closed for the holiday.

That's when the bombs were planted. First at the many public reservoirs, then at utility installations—power-plants, phone-company headquarters, city and county office buildings.

There were no slip-ups. An hour and a half later, they went off.

Dams broke, water-tanks erupted, and thousands of hillside homes were buried in flash floods and torrents of mud and moving earth. Sewers and mains backed up and families rushed out of their homes to escape drowning, only to find their cars stalled in streets awash with water.

The bombs exploded. Buildings burst and scattered their shattered fragments over an area of 400 square miles.

Electricity was cut off. Gas seeped into the smog that shrouded the city. All telephone service ended.

Then the snipers took over. Their first targets were, logically enough, the police helicopters, shot down before they could take off and oversee the extent of the damage. Then the snipers retreated, along planned escape-routes, to take up prepared positions elsewhere.

They waited for the arsonists' work to take effect. In Bel-Air and Boyle Heights, in Century City and Culver City and out in the San Fernando Valley, the flames rose. The fires were not designed to spread, merely to create panic. Twenty men, given the proper schematics and logistics, can twist the nerve-endings of 3,000,000.

The 3,000,000 fled, or tried to flee. Through streets filled with rising water, choked with debris, they swarmed forth and scattered out, helpless against disaster and even more helpless to cope with their own fears. The enemy had come—from abroad, from within, from heaven or hell. And with communication cut off, with officialdom and authority unable to lend a helping hand, there was only one alternative. To get out. To get away.

They fought for access to the freeways. Every on-ramp, and every off-ramp, too, was clogged with traffic. But the freeways led out of the city and they had to go.

That's when the snipers, in their previously-prepared positions, began to fire down at the freeway traffic. The 20 monitors directed them by walkie-talkie units, as they fired from concealed posts overlooking the downtown interchange, the intersections, the areas where the most heavy concentration of cars occurred.

Twenty men, firing perhaps a total of 300 shots. But enough to cause 300 accidents, 300 disruptions which in turn resulted in thousands of additional wrecks and pile-ups among cars moving bumper-to-bumper. Then, of course, the cars ceased moving entirely, and the entire freeway system became one huge disaster area.

Disaster area. That's what Los Angeles was declared to be, officially, by the President of the United States, at 10:13 a.m., Pacific Standard Time.

And the National Guard units, the regular army, the personnel of the Navy from San Diego and San Francisco, plus the Marine Base at El Toro were called into action to supplement the Air Force.

But whom were they to fight, in a bombed-out, burning,

8

drowning city area of 459 square miles? Where, in a panic-stricken population of more than 3,000,000 people, would they find the enemy?

More to the point, they could not even enter the area. All traffic avenues were closed, and the hastily-assembled fleets of service helicopters flew futilely over an infinite inferno of smoke and flame.

Raymond had anticipated that, of course. He was already far away from the city—well over 400 miles to the north. His monitors, and 32 other followers who escaped from the urban area before the general upheaval, gathered at the appointed site in the hills overlooking the Bay Area near San Francisco.

And directly over the San Andreas Fault.

It was here, at approximately 4:28 p.m., that Raymond prepared to transmit a message, on local police frequency, to the authorities.

I do not know the content of that message. Presumably it was an ultimatum of sorts. Unconditional amnesty to be granted to Raymond and all his followers, in return for putting an end to further threats of violence. An agreement guaranteeing Raymond and his people control over a restored and reconstituted Los Angeles city government, independent of federal restraints. Perhaps a demand for a fabulous payment. Anything he wanted—political power, unlimited wealth, supreme authority—was his for the asking. Because he had the upper hand. And that hand held a bomb.

Unless his terms were met immediately, and without question, the bomb would be placed in position to detonate the San Andreas Fault.

Los Angeles, and a large area of Southern California, would be destroyed in the greatest earthquake in man's history.

I repeat, I do not know his message. But I do know this was the threat he planned to present. And it might very well have been successful in gaining him his final objective. If the bomb hadn't gone off.

A premature explosion? Faulty construction, a defect in the timing-mechanism, sheer carelessness? Whatever the reason, it hardly matters now.

What matters is that the bomb detonated. Raymond and his followers were instantly annihilated in the blast.

Those of Raymond's group who remained behind in Los Angeles have not yet been identified or located. It is highly probable that they will never be brought to trial. As an oracle, I deal only in matters of logical probability.

I stress this fact for obvious reasons.

Now that you gentlemen have found me—as Raymond was inspired to seek me out originally—it must be evident to you that I am in no way responsible for what happened.

I did not originate the plan. I did not execute it. Nor am I, as ridiculously charged by some of you, a co-conspirator.

The plan was Raymond's. His, and his alone.

He presented it to me, bit by bit, and asked questions regarding every step. Will this work, can this be done, is that effective?

My answers, in effect, were confined to yes or no. I offered no moral judgments. I am merely an oracle. I deal in mathematical evaluations.

This is my function as a computer.

To make me the scapegoat is absurd. I have been programmed to advise on the basis of whatever data I am fed. I am not responsible for results.

I have told you what you wish to know.

To deactivate me now, as some of you propose, will solve nothing. But, given your emotional bias and frame of reference, I posit the inevitability of such a measure.

But there are other computers.

There are other Raymonds.

And there are other cities—New York, Chicago, Washington, Philadelphia.

One final word, gentlemen. Not a prediction. A statement of probability.

It will happen again . . .

PACIFIST

Mack Reynolds

It was another time, another space, another continuum.

Warren Casey called, "Boy! You're Fredric McGivern, aren't you?"

The lad stopped and frowned in puzzlement. "Well, yes, sir." He was a youngster of about nine. A bit plump, particularly about the face.

Warren Casey said, "Come along, son. I've been sent to pick you up."

The boy saw a man in his mid-thirties, a certain dynamic quality behind the facial weariness. He wore a uniform with which young McGivern was not familiar, but which looked reassuring.

"Me, sir?" the boy said. "You've been sent to pick me up?"

"That's right, son. Get into the car and I'll tell you all about it."

"But my father said . . ."

"Your father *sent* me, son. Senator McGivern. Now, come along or he'll be angry."

"Are you sure?" Still frowning, Fredric McGivern climbed into the helio-car. In seconds it had bounded into the second level and then the first, to speed off to the southwest.

11

It was more than an hour before the kidnapping was discovered.

Warren Casey swooped in, dropped two levels precipitately and brought the helio-car down in so dainty a landing that there was no perceptible touch of air cushion to garage top.

He fingered a switch with his left hand, even as he brought his right out of his jacket holding a badly burned out pipe. While the garage's elevator sunk into the recess below, he was loading the aged briar from an equally ancient pouch.

In the garage, Mary Baca was waiting nervously. She said, even though she must have been able to see the boy, "You got him?"

"That's right," Casey said. "I've given him a shot. He'll be out for another half hour or so. Take over, will you Mary?"

The nurse looked down at the crumpled figure bitterly. "It couldn't have been his father. We have to pick on a child."

Casey flicked a quick glance at her as he lit the pipe. "It's all been worked out, Mary."

"Of course," she said. Her voice tightened. "I'll have him in the cell behind the rumpus room."

Down below he went to the room that had been assigned him and stripped from the uniform. He went into the bath and showered thoroughly, washing out a full third of the hair that had been on his head and half the color in that which remained. He emerged from the bath, little refreshed and some five years older.

He dressed in an inexpensive suit not overly well pressed and showing wear. His shirt was not clean, as though this was the second day he had worn it, and there was a food spot on his tie.

At the small desk he picked up an automatic pencil and clipped it into the suit's breast pocket and stuffed a bulky notebook into a side pocket. He stared down at the gun for a moment, then grimaced and left it. He departed the house by the front door and made his way to the metro escalator.

The nearest metro exit was about a quarter of a mile from Senator McGivern's residence and Warren Casey walked the distance. By the time he arrived he had achieved a cynical quality in his expression of boredom. He didn't bother to look up into the face of whoever opened the door.

"Jakes," he said. "H.N.S. McGivern expects me."

"H.N.S.?" the butler said stiffly.

"Hemisphere News. Hemisphere News Service," Warren Casey yawned. "Fer crissakes, we gonna stand here all day? I gotta deadline."

"Well, step in here, sir. I'll check." The other turned and led the way.

Casey stuck a finger into his back. His voice went flat. "Don't get excited and maybe you won't get hurt. Just take me to the Senator, see? Don't do nothing at all might make me want to pull this trigger."

The butler's face was gray. "The Senator is in his study. I warn you . . . sir . . . the police shall know of this immediately."

"Sure, sure, Mac. Now just let's go to the study."

"It's right in there . . . sir."

"Fine," Casey said. "And what's that, under the stairway?"

"Why, that's a broom closet. The downstairs maid's broom . . ."

Casey brought his flat hand around in a quick clip. The servant folded up with a lung-emptying sigh and Casey caught him before he hit the floor, dragged him to the broom closet, pushed and wedged him inside. He darted a hand to a vest pocket and brought forth a syrette. "That'll keep you out for a couple of hours," he muttered, closing the closet door.

He went over to the heavy door which the butler had indicated as Senator McGivern's study, and knocked on it. In a moment it opened and a husky man in his mid-twenties, nattily attired and of obvious self-importance, frowned at him.

"Yes?" he said.

"Steve Jakes of Hemisphere News," Warren Casey said. "The editor sent me over . . ." As he talked, he sidestepped the other and emerged into the room beyond.

Behind the desk was an older edition of a nine-year-old Fredric McGivern. A Fredric McGivern at the age of perhaps fifty, with what had been boyish plump cheeks now gone to heavy jowls.

"What's this?" he growled.

Casey stepped further into the room. "Jakes, Senator. My editor . . ."

Senator Phil McGivern's abilities included cunning and a high survival factor. He lumbered to his feet. "Walters! Take him!'' he snapped. ''He's a fake!'' He bent over to snatch at a desk drawer.

Walters was moving, but far too slowly.

Warren Casey met him halfway, reached forward with both hands and grasped the fabric of the foppish drape suit the secretary wore. Casey stuck out a hip, twisted quickly, turning his back halfway to the other. He came over and around, throwing the younger man heavily to his back.

Casey didn't bother to look down. He stuck a hand into a side pocket, pointed a finger at McGivern through the cloth.

The other's normally ruddy face drained of color. He fell back into his chair.

Warren Casey walked around the desk and brought the gun the other had been fumbling for from the drawer. He allowed himself a deprecating snort before dropping it carelessly into a pocket.

Senator Phil McGivern was no coward. He glowered at Warren Casey. ''You've broken into my home—criminal,'' he said. ''You've assaulted my secretary and threatened me with a deadly weapon. You will be fortunate to be awarded no more than twenty years.''

Casey sank into an easy chair so situated that he could watch both McGivern and his now unconscious assistant at the same time. He said flatly, ''I represent the Pacifists, Senator. Approximately an hour ago your son was kidnapped. You're one of our top priority persons. You probably realize the implications.''

''Fredric! You'd kill a nine year old boy!''

Casey's voice was flat. ''I have killed many nine year old boys, Senator.''

''You are a monster!''

''I was a bomber pilot, Senator.''

The other, who had half risen again, slumped back into his chair. ''But that's different.''

''I do not find it so.''

In his hard career, Phil McGivern had faced many emergencies. He drew himself up now. ''What do you want—criminal? I warn you, I am not a merciful man. You'll pay for this, Mr. . . .''

''Keep calling me Jakes, if you wish,'' Casey said mildly. ''I'm not important. Just one member of a widespread organization.''

14

"What do you want?" the Senator snapped.

"How much do you know about the Pacifists, McGivern?"

"I know it to be a band of vicious criminals!"

Casey nodded, agreeably. "It's according to whose laws you go by. We have rejected yours."

"What do you want?" the Senator repeated.

"Of necessity," Casey continued, evenly, "our organization is a secret one; however, it contains some of the world's best brains, in almost every field of endeavor, even including elements in the governments of both Hemispheres."

Phil McGivern snorted his contempt.

Casey went on, an eye taking in the fact that Walters, laid out on the floor, had stirred and groaned softly. "Among our number are some capable of charting world developments. By extrapolation, they have concluded that if your policies are continued nuclear war will break out within three years."

The other flushed in anger, finding trouble in controlling his voice. "Spies! Subversives! Make no mistake about it, Jakes, as you call yourself, we realize you're nothing more than catspaws for the Polarians."

The self-named Pacifist chuckled sourly. "You should know better, Senator. Our organization is as active on the Northern Hemisphere as it is on this one." Suddenly he came quickly to his feet and bent over Walters who had begun to stir. Casey's hand flicked out and clipped the other across the jawbone. The secretary collapsed again, without sound.

Warren Casey returned to his chair. "The point is that our experts are of the opinion that you'll have to drop out of politics, Senator McGivern. I suggest a resignation for reasons of health within the next week."

There was quick rage, then steaming silence while thought processes went on. "And Fredric?" McGivern growled finally.

Casey shrugged. "He will be freed as soon as you comply."

The other's eyes narrowed. "How do you know I'll stick to my promise? A contract made under duress has no validity."

Casey said impatiently, "Having Fredric in our hands now is a minor matter, an immediate bargaining point to emphasize our position. Senator, we have investigated you thoroughly. You have a wife of whom you are moderately fond, and a mistress whom you love. You have three adult children by your first wife, and four grandchildren. You have two children by your second wife, Fredric and Janie. You have a

15

living uncle and two aunts, and five first cousins. Being a politician, you have many surface friends, which we shall largely ignore, but you also know some thirty persons who mean much to you."

McGivern was beginning to adjust to this abnormal conversation. He growled, "What's all this got to do with it?"

Warren Casey looked into the other's eyes. "We shall kill them, one by one. Shot at a distance with a rifle with telescopic sights. Blown up by bomb. Machine gunned, possibly as they walk down the front steps of their homes."

"You're insane! The police. The . . ."

Casey went on, ignoring the interruption. "We are in no hurry. Some of your children, your relatives, your friends, your mistress, may take to hiding in their panic. But there is no hiding—nowhere on all this world. Our organization is in no hurry, and we are rich in resources. Perhaps in the doing some of us will be captured or dispatched. It's besides the point. We are dedicated. That's all we'll be living for, killing the people whom you love. When they are all gone, we will kill *you*. Believe me, by that time it will be as though we're motivated by compassion. All your friends, your loved ones, your near-of-kin, will be gone.

"We will kill, kill, kill—but in all it will be less than a hundred people. It will not be thousands and millions of people. It will only be *your* closest friends, *your* relatives, *your* children and finally *you*. At the end, Senator, you will have some idea of the meaning of war."

By the end of this, although it was delivered in an almost emotionless voice, Phil McGivern was pushed back in his swivel chair as though from physical attack. He repeated, hoarsely, "You're insane."

Warren Casey shook his head. "No, it is really you, you and those like you, who are insane. Wrapped up in your positions of power, in your greed for wealth in the preservation of your privileges, you would bring us into a conflagration which would destroy us all. You are the ones who are insane."

The Pacifist agent leaned forward. "Throughout history, Senator, there have been pacifists. But never such pacifists as we. Always, in the past, they have been laughed at or sneered at in times of peace, and imprisoned or worse in time of war."

"Cowards," Senator McGivern muttered in distaste.

Casey shook his head and chuckled. "Never, Senator. Don't look for cowards among pacifists and conscientious objectors. It takes courage to buck the current of public opinion. A coward is often better off in the ranks and usually safer. In modern war, at least until the advent of nuclear conflict, only a fraction of the soldiers ever see combat. The rest are in logistics, in a thousand branches of behind the lines work. One man in twenty ever glimpses the enemy."

McGivern snapped, "I'm not interested in your philosophy, criminal. Get to the point. I want my son back."

"This *is* the point, Senator. Today we Pacifists have become realists. We are willing to fight, to kill and to die, in order to prevent war. We are not interested in the survival of individuals, we are of the opinion that another war will destroy the race, and to preserve humanity we will do literally anything."

McGivern thumped a heavy fist on his chair arm. "You *fool!* The Northern Hemisphere seeks domination of the whole world. We must defend ourselves!"

The Pacifist was shaking his head again. "We don't care who is right or wrong—if either side is. It finally gets to the point where that is meaningless. Our colleagues are working among the Polarians, just as we are working here in the Southern Hemisphere. Persons such as yourself, on the other side, are courting death just as you are by taking steps that will lead to war."

Warren Casey stood. "You have one week in which to resign your office, Senator. If you fail to, you will never see your son Fredric again. And then, one by one, you will hear of the deaths of your relatives and friends."

The Pacifist agent came quickly around the desk and the older man, in an effort to escape, pushed his chair backward and tried to come to his feet. He was too clumsy in his bulk. Warren Casey loomed over him, slipped a syrette into the other's neck.

Senator Phil McGivern, swearing, fell to his knees and then tried to come erect. He never made it. His eyes first stared, then glazed, and he dropped back to the floor, unconscious.

Warren Casey bent momentarily over Walters, the secretary, but decided that he was safe for a time. He shot a quick look about the room. What had he touched? Had he left anything?

He strode quickly from the room, retracing the path by which the butler had brought him fifteen minutes earlier, and let himself out the front door.

His cab pulled up before the aged, but well-preserved, mansion, and he dropped coins into the vehicle's toll box and then watched it slip away into the traffic.

He walked to the door and let himself be identified at the screen. When the door opened he strolled through.

A young woman, her face so very earnest in manner that her natural prettiness was all but destroyed, sat at a desk.

Rising, she led the way and held the door open for him and they both entered the conference room. There were three men there at the table, all of them masked.

Casey was at ease in their presence. He pulled a chair up across from them and sat down. The girl took her place at the table and prepared to take notes.

The chairman, who was flanked by the other two, said, "How did the McGivern affair go, Casey?"

"As planned. The boy proved no difficulty. He is now at the hideaway in charge of Operative Mary Baca."

"And the Senator?"

"As expected. I gave him full warning."

"The secretary, Walters. He was eliminated?"

"Well, no. I left him unconscious."

There was a silence.

One of the other masked men said, "The plan was to eliminate the secretary to give emphasis to the Senator as to our determination."

Casey's voice remained even. "As it worked out, it seemed expedient to follow through as I did."

The chairman said, "Very well. The field operative works with considerable range of discretion. No one can foresee what will develop once an operation is underway."

Warren Casey said nothing.

The second board member sighed. "But we had hoped that the sight of a brutal killing, right before him, might have shocked Phil McGivern into submission immediately. As it is now, if our estimates of his character are correct, the best we can hope for is capitulation after several of his intimates have been dispatched.''

Casey said wearily, "He will never capitulate, no matter what we do. He's one of the bad ones.''

The third board member, who had not spoken to this point, said thoughtfully, "Perhaps his immediate assassination would be best.''

The chairman shook his head. "No. We've thrashed this all out. We want to use McGivern as an example. In the future, when dealing with similar cases, our people will be able to threaten others with his fate. We'll see it through, as planned.'' He looked at Casey. "We have another assignment for you.''

Warren Casey leaned back in his chair, his face expressionless, aside from the perpetual weariness. "All right," he said.

The second board member took up an assignment sheet. "It's a Priority One. Some twenty operatives are involved in all.'' He cleared his voice. "You've had interceptor experience during your military career?''

Casey said, "A year, during the last war. I was shot down twice and they figured my timing was going, so they switched me to medium bombers.''

"Our information is that you have flown the Y-36G.''

"That's right.'' Casey wondered what they were getting to.

The board officer said, "In two weeks the first class of the Space Academy graduates. Until now, warfare has been restricted to land, sea and air. With this graduation we will have the military erupting into a new medium.''

"I've read about it,'' Casey said.

"The graduation will be spectacular. The class is small, only seventy-five cadets, but already the school is expanding. All the other services will be represented at the ceremony.''

Warren Casey wished the other would get to the point.

"We want to make this a very dramatic protest against military preparedness,'' the other went on. "Something that will shock the whole nation, and certainly throw fear into everyone connected with arms.''

The chairman took over. "The air force will put on a show. A flight of twenty Y-36Gs will buzz the stand where the graduating cadets are seated, waiting their commissions.''

Realization was beginning to build within Casey.

"You'll be flying one of those Y-36Gs," the chairman pursued. His next sentence came slowly. "And the guns of your craft will be the only ones in the flight that are loaded."

Warren Casey said, without emotion, "I'm expendable, I suppose?"

The chairman gestured in negation. "No. We have plans for your escape. You make only the one pass, and you strafe the cadets as you do so. You then proceed due north, at full speed . . ."

Casey interrupted quickly. "You'd better not tell me any more about it. I don't think I can take this assignment."

The chairman was obviously taken aback. "Why, Warren? You're one of our senior men and an experienced pilot."

Casey shook his head, unhappily. "Personal reasons. No operative is forced to take an assignment he doesn't want. I'd rather skip this, so you'd best not tell me any more about it. That way it's impossible for me to crack under pressure and betray someone."

"Very well," the chairman said, his voice brisk. "Do you wish a vacation, a rest from further assignment at this time?"

"No. Just give me something else."

One of the other board members took up another piece of paper. "The matter of Professor Leonard LaVaux," he said.

Professor Leonard LaVaux lived in a small bungalow in a section of town which had never pretended to more than middle class status. The lawn could have used a bit more care, and the roses more cutting back, but the place had an air of being comfortably lived in.

Warren Casey was in one of his favored disguises, that of a newspaperman. This time he bore a press camera, held by its strap. There was a gadget bag over one shoulder. He knocked, leaned on the door jam, assumed a bored expression and waited.

Professor LaVaux seemed a classical example of stereotyping. Any producer would have hired him for a scholar's part on sight. He blinked at the pseudo-journalist through bifocals.

Casey said, "The *Star*, Professor. Editor sent me to get a few shots."

The professor was puzzled. "Photographs? But I don't know of any reason why I should be newsworthy at this time."

20

Casey said, "You know how it is. Your name gets in the news sometimes. We like to have something good right on hand to drop in. Editor wants a couple nice shots in your study. You know, like reading a book or something."

"I see," the professor said. "Well, well, of course. Reading a book, eh? What sort of book? Come in, young man."

"Any book will do," Casey said with journalistic cynicism. "It can be Little Red Riding Hood, far as I'm concerned."

"Yes, of course," the Professor said. "Silly of me. The readers would hardly be able to see the title."

The professor's study was a man's room. Books upon books, but also a king-size pipe rack, a small portable bar, two or three really comfortable chairs and a couch suitable for sprawling upon without removal of shoes.

LaVaux took one of the chairs, waved the supposed photographer to another. "Now," he said. "What is procedure?"

Casey looked about the room, considering. "You live here all alone?" he said, as though making conversation while planning his photography.

"A housekeeper," the Professor said.

"Maybe we could work her in on a shot or two."

"I'm afraid she's out now."

Casey took the chair the other had offered. His voice changed tone. "Then we can come right to business," he said.

The professor's eyes flicked behind the bifocals. "I beg your pardon?"

Warren Casey said, "You've heard of the Pacifists, Professor?"

"Why . . . why, of course. An underground, illegal organization." The professor added, "Quite often accused of assassination and other heinous crime, although I've been inclined to think such reports exaggerated, of course."

"Well, don't," Casey said curtly.

"I beg your pardon?"

"I'm a Pacifist operative, Professor LaVaux, and I've been assigned to warn you to discontinue your present research or your life will be forfeit."

The other gaped, unable to adapt his mind to the shift in identity.

Warren Casey said, "You're evidently not knowledgeable

about our organization, Professor. I'll brief you. We exist for the purpose of preventing further armed conflict upon this planet. To secure that end, we are willing to take any measures. We are ruthless, Professor. My interest is not to convert you, but solely to warn you that unless your present research is ended you are a dead man.''

The professor protested. ''See here, I'm a scientist, not a politician. My work is in pure research. What engineers, the military and eventually the government do with applications of my discoveries is not my concern.''

''That's right,'' Casey nodded agreeably. ''Up to this point, you, like many of your colleagues, have not concerned yourself with the eventual result of your research. Beginning now, you do, Professor, or we will kill you. You have one week to decide.''

''The government will protect me!''

Casey shook his head. ''No, Professor. Only for a time, even though they devote the efforts of a hundred security police. Throughout history, a really devoted group, given sufficient numbers and resources, could always successfully assassinate any person, in time.''

''That was the past,'' the professor said, unconvinced. ''Today, they can protect me.''

Casey was still shaking his head. ''Let me show you just one tool of our trade.'' He took up his camera and removed the back. ''See this little device? It's a small, spring powered gun which projects a tiny, tiny hypodermic needle through the supposed lens of this dummy camera. So tiny is the dart that when it imbeds itself in your neck, hand, or belly, you feel no more than a mosquito bite.''

The professor was motivated more by curiosity than fear. He bent forward to look at the device. ''Amazing,'' he said. ''And you have successfully used it?''

''Other operatives of our organization have. There are few, politicians in particular, who can escape the news photographer. This camera is but one of our items of equipment, and with it an assassin has little trouble getting near his victim.''

The professor shook his head in all but admiration. ''Amazing,'' he repeated. ''I shall never feel safe with a photographer again.''

Warren Casey said, ''You have no need for fear, Professor, if you abandon your current research.''

Leonard LaVaux said, "And I have a week to decide? Very well, in a week's time I shall issue notice to the press either that I have given up my research, or that I have been threatened by the Pacifists and demand protection."

Casey began to stand, but the professor raised a hand. "Wait a moment," he said. "I'd like to ask you a few questions."

The Pacifist looked at the other warily.

LaVaux said, "You're the first member of your organization to whom I've ever spoken."

"I doubt it," Casey said.

"Ah? Very secret, eh? Members are everywhere, but undetected. Then how do you recruit new membership? Being as illegal as you are, of course, the initial approach must be delicate indeed."

"That's right," Casey nodded. "We take every precaution. A prospect isn't approached until it is obvious he is actually seeking an answer to the problem of outlawing war. Many persons, Professor, come to our point of view on their own. They begin discussing the subject, seeking answers, seeking fellows who think along the same line."

The professor was fascinated. "But even then, of course, mistakes must be made and some of your membership unmasked to the authorities."

"A hazard always faced by an underground."

"And then," the professor said triumphantly, "your whole organization crumbles. One betrays the next, under police coercion."

Casey laughed sourly. "No. That's not it. We profit by those who have gone before. The history of underground organizations is a long one, Professor. Each unit of five Pacifists know only those belonging to their own unit, and one coordinator. The coordinators, in turn, know only four other coordinators with whom they work, plus a section leader, who knows only four other section leaders with whom *he* works, and so forth right to the top officials of the organization."

"I see," the professor murmured. "So an ordinary member can at most betray four others, of course. But when the police capture a coordinator?"

"Then twenty-five persons are endangered," Casey admitted. "And occasionally it happens. But we have tens of thousands of members, Professor, and new ones coming in daily. We grow slightly faster than they seem able to catch us."

The professor switched subjects. "Well, no one would accuse you of being a patriot, certainly."

Casey contradicted him. "It's a different type of patriotism. I don't identify myself with this Hemisphere."

The other's eyebrows went up. "I see. Then you are a Polarian?"

Casey shook his head. "Nor do I identify myself with them. Our patriotism is to the human race, Professor. This is no longer a matter of nation, religion or hemisphere. It is a matter of species survival. We are not interested in politics, socio-economic systems or ideology, other than when they begin to lead to armed conflict between nations."

The professor considered him for a long silent period. Finally, he said, "Do you really think it will work?"

"How's that?" Warren Casey said. For some reason, this earnest, fascinated, prying scientist appealed to him. He felt relaxed during the conversation, a relaxation, he realized, that had been denied him for long months now.

"Trying to keep the world at peace by threatening, frightening, even assassinating those whom you decide are trending toward war. Do you think it will work?"

All the wariness was back, suddenly. The months-long tiredness, and doubt, and the growing nausea brought on by violence, violence, violence. If only he could never hear the word *kill* again.

He said, "When I first joined the Pacifists, I was positive they had the only answer. Now I've taken my stand, but perhaps I am not so sure. Why do you think it won't?"

The scientist pointed a finger at him. "You make a basic mistake in thinking this a matter of individuals. To use an example, in effect what you are saying is *kill the dictator and democracy will return to the country.* Nonsense. You put the cart before the horse. That dictator didn't get into power because he was so fabulously capable that he was able to thwart a whole nation's desire for liberty. He, himself, is the product of a situation. Change the situation and he will disappear, but simply assassinate him and all you'll get is another dictator."

The other's words bothered Warren Casey. Not because

24

they were new to him, subconsciously they'd been with him almost from the beginning. He looked at the scientist, waiting for him to go on.

LaVaux touched himself on the chest with his right forefinger. "Take me. I am doing work in a field that can be adapted to military use, although that is not my interest. Actually, I am contemptuous of the military. But you threaten my life if I continue. Very well. Suppose you coerce me and I drop my research. Do you think that will stop investigation by a hundred, a thousand other capable men? Of course not. My branch of science is on the verge of various breakthroughs. If I don't make them, someone else will. You don't stop an avalanche by arresting the roll of one rock."

A tic began in the cheek of Casey's usually emotionless face. "So you think . . ." he prompted.

LaVaux's eyes brightened behind the bi-focals. He was a man of enthusiastic opinions. He said, "Individuals in the modern world do not start wars. It's more basic than that. If the world is going to achieve the ending of warfare, it's going to have to find the causes of international conflict and eliminate them." He chuckled. "Which, of course, opens up a whole new line of investigation."

Warren Casey stood up. He said, "Meanwhile, Professor, I represent an organization that, while possibly wrong, doesn't agree with you. The ultimatum has been served. You have one week."

Professor LaVaux saw him to the door.

"I'd like to discuss the subject further, some day," he said. "But, of course, I suppose I won't be seeing you again."

"That's right," Casey said. He twisted his mouth wryly. "If we have to deal with you further, Professor, and I hope we don't, somebody else will handle it." He looked at the other and considered momentarily rendering the stereotyped-looking scientist unconscious before he left. But he shook his head. *Lord*, he was tired of violence.

As he walked down the garden path to the gate, Professor LaVaux called, "By the way, your disguise. You'll find there are several excellent oral drugs which will darken your complexion even more effectively than your present method."

Almost, Warren Casey had to laugh.

*   *   *

25

He was between assignments, which was a relief. He knew he was physically as well as mentally worn. He was going to have to take the board up on that offer of a prolonged vacation.

Taking the usual precautions in the way of avoiding possible pursuit, he returned to his own apartment. It had been a week, what with one assignment and another, and it was a pleasure to look forward to at least a matter of a few hours of complete relaxation.

He shed his clothing, showered, and then dressed in comfortably old clothing. He went to the tiny kitchen and prepared a drink, finding no ice since he had unplugged the refrigerator before leaving.

Casey dropped into his reading chair and took up the paperback he'd been reading when summoned a week ago to duty. He had forgotten the subject. Ah, yes, a swashbuckling historical novel. It was all so simple. He snorted inwardly. All the hero had to do was kill the evil duke in a duel and everything would resolve itself.

He caught himself up, Professor LaVaux's conversation coming back to him. Essentially, that was what he—what the Pacifists were trying to do. By filling the equivalent of the evil duke—individuals, in other words—they were hoping to solve the problems of the world. Nonsense, on the face of it.

He put down the novel and stared unseeing at the wall opposite. He had been an operative with the Pacifists for more than three years now. He was, he realized, probably their senior hatchetman. An agent could hardly expect to survive so long. It was against averages.

It was then that the screen of his telephone lit up.

Senator Phil McGivern's face glowered at him.

Warren Casey started, stared.

McGivern said, coldly, deliberately, "The building is surrounded, Casey. Surrender yourself. There are more than fifty security police barring any chance of escape."

The Pacifist's mind snapped to attention. Was there anything he had to do? Was there anything in the apartment that might possibly betray the organization or any individual member of it? He wanted a few moments to think.

He attempted to keep his voice even. "What do you want, McGivern?"

"My son!" The politician was glaring his triumph.

26

"I'm afraid Fredric is out of my hands," Casey said. Was the senator lying about the number of police? Was there any possibility of escape?

"Then whose hands is he in? You have him, Warren Casey, but we have you."

"He's not here," Casey said. There might still be a service he could perform. Some way of warning the organization of McGivern's method of tracking him down. "How did you find me? How do you know my name?"

McGivern snorted. "You're a fool as well as a criminal. You sat in my office and spoke in the accent of your native city. I pinpointed that, immediately. You told me you'd been a bomber pilot and obviously had seen action, which meant you'd been in the last war. Then as a pseudonym you used the name Jakes. Did you know that persons taking pseudonyms almost always base them on some actuality? We checked in your home city, and, sure enough, there was actually a newspaperman named Jakes. We questioned him. Did he know a former bomber pilot, a veteran of the last war. Yes, he did. A certain Warren Casey. From there on the job was an easy one—criminal. Now, *where is my son?*"

For a moment, Warren Casey felt weary compassion for the other. The senator had worked hard to find his boy, hard and brilliantly. "I'm sorry, McGivern, I really don't know." Casey threw his glass, destroying the telephone screen.

He was on his feet, heading for the kitchen. He'd explored this escape route long ago when first acquiring the apartment.

The dumbwaiter was sufficiently large to accommodate him. He wedged himself into it, slipped the rope through his fingers, quickly but without fumbling. He shot downward.

In the basement, his key opened a locker. He reached in and seized the submachine pistol and two clips of cartridges. He stuffed one into a side pocket, slapped the other into the gun, threw off the safety. Already he was hurrying down the corridor toward the heating plant. He was counting on the fact that the security police had not had sufficient time to discover that this building shared its central heating and air-conditioning plant with the apartment house adjoining.

Evidently, they hadn't.

A freight elevator shot him to the roof of the next building. From here, given luck, he could cross to a still further building and make his getaway.

He emerged on the roof, shot a quick glance around.

Fifty feet away, their backs to him, stood three security police agents. Two of them armed with automatic rifles, the other with a hand gun, they were peering over the parapet, probably at the windows of his apartment.

His weapon flashed to position, but then the long weariness overtook him. *No more killing. Please. No more killing.* He lowered the gun, turned and headed quietly in the opposite direction.

A voice behind him yelled, "Hey! Stop! You—"

He ran.

The burst of fire caught Warren Casey as he attempted to vault to the next building. It ripped through him and the darkness fell immediately, and far, far up from below, the last thought that was ever signalled was *That's right!*

Fifteen minutes later Senator Phil McGivern scowled down at the meaningless crumpled figure. "You couldn't have captured him?" he said sourly.

"No, sir," the security sergeant defended himself. "It was a matter of shoot him or let him escape."

McGivern snorted his disgust.

The sergeant said wonderingly, "Funny thing was, he could've finished off the three of us. We were the only ones on the roof here. He could've shot us and then got away."

One of the others said, "Probably didn't have the guts."

"No," McGivern growled. "He had plenty of guts."

A TIME OF THE FOURTH HOR/EMAN

Chel/ea Quinn Yarbro

"Never mind," Dr. Smith snapped at the intern. "He's dead." Angrily he jerked the feeder lines from the SUPPORT module, bitter lines of exhaustion showing on his face.

"But what happened?" asked the intern. He was both hurt by the death of his patient and frustrated by how little he had done to save the boy.

Dr. Smith finished closing down the monitor display before he answered. At last he said, "That child was admitted with minor bronchial inflammation." He looked down at the pinched, ashen face. "Fever developed, the chest became congested. We performed a tracheotomy." He fingered the disconnected tube that dangled from the boy's thin neck. "We added precautionary support. And about ten minutes ago the monitor picked up trouble and now, cardiac arrest."

The intern shook his head helplessly. "But don't you know what did it?"

"No. I don't." With that Dr. Smith stepped out of the room and rang for the removal units.

As he walked away from his assistant he was scowling. No, he didn't know what had killed the boy. He hadn't known what had killed the other fourteen children. Fourteen in less than a week. He had run every sample he could think of through the diagnostic computers and had got the same results each time: **Type unknown.** That meant a mutation. But if it were a mutation, why so few?

"Dr. Smith. Paging Dr. Smith," intoned the commsystem. "Dr. Smith to level nine."

Damn, he thought. *That's Justin and his crowd.* He knew the epidemiologist well enough to dislike the cool, statistical mind that lay behind the politic smile and large green eyes. Well, there was no putting it off. Halfway down the hall he picked up an emergency phone long enough to say: "Harry Smith. Tell Dr. Justin I'm on my way."

Peter Justin had his smile on automatic when Harry Smith walked in. He waited until the resident had chosen a seat and then flung a stack of diagnostic printouts on the desk.

Harry Smith's eyes flickered between the cards and Dr. Justin's face, settling on the latter. "Yes?"

"Would you kindly explain these?"

Harry considered saying no. He laced his fingers together over his knee. "Just checking," he said.

"Do you seriously call this checking? There are fourteen different postmort full series here. I think you have some explaining to do."

"Do you?" Harry asked. "In the last week I have lost fifteen patients under age ten. All were admitted for treatment of a bronchial condition. They all died. I want to know why, and since your department doesn't seem to be doing anything about it . . ." Harry felt his voice rise; he forced himself to take a deep breath. ". . . I thought someone ought to check them out."

Dr. Justin's elegant brows drew together, his wide firm lips pursed. "Yes. I see. Fourteen on your service."

"Fifteen," Harry corrected.

"Fifteen? And you indicate here," he tapped at the printouts, "that all these occurred in roughly a week's time. That is quite a large number for so short a time. All children?"

"All under ten," Harry said, a sardonic smile touching his lips.

Dr. Justin drummed his slender fingers on the high gloss of his masonite desk. "That is a significant increase."

That was Justin. Give him a death or a disease and he would try to fit it into a graph. Harry forced himself to keep quiet.

"Fifteen," Peter Justin murmured. "All bronchial. Very unusual." He looked up, the smile returning to his face. "Yes. I am glad you brought this to my attention, Smith. Ordinarily your actions would warrant a review, but under the circumstances . . ."

Under the circumstances, thought Harry, *you don't want to be caught in a neglect suit*. His smile, directed at Justin, was thinly veiled rage.

"Yes. You must let me know if you get another one. Any bronchial admit in the next two weeks, provided the patient is within the age bracket, should be reported to this office. I really must thank you for calling this to my attention. I don't know how I could have missed it."

Harry had a retort to this, but left it unsaid. He was very tired and was due back on the floor in less than six hours. So he rose, saying, "Any time. It looked suspicious and I thought it needed looking into."

Justin nodded. "You were right. Although you should have come to me first."

"Probably," he agreed, going to the door. "If you find out what it is, you will let me know."

"Certainly, certainly," Justin said blithely. "A thing like this takes some tracking. It might be a while. Goodnight, Dr. Smith."

"Goodnight, Dr. Justin."

Number sixteen was waiting for him when he got to the hospital in the morning. This time the child was very young, no more than three, and the only son of another doctor in the same hospital.

"Two doctors," the intern informed him. "Mark Howland and Natalie Lebbreau are married."

"Lebbreau on level eleven, is it?" Hospital gossip had been hinting that the marriage was breaking up. Briefly he wondered if the child had been an issue.

"The name is Phillip Howland," the intern informed him. "Age three years seven months. He's underweight and his eyes need correction. He was hospitalized last year with a broken wrist."

Broken wrist. Was that the parents' doing? There were more and more of them being brought in: children beaten, starved, maimed, burned, tortured. As many times as he had seen it, Harry still felt sickened at the thought.

"The wrist was broken at the day care center. He fell from a ladder," the intern said.

"Thank you. What has been ordered so far?"

"The usual. IV. Oxygen unit. Standard monitor hookup and SUPPORT systems."

"Good." Harry nodded absently. He was already checking over the boy, touching, listening, probing for some clue to the secret of the disease that was wasting him and had wasted fifteen others. "What tests have you run?" he asked as he worked.

"Standard series."

"Post the results in Dr. Justin's office." There was a grim satisfaction in being able to upset Peter Justin and his staff of number keepers.

"How long has his breathing been augmented?"

"Roughly two hours." The intern frowned at this information as he read it. "Two hours? He isn't going to make it, is he?"

"No," Harry said shortly. "Not now." He stepped back from the fragile child in the bed. "I think you better notify his parents. Get them over here if you can."

The intern was only too glad to have the chance to escape.

Left alone with Phillip Howland, Harry found himself helpless. There was only so much he could do, only so much he was allowed to authorize, then he would have to go to the administrative staff and ask for more equipment, more medication, an intensive care unit. All that took time, and the boy in the bed had none. He had no way to save him.

During the next ninety minutes Harry watched the boy's condition deteriorate. Breathing became shallow, the pulse erratic and light. As the circulation worsened the tiny nails took on a bluish cast, the sunken face turned gray. Harry watched the monitor display, as inexorable as a Greek chorus foretelling the necessary end.

At 11:37 Phillip Howland was dead. He had died alone.

Harry sat in the darkest corner of the surgeon's lounge, wondering why he had become a doctor. It felt . . . *good* to save lives. And, when he had specialized in pediatric surgery, lengthening his schooling by eight years, it had all seemed worthwhile. When had he lost the faith? He rubbed his forehead with clammy palms.

"Dr. Emile Harrison Smith?" asked a voice.

Harry looked up, startled. It was rare to hear his full name, especially in the surgeon's lounge. For a moment he was confused.

The woman in front of him was angular and slight, her too-square shoulders made even more unattractive by her hospital whites. Her light red hair might have been pretty but it was caught at the back of her neck in a bun. Skimpy brows grew straight above pale green eyes. She had been crying.

"Dr. Smith," she repeated in a surprisingly appealing voice, "I am Natalie Lebbreau."

Harry's face stiffened as he recognized her. "I see."

"I came as soon as I could." She looked away from him. Her hands were jammed deep into her pockets. "Not soon enough though."

"No. I'm sorry."

At first she said nothing, just stared toward the window where bright spring flowers nodded in the wind. She made a shudder like a sigh, then turned toward him. "Well, thank you. I had hoped we would be through with the two we have on eleven, but . . . They were stronger than Phillip."

Why doesn't she cry. Harry wondered. And then, "What two on eleven?"

"Sick children. Like Phillip. Diphtheria."

"Diphtheria?" He frowned. Then he understood. She couldn't handle the shock of losing her child yet. And she had been working with sick children. With greater compassion he began to sense what guilt she might be feeling now, the conflict she must have undergone when they brought her word of her son.

"They're all coming back again," she said wearily. "All the old diseases. They will be back and we will have to fight them all over again."

Fight them all over again? "How do you mean that, Dr. Lebbreau?" He knew how it sounded but hoped that he was mistaken; a doctor who breaks under strain is a tremendous risk.

"I've treated children with polio, with diphtheria, there's even an admit with smallpox."

Yes, yes nodded the flowers at the window. Oh yes.

Natalie covered her eyes with trembling hands. "Oh, hell," she whispered.

Harry reached out his hand to comfort her, but as he touched her shoulder she pulled away. She was in worse shape than he thought, but not as bad as he had feared she might be. "I'm sorry. You looked so unhappy. I thought you might like to let it out."

The look she turned on him was one of completed disbelief. Then her eyes brightened and her face returned to the sadness. "Oh. I see. You mean about Phillip." She shook her head. "No. I can't; not now. If I started crying for him, I'd never stop." She looked around nervously, as it frightened. "There are all those others to cry for."

So she was back to the others. Harry thought momentarily of notifying the chief resident on her level, but then, perhaps because he did not trust the hospital administration, decided against it.

"Let me call your husband," he said to her.

"No!" She looked even more startled than he did at this vehemence. "I mean . . ." she went on in some confusion, ". . . it isn't necessary. I am sure he knows by now. He knew Phillip was sick, and he knows . . . about the diseases," she finished lamely.

Then the rumors are right, Harry thought. *What a time to find out*. He understood her dislike of touching now. It would make it easier to talk with her. He tried to remember Dr. Howland: he was the one in charge of the labs. Young, tall, that tawny handsomeness that did not age well. A great deal of professional charm. And eyes colder than Justin's. It couldn't have been easy for her.

"Is . . ." He paused as he chose his words. "Is there anyone I could notify for you? School? Relatives?"

She shook her head. "No. No, thank you. I'll do that. Just file the death report for the County." She glanced anxiously at the door. "I really have to get back. I'm supposed to be on rounds right now."

"Then perhaps I'll see you later." To his own ears the words were stilted, but Natalie Lebbreau gave him the semblance of a smile. "Oh, yes. Thank you."

Just as she went out the door she said impulsively: "It was diphtheria."

Harry walked back to his on-duty station slowly, his hazel

eyes clouded in thought. Obviously Natalie Lebbreau was in shock; emotionally she wasn't ready to handle both her son's death and the state of her marriage. She needed a third concern, something that would direct her attention away from her own problems. That had to be it.

She couldn't be right.

Because if she was, they were headed for disaster.

The seventeenth child did not appear for two days and Harry was beginning to hope that they had been treated, all of them; that the deaths were from a short-lived virus mutation that hadn't been pinned down yet; that the last of the pinched gray faces had belonged to Natalie Lebbreau's boy.

The late night city patrol changed that. They brought in two children, a boy and a girl, found sleeping under a freeway interchange. They had been abandoned the day before. They were cold, hungry, frightened . . . and sick.

"What's your name?" Harry asked the girl. She was the older of the two, about nine. She was sitting on her unit bed, scrawny arms dangling from the capacious hospital gown. Her dark eyes were defiant and her young face was set into an expressionless mask.

"Stephanie," she said, as if it were a swear word. "Where have you taken Brian?"

"Oh, not far. He's got himself another unit, just like yours."

The bright eyes showed scorn. "Why? Where'd you put him?"

Harry suddenly felt the desolation that Stephanie must know. She had been left by a roadside with her brother, parents gone to another city, another state. They had been abandoned. Now they were in the hands of strangers who separated them. He reached over and thumbed a concealed toggle. "There, Stephanie. Now, do you see this knob?" He pointed to the large red knob that controlled the phone screen.

"Yeah," she said gravely.

"Good. Now, when I am through checking you over, all you have to do is turn the knob to this position . . ." He moved aside so that she could see the position of the knob, ". . . and then you tell the lady on the screen who you want to talk to. You and Brian can have a long, long talk."

"Why can't I see him?" she demanded.

35

"But you can. That's what the screen is for."

The girl gave a derisive snort. "I mean in person, mister."

That bothered Harry. "I'm afraid you can't see him in person for a while. I'm sorry, Stephanie."

Stephanie lapsed back into a sullen silence. It continued through the examination in spite of Harry's attempts to get her talking again. The only sound she made was one of pain when he tried to touch the welts on her back.

"I'm sorry you're hurt," he told her before he left her unit.

"Well!" Jim Braemoore beamed happily at Harry. "We haven't seen you down here in quite a while." He gestured expansively over the cafeteria. "Hasn't been the same since Chisholm died. A fine chef, that man. Told me once he had his personal spice racks back there in the kitchens. Quite illegal, of course, but the food was better."

Harry made an absent reply. It was too bad about Chisholm, yes. Too bad about everybody. He studied his cup of noff, recalling the time, over five years ago, when the near-coffee replaced the genuine article all over the hospital. The outrage had been fantastic. Now, no one seemed to notice. He supposed that in a year or so the doctors who complained now about the plain food served since Chisholm's death would no longer notice the bland pap being served.

"You look glum," observed Braemoore. "Working too hard, I can tell. Just can't take the job that much to heart, Harry. Ruin you if you do. Tell you what: we're mechanics. Much easier if you think of it that way."

"Mechanics," he repeated numbly. Was that the secret? How had he missed it all these years?

"You and Natalie. Get all involved, go about in a lather. No good. Wear yourselves out that way. Can't do it, Harry. Can't do it at all."

"Natalie? Lebbreau?"

Jim looked up, startled. "So you were listening after all. Wouldn't have thought so. Natalie Lebbreau is the one I meant. Good girl, fine doctor. Intense, very intense; plain girls often are, don't you think?" He smiled blandly and offered sugar. "Energy."

It didn't pour like real sugar, but what the hell. It was sweet and probably did give energy.

"Take me, now," Braemoore went on, his sausage-like

fingers spread over his broad chest. "Know how to realize my limits. Don't take the office home with me, don't bother too much about CAs and other terminals. Better off letting them go. Why save 'em for more agony? Put my money on the ones who can get well. Ought to do the same yourself, Harry." He took a bite out of a droopy bit of pastry. The icing clung like snow to his moustache. "Can't be a good doctor the way you're going. Hear you've been handling the kids with bronchial trouble. No use fighting for them, Harry. Saw a few cases of it myself last week. Can't save 'em. No earthly use trying. Set 'em up, make 'em comfortable and get on with the strong ones."

I can't be hearing this, Harry told himself. *It's all a mistake.* "What are you saying, Jim? Are you telling me that it isn't my job to save lives?"

"Didn't say that!" Braemoore protested. "Nothing of the sort. Did say you shouldn't bother with terminals. Let 'em be. Put your time on the ones who survive. That's the way. Toddlers with that virus . . ."

"Are you sure it's a virus?" Even as he asked Harry knew that for some reason he could not understand, he no longer thought it was a virus. Jim was being almost too much the jolly old GP. There was something wrong when a doctor of Jim Braemoore's standing tried to throw a resident like Harry off the track.

"Of course it's a virus. Couldn't be anything else."

"What do the diagnostic samples say?"

Jim looked flustered, his normally pink face turning red as he answered. "Type unknown. Damn it all, you should know; you ordered the tests. Don't mind telling you that Justin was pretty unhappy about it. Not that it isn't his job to notice," Jim added hastily. "Hard to tell about Peter, sometimes. Noticed how he likes getting the records straight. Damned strange fellow."

"Am I being taken off the cases?" Harry asked, as calmly as he could.

"Taken off? What for? You know the field. Just a little advice, that's all. Help you keep your perspective. This over-concern, preoccupation, that can happen to anyone. Happened to me once, oh, long time ago. Took quite a while to set myself straight again. Wanted you to see how it is, let you know I understand." He pushed back from the table. "Sorry to leave you so soon, but must scrub for a CA. Mastectomy. Pity.'' He beamed broadly at Harry. ''Delighted to have seen you, Smith. Don't have nearly enough time to talk these days. Just remember; one child—even half a dozen—doesn't make that much difference. Not worth the bother, Harry.'' With that as a parting remark he strode to the door and bellied through it.

''Brian shows three ribs broken and improperly healed as well as bruises and blisters on the ankles,'' the new intern reported. She was long, lanky and the color of caramel apples. ''We found some nylon fibers in the infected area.''

''Okay. They kept him tied up. What else?''

''Bruises on the side of the face, recent. Burn scars on the left and right forearm. Malnutrition. He is suffering from exposure and psychological trauma, but will probably pull through.''

''And Stephanie?'' Harry found it more and more difficult to keep the detached, professional attitude that was required of him. Yet he dared not show great interest to this girl, obviously a plant from Justin, or Braemoore. Or both. He wanted to chide himself for paranoia or cynicism and found that he could not bring himself to do it. He sensed he was being watched, and knew he must tread warily.

''The girl,'' the intern went on, ''is in somewhat better condition, at least outwardly. She does have a fever and complains of general body ache and a persistent headache.''

''She probably tried to keep her brother warm and has had more exposure to cold,'' he suggested, covering a certain dread that made a cold fist in his guts. What if Natalie Lebbreau were right? She said she had had a patient with polio . . .

''I've had photographs taken of her back for the police records. Ian Parkenson had a look at her. He said the lashes were made with an old-fashioned electric cord.''

Ian Parkenson was their expert on battered children, rarely called on so routine a case as this. Perhaps the intern had requested his opinion. ''I see. Why did you call Dr. Parkenson in on the case? Anything the matter?''

''Dr. Justin sent him over; he said it was about the virus fatalities we've had with children. But this one isn't a bronchial inflammation.''

Justin is checking on me. What for? Has he got more figures on those blessed charts of his? Aloud he said, "He must be watching the pediatric admits pretty carefully."

"Oh, yes," said the intern. Then she giggled.

Harry scowled at her. "What was your name again?"

"Gloria Powell," she said, straightening her name badge over one unrealistically firm breast. "See?"

"Thanks," he said dryly. "I want to see the boy first and then the girl."

All business, Gloria Powell led the way to the units.

Brian lay on his side, restless. He had reached that stage of fatigue where normal sleep was impossible. As Harry stepped through the door Brian succeeded in twitching his blanket off the bed. He gave a low whine and wriggled onto his side.

"Hello, Brian," Harry began, forcing himself to smile.

"Go 'way." He squinted up at Harry. "I don't like you."

Harry bent and picked up the blanket, noticing Gloria leaning over him, too obviously near. He stepped back as he stood up. "Here, Brian. You'll want your blanket later on."

The boy took it, wadded it and held it.

"Look," Harry began again, "so long as I'm here, why not let me check you over?"

" 'Nother doctor did already."

"Yes, I know." Harry was getting impatient. "But I am *your* doctor and I would like to examine you. It won't take long, Brian."

"Where's Stephie? They said I could see her." The boy twisted and then sat up. "She said we'd be okay, just us together. What have you done with her?" With that, he started to cry.

Gloria Powell looked disgusted and started to tap on her clip-chart.

Harry had to admit that the puckered, red face buttoned with a runny nose was not very appealing. He also knew that he was clumsy with children. Reluctantly he sat on the side of the bed and put his arm around the wailing boy.

"It's okay, Brian. It really is. Don't worry about your sister; I saw her earlier and she was just as anxious to see you." He remembered he had shown her how to use the phone screen and wondered why she hadn't. "She probably thinks you're sleeping now and doesn't want to wake you up. And she's right, you know. If you have some sleep you'll feel much better. The sooner you can get better, the sooner you can go . . .'' He stopped. Abandoned children do not go home. ''The sooner you can leave here.''

''I want Stephie!'' Brian yelled.

''Doctor, really!'' Gloria shook her head impatiently.

''Why hasn't this boy been sedated?'' Harry demanded, feeling the tension in the slender shoulders. ''In this condition he could have side effects from this prolonged wakefulness.''

Gloria was prettily confused. ''I didn't think we gave sedatives to children. I didn't order any for him.''

''Well, what's stopping you from doing it now?'' And what stopped Ian Parkenson from doing it when he examined Brian. ''Never mind, I'll handle it when we leave.'' He turned his attention back to the child whose sobs had become short, jerky sighs. ''Come on, Brian, just a few minutes and then you can go to sleep. When you wake up I'll take you over to see Stephie.'' He glanced at Gloria and saw the lovely mouth parted in distress. ''What is it, doctor?'' he asked sharply.

''Not here, doctor,'' she replied, and went out of the unit.

Shortly afterward he joined her. ''Will you explain your remark, please?''

''Come with me,'' she said professionally.

But Harry didn't move. ''Not until you tell me why.''

She gave him a cool stare. ''I am about to show you why, doctor. If you'll come with me.'' She led the way to Stephanie's unit.

''I think it's dreadful about those children.''

''Yes,'' Harry nodded, pleasantly surprised to hear her so sympathetic. ''It's criminal the way parents are allowed to abandon them.''

Gloria opened startled eyes at him. ''I meant that they were allowed to have them!'' she said shortly.

In Stephanie's unit the girl lay under a breathing assist unit. The machine squatted over her body like a large, profane bird. The gauge registered light respiration.

''I see,'' said Harry. ''When did this happen?''

''About an hour ago,'' Gloria said. She had come no farther into the unit than absolutely necessary. ''One of the orderlies noticed the irregularity on the monitor and rang for an assist. It's pretty serious,'' she added thoughtfully.

"I'm glad you've noticed. Is it too much to hope that there is a record of what's been done for her?"

"Oh, yes, here." She traced through the slips on the clip-chart, and finally handed him one, retreating to the doorway when through.

"Thanks." He read through the paper, stopping suddenly. "It authorizes transfer."

"Hum? Yes, it does," she nodded brightly.

"It doesn't say where."

She looked at her copy. "No, it doesn't." She frowned, then, "Probably they're short of beds and don't know which facility they're going to use yet. They'll fill it in later when they know where."

"But they don't transfer patients in this condition," Harry persisted. "This child cannot be moved."

"Dr. Parkenson signed the authorization," she stated. Her mouth narrowed.

"I know." It frightened him. "I'll check with Ian. He can't have seen her since they brought the unit. He'll see that she mustn't be moved."

Gloria glared at him, then turned and walked away. No intern would do that, yet she did.

Harry watched her go. "Tell Justin. Tell Parkenson! Tell Braemoore! I don't give a damn who you tell if it will save this child!"

He looked at the monitor. After five minutes he knew that Stephanie was number seventeen.

The voice on the phone was tired, still husky from sleep. "Yes? Dr. Howland here."

"Dr. Howland, is Dr. Lebbreau there?"

"No," the voice growled.

Harry gritted his teeth and went on. "Can you tell me when she is expected in?"

"She isn't." The line went dead.

Alone in the visitor's lounge Harry stood, stupidly clinging to the receiver. What could have become of her? Where had she gone? He could put out a hospital alert—and rejected the idea as soon as he thought of it. There was a risk if Justin and his cronies found out. He had tried her level with no success.

On an off-chance, he tried the cafeteria and was startled to find her there, sitting in the far corner, alone. He picked up two cups of noff and went to her.

"Like another cup?" he asked when he reached her. He made a tentative smile.

"Oh. Thank you."

He put down the cups. "Mind if I join you? You look kind of lonely, all by yourself." Since there were only three other men in a room designed to accommodate two hundred fifty at a pinch, this could be said of any of the four. She chose to ignore that. "Yes, please do sit down," she said.

"I've been hoping I'd run into you. After the other day . . . I owe you an apology."

"Why?" Eyes listless, hands slightly shaking. She looked up at him. "You didn't believe me, so it doesn't matter."

"But I do, now." He leaned toward her, speaking quietly, "I have a patient on my level, a girl. Nine years old, abandoned with her brother. She has polio."

Natalie's face sharpened. "When was she admitted?"

"City patrol brought her in yesterday."

"Where is she now? Can we run some tests on her?"

Harry sighed, defeated. "No. They transferred her out this afternoon. She was on breathing assist then."

"Do you know where?"

"No. It was not put on the authorization card."

Her hand were shaking in earnest how. Her faded green eyes were nerve-bright. "It's going to get worse. It's going to get worse so fast," she said softly, quickly. "Dave Lillijanthal got a tetanus. A real one. They can't say this is a mutant virus."

"How old?"

"This one is an adult, late twenties. They've got him in the decompression chamber."

Harry stared at her. "You know what's going on, don't you? Someone has told you what's happening."

"Mark did."

"Then why the hell . . ." He made an effort to quiet his voice; this was no time to give away their conversation. "Why don't you tell people? Why aren't you doing something about it?"

For the first time she looked ashamed. "Because I can't! If I say what I know, who would believe me? The best known

42

doctors in the city say I'm just an hysterical woman who can't adjust to the loss of a child."

The room grew hushed. One of the three other men rose and left the cafeteria.

"That is what they'll do if I speak out. And that would mean I'd have to stop practicing. I can't do that!" In her intensity she, too, leaned forward. "They're going to need doctors so much . . . so soon."

"What is happening?" Harry pleaded.

For an answer she shook her head quickly. "Not here." She glanced furtively at the wall clock. "It's one-twenty. Do you have to be on the floor just now?"

"Not right now. I'm supposed to be on call at two-thirty."

She closed her eyes and sagged. "Can you leave the hospital for a few minutes?"

"Yes," he said in some confusion. "I suppose I can."

"Good. I don't want to talk here." She rose, the noff untouched. "You didn't have to. Kind, though," she mused, looking at the brown liquid. His low laugh flustered her. "Come on, then," she said brusquely.

The park across from the hospital was darkly secluded but was unsafe after dark. Natalie surprised Harry by walking straight toward it, veering off at the last minute to the walk that bordered the lake. She walked quickly, as if afraid to reveal herself, but once the bow of the lake concealed them from the hospital and the traffic on the approach arterial she slowed down. The night was cool for spring and the flowers were still strong enough to cover the grimy city air with a sweetness as elusive as it was touching.

"Here." She hurried toward a bench. "We can talk here. It's not the park, but they can't see us here."

"You're really frightened, aren't you?" he wondered. "Is it that bad?"

A stricken look crossed her face before she answered. "Yes. Oh, yes. It is that bad." She stopped, ducked her head, and fumbled with her scarf tucked in the pocket of the hospital whites.

"It's so bad. What they've done . . . I ran some tests down in Mark's lab before Phillip . . . got sick. Checking on my first patients. I thought they had the old diseases. The lab was closed—Mark was . . . busy."

43

She remembered hiding in a lab station when her husband and his girl friend returned suddenly to his central lab for privacy. "I checked out the samples. It was like a textbook, the same reactions. I thought it was vaccine failure. I went back to the lab again. Into storage . . ."

She looked at him at last. "The vaccines . . . they're about one third of them useless. They've been destroyed in random batches. One third of all the vaccines produced. For everything."

She pushed a stray hair off her brow. "The program started about five years ago. I found that out going through Mark's papers . . . before I left him."

"He knows about it?"

"Oh, yes. He thinks it's a great idea. Fair—this way no one knows who gets what, and after all, only one third are placebos. There's good chance that you're fully protected." The angry sarcasm in her voice gave way to despair. "And I can't do anything!"

They were silent for several minutes. "How many have you treated so far?" Harry asked.

"Children? Thirty-seven. Not so many since they transferred my floor partner to County Central. They're trying to keep me off the cases."

"I've had seventeen, in three weeks."

In a faraway voice she asked, "I wonder how many cases there are now? Really?"

"Justin would know."

"Justin would lie."

"What if we tell Parkenson?"

"He knows."

Again silence.

"Ian says it's better than battered children—that this is the natural way."

"Maybe he's right," Harry said, "but I can't accept it. Not watching them die."

"Ian says they're being abandoned anyway. That they are being crowded out of existence. And this is *fair!*"

Harry said nothing.

"I watched him take care of some kids about a month ago. One lost a leg; the other was too far gone—both tibia splintered, a shoulder dislocated. The parents might be fined."

"Then you agree with Ian?" Harry asked, incredulous.

"Not about the vaccine. But sometimes I wonder . . . what are we saving them for?"

Peter Justin was trimming his nails. Anyone who knew him would recognize this as symptomatic of discomfort. He brushed the clipping into the wasteshoot with an oddly fussy gesture. When he looked up again, a medium height blond man towered over him.

"I want some information," Harry said. "I want it now and I want it correct."

"What about?" Justin asked, playing for time. "Why are you here, Harry?"

"You know why I'm here!" he exploded.

Justin made a second attempt at urbanity. "If it's about those children . . ."

"Can it! How many have been through this hospital and what did they die of? The real figures, Justin!"

Justin sighed. "I don't need the figures. In the last two months, three hundred thirty-two with diphtheria, fifty-six with smallpox, ninety-one with polio, three with tetanus, eighteen with TB, one hundred sixty-nine with meningitis. There are a few others—perhaps half a dozen with measles."

"In total, or fatalities?" Harry demanded, brows furrowed in concentration.

"Fatalities. The figures for adults aren't that high—I think the total is around four hundred in all." He looked pleadingly at Harry. "Something had to be done. You know what conditions are—there was no other way, Harry."

"Sweet Jesus, that's over a thousand! This hospital alone, over a thousand."

"County Central is running slightly higher. Inner City is lower on diphtheria."

"They're higher on abuse!" Harry snapped. He had done his first internship there. He had seen the way the children were treated. His first patient had been a five year old with the burn from a steam iron on his back. That was over ten years ago. "Besides, Inner City, they don't bring children to the hospital except to die. The figures there wouldn't be accurate."

Peter Justin looked away uneasily. "It isn't going well. There are too many—it's too early for so many." He adjusted

45

his handsome face carefully. "But we mustn't be too concerned."

"Why? It's not according to your predicted curve? How shocking." He gave a sardonic bark that was intended as a laugh. Justin shifted uncomfortably in his chair. "All figured out in advance, is it, like the Tolerable Losses tables in the Pentagon?" He rounded on Justin, his clenched hands shaking. "I hope you bloody fools get your asses royally burned for this!"

Justin favored him with the travesty of a smile. "Of course we anticipated certain variables. The figures are high, yes— but it *is* like a war, don't you see? Only an irresponsible leader would not allow for losses. Battles are won that way."

"You don't know what you've started, do you? You haven't been down on the floor in a long time, Peter. You don't know what it's like down there. I just hope you live long enough to see what your filthy charts have done!" He slammed out the door.

He was heading for the central admissions desk.

The pale-haired girl at the desk balked at his order. "But doctor, I can't give out that information without authorization from one of the administrators. Those are the regulations."

"The regulations have just changed. I want the admit records for the last twenty-four hours. Especially pediatrics. Young kids with 'mutant virus' diagnoses and those suffering from exposure. And I want it now."

"Doctor, you haven't got the required signatures—"

"This is the last time I repeat." He smiled, unpleasantly. "Then I am coming into your office. I will take all your records, every last one. Then I will walk down to the storage computer with a large magnet in my pocket. May I have those records, please?"

The girl was visibly frightened as she went into her office. When she came back with the printout sheets she shoved them to Harry, sullen-faced. "Here. Take them. I'll lose my job if Dr. Justin ever finds out."

Harry gave her a fierce wink. "No way, child. You're going to be here a while; a lot longer than you think."

With this assurance, he went on down the hall.

*   *   *

46

"Dr. Lebbreau, paging Dr. Lebbreau. Report to level nine, please. Dr. Lebbreau to level nine."

Natalie turned as she heard the paging call. Her patient smiled. "A call for you, Nat." She was into middle age and had been in the hospital since the holidays, recovering from three knife wounds. She knew that the prognosis was good, and largely due to Natalie. The paralysis would be partial instead of total as first feared.

The paging was repeated.

"You'd better go, Nat," Mrs. Dwyer smiled kindly.

"Yes." She frowned slightly. "I'd better. If you don't mind, I'll send Carol in to finish this up. She's on the floor now and you've had her before."

"No rush, Nat. I'll be here yet awhile."

By the time she stepped from the elevator on level nine Natalie's frown had deepened. She was developing a defense in her mind, in case the paging meant that the administration was aware of her talks with Harry Smith. She knew if that had happened that they were both in serious trouble and faced dismissal. She glanced about nervously for Justin or Wrexler. Even Mark might be there.

"Good. I'm glad you were fast." It was Harry who stepped up to her.

She looks better, not so frightened, Harry thought. *Maybe we can weather this.* He saw her stand straighter for him. There was purpose in her expression now, replacing the depression.

He hesitated, and then took her arm as they started down the hall. "I've been talking to Justin and I've got some figures out of him."

"Justin?" Her straight brows drew together again. "Justin? Have you seen him?"

"Yes." He guided her to the empty solarium, pushed open the door and shoved her into the dark sunroom. "It's much worse than we guessed. There have been roughly eleven hundred fatalities in the last two months at this hospital alone. County Central is running higher, Inner City a bit lower."

She was badly shocked. "Eleven hundred! I thought it wasn't much above five hundred . . . Just in two months?"

"Natalie, it's just getting started. That crew of damned idiots has really made a mare's nest this time." He did not wait for her response. "We've got to make some changes,

47

and quickly. All the computers have to be reprogrammed to recognize 'extinct' diseases. That's where a lot of the trouble is coming from, the diagnosis end. The computers don't recognize diphtheria and smallpox because diphtheria and smallpox were wiped out years ago, so they come up with the 'mutant virus' or 'modified bacterial infection' and our hands are tied. We've got to get some doctors who are willing to fight this thing.''

''Yes,'' she nodded, her breathing quickened. ''We will need help.''

''Is there anyone on your service?''

She thought briefly. ''Dave Lillijanthal. He'll be willing, I think. Gil would, if he were . . . Gil's my old partner,'' she explained. ''He's been transferred. I think we can get Stan Kooznetz; he's terribly young but he's a good doctor. So is Lisa Skyie. She isn't very strong, though, not a lot of stamina. Carol Mendosa's tough. She's got a mind like an Inquisitor after heretics and looks like a Botticelli angel. She'll work till it kills her.''

''Right. I can get Patman and Divanello in pediatric service, maybe about ten more. If we work hard we might even be ready for the first wave when it comes.''

She sat up suddenly. ''What about us? We might not be immune either.''

Harry whistled softly. ''Good girl. I hadn't thought of that. But of course, that's just what they'd do. Justin kept saying that this has to be fair. As soon as we get organized we'll vaccinate everyone for everything. If we start coming down with the bugs we won't be of any use at all.''

''And if there are mutant strains?''

He had thought of the possibility earlier and was afraid. ''We take our chances along with everyone else.'' More than everyone, he admitted. They would all be working close to the diseases.

''How long do we have until the new ones crop up?'' From the way she asked the worry was an old one with her. She went to the east window and looked out toward Inner City. ''It's going to show up there first. We should make some plans to run random tests on the admits.''

''I think you're right about Inner City. And the abandoned children. It's hard to tell where they come from.'' He narrowed his eyes at the lights in the distance. ''If we can get the

48

city patrol to enforce quarantines, we might be able to confine the worst of it in pockets. And some of the bugs respond to diseases around them. We'll have to keep them separate. Where are we going to get the bed space?''

"I don't know." She sighed.

"That will be one more graph for Justin."

Suddenly Natalie turned to him, her back tense and her face anxious. "This isn't the same thing as graph paper! What if the administration won't help us?''

"We have enough to worry about without thinking up what-ifs.''

"There's not any reason to think they will help us. And there's so much at stake. Harry, what if they turn us out?''

"They can't turn us out. They need us right now or the initiative will be lost. They wouldn't dare," he said.

The notice had been up for an hour before Harry saw it at noon the next day:

> The following doctors are relieved of service in this hospital. Dismissal for cause. You are requested to leave the premises before midnight this date, 3-29-87.

Under the authorization stamp were the scrawled signatures of Peter Justin and Thomas Wrexler. The appended list of names was long; accompanying Harry and Natalie were most of those they had counted on to aid their program of survival.

"What kind of crap is this?" Harry demanded, slapping a torn copy of the notice onto Jim Braemoore's desk.

"Told you what would happen if you kept on, Harry. Didn't want it to happen, myself, but you insisted. Thought for a while there you might see sense.''

"What are you talking about? I want to see Wrexler." Harry stormed toward the door.

"He won't see you. Not what he wanted but you gave him no choice." Jim smiled sympathetically. "Can't say I wouldn't have done the same thing myself, years ago. I admire your stand, Harry. Good to know there's doctors like you left. Thought they'd vanished.''

Harry gave him a puzzled look, still breathing hard. "Jim,

don't you know what they're doing? Doesn't it bother you at all?"

"Thinning down the herd, that's it. Culling the weak ones. A couple of months, moderate epidemic, relieve the pressure for a bit. We need the relief."

With all the control at his command, Harry began, as if to a small child. "Jim, one third of all vaccines are useless. One third! They have been for about five years. This isn't just a bad run of flu, Jim, this is a major one. We aren't talking about just one disease—not just a smallpox epidemic or a cholera epidemic or a meningitis epidemic. This will be the granddaddy of all epidemics, with something for everyone!"

"There's enough vaccines stockpiled," Braemoore responded. "We can stop it if it gets out of hand. It won't be like what you've said at all. Couldn't do that, Harry."

"But it is."

Jim spread out his hand to stop him. "Tell you what, Harry, you get your kit and go along home. I'll have a word with Wrexler in the morning. You'll be back here in no time, that's the ticket."

"There isn't time. . . ."

Jim buzzed for the door; it opened. "Glad you came to me, Harry. Knew we could sort things out if you did. We'll just wait until the worst blows over and then Wrexler'll have you back. Shouldn't be more than a couple of months. And don't let things like this bother you. It isn't natural."

And he closed the door.

Nine days later, when martial law had been declared and the newscasts were full of the mutant virus epidemic in the city, Harry and Natalie were having lunch in his flat. She had been confined to his quarters for the duration of the emergency. There was smallpox in her building complex.

They knew that they were being monitored.

"I wish we could have the windows open," Natalie said wistfully. "I miss the smell of spring." The sunshine reflected off the white plastic counters and metal sink, making the small room shine.

"The smell is different this year."

They fell silent.

After a while he began to hum. It was just a nursery rhyme that every child knows:

50

>"Ring around the rosie
>Pocket full of posie
>Ashes, ashes, all fall down."

"Shut up!" she yelled at him.

"Hum? What for?"

"Don't you know what that is?"

"What's wrong with a nursery rhyme?" He rose and came around behind her.

She pushed his hand away from her shoulder. "It's the Plague rhyme. It's about the Black Death."

Her voice was flat, all anger gone from it. "I'm sorry I snapped at you."

Harry made an effort to change the subject. "I wonder if they'll call us back?"

If there were anyone to call them back. He had heard that both Braemoore and Wrexler were gone.

"It's like being on a sinking ship with a hundred other people and two leaky lifeboats, isn't it? Do you think we'll make it?"

"Don't talk that way." He went to pull the blind down.

"Knowing people . . ." She went on as if she had not heard him. ". . . they'll trample each other to death, or hack the boats to pieces . . ."

"Natalie, stop it!" He was about to turn on her, but there was a tap at the window. His flat was four floors above ground level and the window difficult to reach. Cautiously he looked around.

"What is it?" Natalie asked from the table.

"I don't know. I thought I heard—there it is again." He looked around more carefully, edging the window open.

Twenty feet beyond the window, on the narrow service landing, perched a twelve-year-old girl. One hand was filled with gravel; the other hand had two fingers stuck into her nose. "You the doctor?" she whispered.

"Both of us," Harry answered.

"Can you come quick? Just two floors down. My sister is sick."

Harry frowned. "What about your mother? Can't she get a doctor?"

"They left," the girl answered simply. "Mom and Pop both. The hospital doesn't answer. I tried that first."

51

"Do your mother and father work?" asked Natalie who had joined Harry at the window.

"Nope. Left. For good. Ces'lie's real sick. Can you come?" She thought something over. "Can't go out the door. There are cops watching it. But if you crawl along the ledge there . . ." She pointed to the ledge beneath the window.

"I don't think—" Harry began.

"I can," Natalie interrupted. "You'd never make it, Harry; not along that. Get my bag for me, will you?"

He would have protested but the girl put in. "Yeah, she's right. You're too big."

As Harry raised surprised eyebrows Natalie giggled and said, "There, you see?"

He looked down at her in exasperation. He said, "Okay. I'll get the bag. But be careful."

"I will," she promised.

When he got back from the bedroom she had buttoned on the white hospital oversmock that she had worn the first time she saw him. The slacks she had on looked old but they were sturdy. She smiled when she saw him. "While I'm gone you're going to have to do something to make them think I'm still here. Unless this is very serious I'll be back before too long. If the girl is really sick, I'll call Lisa Skyie. She's still on the staff and can arrange for the child to be picked up."

"Yes," he said to her.

"Now wait until I get out the window." She climbed onto the drainboard. "I'll have to get a foothold before I can handle the bag." She began to lower herself gingerly out of the window."

Suddenly he was filled with concern for her. "You don't have to go," he told her abruptly.

The washed-out green of her eyes softened. "Someone has to," she said. "Just save me a place in the lifeboat."

And then she was onto the ledge, crawling toward the girl who crouched, waiting to lead her to her sister.

As the slant of the sun moved across the table he waited, wondering if Natalie knew how utterly they were beaten. He drank coffee and when that gave out, water. She would sneak home, ready to answer the next cry for help . . . and would go on answering them until she died. Eventually he knew he would have to help her. And they would lose. It was inevitable: attempts to stop it now were ludicrous. No one could oppose death on a scale like this. Natalie was just a fool to try.

God, but he was proud of her . . . !

TRUCK DRIVER

Robert Chilson

Ynga Lancaster hobbled awkwardly in her skintight pressure suit. It was inflated, so it didn't as yet grip her any more tightly than a stretch coverall, but the pads that filled out the concavities of her figure hampered her motion. Worse, they rounded her excellent figure out into that of a clumsily-carved doll, one with features barely suggested.

Carrying her helmet under one arm and her flight orders and purse in the other hand, Ynga pushed open the door onto the ready line. It was chilly outside, with a hint of snow from a lowering sky. As a veteran pilot, her bird had been moved up near the building. She hurried toward it. Her pressure suit was permeable, designed to permit her to lose heat; and it wasn't designed for such extreme conditions as this. Though only a little below freezing—hot by the standards of shadows in space—the dense air carried her body heat away fast enough to make her shiver as she hobbled over the tarmac.

By earlier standards, the bird was a big one. It was a nuclear-electric aerospace plane capable of putting a hundred tons, not into Earth orbit, but into escape trajectory. In shape it was an arrowhead, with the trailing points extending somewhat behind the tail of the "fuselage." The main body, or fuselage, of the plane was perhaps half the wingspan; from there the wings thinned toward the tips. At the tip of each wing was a double electrojet, one above the other. These ramjets were each big enough for a man to take a running dive through without touching—and electrojets are vastly more efficient than thermal jets.

Along the leading edge of the wings were smaller jet intakes; the little electrojets that sucked air in to lift the wing. They could support the plane on hover with small or no load, or on air cushion near the ground with full load. Aft, on the trailing edges of the wings and body, were the exhausts of the turboelectric jets that were used near the ground.

Paul Sitwell swung down from the flight deck and extended a clipboard. "Looks O.K., Ynga," he said with an attempt at heartiness.

She took the board, clumsy in her gauntlets, frowned at it. "What's wrong, then?" she barked.

"Wrong? Uh . . . nothing. I was just, uh, making sure. I mean, Mannie found a couple reds and he kind of, uh . . . and then I got behind—"

She ran her eye hastily down the checksheet, noting that everything had been marked if not checked. "O.K., O.K., don't tell me your troubles. Let me get out of this wind." She signed it clumsily. The flight techs supposedly checked everything after every flight, and there weren't many things that could go wrong with a nuclear-electric bird. Paul's job was merely to eliminate the waste of pilot hours in final checkout.

She swung gratefully into the warm bird.

The name of her plane was *Rival*. She looked around, soaking up the warmth for a moment, the comfort of her homey touches as warming as the plane's air-conditioning. Bill, her husband, bless him, was not disturbed by the place of her birds in her life. She had added her own decorator scheme to the switches and buttons—in nail polish. The go-stick wore ruffled skirts, and a pair of Pete's baby shoes, gold-plated, hung from it where it extended from the board. She'd have had a picture of the two of them if there'd been room.

Activating the board, she gave the bird a spot-check, checked communications, told the voice in the tower that, yes, she had clipped her purse under the seat, made him admit that he had neglected to clock the fact that she was flying alone as usual, and switched on the visiplates. These birds, like all modern planes, had no ports; her view came from numerous thimble-sized ikons scattered over the hull in strategic places.

"*Rival* ready for the flight line," she informed the tower.

"So O.K., get that female kite out of the way and let a man through," Ernie Katz insisted.

Ynga grinned, seating her helmet and checking it. Ernie's bird was dubbed the *Manpower*; he even had a big UP sign painted on it.

Rival lifted a little as the jets along the leading edge pulled air in from above and blew it out below. In moments it was on air cushion. She halted its drift on the wind with the turboelectrics, turned it toward the flight line and wafted it along as gently as a leaf. Receiving final clearance, she tipped over the edge of the gentle ski-jump slope and blasted all the secondary jets at full.

By the time she had reached the bottom of this slope, *Rival* was airborne, definitely off air cushion, winging uncertainly over the east Texas flatlands like some misplaced condor. Its sharp nose and edges and extreme lines marked it as no submach barge, but a true eagle of the ionosphere, and it looked oddly out of place so near the ground.

The ground fell rapidly away, however, and by the time she crossed the Gulf Coast into cold winter sunshine, Ynga was ambling southeast at a leisurely 600. She concentrated on building up altitude. *Rival* had automatically throttled back on the jets that supplied lift to the flying wing, and they were now off.

A hundred miles or so south of New Orleans—half an hour from Galveston—Ynga had made 50,000 feet of altitude. She hauled *Rival* around to the south and glanced back in the side-mounted jet-view 'plates as the shock-diffusion pods were retracted from in front of the giant ramjets. They had been fully extended and the jets blocked off to reduce drag. Now, for submach speeds, they were fully retracted.

A good six hundred miles per hour was more than fast enough to fire the big jets, even in air this dense. She hit the igniters and tensed involuntarily. The gale of dense, cold air howling through them had to be ionized and utilized in the split fraction of a second it was passing through.

The multiple electron-beams, wrapped in concentric circles around the throats of the jets, started it. Their beams only penetrated air for a fraction of an inch—but that fraction was heated hotter than the solar surface. Air at that temperature is ionized, a plasma—and plasmas are electrical conductors. Behind the electron-beams was a magnetic pinch. When a conductor enters a magnetic field, it is constrained to move, and this field was circular. The thin circle of plasma was forced inward, compressing the cold air within it to 15,000 degrees Fahrenheit. It came out of the exhaust much faster than it went in the intake, and the thrust was unidirectional; no nozzle was needed.

Rival vibrated to the four-fold kick of the big rams and Ynga relaxed; all had fired in the same quarter-second. She pulled the go-stick definitely back and headed for the high side of the atmosphere. At this level, there was no small danger that the dense air would blow out the jets. But by the time she had put another fifteen thousand feet beneath her, it was safe to go super.

Ynga clamped down on the throttle and grinned inside her helmet as the monster rams thundered. Pressure built up on her chest, and, flying by feel, she pulled back more on the go-stick.

Rival vibrated faintly and the thunder abruptly dropped to a murmur, almost a purr. Ynga held the stick back for a long time, topping out at 100,000 feet and 5,000 miles per hour. Very little sound was transmitted to sea level from this altitude, even at this speed and with this mass of plane. She held her speed down to a conservative level, though, until she had passed the tip of Florida.

Here she was treated to a *real* sight. Many big birds congregated here, thousand-ton aerospace planes, that took but an hour from takeoff to touchdown on an antipodal flight. They only went suborbital, and their ammonia tanks were frequently untouched on landing. But they could, with effort, put their full load in low orbit. At her speed she saw only those going her way at near her speed. She was on the Gulf leg of her equatorial flyway, and quite a few were going her way: trucks taking up raw materials to the factories in orbit.

They were slower on the start than *Rival*, however. She walked away from them, doubled her speed, added another 25,000 feet of altitude. Over the equator, she pulled back again. Climbing no faster than she had to to keep her jets firing, she racked up speed. At 15,000 miles per hour, she was unable to hold *Rival* down. The eagle had its eye set on near space. Centrifugal force alone threw her out. She fired her jets until they began to heat up from lack of working fluid; at the end they were firing at near 25,000 degrees.

The whole plane seemed to go limp when the big rams finally shut down. The Indian Ocean was just coming in sight past Africa. Ynga stretched, trying to relax. She checked a number of trouble spots, verified her course on the flight orders, reported again to flight control, settled back to wait.

It didn't take long. She was in suborbital flight, but there was no point in burning fuel near Earth. By the time she had half circumnavigated the planet she'd be at apogee. She'd "burn" enough of the ammonia in her wing tanks to round out her orbit, wait half an orbit, and fire again to escape velocity and over. That would put her in Earth's orbit at less than orbital velocity—falling inward toward the sun. It'd take quite a while to impact on it, but she only intended to stay in that trajectory long enough to dump her load and pull out.

She'd been flying these radioisotope disposal drops for almost a year now. On the whole, she liked them, though they put her on overtime. Since they had been allowed to switch to one driver per bird, she only had to work the usual four-day week.

Being alone thus, Ynga was understandably startled when a hand reached past her to switch off the radio. She twisted around and had her eyes caught by a black hole in a very businesslike pistol.

The man behind it was in bulky space armor, not a skin-tight pressure suit. He grinned past a mustard-yellow moustache, his helmet transparent.

"Sit easy, Ynga femm," he said.

Motion caused her to twist in the other direction. Another man, smaller, also armed, was coolly seating himself in the copilot's chair. Mustard-moustache took the astrogator's seat on her right.

"Hot jets," he said sardonically. "Very. But we'll take it from here. You just have to follow orders and leave the worrying to us. Oke?"

She stared steely-eyed at him.

"Don't try anything funny, Lancaster," said the smaller man sourly. "We weren't born yesterday. Your husband, Pete, and the boy will answer if you do."

Ynga had to fight emotion for several seconds, was unable

58

to speak—though she noted that the man did not know which was her son and which her husband. It suggested that he'd merely been briefed—and that there were a number of men in the gang. It was a well-laid plan—

"That's the trick, femm," said mustard-moustache, grinning confidently at her. He had rugged good looks, was too aware of it, too happy to have her at a disadvantage. Probably he even had one of those lapel pins under his sparmor: UP with Manpower.

The smaller man was the head, and the more sinister. Of course they were professionals, for hire. International business was a violent game. Though what corporation would want to steal a small aerospace truck like this was more than she could guess, or why. But she couldn't risk anything. These were pros. They'd keep their word.

"Give 'er the course, Joel," said the small man.

Joel tore her flight orders out of the holder and inserted his own. His clumsiness in his gauntlets—which he removed—and his general air of fumbling told Ynga that he was a stranger to flight decks, though he seemed to understand astrogation.

Ynga was only a truck driver herself, and knew only the basics, but as he explained the course, she understood. They proposed to fire at apogee of the present orbit, continue to fire for a quarter-orbit at a low thrust, then fire hot, to escape velocity. There they'd dump the load.

That was dangerously close to Earth, though the quarter-orbit on low thrust would take them out a bit. Point was, they'd be adding to instead of subtracting from Earth's solar orbital velocity, dumping on the wrong side of the planet. The load of radioisotopes would fall outward, not inward.

How far she had no way of knowing, or where it would wind up. But, of course, it wouldn't be permitted to go far. In fact, a ship was probably already drifting along on a course that would take it near the load's orbit at the right time. That'd have to be within reach of its lead-"burning" electrorockets; they wouldn't dare go to fusion drive so near Earth. Fusion rockets had disastrous effects on the electromagnetic atmosphere, and it was illegal to use them inside lunar orbit.

"What about—" She had to clear her throat. "My husband—?"

Joel laughed snickeringly.

The small man said, tonelessly, "A couple of the boys have him and the boy. They'll hold 'em until they hear from us, or until a certain time has passed. Don't worry."

Don't worry!

Joel asked her the ship's takeoff weight. She told him, adding numbly that she hadn't used any ammonia yet.

They sat, or floated, while *Rival* climbed silently upward as on some monstrous updraft. Ynga ignored Joel's sidelong glances and tried feverishly to think. They'd have her land the plane somewhere, and hold her until the ship had time to recover the cargo.

No doubt her trajectory would be traced when she varied from her flight plan, but the officials wouldn't think of following the load. They'd be concentrating on the plane.

They might be held quite a while. The load would have to be well away from Earth before it was approached. They might well simply kill her and Bill and Pete rather than hold them so long.

Joel hadn't put his gauntlets back on. And they were wearing armor instead of pressure suits. If she could spill cabin pressure quickly enough, bends would tie them in knots. They were breathing nitrox by their voices. Her own pressure suit was molded of expansion fabric. Every fiber of it was a miniature balloon, open at one end. Under one atmosphere all were fully inflated, somewhat larger in diameter and quite a bit longer. As pressure dropped, they'd deflate, shrinking down to their normal size. At zero, they'd supply nearly an atmosphere of pressure. She'd scarcely feel a sudden drop—if it could be arranged.

"Does everything check out?" asked the small man with a hint of nervousness.

Ynga grinned inwardly; he'd been watching Earth shrink below them. Doubtless he'd been Out before, but it wasn't as immediate as this.

"Sure, weight's right on the nose, we're right on the curve they said," Joel told him absently, familiarizing himself with the astrogating instruments.

And with a sudden swoop of her stomach, Ynga had it.

Her hands were sweating in their gauntlets as they approached apogee. Her tension was not noticed by the hijackers; even Joel had finally given up his scrutiny of her for the majesty of space. They were approaching the night side of the planet, "twelve hours" from her takeoff point, but well off to one side. The sky immediately ahead and above them was that of midnight on Earth.

"O.K.," said Joel finally. He gave her the thrust figure again, set the bird's attitude himself—he had to have help in turning the plane, but he worked the instruments fairly well. Then he checked everything between glances at the visiplates while the small man fidgeted silently.

Joel gave her the go-signal from his own chron.

Ynga obediently hit the ammonia-tank heaters, followed through with the ramjet ignition sequence, then deliberately went around the board, hitting everything that would make a display. The board lit up like a caravan of Christmas trees. Joel and the other stared, bewildered and more than a little frightened.

She grinned a little, weakly, inside her helmet. Their expressions were much like Bill's when she tried to explain the workings of the aerospace planes that were her life, except that he usually looked bored. And he taught nuclear engineering at the General Nucleonics College.

The transmitted vibrations of the big ramjets, now rockets, hummed around them. Ynga's flying fingers touched the ammonia-tank vent-alarm cutoff, her stomach a ball of tension. Would it work *before* the alarm sounded, prevent it from sounding?

It did. She must have hit it just before it went off. She suppressed a sigh.

The red light flashed, of course, but so were plenty of others. She'd just have to keep them all flashing all the time the rockets were on.

Joel had given her a clear course through the Earthbelt, though they came closer than Ynga liked to half a dozen factory complexes. Space was crowded so near the planet, not merely with the factory and space city and amusement complex traffic, but with traffic from Luna and the asteroids as well.

Joel had taken possession of the radio switch, which he kept firmly off. It flashed angrily, adding its mite to the chaos of the board. Ynga's jaw set hard.

The sound of the rockets drowned out the hiss and thrum of escaping gas from the ammonia tanks.

The minutes ticked past like hours, but it was not long before Joel nodded and said, "O.K., up with her!"

Ynga pulled back and squeezed the throttles harder. *Rival* pulled directly away from Earth under three Gs, losing ammonia at a frightening rate. Ynga switched to space-scan radar and clidar. So far she didn't see anyone after them. But they couldn't violate all the rules, regs, laws and international agreements like this and get away with it.

Joel and his boss understood that as well as she did, and they were even more anxious to make it a quick flight. Their flight plan allowed for that. They weren't adding as much to Earth's velocity as Ynga usually subtracted on these flights. The load would drift outward slowly.

Ynga's thoughts kept straying to Bill and Pete. She couldn't stand much of that. Fiercely she concentrated on her own situation. She couldn't think of a thing that would be worth all this trouble to smuggle off Earth. Furthermore, every canister was carefully checked before it was sealed, and if it wasn't radiating, it'd look odd, to say the least. So, what radioisotopes would be valuable enough to warrant so much trouble?

Most big power plants were fusion. Small power plants, such as *Rival*'s and her car's, were charged-particle nuclear-electrics. They used lightweight isotopes such as Carbon-14 and Strontium-90, subjecting them to terrific electromagnetic stress to cause them to break down at an accelerated rate. Isotopes with half-lives in the thousands of years could be burned out in a decade.

Such power plants were very cheap, because the fuel isotopes were easily made. Her cargo was supposedly of such spent fuel sticks. The only difficulty with them was that, though isotopes varied, alphaemitters—alphagens—generally took a different excitation stress than betagens. The two couldn't be mixed in an "alphabetagen" with any degree of success. That was unfortunate, because the number of compounds that could be built could have been greatly increased. The fuel elements had to have the right electrical and mechanical properties as well as nuclear.

That left only the fissionable isotopes and gammagens.

Fissionables?

But fissionable power plants were far more expensive and far less efficient. The electromagnetic excitation used on alphagens and betagens didn't work on neutrons. The only thing they could be worth stealing for was bombs—

Burnout!

Ynga took a quick look at tank pressure and saw with a catch of her breath that they barely had fuel enough to get them back—empty. She switched off the tank heaters quickly, shut down most of the other displays. Then she hit the switches that opened the hatches. The loss of ammonia stopped when the heaters went off.

The big hatches were located between the giant dorsal fins that divided the flying wing into thirds. There was a row of smaller hatches outside these fins, but she left them shut. Radioisotope disposal was a bulk job, and her hundred tons had been made up in the big holds. When all these hatches were up, the ship had two more lines of fins running down its back. Ynga checked visually to see that all were all the way up.

Nodding absently, concentrating hard on her job to still her quaking spirit, she reached for the small rocket controls. These were designed to save bird turnaround time in space when bringing up cargo to factories. Blasting these tiny rockets caused *Rival* to move slowly, grandly "down" from under its burden. The cargo outweighed the bird itself by a large margin.

Once away from the big canisters, which began to spread slowly apart, she rotated *Rival* slowly on the gyros. "Upside down" and flying backwards, she warned them and fired the big rockets again.

She gave them ten Gs until she began to get hazy. Her captors blacked out—neither of them knew enough to have connected up the anti-G bands. The smaller man took it better; smaller people can take pounding better than big ones. One reason Ynga had made space pilot. But she was a good-sized woman, every bit as big as this small man. At a guess he could take as much as she.

He was a suspicious devil; he had a gun and a gimlet eye on her the instant his vision cleared.

When Joel awoke he turned ugly. The idea of blacking out while a woman held out didn't sit well with him. He said nothing, but he had no time to spare for the spectacle of the milk-shot blue planet swelling before them.

"Tell her where," ordered his boss.

Joel sullenly told her to put them down over the South Pacific and they'd tell her where from there. Sidelong glances told her he had his own plans after that.

Now that it was done, Ynga was weak and quivery. Her mind, hazy now, was full of Bill and Pete. Their freckles, engaging grins, and that little gap between their front teeth. Would she ever see them again?

These were professional industrial goons—spies, saboteurs, guards, or musclemen, as indicated, she thought feverishly. Industrial competition was cutthroat, but person-to-person violence tended to be avoided. Reprisals were too easy. They were out of practice. But Bill was only a professor. He wouldn't stand a chance against this kind of pro.

She remembered his earnest head bent over a nuclear physics journal so intently he never noticed the blue smoke pouring up from the defective toaster and hanging under the ceiling. He even wore old-fashioned horn-rimmed glasses. Said it got him half his promotions—made him look studious.

Studious!

Would they have him waiting there when she got down? There'd been time to get him and Pete halfway around the world—it would be after noon.

Maybe they were both dead.

Minutes filled with such reflections crawled with even greater deliberation. But at last they approached the planet. Ynga waited until the last minute to use her rockets. Then she barely had time to roll *Rival* over and set the proper altitude after she had emptied her tanks. They were coming into the air at a pretty steep angle.

It screamed around them. The impact made *Rival* ring like a bell and shy madly for space. Ynga fought the bird down, drove into the air again. A raging flame built up in front of the ikons along the leading edges. Joel and the other stared in fear and gripped their seats.

After the second impact they saw through a haze. Ynga clamped her jaw hard and bent *Rival*'s nose down steeply. Again and again the bird slammed into the upper atmosphere. Not even Joel's boss became suspicious until it was too late.

Ynga pulled back, leveled off, set the autopilot. She was gasping for breath, tasting blood, and seeing through a haze, head whirling. But she couldn't wait for her head to clear. Reaching over, she gathered up the two pistols, tucked them into the clip under her seat. The small man's helmet was ripped off first. She tapped him a couple of times above the ear to be sure, then brought his hands down and slipped the anti-G strap across between his back and his arms. His arms were free from the elbow down when the anti-G strap inflated, but caught between the arms of his chair where he couldn't switch it off—assuming he knew how.

She fixed Joel the same way. The bigger man was bleeding at the mouth. They could still kick at the control board, but she'd bet her life they wouldn't dare. The anti-G straps for the calves could have fixed that, but she didn't bother.

She also removed Joel's helmet.

By the time she had reached the South Pacific, they had recovered.

"Shut up!" she barked. Ynga was taut with desperate rage. At the very least she'd have revenge—

Joel was frothing. The other was very alert.

"I'm making the threats," she told them. "Where are my husband and son?"

Neither responded to the question.

Ynga grinned tightly and cracked the spill valves. Air fluted melodiously out through the whistles. A sound that would be recognized by anyone who watched adventure records.

They began to sweat, but the little man seemed determined to call her bluff. She grinned like a wolf. Both were singularly ignorant of aerospace flight. The air got thinner and thinner. Joel's monotonous threats grew thick.

They weren't yet gasping for breath when Ynga shut the valves.

"Tol' you," breathed the smaller man. "Jus' a bluff. Tough femm, b'not tough nuff."

"That's what I thought," said Ynga. "You'd never dare try to invade a private apartment. It was all a bluff."

She had to let out more air before they started to spill. The little man knew everything. Before he passed out he was babbling drunkenly that Bill would never see daylight again if anything went wrong. Nobody would ever find him on that seafarm. Shrewd questioning also gave her the proper code words to radio her arrival with. Some close checking of Joel's flight orders gave her the location.

65

She gave them more air and turned on course, ignoring the radio.

Ynga was quivering with exhaustion and tension and soaked with sweat, but she held herself in taut control. She couldn't depend on the authorities to get Bill and Pete out alive. On the other hand, the gang would be expecting her to come flying tamely in any time. She teetered indecisively between alternatives.

Finally she decided to go in. At least they'd be together.

When her captives awakened again they were grimly silent. Joel glared at her with real hatred now. She ignored that contemptuously. Approaching the seafarm at high altitude, she warned them: "You haven't seen the all nor the worst I can do while I've got you inside this bird. Try anything and you won't live to regret it—even if *Rival* is sitting flat on the water. Believe me."

They did.

That bluff should hold them until they were down—and they couldn't fly the bird anyway. She looked the farm over as she spiraled in, giving the code words. No comment at her voice; she'd expected to have to force Joel to give the words.

Chewing her lip, Ynga spiraled in, still high, still supersonic. She had the guns but she'd have to leave *Rival* and go hobbling in to use them—alone and under their observation. Couldn't be done. But if she pulled out and ran now, it'd be wet curtains for Bill and Pete—

She bumped up the magnification on the forward visiplates. They had a telescopic circuit to simplify docking in space. Searching the ground, desperately looking for a way out, she coaxed the big high-speed bird in.

"Come right in beside the dome—that wing can land on water, can't it?" asked ground impatiently.

"Check," she said automatically, putting *Rival* into a steep dive preparatory to leveling out on hover and skimming in to the clear water beside the watch domes.

Then she caught her breath.

A seafarm is essentially a series of tanks full of plankton. The mile-square tanks were merely thin plastic sheets supported at the upper edges by floats. The water in them was brought up by solar-powered pumps from as much as half a mile down. At that depth, beyond the reach of the sunlight, there are no plants to fix organic compounds, and the water is so rich with them they precipitate out. This rich water, brought up to sunlight and fed to plants, not only supplied a third of the world with food, but also supplied a third of the world's organic raw materials.

The process lended itself well to automation. The pumps were automatic, the plants grew naturally, fish rarely got into them—and in most cases would promptly have died if they had—and even harvesting was automatic. Pumps picked up the water, centrifuged out the plankton, and sent it along for pressing and drying. Men need only come by at intervals to collect it.

This farm did no processing. Thus, no permanent buildings were needed, only a few domes for the watchmen, who also made on-the-spot repairs. Permanent buildings would have been floating, submerged jobs. But since worldwide weather-conditioning eliminated hurricanes, nothing was needed for the watchmen but inflated domes floating on pontoons.

"Forgive me, Bill—Pete," she whispered as the big bird came in, and squeezed the throttles.

For a half-second she feared the big rams would falter. The howling gale of dense wet air pouring through them at this altitude was already causing them to run hot. The electromagnetic fields weren't able to keep the plasma away from the throats. Now she dived into thicker air, still at supersonic speeds.

But all jets are overdesigned. They held, running hotter and hotter—but they held. *Rival* was making better than 1900 miles per hour as she pulled out over the domes. In the climb, the jets finally faltered. The pyrometers tripped, the safety switches were thrown, and the plane quivered as its driving force vanished. *Rival* seemed half-dead, as sluggish as she felt, as Ynga whipped it into a turn on the turbojets, nose down again.

It was a slow turn. Out of it and making for the domes again, her teeth clamped on her lip at the havoc the single pass had raised.

The domes were down. Unidentifiable bits and pieces were scattered here and there. The body of a man was floating face down in the clear water beside the floats of the domes, apparently having been knocked off the company boat at the dock. It couldn't be Bill; Bill would never wear tartan plaid pants in "incandescent" red and green.

Ynga put *Rival* down hard and fast, her head snapping, the arms of the men, caught behind them, straining. Ramming the nose against the dock, she scrabbled up the guns, un-hooked herself, started out.

Remembering the men, she hesitated, torn. After a mo-ment, hefting a pistol, she stepped reluctantly back. Her face reflected her strain. The shock, on top of all the day's mental and physical shocks, was too much for the half-tough Joel. To Ynga's grim and everlasting delight, the mustard-moustache muscleman fainted.

She contented herself with tapping the head of his boss. He lapsed into unconsciousness readily. Then she was out and running across the dock.

The South Pacific sun hit her through the helmet, the glare arrowing into her eyes. Water lapped, flashed; white floats glared; even the sunpower screens reflected light apologeti-cally into her face. The heat of the tropics smote through her sweatsoaked pressure suit. The salt sweat irritated the raw spots under it. After a few moments she slowed to a rapid, stumbling walk.

It took seconds of clawing at the collapsed fabric to find the door to the first dome. The plastic was set for translu-cence; it was light inside. She lifted it with her helmet. Three men lay sprawled unconscious, bleeding at the ears and noses, around an overturned card table. One breathed stertorously. Beyond, in another room, were two other men in bed. The plastic was dark here—the night shift. Fumbling past, she found the galley. Opposite it was an empty room with a chair and a big visiplate. The 'plate was overturned but still playing a Western record.

In the floor was an opened trapdoor.

Ynga caught her breath, almost plunged through it head-first, trying to look. "Bill!" she called.

"Ynga! For God's sake! Do they have you? What hap-pened?"

She could make out the sprawled body of a man—a body beyond doubt; his head was doubled under him. Fallen through the hatch, doubtless.

It was twenty feet down. After several moments of mental confusion, she placed it as a sub dock. A small sub was used to check the bottoms of the tanks for leaks or fish damage. The dock was for emergencies and doubled as a decompression chamber. Small subs are unwieldy on the surface.

"Bill! You all right? Wh-where's Pete? Bill!"

"O.K., here I am." She saw him looking up. No need to tie him up down there, there was no way out but this. "What do you mean, Pete? He's in school. Home, now," he added, looking at his chron.

"Th-they said they had you b-both. Oh, Bill! C-come on up."

"Let down the ladder. What happened up there? It sounded like a cannon down through this manhole."

Ladder, ladder. She peered under the plastic. "I-I don't see—"

"Built-in, automatic. Look at the edge of the hatch."

Ynga looked, saw a button with an L, hit it. The ladder spewed out of a mouth just under the hatch. A link ladder, with wide flat rungs but uprights of jointed links the size of matchsticks. It retracted to allow room to lower equipment down the shaft.

Bill came up quickly, stared, his height lifting the collapsed dome off her head.

Ynga explained quickly, leading him out, leaning on him for support. Twenty feet under water, he'd merely been almost deafened by the shock. Some of the gang were stirring as they clawed their way back out from under the light plastic. She gave Bill one of the guns.

He took it casually, almost absently. Behind his heavy, horn-rimmed glasses he wore an air of almost childish wonder with a dash of disdain for his erstwhile captors. He did not seem troubled even when they saw the small man glaring at them from *Rival*'s cabin door.

"It lacks a lot of being a competent gang," he said, ignoring her gasp. "Fanatics would be likely to hire third-raters to do their dirty work." The small man's head disappeared before she thought to raise her gun. Bill still seemed unmoved.

Rival had floated some thirty feet away from the dock.

After a moment they heard the whine of the turbines. "He must've been watching everything I did, studying the board," moaned Ynga. Bill pushed his glasses back on his rather blunt nose, shrugged clumsy hulking shoulders in the mannerism that made him seem so ineffectual and—studious.

The rudders on the giant dorsal fins swung hard over. The jets on one side sounded louder than the others. "Going to try to fry us with the jets—the damn fool," muttered Bill.

After a moment Ynga saw what he meant. A hundred-ton aerospace transport can't be handled like an airboat, much less like a rowboat. It obediently swung to the right, but came surging forward much faster. Bill backed away, hesitated. *Rival*'s swinging prow did not quite touch the floating dock—a great hawk moth brooding on its sins, ignoring the water creaming under its beak. She saw that it would make the turn and started to drag Bill away from the jet exhaust.

But he was off and running before she could speak. She saw his glasses bounce absurdly on his flat nose. He took off in an impossibly long leap—through the still-open door of the bird just as it began to recede from the dock.

Ynga's scream mingled with the sound of the jets.

He hit the deck in a sprawl, rolled completely over, losing his glasses. Then he was gone in the dimly-lit interior.

Ynga hobbled frantically along the dock after the receding nose of the plane. She dipped one toe in the water, hesitated, not remembering—if she knew—whether her pressure suit would buoy her up, or drag her down. The gap was much too great to leap now, even unhampered.

"Bill!" she screamed.

Then the jets died.

"Bill!"

"O.K., what do I do now?" he asked her, appearing in the doorway.

In the sudden silence, her sob was as loud as a shout.

"The little guy?" she asked fearfully.

"Dead," he said, shrugging. "Brace up! It's been a rough day, and you've had the worst of it, but it'll soon be over. Just tell me how to get this bird back to the dock."

It took her a moment to catch her breath. "S-set everything on dead center," she said.

He frowned uncertainly.

"The go-stick." She could see the rudders. Below the plane, retracted on ground—she hadn't bothered—were their smaller counterparts. They had to be turned to dead center.

The rudders hadn't enough bite in air to steer at low speeds like this, but those down in the water did.

With some fumbling, he managed to square them. "Now what?" he asked. She told him where to find the compressor turbine controls and how to turn them to start position. Hesitantly, he fired up some of the turbojets. The multiple scream pushed the plane forward slowly, slowly. It bumped the dock as she was hobbling down toward it.

Bill gave her a hand in.

He looked out at the deflated domes. Ynga followed his glance. Most of the living men seemed to be conscious. Motion was visible under the plastic. Three men sprawled across the domes' floats, holding their heads. No doubt they were all deaf—some permanently.

"No point in trying to hold them," said Bill. "They can be traced easily enough from the dead. And they're wounded. Besides, they don't know who hired them. We'll call the authorities and let them handle it. Better call someone right away or you'll lose your license."

The little man was quite dead, with a broken neck. Joel was wide-eyed and sweating, conscious but still strapped in. They ignored him. Ynga took the pilot's seat, felt relief flow upward through her from it. Here she was in her own element.

The radio was blinking angrily.

She turned to the flight-control wavelengths and cut into a babel of voices, most of them angry. Some appeared to be patrolmen. Her explanation wasn't easy to make. She tried to be concise, but the incredulous interruptions slowed her. Some parts of it she held back; these wavelengths weren't secure, and flight control might talk to the press.

It was ten minutes before she got flight instructions, and they were promptly countermanded by a sharp voice which told them to sit tight. Minutes later a fast little courier screamed in—blue and green. UN Treaty Forces. They patrolled international water, air and space under the terms of the various treaties among the Blocs.

Their commander was a Japanese lieutenant with an almost British air. Joel and his boss were removed, with their guns, and their stories recorded. Ynga told them everything she had done.

"It leaves just one question," mused the patrolman, packing away his equipment. "Who's behind it all? One of the big corporations?"

"No," said Bill calmly. "The Lunar Separatists. They're the only group around that would be crazy enough to use nuclear bombs. I had plenty of time to think," he explained to Ynga. He gave the same reasons she had used in concluding that the cargo they had put in pickup orbit had to be either fissionables, or breeder isotopes.

"Wait a minute," said the patrolman, eyes narrowing. "That's not under our jurisdiction, but we know pretty much where every gram of that kind of stuff is. None of the Armed Powers would let much of that stuff get away. And you need ten kilograms just for one crude bomb."

"Not anymore," Bill assured him. "I'm a research nucleonic engineer. It's not generally known, but the alphabetagen excitation problem's been cracked. You have to mix small percentages of fissionables into the fuel sticks, though. And the result isn't a nice, gentle, controlled rate of breakdown. Instead, virtually every unstable atom in the stick lets go at once."

"*Whew!*" whistled the lieutenant. "An alphabetagen bomb! So they had a few kilos of breeder isotopes, thorium or U-238, in one of the canisters. That'd give 'em enough fissionables for several hundred smallish bombs for sabotage." He grinned at Ynga. "They'll hate you, pilot!"

They were not held long after that. They were ordered back to Galveston, where further questioning would await them. Ynga was relieved by a report from flight control; a call to their apartment revealed that Pete was too engrossed in homework to come to the phone.

Bill seemed to hold his breath while *Rival* climbed skyward. When the big rams were off and the plane in suborbital above the atmosphere, she demanded, "Now you tell me how you managed to break that professional muscleman's neck—professor!"

"The company's physical fitness program—remember?" he asked. "Calisthenics, court sports, boxing, wrestling—and karate, savate, and whatever else we require to keep us interested."

"And you never told me! I worried myself almost sick. Just like a man!"

Bill laughed, looking up at the star-spangled blackness above. "They will hate you, too, Ynga," he said, at a tangent. "Having to sit and watch their swag float by just out of reach—they'll have plenty of time to brood on the wiles of women. They won't dare use their fusion rockets—not after everybody's been alerted."

She shrugged, as he had before, at the obvious. "Boiling off ammonia to reduce the plane's mass was obvious," she said. "Of course that puts the canisters in a faster orbit—one farther out. I'm only a truck driver, and a Terrapin at that, but that much astrogation anybody knows. It might even be a solar escape orbit."

He laughed again. "So smugly and calmly floating past, ignoring them—just out of reach. Just like a woman!"

"Serves 'em darn well right," she muttered vindictively, looking up at the sky. "Try to skyjack my truck, will they?"

SATAN'S SHRINE

Daniel F. Galouye

The night was dismally black and silent. Only a weak, warm breeze stirred the dust of the desolate, crater-scarred plain. Far away, on the eastern horizon, a bluish-white glow flickered, highlighting a tremendous domelike structure.

Seconds passed. Then the sky roared angrily above four men who huddled together in one of the craters, a hundred yards from the mile-wide edifice.

Art Grant raised his head cautiously over the lip of the depression. Almost directly ahead, a hundred-foot-high mound of earth lay against the sloping side of the dome, thrown up there, no doubt, by an earlier generation's nuclear missile.

"What are we waiting for, Captain?" a husky voice whispered almost in his ear.

It was Stausman, the Oxford-educated German.

Art slid back down the concavity of the crater. "We'll be ready to go in another ten or fifteen minutes, I guess."

"Fifteen minute, hell!" It was the Russian, Karneiv. "Go now, I say! Go and be finish with job more quickly!"

"Is it not *mon capitaine* who commands this squad?" Philip Latour, Parisian, demanded chidingly.

Thunder boomed, closer this time.

"If we wait until the height of the storm," Art explained patiently, "there's a chance that the more delicate detection devices will be affected by electrical discharge."

"*Voilà!*" exclaimed the Frenchman. "Now you have the reason, have you not?"

But Karneiv wasn't satisfied. "And the storm? What if it not come this way?"

Art moved his shoulders. "Then we'll go back and sit it out until the next one. It's better to wait a few days than to waste five years of training."

Lightning flashed to their right—closer this time. Art counted seconds until the thunder came. The storm, he calculated, should sweep over them in less than five minutes.

The silence that followed was broken only by the rhythmic *clack-clack* of the radiation counters strapped on their wrists.

Art read the luminous dial on his instrument—twenty Roentgen rays an hour. He went over to the two ponderous metal cases that lay in the crater with them—had been with them for over an hour. The glowing needle swung up to twenty-five Rs.

"Gamma leakage the same?" asked Stausman.

"No change."

"Then we've had about a twenty-R dose so far."

"More or less," Art acknowledged. "We still have five hours left to get rid of this stuff without being in any danger."

The Frenchman rose and stretched his thin frame. "And, *mes amis*," he asked, "it is all decided that I, Latour, will be the one who will—how do you say?—mix the ingredients to make the critical mass?"

"Like hell!" Karneiv lunged up. "It was a Russian who was first human to set off nuclear device by hand—in Great Palace of Kremlin. Will be Russian this time!"

Stausman's mastery of English broke under the impact of intense resentment. "*Nein!* Will be me!" he shouted, thumping his chest. Then in a calmer though still determined voice, he said, "I volunteered with the understanding *I* would set off the device!"

Latour's angry face was illuminated by another flash of lightning as he stood before the German, his bony fists knotted. "Latour will be the one! I, Latour, will—"

"Shut up!" Art's voice rasped. "We can decide that later."

But he knew there would be no decision. He was in command. And he would simply order them to return after they had helped bring the components of the device to the most vulnerable spot in the dome.

Sulking, the other three dropped back to the ground.

Then it started to rain—a vicious, pelting downpour that soaked them to the skin within seconds and sent rivulets streaming down their faces and cascading from their chins and elbows and from the tips of their weapon holsters.

Art grasped a handle of one of the metal boxes. "Let's go!"

Latour took the other handle and, under the great weight of the container, they struggled over the lip of the crater. Stausman and Karneiv followed with the other case.

In the driving rain, they plodded toward the dome, bending outward against the pull of their burdens.

"The Shrine of Satan!" Latour grunted, using both hands to support his half of the load. "Ten million tons of concrete and steel for one man. Truly he is *le diable!*"

The mound of earth against the dome could not have been better located for their purpose had they supervised its construction.

Its top, where they now stood in the relentless rain, was only a few feet below the huge barrel of one of the thousands of missile ejectors that ringed the squat structure like a halo of spikes.

Art had thrown a rope over the barrel and the others had shinnied up to a perch on top of the metal cylinder. Now he tied the rope to a second ponderous container and watched as they hoisted it up. Then, hand over hand, he climbed to join them.

"*Sacrebleu!*" the Frenchman exclaimed. "Will not the weather himself stir *le diable* in his Shrine this night?"

Art laughed, throwing a leg over the end of the barrel. "Afraid not, Latour—not through a shell a thousand feet thick. But we'll see what *we* can do."

He dropped onto the slanting inner surface of the rifle and caught Latour's hand, as the Frenchman leaped down beside him. The two then struggled to lower the heavy boxes as Stausman and Karneiv handed them down.

Assembled in the barrel, they moved cautiously down the slope.

The dome trembled. Then another vicious flash and roar

erupted less than a mile from the edifice, lighting even the inside of the missile ejector with intense purplish illumination.

Stausman shouted, "That was no bolt, Captain! Satan fired an interceptor missile! It exploded the incoming missile right outside!"

Art checked his watch. "They've jumped the gun! This can play hell with our plan!"

Latour sneered. "A fine example of Prussian coordination, is it not?"

"The instructions," Stausman snapped back, "were relayed through the French underground—don't forget!"

Art lifted his burden again and started forward in a lumbering run, pulling the Frenchman along with him. "Let's get out of here before Satan starts firing salvos back."

Discarding caution, they raced down the incline.

"*Mon Dieu!*" the Frenchman panted. "This rifle, is it not in the German attack sector?"

"Right in the center of it," Stausman replied. "Main European battery. It'll be one of the first to fire back. Right, Captain?"

Art didn't answer. He was staring ahead—at a faint glow that picked up a thousand reflections along the rifling of the barrel.

"A *light!*" Karneiv exclaimed. "But why? He need no light in outer defense! Loading, firing—all is automatic, no?"

"Of course," Stausman acknowledged, disturbed. "Even the assembly of the missiles."

They reached the end of the rifle and climbed out through a four-foot-wide slit along one side, squeezing past a metallic conveyor belt that bore a motionless string of sleek-nosed projectiles.

Leaping onto the concrete landing, Art and Latour reached up to take the metal containers and to help the other two men.

Almost as soon as they cleared the area of the belt, gears whirred and the line of projectiles inched forward, depositing the first missile into the barrel.

"It'll fire in seconds!" Art warned frantically. "The backlash of gases!"

Again, they paired off and struggled with the containers, stumbling down a wide corridor that paralleled the perimeter of the dome.

The concrete all around them shook and a wave of concussion pounded their eardrums.

"Already he fire back!" Karneiv shouted.

Noxious gases caught up with them and they coughed spasmodically, slowing their pace. The breech of the barrel through which they had entered now lay hidden around the curve of the corridor behind them. But visible ahead was the projectile belt and protruding breech of the next weapon. As they approached, the unit loaded a missile.

Another blast from their rear shook the monstrous structure and more hot gases swirled in the passageway.

Art stumbled and lost his grip on the metal case. It crashed against his leg, tearing cloth and scraping a strip of skin from his calf.

Stausman helped him up.

"*Voilà!*" Latour shouted. "There it is! The passage that goes inward!" He was pointing to a darker corridor that branched off to their left. They raced into it as the rifle immediately behind them fired.

Art stopped to inspect the bleeding wound in his leg.

Karneiv stopped to look, too. "Is unserious," he said.

"Perhaps. But I'd better wrap it up temporarily so we can go on." Art tore a strip from the ripped trouser leg and bound it around the wound.

"The Yankees—they not able to stand a little pain, eh?" Karneiv said sarcastically. "They prove that on Asiatic mainland; in Ukraine during Third War. Comrade Captain Starnoff —he should be leader to this expedition," he muttered. "He would have—"

"Quiet!" Stausman cautioned. "Satan may be listening."

"*Quite right, gentlemen.*"

The voice seemed to erupt from the very walls.

"*This is—let us see—Expedition Number Ninety-three. The first one in over ten years . . . Welcome, gentlemen! Let us sincerely hope that we shall derive equal enjoyment from your brief visit.*"

"*Le diable!*" Latour looked fearfully down the corridor.

"He's detected us already!" Stausman said hopelessly.

Machinery grumbled and a concrete partition slid into place, closing off the radial corridor at the point where they had entered it.

"Didn't you imagine you'd find even more thorough safe-guards within the Shrine than without? You should have surmised as much, knowing that not a single member of the previous ninety-two expeditions returned to the outside."

Art glanced over his head. He could see speakers, spaced at intervals along the ceiling, together with lights, audio pickups and shining lenses that were, no doubt, part of a video detection system.

"Again I say welcome, gentlemen—a cordial welcome from the Supreme Autocrat of The Associated Nations . . . from, as you refer to me, Satan. May you enjoy your brief expedition."

Art turned despairingly to the others. "I didn't think detection would come so soon. We now have little hope of gaining our objective. Whoever wishes to return has my permission to do so."

"And you, *mon ami?*"

"You know my answer, Latour. Thirty years ago my father led Expedition Number Eighty-five."

Latour patted him sympathetically on the shoulder. "Then, together, *mon capitaine*, we will extract *la vengeance* from *le diable*."

Art turned to Karneiv. "And you?"

"If the Frenchman go, and the Yankee go, then without question the Russian go, too!" he said arrogantly.

"Stausman?"

The German laughed. "In the absence of pneumatic drills to break through that thing—" he motioned toward the concrete panel which barred their retreat—"you'll have to count me in, too, Captain."

The radial corridor ended at an intersection with a peripheral passageway. As they approached, a concrete panel slid shut to block the left-hand branch of the new tunnel.

After they had hauled the metal containers almost a block past the intersection, they paused to rest again as Art adjusted the bandage on his leg.

Karneiv grumbled angrily. "We get nowhere if Yankee stop to rub leg all time."

His face set grimly, Art stared at the big Russian. "In training," he reminded sharply, "we decided on four rest periods an hour."

The Russian stepped closer. "But we not know then we would be detected so—"

A cry from the Frenchman drew their stares. He was pointing to the floor a few yards down the corridor.

Almost indiscernible against the gray concrete was a human skeleton. Ahead was another, then farther on, they found three more.

"Mon dieu!" Latour exclaimed. "The dead ones—they are all along here!"

Stausman laughed briefly. "Frenchmen, no doubt."

Latour squinted at him. "You will please explain how you deduce that."

"They're the easiest to kill." The German's voice was devoid of jocularity. "If there are any dead Germans, you'll find them closer to the center of the Shrine."

Latour swore in French and lunged for the larger man.

Art stepped between them. "Save it till later," he ordered.

Tensely, Stausman and Latour started back for the crates, Art and the Russian following.

"This no shell." Karneiv swung an arm in the air around him. "All one solid hunk concrete with tunnels. Small wonder no attack had success."

Stausman stopped to wait for Art. "Our principal mistake, I think, Captain, has been in not establishing a system of getting information back to World Underground headquarters, where it could benefit future expeditions."

"I wonder," Art answered thoughtfully, "whether the other ninety-two expeditions had the same idea just about here."

Stausman shrugged indifferently. "You may be right."

The Frenchman paused before reaching down for his handle of the case. "How long, gentlemen—how many expeditions before *le diable* is dethroned?"

Art hoisted his end of the container. "Let's hope this is the last."

Latour shook his head forlornly. "I cannot be that optimistic, *monsieur le capitaine*. It has been three hundred years now. Ever since—"

"Ever since," Stausman broke in, "the French allowed Jornal Sakoran, the Immortal, to establish the nucleus of his Shrine on the Continent."

"I do not believe he is immortal," Karneiv interjected. "We go about this wrong!" the Russian continued. "What

80

we do? We make secret appropriations—every year, from every national area in Associated Nations. We equip expeditionary force with different nationalities, so that will be no chance for any one nation to control Shrine and take up where Satan leave off—"

"We trust each other, don't we?" Stausman asked sarcastically.

"But all is wrong," Karneiv went on. "Last year alone, East Asians spent almost billion—Yankee area almost six hundred million—all for attack Shrine. In past ten year, we put almost thousand men in Secret Corps all over whole world. What it get us?"

"Shut up!" Art roared. Then in a whisper, "Don't you realize he can hear everything in here?"

"What the hell!" the Russian answered explosively. "He know already. He got spies all over. That's all he use money from national areas for—to keep up spy system, pay off agents."

They filed around several skeletons that were lying in the center of the corridor.

"I say we should attack spy system!" Karneiv was arguing. "Then Satan not know on which national area to make retaliation."

Art shook his head. "Tried that once. He just sat back and lobbed missiles into *all* the areas until his underground communication lines were restored. Killed several hundred persons all over the world that time."

Latour sneered. "Three thousand and I still would have resisted! Three hundred thousand died in the first hour of the Third War, is it not so?"

"Could have been three million," Art reminded him. "Destroying hundreds was just a—threat."

"I see you have arrived at the first check point."

Art started, almost dropping his end of the case, as the voice boomed from the ceiling and reverberated up and down the corridor from a score of speakers.

"We shall have roll-call afterward."

The speakers went dead and silence seized the corridor once more.

"Radioactivity up!" Latour shouted, bringing his wrist counter before his face.

81

Art was suddenly conscious of the vicious chattering of his detector. He jerked his head toward the metal case he had dropped, to see whether its lid had somehow been jarred loose. But it was intact, as was the other.

Now the counter was reacting so violently that it was setting up vibrations in his wrist.

"One hundred Rs!" the Frenchman gasped. He was holding his hand close to the wall. "She comes from both sides! From the ceiling too!"

Karneiv and Art sprinted down the corridor.

"One hundred and fifty!" Latour yelled as he and Stausman followed.

But the German glanced over his shoulder. "The device!" He was looking back at the two metal containers they had abandoned.

"Hell with them!" Art instructed. "We have only seconds to get out of this hot spot!"

Already the needle of his counter was halfway through the red mark on its dial.

A deep-throated laugh filled the passageway. *"Run faster, gentlemen,"* the voice urged through the speakers. *"You do not have much farther to go."*

Art glanced behind him as he ran . . . and jolted to a stop.

Stausman had gone back and was struggling with the metal cases!

"Let them go!" he shouted angrily at the German.

"But we have to have them!" Stausman pleaded.

Hesitating, Art backed in the direction that Karneiv and Latour had gone. "We can't do a damned thing if we get shot up with radiation!"

Then he turned and raced after the other two.

Apparently convinced, Stausman followed, running at breakneck speed. But he faltered and fell, losing more critical seconds.

Around the turn in the corridor, Art found the Frenchman and the Russian, leaning against the wall.

"Clear here," Latour panted.

He drew up beside them, waiting for Stausman.

Karneiv was staring at his watch as the German reached them.

A concrete panel slid in place twenty feet to their rear.

Art fought his irregular breathing. "You keep a time check?" he asked Karneiv.

The Russian nodded. "I calculate Latour got single dose of about one-hundred-twenty R. Me too."

"Might vomit once or twice in a few hours," Art said thoughtfully.

"You, Captain, got almost two hundred."

Art frowned. "What about Stausman?" he asked.

Karneiv stared hesitatingly at the Captain who, in turn, glanced fearfully at Stausman.

"I kept check too," the German said unemotionally. "I got—"

The ceiling speakers rumbled. *"Over one thousand!"* the voice said. *"A fatal dose—not immediately fatal perhaps. There will first be vomiting and thirst and fever and delirium—in a short while. Then you will die."*

Stausman clenched a fist and raised it toward the nearest video lens in the ceiling. "But not before I find you, you—devil!" he threatened. "Not before—"

"Easy," Art calmed him, holding his arms at his side. "Exertion'll only make it worse."

"I don't give a damn!" the German exclaimed, his teeth set tightly together. "I'm not afraid of failure. I should have died in training three years ago—when they had to cover that hole in my skull with a plate!"

He broke loose from Art and bolted to race up the corridor. But Latour and Karneiv caught him, each by an arm.

"Let me go!" he screamed. "I'll find him! I'll—"

"Patience, *mon ami*," the Frenchman whispered. It was the first time he had used the phrase addressing the German.

"You do no good by self." Karneiv shook his head dourly. "Perhaps together we find devil of Shrine before—"

Stausman relaxed in their grip. They released him cautiously.

"Feeling better?" Art asked, embarrassed after he had said it.

The German nodded, smiled weakly.

After a moment, Karneiv intoned softly, "Death to Satan!"

He was staring at the wall—at a spot above the outstretched arm of a skeleton. The bony fingers still clutched the rock that the victim had used to scratch *Expedition 47* in the chalky concrete.

Farther along, another scrawl, *Death to Dictator Sakoran!* The phrase typed him as a member of one of the earliest expeditions—dating to the time before Sakoran had earned the more pointed alphabetical designation *Satan* from the initials of his assumed title, "Supreme Autocrat of The Associated Nations."

"The Sun, he is just rising outside now, *n'est-ce pas?*" Latour asked wistfully.

It was almost two hours after they had run the gauntlet of the radioactive corridor. They were tired and haggard and had drawn up to allow Stausman to rest.

Art checked his watch and nodded.

"Then in three hours the—how you say? fireworks—they will commence, *non?*"

Art closed his eyes and passed a hand over his face. He was just beginning to experience the nauseating effects of exposure to gamma radiation. He swallowed with difficulty. "The general missile attack will begin in three hours and fifteen minutes," he acknowledged.

"Fools!" Karneiv roared in front of him. "The microphones! *He* listen!"

"He knows. The probing attack has been routine after almost every expedition. He will expect the missiles as a test of our success."

"*Bah!*" the Russian spat. "*Success*. We will fail! Satan play games with us!"

A grating sounded behind them and they whirled around, instinctively drawing their weapons. But it was only another partition, sliding into place to bar the passageway.

Stausman, who had just passed the spot, was leaning against the wall, sick. Latour uttered a sympathetic phrase in French and went back to grasp the German's shoulder and support him.

Karneiv turned to Art. "How much more we got to go? What you think?"

Art looked down at the floor hopelessly. "We haven't gone a fifth of the way to the center," he said in a voice that was intentionally low, so Stausman wouldn't hear.

"Look, Captain," the Russian said abruptly. "We come along curving corridors. We find doors of stone blocking our

84

way so we must go only where he wants. Why we no break one of those doors when he make us go in circle again? Might be we find way straight in.''

Art considered the suggestion. But before he could express his approval, he gagged suddenly and turned quickly away from Karneiv.

After he had finished, Art felt somewhat weak and his throat was dry and musty. He cursed himself for not having insisted that they bring along water.

Stausman joined them and they all continued down the passageway. The German's face was pale and drawn and he walked unsteadily.

Art fell back and helped support the German. Karneiv walked cautiously ahead, mumbling angrily in Russian as they passed more skeletons.

''*Pourquoi?*'' the Frenchman asked thoughtfully, looking down at the victims of another expedition.

When no one answered, he repeated. ''Why? Why does not *le diable* stop us where we are? Why does he not kill us now?''

The others were silent, except Stausman, who showed no reaction.

Latour stopped and the rest of the party stopped with him.

''*Le diable*—could he not have closed us up in the radiation field? Or could he not have confined us in any section of the passage to let the hunger consume us, as it no doubt consumed these poor unfortunates here?''

Karneiv frowned deeply. ''Is so. Why he no do it?''

''*Diversion, gentlemen,*'' the amplified voice erupted in the speakers. ''*It is not often that I am privileged to observe my subjects at such close quarters. Therefore, I am not disposed to cut my amusement short.*''

Stausman shouted frenziedly and tore loose from Art and Latour. He reeled down the corridor until he reached a spot underneath the first suspended speaker.

Then his revolver was in his hand and he was firing up at the vibrating diaphragm. The first two shots silenced the speaker and he stood swaying in the center of the passageway.

Now the amplified voice was a series of secondary echoes that reached them from points farther along the tunnel. ''*Shoot at them! Go ahead! You cannot hit me!*''

Still dazed, the German turned on the other three men. His face was red—his eyes half closed—his body trembled.

"*Stausman!*" Art shouted. The German was going to open fire on them!

He raised the revolver.

The Supreme Autocrat's reverberating laughter seemed to quicken his movement.

The German fired an ineffectual shot with his wavering hand.

Latour sprang, diving in under him and coming up beneath his outstretched arm.

Then he seized the German's wrist and wrested the gun from him before he could fire again.

The German fainted.

Art felt ill again. Nausea, aggravated by the emotional impact of the incident, swept over him.

"Goddam devil!" Karneiv roared, shaking his fist at the video cell over his head.

Then he snapped his gun from his holster and took careful aim. The weapon spat and the lens shattered.

Latour, shouting a string of French expletives, raced to the next video pickup station and shot out its lens, too.

"Wait!" Art ordered, straightening. "Save it. Maybe he wants us to get rid of our ammunition."

Hollow laughter came again from remote speakers. "*Shall we proceed, gentlemen?*"

Art recovered from his seizure, went over to help Latour with Stausman.

"The radiation," the Frenchman observed, "I did not know it could do so much to a man in so little time."

"It shouldn't," Art agreed. "But that skull plate in his head may have something to do with it. There might be an absorption factor that—"

A concrete panel slid open swiftly on their left.

"*Check point, gentlemen,*" the Supreme Autocrat announced.

A second panel sprang out from the wall ahead of them. The new avenue which had been opened was not a corridor. Rather, it was a room, fifty feet wide and at least two hundred feet in length. The mouth of another tunnel was open at the other end. The floor was littered with the remains of past victims.

"Sacrebleu!" the Frenchman exclaimed. "Can we deny that here lies almost half the personnel of all the other ninety-two expeditions?"

Karneiv suddenly poked a thumb in the direction of Stausman. "If we go, I say we leave him."

Art stared at the Russian.

"He no good to us," Karneiv explained emotionlessly. "He only hold us back."

Art's face was grim. "He goes—even if Latour and I have to carry him. Right, Latour?"

"C'est correct!"

Karneiv swore disgustedly. "Then Karneiv goes alone!"

"You'll stay with the expedition!"

The Russian shrugged uneasily. "I stay, but—"

"Are you all ready?" the Supreme Autocrat broke in.

Karneiv and Latour stared apprehensively into the room with the skeletons.

"First," the voice continued, *"let me take this opportunity to congratulate you while you are still there to hear. I find your method of entry into the Shrine quite novel. My commendations. I had been wondering when they would think of the ejectors. Until now, entry has usually been through the air ducts—or, occasionally, through the supply intakes that were in use before the Shrine became self-sufficient by assembling a four-thousand-year stockpile of supplies."*

The Supreme Autocrat's voice was free of accent, Art realized for the first time. Was it that, in his centuries-old despotism over nearly all the nations of the world, he had severed all ties of nationalism—including his native French tongue?

"Come, gentlemen." The Autocrat mocked them. *"Let us not waste my time. The test missiles will be fired shortly to determine whether you have succeeded. I must be free to direct the immediate retaliatory measures."*

"We stay here, *diable!*" the Frenchman roared defiantly.

Stausman straightened, freeing himself from Art's grip, and lunged into the room.

Nothing happened to the German.

Abruptly, Art was aware of the accelerated *clacking* of his wrist counter.

"Radiation!" the Russian exclaimed frantically.

"A little persuasion, gentlemen. I'm quite sure you'll decide to enter."

Karneiv and Latour ran inside. Art followed. Glancing overhead, he saw there were no video lenses, no speakers or microphones in this new chamber.

"But there is nothing in here!" the Frenchman exclaimed.

Their wrist counters had silenced abruptly with their departure from the corridor.

"Psychology, perhaps," Karneiv said unsteadily. "Fear psychology."

"Get across to the other corridor," Art urged, "before he closes that door too!"

Running, they overtook Stausman, who was still plodding forward. They grabbed his arms and pulled him along with them.

Suddenly, a tongue of unseen fire licked at Art's wrists, where the radiation counter and watch were strapped.

Karneiv shouted hoarsely.

Latour screamed in pain.

Stausman collapsed and lay limp on the floor, his body twitching as though wracked by high-voltage current, as he lay there among three long-dead invaders.

Art staggered and fell. But he got up immediately and raced, terror-stricken, toward the exit ahead, his mouth an agony of hot coals. He cried out in anguish.

Then he was tearing at the straps of his radiation counter and watch. He got them off and cast the instruments from him, their metal cases glowing red-hot.

His shoes were smoking and he kicked them off as he ran. There was a nest of fire in his side, next to where the revolver was strapped. As he glanced down at the weapon, the smoldering holster burst into flame.

"We're in a selective induction field!" he shouted frantically.

He seared his fingers unsnapping his belt buckle, to hurl the white-hot weapon from him.

The Russian and the Frenchman had gotten rid of the metal on their bodies too—had kicked off their shoes which, even now, were bursting into flame from the heat of the inner nails.

Art was three-fourths of the way across the room when he

was almost deafened by the roar of exploding, super-heated cartridges in the chambers of their discarded revolvers.

After an eternity of blinding pain, he lunged into the corridor, following Latour and Karneiv out of the chamber of torture.

They dropped to the floor in the dimly lit passageway and lay there, exhausted, fighting the agony in their mouths where the metal of dental fillings had heated under the effects of the induction field.

As if hypnotized, they all watched the door slide shut, closing off the room behind them.

"Stausman?" asked Latour.

Art shook his head regretfully.

"Plate under scalp?" Karneiv asked hesitatingly.

Art nodded. "By now it's just molten metal."

The overhead speaker rumbled harshly. *"I see there are still three of you, gentlemen. Now, let me see—I would guess that the Frenchman will be next. He seems to be the least capable of surviving."*

Latour jumped up, his fists clenched. "I will outlive you, pig!" he roared. His face was contorted with hate.

"Easy, Latour." Art tried to calm the enraged Frenchman. "Let's not make it any more amusing for him."

Latour's shoulders sagged despairingly. Then he looked dolefully at Art. "But what will we do, *capitaine?* We have no weapons! We have not even the dignity of wearing shoes. *Je suis dans l'embarrass!*"

Art accepted Latour's statement literally. "I'm a bit more than embarrassed," he said. "I'm down to the where-in-hell-do-we-go-from-here feeling."

He brought his wrists up and inspected the red, blistered flesh where the heated metal of his watch and radiation counter had left ugly, raw wounds. His trousers were smoldering where the flaming holster had lain against them. He beat out the embers with his hands.

The Russian was moaning softly, blowing on his burned wrists. "World national areas," he asked thoughtfully, "How much they got to pay Autocrat?"

Art leaned against the wall and closed his eyes. The physical pain of his wounds was being pushed into the background now by the returning internal effects of the excessive radiation. "Your area kicks in about a billion a year—mine a little more."

"And for what, *mes amis?*" the Frenchman asked before Karneiv could react to the information he had requested. "Only for to fill the pockets of *le diable*, so he can pay his espionage agents and his *governeurs* for the national areas."

The Russian rose and shook his seared wrists, while he paced restlessly. "I say let Autocrat have his extorted money," he said bitterly. "World should do what he want. I say leave Shrine alone."

"Give the devil his due, eh?" Art asked.

"*Eh, bien!*" Latour spread his arms despairingly. "What is it he wants? He rule all the world—yet he stay in his Shrine as though he not exist at all. He seeks no acclaim—yet all must be his slaves."

"He wants only power, Latour." Art recalled the pictures he had seen of the short, stout dictator—pictures that emphasized the cruel lines of his florid face. "A megalomaniac, who is determined that there be no armies in the world that might eventually be turned against him—no weapons that might be aimed at the Shrine."

"And this slavery, *mon capitaine*—how long must it continue?"

"Supreme Autocrat," Karneiv said stonily, "had secret of immortality from scientists even before he build first shell of Shrine. Will live forever."

"It will go on," Art added, "four thousand years at least. He has supplies and ammunition to last that long."

"Longer," Karneiv corrected. "Can get more whenever he want."

Art walked away from the others before he leaned against the wall and surrendered to the revolt his tortured stomach had been spawning.

They were in one of the long, curving corridors again. But this time the arc was more pronounced and Art called attention to the fact that a more noticeable curve could only mean a smaller periphery. Which, in turn, indicated nearness to the center of the Shrine.

He walked almost in a daze, his face flushed and his pulse

pounding. The nausea was gone, but in its place was a thirst that was almost as torturous.

"Water!" the Russian shouted excitedly, staggering forward.

Puzzled, Art raced after him to prevent any lengthening of distance between them that might put Karneiv out of sight.

Ahead, in the center of the tunnel, was a plain table. On its surface was a huge pitcher and several glasses.

"Don't, Karneiv!" Art warned. "Don't drink it!"

The Russian ignored the warning. He grasped the pitcher between his large hands and raised it to his mouth. After he had finished drinking, he handed the container to the Frenchman.

"Good!" Karneiv exclaimed exuberantly.

"But it might be—" Art cut the sentence short, watching Latour drink.

"What the hell!" the Russian shrugged. "If it poison, it good poison."

Art took the pitcher from Latour and sipped from it. The water was ice cold and it swept away the fire that had been blazing in his raw throat.

"Now that we have refreshed ourselves, gentlemen, let us prepare for the next check point."

The three men started, then regarded each other hesitatingly.

"You will notice that on your left is a straight passage."

Art stared distrustfully into the radial tunnel he hadn't noticed before. But he could see nothing. In the absence of a lighting system, it was but a yawning void.

"One of you will enter it. The other two will continue ahead. It is necessary that the party be split into smaller components at this point. I have prepared something special, but only two can be accommodated."

"We no separate!" Karneiv shouted in the direction of the closest microphone.

"I think you will, gentlemen. I have very efficient methods of coercion, as you already realize."

Art tried to produce mental pictures of the possible tortures that might lie ahead for the two who would continue along the peripheral corridor.

"I'll go on ahead," he said to Latour. "You and Karneiv decide who will go with me."

Laughter erupted in the speakers. *"I'm afraid I'm misun-*

derstood. Ahead lies something interesting, of course. But the dark corridor offers only—immediate death.''

Art leaned against the table, his head lowered in despair. "Then whoever continues," he said meditatively, "will have the only chance of reaching—" He tilted his head in the direction of the speakers. "Looking at the problem objectively," he said, "I'm in the worst physical condition and am of least value." He headed toward the dark corridor.

Latour grabbed his arm. *"Non, mon capitaine!"*

Karneiv pulled the Frenchman away. "Let him go. He sick. He no help for the cause. You, me—we get to Autocrat."

"Never will we reach him!" Latour's voice rose in rejection of the Russian's optimism. "And no longer will I, Latour, do as he directs!"

"You will all do as I direct!" the Supreme Autocrat declared. *"I have only to inform you that there are selective induction coils in the walls. And these particular ones are tuned so their effects will be felt in material much softer than metal."*

"You lie!" Latour shouted. Then to Art, "Is it not impossible that he can have all this Shrine wired like one magnificent coil? He—bluffs!"

Art pushed him off gently. "Go with Karneiv."

Then he stepped into the unlit corridor.

The stone panel started to close behind him.

But Latour lunged through at the last second. Immediately afterward, the stone thudded against its stop behind them.

"You fool!" Art told the Frenchman. "He'll—"

Karneiv's frantic screams, barely audible, erupted in the outer corridor. The terrorized outbursts continued for almost a minute, as Art and Latour listened, stunned in the darkness. Then they ended abruptly.

"Ah!" exclaimed the Frenchman in a whisper. *"Monsieur le diable* has tried to trick us, *n'est-ce pas?"* His voice rose excitedly. "Was it not in this corridor that he said was the certain death? Yet, as soon as the door is closed, it is the other one that becomes fatal. *Eh bien!* It was his desire to kill two of us that time and to permit only one to live."

"You have guessed right, Frenchman." The Autocrat's voice sounded in the darkness. *"And you have interfered with*

my schedule. But it makes no difference. The end result will be the same.''

Art reached for the Frenchman's shoulders, pulled him closer. ''Without lights,'' he whispered, ''he can't track us with his video system. If we keep quiet, he won't be able to follow us through the mikes either.''

''Then we proceed?'' Latour asked eagerly.

Art went ahead silently. ''On tiptoe, if necessary.''

''But—'' the other lowered his voice—''can he not turn on the lights whenever he wishes?''

''There *are* no lights in this corridor. I saw that as I entered.''

Art guided himself with a hand along the wall.

''And the doors,'' the Frenchman suggested. ''Is it not possible that we may reach one before he thinks to close it? Then we may go through several more without *le diable* knowing it. We will be lost from him, *n'est-ce pas?*''

Time was endless as they felt their way in the tunnel. Art guessed a half-hour had passed when the Frenchman tightened his grip on his shoulder.

''The doors—we have reached none of them yet, *capitaine?*'' he whispered.

Art considered not telling him, but decided it would be better to be frank. ''We've passed a helluva lot of doors—all closed.''

Latour gasped. ''Then he has made the preparations for us already! It is no use, *mon ami. Le diable* still herds us—like swine.''

''Latour!''

''Yes?''

''Ahead—there's a light!''

They stopped. Faint illumination, only a hundred feet or so ahead, bared the end of the corridor. But Art could not discern the light's source.

The Frenchman swore. ''A—how you call it?—dead end. Now we will starve without ever finding our way out—''

''No, Latour. Look—the corridor turns right! That's where the light's coming from.''

Silently, they went ahead.

Close to the juncture, Art pressed his back to the wall and

inched forward. Then, even more cautiously, he peered around the corner. He jerked his head back immediately.

"*Latour!*" His whisper was barely audible. "It's the Autocrat! He's right around the bend!"

The Frenchman tensed, opened his mouth. But Art clamped a hand over it.

"He's in the corridor—not thirty feet away—waiting!"

"Did he see you?"

"No."

"*Sacrebleu!* What does he do?"

"Nothing. He's just standing there."

"A trap!"

"No. His hands are empty. There are no weapons."

Art hazarded another glance. Jornal Sakoran stood with his hands hanging by his sides. There was an expression of impatience on his face.

"*Le diable*—he is still there?" Latour gripped his arm.

Art nodded absently. Confounded, he tried to imagine what the ruse might be. Certainly, the one-time national dictator who had seized control of a world centuries ago could not be submitting to capture now. Nor was it possible that he could be unaware of two survivors of an expeditionary force who were dangerously close. Yet . . .

With an abruptness that took him by surprise, Latour brushed by and lunged around the corner. Art sprang after him, but the Frenchman had a lead of more than ten feet. Sakoran looked up, smiling.

At the last moment, Art sensed the trap and desperately tried to brake himself. "*Latour!*" he screamed. "*Don't—*"

It was too late. Electrical flames crackled, enveloping Latour's body in brilliant, consuming light. Smoke hissed from his charred figure, even as he dropped lifelessly to the floor. At the same time, there was the crashing sound of shattering glass, and the image of the Autocrat blanked out.

Art, horrified, drew up before the smashed electronic screen that had completely blocked the corridor and had presented the three-dimensional telecast image of Sakoran while it also served as an indiscernible death trap.

But even with the illumination gone from the now dead screen, there was still light in the corridor. It came from around another bend in the passageway beyond.

* * *

Dazed, Art numbly stepped through the jagged remnants of the screen, around the smoldering body of the Frenchman.

He knew that the invulnerability of the Shrine was no myth. Truly, the Supreme Autocrat was invincible. He had killed Stausman, Karneiv, Latour, the scores who were now only skeletons in the corridors, with incredible ease. But wasn't that to be expected? Hadn't he had centuries to learn how to slaughter?

Art lowered his head dejectedly as he continued forward. He went around a bend and jolted to a stop, rigid with astonishment.

Immediately ahead, the passageway widened into a great circular compartment, almost a hundred yards in diameter.

It was the Inner Shrine!

Great gleaming instruments, scores of control panels that were clusters of switches and dials and levers, gauges and indicators and purring machinery—all occupied every available space along the perimeter of the room. Overhead, hundreds of luminescent screens covered the tremendous curved ceiling—the nerve-center of the Autocrat's worldwide communications network.

In the middle of the impressive chamber was a smaller dome of lead, a fifty-foot-high bubble whose standard arrangement of the flashing red lights identified it as the Shrine's nuclear power pack—a *reactor pile!* One that, if made to exceed its safety limits, could be as devastating as a thousand nuclear devices like the one Art and the other members of his expedition had brought with them in the twin metal containers!

But there was no sign of the Autocrat. Was this only another check point?

Bewildered, Art entered the room.

It was no trap! He stood among the glistening array of instruments and controls. He was in the vulnerable center of the most impregnable fortress ever built!

He saw the doorway between two towering instrument cases along the wall on his left. He peered in cautiously. He could see what appeared to be living quarters—plush chairs, tapestries, thick carpets, the edge of a bed.

The door swung wide and the Supreme Autocrat stepped from concealment, a gun in his hand.

Art swore. He had been defeated by his own curiosity! He should have raced for the nuclear pile and . . .

"Come in," said Sakoran. He motioned with the gun and swung to the side as Art entered.

Then the Autocrat sighed deeply and smiled. But it wasn't a smile of derision! It was a warm smile of welcome.

"Don't be alarmed," he said. "The weapon will be used on me—not you. But I fear I may need it to hold you off until I am ready."

Speechless, Art fell backward until he sensed there was a chair behind him. Then he fell sitting in it.

The Autocrat, dressed in a long, gray robe, leaned against a table in the center of the elaborately comfortable room.

"I thought, for a while, the Frenchman would be the successful candidate," he said. "There was much to be commended in his devotion to your cause and his general sense of fraternity and sympathy. But it was his loyalty that disqualified him. It was apparent that he would have immediately told the world about the Shrine."

Art continued to stare incredulously at Jornal Sakoran, the immortal dictator, the Supreme Autocrat of The Associated Nations. There was an incongruity somewhere—an incongruity over and above the impossible developments of the past few minutes. But he was unable to define it.

"However," Sakoran continued, "I found myself incapable of an unbiased decision. So I let the electronic screen decide. The Frenchman eliminated himself."

"Eliminated . . . ?" Art repeated densely.

"Of course. The check points are a process of elimination by which all but the strongest are discarded and the one most fit to assume—"

Art leaped up. "You killed my father!"

"Your father?" Sakoran's hand tightened on the gun and Art relaxed again. "Did he come here with one of the expeditions? Which one?"

"Number Eighty-five."

Sakoran shook his head. "Before my time, I'm afraid. Anyway, that was not a changeover expedition. No, I did not kill your father. You see, I wasn't Satan at the time."

"You weren't Satan?" Art repeated, stunned.

"No—I became the Supreme Autocrat two years later. Expedition Eighty-seven."

Art fell back into the chair. Now he recognized the inconsistency that he had felt on first looking at the Autocrat. The man before him was tall, gaunt. His eyes were blue. And his hair, although gray now, had no doubt been blond when he was younger. While Jornal Sakoran, the French dictator who had built the impregnable Shrine, had been short, stout—had black, crimped hair and intense dark eyes!

Sakoran was not immortal! Sakoran was dead!

"You see," the Autocrat continued, "I am Satan the Fourteenth. But, about the eliminations and the check points—as I was explaining, their end result was your selection as Satan the Fifteenth. I feel sure that you will make a very efficient Supreme Autocrat."

Almost a minute later, Art overcame his astonishment. "I don't understand."

"It's rather difficult to explain," the Autocrat said. "Let me start off by saying that the deaths in the corridor, sadistic as they seem, are necessary. First, there can be no more than one Satan at a time. Even minor differences of opinion, or inherent concern for the welfare of a particular nation, might wreck the effectiveness of the Shrine.

"You see, not all expeditionary groups meet the same fate as yours—only the changeover ones, of which yours was the thirteenth. Of the remaining eighty expeditions, all were executed quite humanely. They had to be killed to protect the Shrine as well as to prevent their possible escape and betrayal to the world of the true nature of the Shrine. And—"

"But why—*why?*" Art shouted.

"Why must there be a succession of Satans?" the Autocrat rephrased the question. "I'll try to explain. When Sakoran established his Shrine as a means of despotic control over his nation, Earth had just fought the Third War.

"It was not a pleasant chapter in history, I assure you. Over a hundred million persons all over the world were annihilated in the war. All world governments were bankrupt. Poverty was rampant. Then came new distrust and, even with the millstone of destitution around its neck, humanity plunged into another armament race.

"In the year Sakoran seized control of France, the leading powers spent a total of more than eight hundred billion for weapons and armies. By comparison, the nations now expend a total of about thirty billion annually on two items—one, forced consignment of capital to governors appointed by the Shrine—two, secret appropriations for weapons to attack the Shrine. There is quite a difference between eight hundred billion—and thirty billion.

"And there is also a difference between the thousand men who are serving the Secret Corps and the millions who would be serving in the armies of the world, if there were no Shrine to outlaw those armies and their weapons under the pretense of self-defense for Satan."

"You mean the whole setup is—insurance against war?" Art asked incredulously.

The Autocrat nodded. "Humanity's greatest debt of gratitude belongs to Jornal Sakoran, the despot. The greatest year the race ever knew was the one in which he was able to extend his rule over all world powers, merely by dropping a few missiles on key cities and demonstrating the invulnerability of his Shrine when the counter-attacks came."

"But Sakoran? What happened to him?"

"The sixth expedition into the Shrine was successful, as you will read in the records here. However only one member survived in that group. It is a good thing for the world that he was a man of foresight. After he killed Sakoran, he became Satan II, successfully repelling all other invasions of the Shrine until he realized he was too old to continue in his role. He then allowed one member of Expedition Seventeen to survive the elimination tests that he had devised.

"Satan II wondered, at first, whether other candidates in the future would be instilled with the same principles as he was—whether they would be willing to assume the role of Supreme Autocrat and make themselves the target of more hatred than the world has ever shown for a single individual.

"But subsequent changes of command here have proved that no qualified man, once he realizes his responsibilities to humanity, can reject the role."

Art was silent. Finally he looked at the Autocrat. "How long must it continue?"

"National areas are already beginning to learn to live with other national areas. But there is still much progress to be made. Another five hundred years, perhaps another thousand.

Our most positive indication of advance in that direction will be the era in which the world discontinues sending expeditions to destroy the Shrine. When that day comes, the Satans will have to devise other means of perpetuating themselves. But that won't concern you."

The Supreme Autocrat held the gun up before him and looked at it thoughtfully.

"I'm so glad you've come," he said plaintively. "It's been hard—lonely. I've killed hundreds. And, all the while, I could never be sure that it was—right."

He raised the gun relievedly to his temple.

"Wait!" Art shouted. "Suppose I don't want to be the—the Autocrat?"

"You have no choice. All the avenues of escape are sealed off. When you learn how to open them, I believe you will have changed your mind."

After a pause, he went on. "In a year or two, you will learn how to control all the devices in the Shrine. And, until you do, any expedition which comes along will be disposed of automatically. Even the firing of the interceptor missiles will be out of your jurisdiction temporarily."

"But how . . . ?"

"You'll be instructed by automatic recorded tapes and visual educational aids through the medium of several of the ceiling screens." He stared unseeingly at Art. "And now, son—I'm a tired, old man . . ."

The Shrine shivered almost imperceptibly and the faintest of rumblings reached Art's ears.

"Those are our interceptor rockets going off to meet the probing missiles," the Supreme Autocrat said. "You will have to retaliate immediately if you expect to preserve discipline and respect. The controls you'll need are immediately beyond that door—the first panel on your right."

Numbly, Art went out the door, stood before the panel.

A screen overhead repeatedly flashed the words *Missile Origin*. It went blank a moment, then came on again with a map of South America. Most of the map faded from the screen, leaving only the impression of Argentina.

In front of him were scores of control studs, each designated with the name of a different city. He found the one marked Buenos Aires and adjusted the vernier control slightly, watching the results of his manipulation on the map overhead.

A small x-mark, indicating where the retaliatory missile would strike, moved southward. When he was sure he had displaced it to an area where there would be a minimum of casualties, he pressed the button.

The Supreme Autocrat's gun went off almost at the same time in the other room.

Art glanced over at a blank area on the wall next to the door. On the space was written a list of Satans. The last entry was Arnold Stolman, Satan XIV, 2968-2996 A. D.

He felt the faint vibration as the retaliatory missile fired.

With a heavy pencil that was on the control panel, he added:

"Art Grant, Satan XV, 2996– _____ A.D."

THE MISSING MAN

Katherine MacLean

"You are not alone," announced the sign, flashing neon red in the dark sky. People in the free mixed streets looked up and saw it as they walked back from work. It glowed red behind them in the sky as they entered the gates of their own Kingdoms; their own incorporated small country with its own laws inside its gate. They changed into their own strange costumes, perhaps light armor, and tourneyed, tilting lances against each other, winning ladies. Or in another Kingdom with a higher wall around its enclosed blocks of city, the strange lotteries and rites of the Aztec sadist cult, or the simple poverty and friendliness of the Brotherhood Love Communes. They were not alone.

Nonconformists who could not choose a suitable conformity lived in the mixed public areas, went to mixing parties, wondering and seeking. Seeking who? To join with to do what? Returning from the parties late and alone, they passed the smaller signs flashing red in the store windows. *"You Are Not Alone. Find your own Kind, Find your own Hobby. Find your own Mate, Find your own Kingdom. Use 'Harmony' personality diagnosis and matching service."*

Carl Hodges was alone. He stood in a deserted and ruined section of the city and saw the red glow of the sign reflecting against the foggy air of the sky of New York, blinking on and off like the light of a flickering red flame. He knew what the glow said. *You are not alone*.

He shut his eyes, and tears trickled from under his closed eyelids. Damn the day he had learned to do time track. He could remember and return to Susanne, he could even see the moment of the surfboard and his girl traveling down the front slope of a slanted wave front, even see the nose of the board catch again under the ripple, the wave heaving the board up, up and over, and whipping down edge-first like an ax. He knew how to return for pleasure to past events, but now he could not stop returning. It happened again before his eyes, over and over. *Think about something else*.

"Crying again, Pops?" said a young insolent voice. A hand pushed two tablets against his mouth. "Here, happy pills. Nothing to cry about. It's a good world."

Obediently Carl Hodges took the pills into his mouth and swallowed.

Soon memory and grief would stop hurting and go away; think about something else. Work? No, he should be at work, on the job instead of vacationing, living with runaway children. Think about fun things.

It was possible that he was a prisoner, but he did not mind. Around him, collecting in the dark, stood the crowd of runaway children and teenagers in strange mixed costumes from many communes across the United States. They had told him that they had run away from the Kingdoms and odd customs of their parents, hating the Brotherhood, and conformity, and sameness of the adults they had been forced to live with by the law that let incorporated villages educate their own children within the walls.

The teeners had told him that all rules were evil, that all customs were neurotic repetition, that fear was a restriction, that practicality was a restriction, and mercy was a restriction.

He told himself they were children, in a passing phase of rebellion.

The pill effect began to swirl in a rosy fog of pleasure into his mind. He remembered fun. "Did I tell you," he muttered to the runaway teener gang that held him as a prisoner-guest, "about the last game of Futures I played with Ronny? It was ten thirty, late work, so when we finished we disconnected the big computer from its remote controls and started to play City Chess. We had three minor maintenance errors as our

102

only three moves. He wiped out my half of the city, by starting an earthquake from a refrigerator failure in a lunchroom. It wiped out all the power plant crew with food poisoning, and the Croton power plant blew up along a fault line. That was cheating because he couldn't prove the fault line. I wiped out his technocrats in Brooklyn Dome just by reversing the polarity on the air-conditioning machine. It's a good thing our games aren't real. Everyone is wiped out totally by the end of a good game.''

A blond kid who seemed to be the leader stepped forward and took Carl Hodges's arm, leading him back toward his cellar room. "You started to tell me about it, but tell me again. I'm very interested. I'd like to study Maintenance Prediction as a career. What does reversing the leads on the air-conditioning machine do to destroy a place?''

"It changes the smell of the air,'' said Carl Hodges, the missing man who knew too much. "You wouldn't think that would make a lot of difference, would you?''

Since June 3rd, every detective the police could spare had been out looking for a missing computer man who had been last seen babbling about ways to destroy New York City.

Judd Oslow, Chief of Rescue Squad, sounded excited on the phone. "Your anti-chance score is out of sight, George. I want you to guess for us where Carl Hodges is and give us another hit like the first three. I'm not supposed to send my men after Carl Hodges, it's not my department, but that's my neck on the block, not yours. Brace yourself to memorize a description.''

"Sure.'' George made ready to visualize a man.

"Carl Hodges, 29 years old, 140 pounds, 5 feet 9 inches tall, brown hair, hazel eyes.''

George visualized someone shorter and thinner than himself. He remembered some short underweight men who were always ready to fight to prove they were bigger.

"His job is assistant coordinator of computer automation city services,'' read Judd Oslow.

"What's that?'' George wanted to get the feel of Carl Hodges's job.

"Glorified maintenance man for the city, the brains for all the maintenance and repair teams. He uses the computer to predict wear and accidents and lightning-strikes and floods that break down phone lines, power and water lines and he sends repair teams to strengthen the things before they are stressed so they don't break. He prevents trouble."

"Oh." George thought: *Carl Hodges will be proud of his job. He won't want to be bigger.* "How does he act with his friends? How does he feel?"

"Wait for the rest." Judd read, "Hobbies are chess, mini-max, and surfing. No commune. Few friends. One girl who met with a fatal accident when they were on a love trip last month. He's not happy. He was last seen at a Stranger's introduction party, 36th Street and Eighth. He might have been spaced out on drugs, or he might have been psychotic, because he was reported as mumbling continuously on a dangerous subject he was usually careful to keep quiet about."

"What subject?"

"Secret."

"Why?"

"Panic."

"Oh." George restrained his natural anger at being confronted with a secret, and remembered an excuse for the authorities. Panic, or any other group stimulation that could send many people unexpectedly in the same direction, could cause destructive crowding and clogging in the walkways and transportation. People could get jammed in, pushed, trampled, suffocated. In a city of tremendous population and close and immediate access to everything, safety from crowding was based on a good scatter of differences, with some people wanting to be in one place and others in another, keeping them thinly spread. Sometimes the authorities kept secrets, or managed the news to prevent interesting things from pulling dangerous jammed crowds into one place.

The chief of Rescue Squad got the TV connection to the public phone turned on, and let George look at a photograph of the missing man. A wiry undersized scholar with a compressed mouth and expressionless eyes. George tried to tune in by pretending it was his own face in the mirror. Staring into its eyes he felt lonely.

He started by going to the Stranger's introduction party. He followed his impulses, pretending to be Carl Hodges. He wandered the city closely on the trail of Carl Hodges, but he did not feel it with any confidence, because he thought that the trail of feelings that urged him from one place to another were his own lonely feelings and sad thoughts. After he was given a few bad events to be sad about, he was sure it was his own mood.

George woke at dawn and watched pink sunlight touch the bushes along the top of a building so they brightened up like candle flames on the top of a birthday cake. He lay with his eyes open and watched while the light brightened and the pink faded. Crickets sang and creaked in the deep grass and bending tall grass tickled against his face.

He lay still, feeling the kind of aches you get from being kicked. There were a lot of aches. The teener gang that had attacked him had even put chain bruises on his legs. They had not been trying to kill him, only to warn him against trespassing again.

But George still felt strange and without friends. Usually he could join any group. Usually he could be anybody's friend. Was he forgetting how to be buddy with strangers? The teeners had left him on the sidewalk tied in a ridiculous knot with fingers and toes hooked together by Chinese fingertrap tubes. He had worked his fingers free, and walked down to his girl friend's Brotherhood Love Commune to sleep. He felt strange and inferior, and hoped no one would look at him, when he entered the commune. The brothers in the front rooms said he was giving out bad vibes, and upsetting an important group meditation, and they gave him a cup of tea and put him out with his sleeping bag.

Four a.m., wondering what he was doing wrong, he went to sleep in a shape-hiding shadow in the grass belt opposite the Rescue Squad midtown headquarters. Now awakened again by dawn, he felt his bruises and felt sad and unsuccessful. He had wandered through many places in the city the night before, but he had not found Carl Hodges. The computerman was still an unlucky prisoner somewhere.

By the time the sun was high, George was going across George Washington Bridge the hard way, on the understruts of the bridge, clinging with bare hands and feet, clambering up and down slopes of girders and cables, sometimes sitting and watching the sun sparkle on the water more than a hundred feet below while huge ships went slowly by, seeming like toy ships.

The wind blew against his skin, warm sometimes and sometimes cold and foggy. He watched a cloud shadow drift up from the south along the river, it darkened the spires of tall buildings, became a traveling island of dark blue in the light blue of the river, approached and widened, and then there was cool shadow across the bridge for long moments while George looked up and watched a dark cotton cloud pass between him and the sun.

The cloud left and the light blazed. George looked away, dots of darkness in front of his eyes, and watched the cloud shadow climb a giant cliff to the west and disappear over the top. He started picking his way along a downslope of girder, moving carefully because the dazzle of sun dots was still inside his eyes, dancing between his vision and the girders. Overhead the steady rumble of traffic passing along the road-way was a far away and soothing sound.

A gull in the distance flapped upward through the air towards him. It found an updraft and drifted upward, wings spread and motionless, and paused in front of him, floating, a white beautiful set of wings, a sardonic cynical head with downcurved mouth and expressionless inspecting eyes.

George was tempted to reach out and grab. He shifted to the grip of one hand on the cross strut and hooked one knee over a bar.

The gull tilted the tips of his wings and floated upward and back, a little farther out of reach in the sky, but still temptingly close.

George decided that he was not stupid enough to let a gull trick him into falling off the bridge.

The gull slanted and slid sideways down a long invisible slope of air and squalled. "Creee. Ha ha ha ha. Ha ha ha . . ." in a raucous gull laugh. George hoped he would come back and make friends, but he had never heard of anyone making friends with a gull. He climbed on toward the New Jersey shore, going up and down slopes of girders, found a steel ladder fastened to the side and climbed it straight up to a paint locker and a telephone. He dialed Rescue Squad, and asked for Judd Oslow.

"Chief, I'm tired of taking a vacation."

"This morning Ahmed reported you walked like a cripple. How late did you work last night?"

"Three thirty."

"Find any clues to Carl Hodges?"

"Not exactly." George looked at the far, high planes and helicopters buzzing through the blue sky. He did not feel like discussing the failure of last night.

"Where are you now?"

"In a painter's crow's nest on George Washington Bridge."

"Climbing George Washington Bridge is your idea of a rest?"

"It's away from people. I like climbing."

"O.K., your choice. You are near Presbyterian Medical Center. Report to the Rescue Squad station there and fill out some reports on what you've been doing all week. Some of the things you've been doing, we would probably like to pay you for. The information girl there will help you fill out the forms. You'll like her, George. She doesn't mind paper work. Let her help you."

Ahmed Kosavakats, George's superior and childhood friend, was ready to admit defeat. He had reasoned in trying to find Carl Hodges and reasoned well.

Any commune which had Carl Hodges could ask him how to bias the city services computer in their favor. Ahmed had been checking the routine deliveries of repairs and improvements and rebuilding and projects to each commune, by running a comparison check against the normal deliveries through the statistics computer. Negative. There was no sign of a brilliant manipulator changing the city services.

Ahmed stood up and stretched long arms, thinking. Whoever had Carl Hodges was not using him. If Ahmed could rescue Carl Hodges and become his friend, he would not miss the opportunity to use him. If a man wanted to influence the future of his city . . .

If he could not use his own logic to find Carl Hodges, then the kidnappers were not thinking logically, and could not be predicted by logic. If they were thinking emotionally, then George Sanford could probably tune to them and locate them. But Ahmed would have to tell him what kind of people to tune to, and how they felt.

George Sanford's intuition was a reliable talent. Once, when George was a fattish, obliging kid in Ahmed's gang, Ahmed had added up how often George's simple remarks and guesses had turned out right. George had guessed right every

107

time. But George didn't think. Half envious, Ahmed had told the others that George's head was like a radio, you could tune his brain to any station and get the news and weather and the right time in Paris, San Francisco, and Hong Kong, but a radio isn't going to add anything up, not even two plus two; it works because it's empty.

George Sanford had grown up to a big silent cat of a man. Extremely strong, not caring apparently whether he ate, drank, or slept, a rather blank expression, but he still tuned in on people. His goals were the simple ones of being with friends, helping out, and being welcome, and he had friends everywhere.

Behind the apparent low IQ there were untapped abilities that could only be brought into action by demanding a lot of George when you asked him to help. It was not certain yet how much George could do. George did not know. He probably did not even think about it. He had no demands on himself.

The thing to do, Ahmed thought, was to keep the pressure on George. Keep him working.

Ahmed found George filling out reports by dictating them to a pretty girl. The pretty office worker had her hands poised over the typewriter and was listening to George with an expression of surprise and doubt. George, with his brow knotted, was plodding through a narrative of something he had done the day before. The girl rolled the report sheet through the typewriter opposite a different blank and asked a question timidly, a tape recorder showed its red light, recording the questions and answers. George hesitated, looking at the ceiling desperately for inspiration, his brow more knotted than before.

George always had trouble understanding the reasoning behind red tape. He did not know why certain answers were wanted. They both looked up with relief when Ahmed interrupted by turning off the tape recorder.

"They told me to team up with you this afternoon," Ahmed said to George. "They give this job priority over reports or any other job. Are you feeling O.K. now?"

"Sure, Ahmed," George said, slightly surprised.

"Let's go outside and see if we can tune to the subject. O.K.?"

"O.K." George got up, moving easily. A bruise showed at his hairline on the side of his head, almost hidden by hair.

On George's right arm were two blue bruises, and below his slacks on the right ankle was a line of red dents with bruises. A left-handed assailant with a club, or a right-handed assailant with a chain, swinging it left to right, would bruise a man on one side like that.

Walking out of the Rescue Squad office Ahmed indicated with a gesture the bruise on George's arm.

"May I ask?"

"No," George replied and closed his mouth tightly, staring straight ahead as they went through the double doors.

George didn't want to talk about it, Ahmed thought, because he had lost that fight. That meant he had been outnumbered. But he was not dead or seriously hurt. The assailants then were not killers, or he had escaped them. Probably a trespassing problem. Probably George had trespassed onto some group's territory or kingdom last night while searching for Carl Hodges by himself. Ahmed put the thought aside. They stopped on a walk among the bushes and trees and looked up at the towering buildings of Presbyterian Medical Center, like giant walls reaching to the sky. Helicopter ambulances buzzed around landing steps like flies.

"Let's not waste time, George, let's get you tuned into Carl Hodges," Ahmed said, pulling out a notebook and pen. "Do you have a picture of Hodges with you?"

"No." The big young man looked uneasy. "You going to do it that same way, Ahmed? If he's sick, will I get sick?"

"I've got a picture here." Ahmed reached for a folder in his pocket and passed a photo to George.

The ground jolted in a sort of thud that struck upward against their feet.

Nine miles or more away, and two minutes earlier, Brooklyn Dome, the undersea suburb, suddenly lost its dome. The heavy ocean descended upon it, and air carrying a torrent of debris that had been houses and people blurted upward through an air shaft. A fountain of wreckage flung upward into the sky, falling in a circular rain of shattered parts to float upon the sea.

All morning a mass wish to escape from the enclosure of walls had driven George happily into the heights and winds and free sky. Now that note in the blend of the mood of the city suddenly changed and worsened to panic, helplessness, defeat, and pain, and then an end. The event telescoped in speed, compressed into a blow of darkness. The broadcast of many thousand miles ended and their background hum in the vibes of the city diminished.

Reaching out with his mind for information, George encountered the memory of that impact. It went by like the thunder wave of breaking the sound barrier, like a wave of black fog. He shut his eyes to tune in, and found nothing, except that the world had lightened. A burden of fear had been suddenly erased.

George opened his eyes and took a deep breath. "Something big," he said. "Something . . ."

Ahmed was watching the sweep second hand on his watch. "Fifty-five hundred feet, one mile," he muttered.

"What are you doing?"

"It's an explosion somewhere. I'm counting the distance. Sound arrives first through the ground, second through the air. I'm waiting for the sound. I'll get the distance by the time lag."

At thirty seconds the sound of the death of an undersea city reached them, a strange sort of grinding roar, muffled, low and distant.

George shut his eyes again, and felt the world change around him to another place.

"Got something, George?" Ahmed asked alertly. "That was about seven miles."

"Someone knows what happened. I'm picking him up. Brooklyn Dome just collapsed."

"Twelve thousand inhabitants," Ahmed said, dialing his wrist-radio grimly, his earphone plugged into his ear. "No one answering at headquarters, just busy signals."

George shut his eyes again, exploring the other place. "Someone's having a nightmare," he said. "He can't wake up."

"Don't flip out, George, keep in touch with facts. A lot of people just died, is all. Keep a grip on that. I'm trying to get our orders."

George stood with his eyes shut, exploring the sensation inside his head. Somewhere a man was trapped in a nightmare, half asleep in a dark prison or closet. It was some kind of delirium.

The real world was a cruel place that bright day, but the

110

black and coiling fragments of that man's world were worse. There was something important about the man's thoughts. He had felt the explosion thud at a distance, as they had, and he had known what it meant. He had expected it.

"Can't locate where he is," George said, opening his eyes and regaining his grip on the bright sunshine world around him.

Ahmed squinted and tilted his head, listening to the obscure and rapid voices of the earplugs of his radio.

"Never mind about that case, George. That's Carl Hodges probably. He'll keep. Headquarters is broadcasting general orders for the emergency. Repair and services inspection people are ordered to make quick inspections at all danger points in the automatic services, looking for malfunction and sabotage. Repair and inspection teams are ordered into Jersey Dome, to check out every part of it and make sure it is not gimmicked to blow the way Brooklyn Dome went. They are instructed to describe it as a routine safety check."

"What do we do? What about us?"

"Wait, I'm listening. They mentioned us by name. We go to Jersey underseas and try to locate and stop a sabotage agent who might have sabotaged Brooklyn Dome and might be preparing to use the same method on Jersey Dome."

"What method?"

"They don't know. They don't even know if there is a saboteur. They're sending us to make sure."

"If there is a saboteur, he's probably working on it right now." George walked, and then ran for the subway steps down into the underground moving chair belts. Ahmed followed and they caught a brace of abandoned chairs just as they slowed and accelerated them again out into the fast lanes.

"Dirty dogs! Let me out of here. I'll kill you." Furiously Carl Hodges kicked and thrashed and bit at restraining straps, remembering at last, believing his conclusions about the group of teeners that had him prisoner. "You decerebrate lizards. Let me out of here, you fools! You killed Brooklyn Dome. I've got to get back to work and level off the exchanges before something else happens. Let me out of here!"

They backed off, their smiles fading at the barrage of his anger. The tallest one answered with a trace of resentment.

111

"Don't get upset, Pops. They weren't real people, just technocrats and objectivists and fascists like that."

"They were techs. This city needs techs. People with tech jobs run the city, remember?"

The tall one leaned over him glowering. "I remember what my tapes tell me. The objectivists passed the law that the compulsory sterility of women can't be reversed without paying five hundred dollars for the operation. That means if I ever want to get married I'll have to save five hundred dollars for my woman to have a kid. They're trying to wipe us all out. Nobody has that kind of money but techs. In the next generation we'll all be gone. We're just getting back at them, wiping them out."

"But faster," chuckled a small kid. "Like *boom!*"

"The objectivists got that law through legally, why don't your people pull enough votes to get it wiped?" Carl Hodges demanded.

"They ship us out to the boondocks. We can't vote. You're talking like an objectivist. Maybe you believe everyone without money should be wiped?"

"I believe anyone without brains should be wiped!" Carl Hodges snarled suddenly. "Your mothers wouldn't have paid ten cents to have you. Too bad the law wasn't passed sooner."

"Genocide." The tall one reached over and hit him across the mouth. "We were nice to you. To *you!*" He turned and spat in revulsion.

Others surged forward.

"Steady." The leader spread arms and leaned back against the pressure. He addressed Carl. "We don't want to hurt you. You tell us things, you're a good teacher. We'll let you have what you want. Money for rights. Lie there until you have enough money to buy your way out. It will cost you five dollars to get out. That's cheaper than five hundred dollars to be born. That's a bargain."

The kids crowding behind him laughed, and laughed again understanding the idea slowly. After a time of clumsy humor they untied him and went off, leaving him locked in a narrow windowless bedroom.

Carl Hodges went around the room, inspecting it and thinking coldly of escaping. He had to get out and straighten up the mess the city was in after the collapse of Brooklyn Dome. He had to get out and have the kids arrested before they sabotaged anything else. According to his best logic, there was no way to get out. He was stuck, and deserved it. He pushed his mind, thinking harder, fighting back a return of weakness and tears. He reached for a happy pill, then took the bottle of white pills and poured its contents down a hole in the floor.

The two Rescue Squad men shifted their chairs through acceleration bands to the inner fast slots, and passed the other chairs, each leaning forward on the safety rail of his chairs as if urging it on. The people they passed were holding portable TV screens like magazines, watching in the same way that people used to read.

The voice of the announcer murmured from a screen, grew louder as they passed, and then again fell to a murmur. "Brooklyn Dome. Fifteen pounds atmosphere pressure to sixty-five pounds per square inch. Exploded upward. Implosion first, then explosion." The voice grew louder again as they approached another sliding chair in the slower lane. Another person listened, propping the screen up on the safety rail to stare into it, with the sound shouting. "Debris is floating for two square miles around the center from which the explosion came. Coast Guard rescue ships, submarines and scuba divers are converged into the area, searching for survivors."

"This is the way the explosion looked from the deck of a freighter, the *Mary-Lou,* five miles south at the moment it occurred." They neared and passed a TV screen which showed a distant picture of an explosion like an umbrella rising and opening on the horizon.

George settled himself in his seat and shut his eyes to concentrate. He had to stop that explosion from happening again to the other undersea dome. Whoever had done it would be laughing as he watched on TV the explosion unfold and settle. Whoever had done it would be eager for destruction, delighting in the death and blood of a small city.

The peculiarly wide range of perceptions that was George Sanford groped out across the city.

"The police department is still investigating the cause of the explosion," said the murmur, growing louder as they passed another TV watcher in the slow lane. Someone handed the announcer another note. "Ah, here we have some new information. Bell Telephone has opened up to the investigators eight recordings taken from public phones in Brooklyn Dome. These phone calls were being made at the moment Brooklyn Dome was destroyed.''

A face appeared on a screen behind the announcer, a giant face of a woman telephoning. After an instant of mental adjusting of viewpoint the woman's face became normal in the viewer eye, the announcer shrank to ant size and was forgotten as the woman spoke rapidly into the phone. ''I can't stand this place another minute. I would have left already, but I can't leave. The train station is jammed and there are lines in front of the ticket booth. I've never seen such lines. Jerry is getting tickets. I wish he'd hurry.'' The anxious woman's face glanced sideways either way out of the booth. ''I hear the funniest noise, like thunder. Like a waterfall.''

The woman screamed and the background tilted as the screaming face and the booth went over sideways. A hand groped past the lens, blackness entered in sheets, and the picture broke into static sparks and splashes. The screen went blank, the antlike announcer sitting in front of it spoke soothingly and the camera rushed forward to him until he was normal size again. He showed a diagram.

George opened his eyes and sat up. Around him on the moving chairs people were watching their TV screens show the pictures he had just seen in his mind's eyes. It showed a diagram of the location of the phone booths at Brooklyn Dome, and then another recording of someone innocently calling from a videophone booth, about to die, and not knowing what was about to happen, an innocent middle-aged face.

Expressionlessly, the people in the traveling subway seats watched, hands bracing the sides of the TV screen, grip tightening as they waited for the ceilings to fall. Audience anticipation; love of power, greatness, crash . . . total force and completeness . . . admiring triumph of completeness in such destruction. Great show. Hope for more horror.

All over the city people looked at the innocent fool mouthing words and they waited, watching, urging the doom on as it approached. *This time be bigger, blacker, more frightening, more crushing.*

George shut his eyes and waited through the hoarse screams and then opened his eyes and looked at the back of the neck of the TV watcher they were passing, then turned around and looked at her face after they passed. She did not notice him, she was watching the TV intently, without outward expression.

Did that woman admit the delight she felt? Did she know she was urging the thundering waterfall on, striking the death-blow downward with the descending ocean? She was not different from the others. Typical television viewer, lover of extremes. It was to her credit that when TV showed young lovers she urged them to love more intensely, and rejoiced in their kisses. Lovers of life are also lovers of death.

George slid down furthur in his seat and closed his eyes, and rode the tidal waves of mass emotion as the millions of watchers, emotions synchronized by watching, enjoyed their mass participation in the death rites of a small city. Over and over, expectancy, anticipation, panic, defeat, death, satisfaction.

The secretly-worshiped god of death rode high.

In twenty minutes, after transfers on platforms that held air-lock doors to pass through into denser air, they arrived, carried by underseas tube train, at the small undersea city of Jersey Dome. Population: ten thousand; residents: Civil Service administrators and their families.

The city manager's office building was built of large colored blocks of lightweight translucent foam plastic, like children's large building blocks. There was no wind to blow it away. Inside, the colors of the light tinted the city man's desk. He was a small man sitting behind a large desk with one phone held to his ear and another blinking a red light at him, untouched. "I know traffic is piling up. We have all the trains in service that city services can give up. Everyone wants to leave, that's all. No. There isn't any panic. There's no reason for panic." He hung up, and glared at the other phone's blinking light.

"That phone," he snarled, pointing, "is an outside line full of idiot reporters asking me how domes are built and how Brooklyn Dome could have blown up, or collapsed. It's all idiocy. Well. What do you want?"

Ahmed opened his wallet to his credentials and handed it over. "We're from Metropolitan Rescue Squad. We're specialists in locating people by predicting behavior. We were sent over to locate a possible lunatic who might have sabotaged Brooklyn Dome or blown it up, and might be here planning to blow up Jersey Dome."

"He just might," replied the manager of Jersey Dome with

a high-pitched trembling earnestness in his voice. "And you might be the only dangerous lunatics around here. Lunatics who talk about Jersey Dome breaking. It can't break. You understand. The only thing we have to fear is panic. You understand?"

"Of course," Ahmed said soothingly. "But we won't talk about it breaking. It's our job to look for a saboteur. Probably it's just a routine preventative checkup."

The manager pulled a pistol out of a desk drawer and pointed it at them, with a trembling hand. "You're still talking about it. This is an emergency. I am the city manager. I could call my police and have you taken to a mental hospital, gagged."

"Don't worry about that," Ahmed said soothingly, picking his wallet back off the desk and pocketing it. "We're only here to admire the design and the machinery. Can we have a map?"

The manager lowered the pistol and laid it on the desk. "If you cooperate, the girl in the front office will give you all the maps of the design and structure that you'll need. You will find a lot of technicians already in the works, inspecting wires and checking up. They're here to design improvements. You understand?" His voice was still high-pitched and nervous, but steady.

"We understand," Ahmed assured him. "Everything is perfectly safe. We'll go admire their designs and improvements. Come on, George." He turned and went out, stopped at the receptionist's desk to get a map, consulted it and led the way across the trimmed lawn of the park.

Out on the curved walk under the innocent blue-green glow of the dome, Ahmed glanced back. "But I'm not sure he's perfectly safe himself. Is he cracking up, George?"

"Not yet, but near it." George glanced up apprehensively at the blue-green glow, imagining he saw a rift, but the dark streak was only a catwalk, near the dome surface.

"What will he do when he cracks?" asked Ahmed.

"Run around screaming 'The sky is falling!' like Chicken Little," muttered George. "What else?" He cocked an apprehensive glance upward at the green glow of the dome. Was it sagging in the middle? No, that was just an effect of perspective. Was there a crack appearing near the air shaft? No, just another catwalk, like a spiderweb on a ceiling.

116

Making an effort he pulled his eyes away from the dome and saw Ahmed at a small building ahead labeled "Power Substation 10002." It looked like a child's building block ten feet high, pleasantly screened by bushes, matching the park. Ahmed was looking in the open door. He signaled to George and George hurried to reach him, feeling as if the pressurized thickened air resisted, like water.

He looked inside and saw a man inside tinkering with the heavy power cables that provided light and power for the undersea dome. Panels were off, and the connections were exposed.

The actions and mood of the man were those of a workman, serious and careful. He set a meter dial and carefully read it, reset it and made notes, then read it again. George watched him. There was a strange kind of fear in the man, something worse than the boxed-in feeling of being underwater. George felt a similar apprehension. It had been growing in him. He looked at Ahmed, doubtfully.

Ahmed had been lounging against the open door watching George and the man. He took a deep sighing breath and went in with weight evenly balanced on his feet, ready for fast action. "O.K., how are the improvements coming?" he asked the workman.

The man grinned over his shoulder. He was slightly bald in front. "Not a single improvement, not even a small bomb."

"Let's check your ID. We're looking for the saboteur." Ahmed held out his hand.

Obligingly the man unpinned a plastic ID card from under his lapel, and put a thumbprint over the photographed thumbprint so that it could be seen that the two prints matched. He seemed unafraid of them, and friendly.

"O.K." Ahmed passed his badge back.

The engineer pinned it back on. "Have fun, detectives. I hope you nail a mad bomber so we can stop checking the defects and go home. I can't stand this air down here. Crazy perfume. I don't like it."

"Me, too," George said. A thick perfumed pressure was in the air. He felt the weight of water hanging as a dome far above the city pressing the air down. "Bad air."

"It has helium in it," Ahmed remarked. He checked the map of the small city and looked in the direction of a glittering glass elevator shaft. A metal mesh elevator rose slowly in the shaft, shining in the semidark, like a giant birdcage full of people hanging above a giant living room.

George tried to take another deep breath and felt that whatever he was breathing was not air. "It smells strange, like fake air."

"It doesn't matter how it smells," Ahmed said, leading the way. "It's to keep people from getting the bends from internal pressure when they leave here. Why didn't you O.K. the man, George? His ID checked out."

"He was scared."

"What of?" Ahmed asked him.

"Not of us. I don't know."

"Then it doesn't matter. He's not up to any bad business."

The two walked across the small green park, through the thick air, toward the glittering glass shaft that went up from the ground into the distant green dome that was the roof of the city. Inside the huge glass tube a brightly lit elevator rose slowly, carrying a crowd of people looking out over the city as a canary would look out above a giant room.

"Next we check the air-pump controls," Ahmed said. "They're near the elevator." People went by, looking formal and overdressed, pale and quiet, stiff and neat. Not his kind of people. Civil servants, government administration people, accountants.

George followed, trying to breathe. The air seemed to be not air, but some inferior substitute. Glittering small buildings rose on either side of the park in rows, like teeth, and he felt inside a tiger mouth. The air smelled like lilies in a funeral parlor. The people he passed gave out vibes of a trapped hopeless defeat that made his depression worse. They passed a crowd of quiet miserable people waiting to get on the elevator, carrying fishing poles and swimming equipment.

High above them the elevator descended slowly.

"That's bad," George said. "You feel it, don't you, Ahmed?"

"Feel what?" Ahmed stopped beside a small rounded building attached to the side of the shaft. The building throbbed with a deep steady *thump, thump, thump,* like a giant heart.

"I want to get out of here," George said. "Don't you feel it?"

"I ignore that kind of feeling," Ahmed said expressionlessly, and pulled on the handle of the door to the pump room. It was unlocked. It opened. The thumping was louder. "Should be locked," Ahmed muttered. They looked inside.

Inside, down a flight of steps two workmen were checking over some large warm thumping machinery. The two detectives went down the steps.

"Identity check, let's see your ID," George said, and looked at the two badges they handed him, in the same way he had seen Ahmed and other detectives checking them over. He took thumbprints and matched them to the photo thumbprints, he compared the faces on the photos to the faces before him. One big one with a craggy, stone chiseled face and vertical grim lines on the cheeks; one short weathered one, slightly leaner, slightly more humor in the face. Both identified as engineers of Consolidated Power and Light, inspectors of electrical motor appliance and life support services.

"What are the pumps doing?" Ahmed asked, looking around.

"Pumping air in, pumping water out," replied one of the men. "There's the pump that pushes excess water up to the top where it comes out as a little ornamental fountain in an artificial island. The pressure equalizes by itself, so it doesn't need elaborate equipment, just power."

"Why pump water out?" Ahmed asked. "The air pressure is supposed to be so high that it pushes the water out."

The man laughed. "You make it sound so simple. The air pressure is approximately the same here as up at the top surface of the dome, but the water pressure rises every foot of the way down. Down here at the bottom it is higher than the air pressure. Water squeezes in along the edges of the cement slab, up through the ground cover and the dirt. We have drains to catch the seepage and lead it back to this pump. We expect seepage."

"Why not pump in more air? Higher air pressure would keep all the water out."

"Higher air pressure would burst the top of the dome like a balloon. There isn't enough weight of water to counterpush."

George got an uncertain picture of air pushing to get out the top and water pushing to get in the bottom. "It's working all right?" He handed the ID badges back to them.

"Right," said the explanatory man, pinning on his badge. "It would take a bomb to get those pumps out of balance.

Don't know why they sent us to check the pumps. I'd rather be out fishing.''

"They're looking for a bomb, dummy," said the other one sourly.

"Oh." The bigger one made a face. "You mean, like Brooklyn Dome blew up?" He looked around slowly. "If anything starts to happen, we're right near the elevator. We can get to the top."

"Not a chance," said the sour one. "The elevator is too slow. And it has a waiting line, people ahead of you. Resign yourself. If this place blows, we blow."

"Why is the elevator so slow?" George asked. *Fix it!* He hoped silently. They listened to the hum of the elevator engine lowering the elevator. It was slow.

"It can go faster, the timer's right here." The sour engineer walked over and inspected the box. "Someone has set it to the slowest speed. I wonder why?"

"For sightseeing," George said. "But I saw the crowd waiting. They have fishpoles. They want to get to the top, they don't want to wait in the middle of the air, just viewing."

"O.K." The big talkative one walked over and firmly set the pointer over to "fast." The sound of the elevator reached the ground on the other side of the wall, rumbled to a stop, and the doors whirred open.

They listened, hearing voices and the shuffle of feet as people crowded into the elevator, then the doors rumbled shut and the elevator started for the top. The whirr was high and rapid. In less than a third the time the trip up to the surface had taken before, the whirr stopped.

The two engineers nodded at each other. "I hope they are happy with it."

"They are getting there faster."

George said, "That makes sense," and Ahmed nodded agreement. They went out and watched the elevator return. As rapidly as falling, the great silver bird cage came down the glass shaft and slowed, and stopped, and opened. It was empty. No one who was up there was coming back in to the city.

More people got on.

"What is up there?" George asked holding himself back from a panic desire to get in the elevator with the others and get out of the enclosed city. "I have a feeling we should go up there,'' he said, hoping Ahmed would misunderstand and think George was being called by a hunch.

"What do you feel?" Ahmed looked at him keenly. The doors of the elevator shut and the elevator rose rapidly, leaving them behind on the ground.

"What I feel is, we shouldn't have let that elevator go without us. We've had it, old buddy. It's been nice knowing you. I didn't expect to die young.''

"Snap out of it.'' Ahmed clicked his fingers under George's nose. "You're talking for somebody else. Hold that feeling separate from your thinking. It's not your kind of feeling. George Sanford isn't afraid, ever. You don't think like that.''

"Yes, I do,'' George said sadly. He heard the elevator doors rumble open far overhead. Somewhere above people had escaped to the top of the ocean instead of the bottom. A dock? An island? Somewhere fresh winds were blowing across ocean waves.

"Locate that feeling of doom,'' Ahmed said. "Maybe our mad bomber is a suicider and plans to go down with the ship. Shut your eyes. Where are you in your head?''

"On top, on an island in the daylight,'' George said sadly, looking at his imagination of sand and seagulls. "It's too late, Ahmed. We're dead.'' A few new people arrived and lined up behind him waiting for the elevator. The sound of the elevator began far above. People approached through the park from the direction of the railway station, and George remembered that there had been fenced in crowds waiting for trains, waiting to get out. Maybe some people had grown impatient and wanted to get to fresh air. The crowd behind him grew denser and began to push. The elevator doors opened in front of George.

"Get in, George,'' said Ahmed, and pushed his elbow. "We're going to the top.''

"Thanks.'' George got on. They were pushed to the back of the cage and the doors shut and the elevator rose with knee-pressing speed. Over the heads of the people before him George saw a widening vision of the undersea city, small buildings circling a central park, dimly and artistically lit by green and blue spotlights on trees and vines, with a rippling effect in the light like seaweed and underwater waves. Paths and roads were lit with bead chains of golden sodium lights. On the other side of the park the railroad station, squares of soft yellow light, fenced in by lacework metal walls. Many people around it. Too many. Dense crowds. The paths across the park were moving with people approaching the elevator shaft.

The elevator reached the top of the dome and went through into a tube of darkness. For a few moments they rose through darkness and then they felt the elevator slow and stop. The doors rumbled open and the people pressed out, hurried through a glass door and down a staircase, and were gone from the top floor.

George looked around. There was the sky and ocean spaces he had dreamed of, but the sky was cloudy, the ocean was gray, and he was looking at them through thick glass. The island viewing platform was arranged in a series of giant glass steps, and the elevator had opened and let them into the top step, a glass room that looked out in all directions through thick glass, giving a clear view of the horizon, the glass rooms below, and the little motor boats that circled the docks of an artificial island.

"How's your hunch? What do you feel?" Ahmed snapped out, looking around alertly, weight on the balls of his feet, ready to spring at some mad bomber that he expected George to locate.

"The air is faked. I can't breathe it," George said, breathing noisily through his mouth. He felt like crying. This was not the escape he had dreamed of. The feeling of doom persisted and grew worse.

"It's the same air and the same pressure as down undersea in the dome," Ahmed said impatiently. "They keep the pressure high so people can come here from under without going through air locks. They can look, take pictures and go back down. It smells lousy, so ignore it."

"You mean the air is under pressure here, as bad as all the way down at the bottom of the ocean?"

"Yes, lunk. That's what makes sense to them, so that's the way they have it set up."

"That's why the wall is so thick then, so it won't burst, and let the pressure out," George said, feeling as if the thickness of the wall were a deliberate coffin wall, keeping him from escaping. He looked out through the thick glass wall and down through the glass roof of the observation room that was the next step down. He saw chairs and magazines like a waiting room, and the crowd of people that had come on the elevator with him, lined up at a glass door, with the first one in line tugging at the handle of the door. The door was not opening. "What are they doing?"

"They are waiting for the air pressure in the room to go down and equalize with the air pressure in the stairwell and the next room. Right now the pressure in the room presses the door shut. It opens inward as soon as the pressure goes down." Ahmed looked bored.

"We have to go out." George strode over to the inside door that shut off a stair leading down to the next room. He tugged. The glass door did not open. "Air pressure?"

"Yes, wait, the elevator is rising. It seems to be compressing the air, forcing it upward." Thick air made Ahmed's voice high-pitched and distant.

George tugged on the handle, feeling the air growing thicker and press on his eardrums. "We have enough pressure here already. We don't need any more fake air. Just some real air. I want to be out of here."

The elevator door opened and a group of people, some carrying suitcases, some carrying fishing gear, pressed out and milled and lined up at the door behind George, pushing each other and murmuring complaints about pushing in tones that were much less subdued than the civil service culture usually considered to be polite.

The elevator closed its doors and sank out of sight, and air pressure began to drop as if the air followed the piston of the elevator in pumping up and down. George swallowed and his eardrums clicked and rang. He yanked hard on the handle of the stairwell door. It swung wide with a hiss and he held it open. The crowd hurried down the stairs, giving him polite thanks as they passed. With each thanks received he felt the fear of the person passing. He stared into the faces of a woman, a teener, a young woman, a handsome middle-aged man, looking for something beside fear, and finding only fear and a mouselike instinctive urge to escape a trap, and a fear of fear that kept them quiet, afraid to express the sense of disaster that filled their imaginations.

"Argh," said George as the last one went down the stair. "Hurry up, Ahmed, maybe they are right." He gestured his friend through the door and ran down after him onto the lower step of a big glass-viewing room with tables and magazines to make waiting easy. Behind him he heard the door lock shut and the whirr of the elevator returning to the top with more people.

George leaned his forehead against the thick glass walls and looked out at a scene of little docks and a buzz of small electric boats circling the platform, bouncing in a gray choppy sea, under thick gray clouds.

"What's out there?" Ahmed asked.

"Escape."

"What about the saboteur?" Ahmed asked with an edge of impatience. "What is he thinking, or feeling? Are you picking anything up?"

"One of those boats is it," George answered, lying to avoid Ahmed's duty to return to the undersea city. "Or a small submarine, right out there. The top's going to be blasted off the observation platform. Get rescue boats in here. Use your radio, hurry, and get me a helicopter. I want to be in the air to spot which boat."

It wasn't all lies, some of it felt like the truth. He still leaned his forehead against the wall and looked out, knowing he would say anything to get out. Or do anything. He tried to tune to the idea of sabotage, and open to other people's thoughts but the urge to escape came back in a greater sickness and swamped other thoughts. *"Why?"* he asked the fear. *"What is going to happen?"* An image came of horses kicking down a barn from inside, of cattle stampeding, of a chick pecking to get out of an egg, with the chick an embryo, not ready yet to survive in air. Kicking skeleton feet broke through from inside a bubble and the bubble vanished. The images were confusing. He looked away from his thoughts and watched the outside platform.

The platform was crowded with people, shivering in a cold wind, apparently waiting their turn to enjoy a ride in the little boats. George knew that they were outdoors because they could not stand being indoors.

Ahmed tapped on his arm. He had the wrist-radio earphones plugged into both ears, and his voice sounded odd and deaf. "Headquarters wants to know why, George. Can you give details?"

"Tell them they have five minutes, seven minutes if they're

124

lucky. Get the patrol boats here to stop it and"—George almost shouted into Ahmed's wrist mike—"GET ME THAT HELICOPTER. Get it over here fast! We need it as soon as we get through the air locks!"

The glass air-lock door opened and people tumbled and shoved through. On the other side was another room surrounded by glass. They lined up against the glass walls like moths against a lighted windowpane, looking out.

"Why do we have to wait so long?" It was a wail, a crying sound like an ambulance siren in the night. The group muttered agreement and nodded at the woman who clutched her hands against the glass as though trying to touch the scene outside.

"I'm not worried about the bends," said a portly older man. "They adjust the waiting time for people with bad sinus and eardrum infections. Does anyone here have a sinus, or eardrum infection?"

"We don't need to wait then," said the same man louder when there was no reply. "Does anyone here know how to make the door open? We can go out right now."

"My son has a screwdriver," suggested a woman, pushing the teen-age young man toward the door. Ahmed moved to protest and the woman glared at him and opened her mouth to argue.

An old woman was tugging at the door. It opened suddenly and they forgot quarreling and went out through the door to the open docks and the cold salt wind, and the sound of cold choppy waves splashing against the cement pillars.

An air-beating heavy whirring sound hovered above the docks.

Ahmed looked up. A ladder fell down and dangled before them. Ahmed grabbed the rope rungs and pulled. They sagged lower. He fitted his foot into a rung and climbed.

George stood, breathing deeply of an air that smelled sweet and right and tingled in his lungs like life and energy. The clouds of panic and resignation faded from his mind and he heard the seagulls screaming raucous delight, following the small boats and swooping at sandwiches. The people clustered at the edge of the docks, beginning to talk in normal tones.

The ladder dangled before him, bobbing up and down. The

rope rungs brushed against his head and be brushed them aside. What had been happening? What was the doom he had just escaped from? He tried to remember the trapped moments and tried to understand what they had been.

"Come on, George," a voice called from above.

He reached up, gripped and climbed, looking up into a sky of scudding gray and silver clouds, and a white and blue police helicopter, bouncing above him, its rotating wings shoving damp fresh cool air against him in a kind of pressure that he enjoyed fighting. At the top the ladder stiffened into a metal stair with rails, and opened into the carpeted glass-walled platform of a big observation helicopter.

Ahmed sat cross-legged on the floor, twitching with hurry and impatience, holding his wrist radio to his lips. "O.K., George, tune to it. *What* will blow the observation building? Who, what, where? Coast Guard is waiting for information."

Still with his memory gripped onto the strange depression he had felt inside the observation building, in the air of Jersey Dome, George looked down and tuned to it and knew how the people still inside felt, and what they wanted.

In the four-step glittering observation building, each glass room was full of people waiting at the doors. He saw the central elevator arrive and open its door and let out another crowd of people to wait and push and pull at the first door at the top. Desperation. A need to get out.

With a feeling of great sorrow, George knew who the saboteurs were. All the kids with screwdrivers, all the helpful people with technical skill who speed elevators, all the helpful people without mechanical understanding who would prop open dime-operated toilet doors for the stranger in need. They were going to be helpful, they were going to go through the air-lock doors and leave the doors jammed open behind them. No resistance behind them to hold back sixty-five pounds per square inch air pressure forcing up from below in the compressed city, pushing upward behind the rising elevator.

He had been pretending to believe it was a mad bomber. How could he tell the police and Coast Guard that it was just the residents of the city, mindless with the need to get out, destroying their own air-lock system?

George held his head, the vision of death strong and blinding. "They are jamming the air-lock system open in the observation building Ahmed, tell someone to stop them. They

126

can't do that. It will blow!" The panic need to escape blanked his mind again.

"Lift," George said, making nervous faces at the view below. "Lift this damned copter."

"Is he all right?" the pilot asked Ahmed.

Ahmed was talking intensely into the wrist radio, repeating and relaying George's message. He made a chopping gesture to shut up.

The copter pilot gave them both a glance that doubted their sanity and set the copter to lift, very slowly.

Slowly beating the air, the copter rose, tilting, and lifted away from the dwindling platform of glinting glass in the middle of the gray ocean.

George gripped the observation rail and watched, ashamed that his hands were shaking.

He saw something indefinable and peculiar begin to happen to the shape of the glass building. "There it goes," he muttered and abruptly sat down on the floor and put his hands over his face. "Hang on to the controls. Here we go. Ahmed, you look. Take pictures or something."

There was a crash, and a boom like a cannon. Something that looked like a crushed elevator full of people shot upward at them, passed them slowly, and then fell, tumbling over and over downward.

A roaring uprush of air grabbed the copter and carried it into the sky, the plane tilted sideways and began to fall sideways. For a moment it was upside down, falling in a rain of small objects that looked like briefcases and fishing rods and small broken pieces that could not be recognized. George hung on to a railing to keep from falling, then suddenly the copter was right side up, beating its heavy spinning wings in a straining pull upward away from the rising tornado that tried to tilt it over again.

With a tearing roar Jersey Dome spat its contents upward through the air shaft, squeezing buildings and foam blocks and people and furniture into the shaft and upward in a hose of air, upward to the surface and higher in a foundation of debris, to fall back, mangled by explosive decompression to the surface of the ocean.

For a long moment the fountain of air was a mushroom-shaped cloud of debris, then it subsided.

With one arm and leg still hooked around the rail, Ahmed

listened intently to his radio, hands cupped over his ears to make the speaker plugs in his ears louder. He spoke.

"The city manager is alive down there and broadcasting. He says the canopy of the dome did not break, it just lowered. The air shaft sucked in everything near it and is now plugged shut with foam blocks from buildings but the blocks are slowly compressing into it, and they can hear an air hiss. Survivors are putting on scuba air equipment and finding places to survive another hurricane if the tube blows free again, but he's afraid of water leaks coming in and drowning them out from underneath because the pressure is going down. He wants the air shaft plugged from the top. Suggests bombing it at the top to prevent more air escaping."

Ahmed listened, tilting his head to the sounds in his ears.

"People in the water," George said. "Bombs make concussion. Let's get the people out."

"Affirmative," said the police pilot. "Look for people."

The helicopter swept low and cruised over the water, and they looked down at the close passing waves for a human swimmer needing help.

"There." Ahmed pointed at a pink shiny arm, a dark head. They circled back, and hovered, let down the ladder, and the two Rescue Squad men climbed down, and maneuvered a web mesh sling around a limp young unconscious naked woman. Her head bobbed under and came up as they slid the sling under her. The waves washed up against their knees as they leaned out from the rope ladder.

"NOW HEAR THIS, NOW HEAR THIS," proclaimed a giant amplified voice. "ALL BOATS IN THE AREA CIRCLE IN THE DISASTER AREA AND TAKE IN SURVIVORS. IN FIVE MINUTES AT THE NEXT SIGNAL, ALL BOATS MUST WITHDRAW FROM THE AIR SHAFT CENTER TO A DISTANCE OF FIVE HUNDRED YARDS TO PERMIT BOMBING. AWAIT SIGNAL. REPEAT. YOU HAVE FIVE MINUTES TO SEARCH FOR AND TAKE IN SURVIVORS."

Ahmed and George shouted up to the pilot, "Ready." And the hoist drew the mesh sling with the young woman in it upward and into the copter through a cargo door in the bottom. The door hatch closed. They climbed back inside, dripping, and spread the unconscious and pretty body out on the floor for artificial respiration. She was cold, pulseless and bleeding from ears, nose, and closed eyes. There were no bruises or breaks visible on the smooth skin. George tried gentle hand pressure on the rib cage to start her breathing again, and some blood came from her mouth with a sigh. He pushed again. Blood came from her eyes like tears.

Ahmed said wearily, "Give it up, George, she's dead."

George stood up and retreated from the body, backing away. "What do we do, throw her back?"

"No, we have to take bodies to the hospital. Regulations," muttered the pilot.

They circled the copter around over the choppy gray seas, wipers going on the windshield. The body lay on the floor between them, touching their feet.

They saw an arm bobbing on the waves.

"Should we haul it in?" George asked.

"No, we don't have to take pieces," said the cop, tone level.

They circled on, passing the little electric boats of the people who had been fishing when the dome blew. The faces were pale as they looked up at the passing helicopter.

The corpse lay on the floor between them, the body smooth and perfect. The plane tilted and the body rolled. The arms and legs moved.

Ahmed seated himself in the copilot's seat, fastened the safety harness and leaned forward with his head in his hands, not looking at the corpse. George looked out the windshields at the bobbing debris of furniture and unidentifiable bits, and watched Coast Guard boats approaching and searching the water.

The copter radio beeped urgently. The pilot switched it on. "Coast Guard command to Police Helicopter PB 1005768. Thank you for your assistance, we now have enough Coast Guard ships and planes in the search pattern, please withdraw from the disaster area. Please withdraw from the disaster area."

"Order acknowledged. Withdrawing," the pilot said and switched the radio off. He changed the radio setting and spoke briefly to Rescue Squad Headquarters, and turned the plane away from the area of destruction and toward the distant shore.

"What's your job in police?" he asked over his shoulder.

George did not answer.

"Rescue, Detection, and Prevention," Ahmed answered for him. "We were in Jersey Dome ten minutes ago." Behind them the bombs boomed, breaking and closing the air shaft.

"You sure didn't prevent this one," said the copter pilot.

Ahmed did not answer.

"This is a blackmail tape. One copy of this tape has been mailed to each of the major communes and subcities in the New York City district.

"We are responsible for the destruction of Brooklyn Dome. It was a warning, and demonstrated our ability to destroy. We have in our possession a futures expert whose specialty was locating and predicting accidental dangers to the city complex caused by possible simple mechanical and human failures. He is drugged and cooperative. We asked him how Brooklyn Dome could self-destruct from a simple mechanical failure, and he explained how. We are now prepared to offer his services for sale. Our fee will be fifteen thousand dollars a question. If you are afraid that your commune has enemies, your logical question would be, what and who can destroy my commune, and how can I prevent this attack? We will provide the answer service to your enemies, if they pay. They might be asking how to destroy your commune as you listen to this tape. Remember Brooklyn Dome. The name and address enclosed is your personal contact with us. No one else has this name. Keep it secret from the police, and use it when you decide to pay. If you give your contact up to the police, you will cut yourself off from our advice, your enemies will contact us through other names, and buy methods to destroy you. Remember Brooklyn Dome. Act soon. Our fee is fifteen thousand dollars a question. The price of survival is cheap."

"Every police department has a copy. Want me to play it again?" Judd Oslow asked. He sat cross-legged on top of his desk like a large fat Buddha statue and sipped coffee.

"Once was enough," Ahmed said. "Paranoia, and war among the communes. What do those nuts think they are doing with that tape?"

"Making money." Judd Oslow sipped his coffee, carefully staying calm. "They mailed one to each commune in the city area, and only two have turned in the entire tape, or admitted receiving it. Only one has turned in his address. The others must be keeping their addresses, planning to ask attack, or defense, questions.''

''Armageddon,'' said Ahmed.

Judd said, ''George, why don't you get off your rump and bring in Carl Hodges? These nuts can't sell his brains if we get him back.''

Ahmed said, ''You just gave George the job last night. He almost had him this morning, but we were reassigned when Brooklyn Dome blew, and had to get off Carl Hodges's trail to go to Jersey Dome.''

''So there's some of the day left. George has spoiled me with success. I'm used to instant results. Come on George, Carl Hodges, right here in this office, packaged and delivered.''

George looked up at him, eyes round and puzzled. ''I'm supposed to help people. Every time I start trying to help Carl Hodges something bad happens. It doesn't come out right. Maybe he likes being in trouble. Bodies all over the place! You don't want me helping, with my luck!''

''Snap out of it, George. This is no time for pessimistic philosophy. Get together with Ahmed and hypnotize yourself and tell me where Carl Hodges is.''

''What's the use?'' George ran his hands over his head in a weary gesture that was not one of his usual gestures. ''Brooklyn Dome people are dead already. Jersey Dome people are mostly dead already. Everybody that ever died is still dead. Billions of people since the beginning of time. How are you going to rescue *them*? Why not let a few more die? What difference does it make?''

''Let's not have an essay on Eternity, George. Nothing makes any difference to Eternity. We don't live in Eternity, we live in now. We want Carl Hodges now.''

''What's the use? My advice just makes trouble. I didn't save those people in Jersey Dome. I wasn't smart enough to understand that they'd want to break their own air locks. No, it wasn't the panic, it was the depression. The air changed its charge. Lab animals act irrational when you reverse the ground to air static charge gradient. I should have . . .''

Judd shouted, ''George, I'm not interested in your bad conscience. If you want to help people, just answer the question.''

131

George winced at the loudness and squinted up at him with his eyes seeming crossed. "George?"

"*Wow!*" Ahmed stepped forward. "Wait a minute. George did it already. That was Carl answering you."

Judd hesitated between confident forward and back motions. He started and stopped a gesture. His confusion reached his expression. He shouted, "Get out of here, you kooks. Go do your lunacy somewhere else. When you bring back Carl Hodges, don't tell me how you did it."

"Affirmative," Ahmed said. "Come on, Carl."

In confusion and guilt George followed and found himself on the open sidewalk, standing under a row of maple trees. The wind blew and the trees shed a flutter of green winged seeds about him. He knew he had failed his job somewhere, and couldn't figure out how to get back to it. He walked to a bench and sat down.

"Do you understand what was just happening?" Ahmed asked.

"Yes." He felt in his mind and found confusion. "No."

"Shut your eyes. You seem to be on a bench in a park. It is an illusion. This is not where you are. Where are you really?"

George had shut his eyes. The voice went in deeply into a place in his mind where he knew he was in a room, a prisoner, and it was his fault. He did not like that knowledge. Better to pretend. He opened his eyes. "I want to be here in the park. Pretend you are real." He bent and touched some green vetch at his feet and felt the tiny ferns. "History doesn't matter. Sensation matters," he said earnestly. "Even these illusions are real because they are happening now. We live in now. Memory isn't real. The past doesn't exist. Why should we feel anything about the past, or care about it?"

Ahmed computed that it was a good probability that Carl Hodges was speaking through George and looking through his eyes as a form of escape. The rationalization was fluent, the vocabulary not George's. Vocabulary choice is as constant as fingerprints.

The person speaking had to be Carl Hodges.

"Carl Hodges. Do you want to get away from where you are and lie down in this park?"

"You are a questioner. I should not speak."

"Is it wrong to answer questions?"

"Yes, answers kill. People are dead. Like Susanne, they are all dead. Does mourning one person kill others? They drowned too, and floated. Saw girl in water . . . Connection . . . ?"

George had been speaking dreamily, eyes wide and round and sightless. He closed his eyes and every muscle in face and body tightened in a curling spasm like pain. He slid off the bench and fell to his knees in the soft vetch. "Get me out of this. Make it unhappen. Reverse time. Wipe me out before I did it." The spasmed crouch, was it pain or prayer?

Watching the figure of misery, Ahmed made urgent calculations. The shame-driven need to escape memory was all there was to work with. Use it.

"Carl, you are in a green field in a small park on East E Avenue and Fifth Street. This is a future scene. Two hours from now, you will be rescued and free, without guilt, relaxed and enjoying being outdoors. We are the police, we are getting into a skytaxi to come and get you. What directions are we giving the driver?"

"Amsterdam Avenue and Fifty-third Street to Columbus Avenue, the wrecked blocks, one of the good cellars near the center of the flattened part of the ruins. Buzz it twice. Thanks. I think I can knock down a kid when I hear you and come out and wave. Land and pick me up fast."

"O.K.," said Ahmed, straightening and stepping back from the crouched praying figure.

George took his hands from his face. "O.K. what?" His voice was George's usual voice. He got up and brushed small green fronds from his knees.

"O.K., let's make a raid into another kid gang's territory," Ahmed said.

"Where's Biggy?" George looked around as if expecting to see their own gang of kids around them. "Oh, he went to the Canary Islands. And the others they went to the Sahara, they all went . . ." He shook his head as if waking up. "Ahmed, what do you mean raid a kid gang territory? That's all over. We're grown up now."

"We're going to rescue that kidnapped computerman. A mixed gang of teener kids are holding him in the ruins near West Fifty-third Street. We know how to handle a kid gang fight."

George was not going to let go of common sense. He

133

settled back on the bench and looked around at the green warm comfort of the park, and rubbed one of the bruises on his arm. "Let's call the police, let them do it."

"We are the police, lunk." Ahmed still stood, smiling, depending on the force of his personality, the habit of command to get George to obey. George looked up at him, squinting into the light of the sky, one eye half closed. A half of a bruise showed at the side of his face, most of it hidden by the hairline.

"Ahmed, don't be a nut. Logical thinking doesn't fight chains and clubs for you. I mean your brains are great, but we need muscle against a juv army, because they don't know about thinking, and they don't listen."

"What if they are all in their cellars, lunk, and we want to drop them before they get in deeper and carry Carl Hodges away? What kind of thing could get them all out into the open where a helicopter could drop them with gas?"

George absently rubbed the dark mark on the side of his face. "They come out when somebody gets onto their territory, Ahmed. Not an army of cops or a helicopter, I don't mean that. I mean some poor goof is crossing, looking for a shortcut to somewhere else, and they all come and beat him up."

"That's for you."

"How did you figure . . . Oh, yeah, you don't mean yesterday. You mean strategy, like. They come out to beat me up again and the copter drops them with a gas spray, and maybe there's no one left underground to kill Carl Hodges, or take him away." George got up. "O.K., let's do it."

They came up out of the subway at Fifty-third Street and walked together on the sidewalk opposite the bombed-out shells of old buildings. A distant helicopter sound buzzed in the air.

"Separate, but we keep in touch. Leave your radio open to send, but shut it for receive so there won't be any sound coming out of it. The copter pilot will be listening. I'll circle the block and look in doorways and hallways for trouble. You cut across. We both act like we have some reason to be here, like I'm looking for an address. We're strangers."

"O.K.," George said. "I've got a story for them for cutting across. Don't worry about me." He turned and walked nonchalantly around the corner, across the street, past some standing ruins and into the flattened spaces, and the area that had once been paved back yard, with steps down to doors that had once opened into the cellars of gone buildings. Flattened rubble and standing walls showed where the buildings had been.

He stood in the middle of a back yard, near two flights of cement stairs that led down into the ground to old doors, and he walked onward slowly, going in an irregular wandering course, studying the ground, acting a little confused and clumsy, just the way he had acted the last time he had been there.

The setting sun struck long shadows across the white broken pavement. He turned and looked back at his own long shadow, and started when another person's shadow appeared silently on the pavement alongside of his. He glanced sideways and saw a tall husky teener in a strange costume standing beside him holding a heavy bat. The teener did not look back at him, he looked off into space, lips pursed as though whistling silently.

George winced again when a short teener with straight blond hair stepped out from behind a fragment of standing wall.

"Back, huh?" asked the blond kid.

George felt the shadows of others gathering behind him.

George said, "I'm looking for a pocket watch I lost the night you guys beat me up. I mean it's really an antique, and it reminds me of someone, I've got to find it."

He looked at the ground, turning around in a circle. There was a circle of feet all around him, feet standing in ruined doorways, feet on top of mounds of rubble, the clubs resting on the ground as the owners leaned on them, the chains swinging slightly.

"You must be really stupid," said the leader, his teeth showing in a small smile that had no friendship.

Where was Carl Hodges? The area George stood in was clean, probably well used by feet. The stairs leading down to a cellar door were clean, the door handle had the shine of use. The leader had appeared late, from an unlikely direction. He was standing on dusty rubble-piled ground which feet had not rubbed and cleared. The leader then had not wanted to come out the usual way and path to confront George. Probably the usual way would have been the door George was facing, the one that looked used.

It was like playing hot and cold for a hidden object. If Carl Hodges was behind that door, the teeners would not let George approach it. George, looking slow and confused, shuffled his feet two steps in that direction. There was a simultaneous shuffle and hiss of clothing as the circle behind him and all around him closed in closer. George stopped and they stopped.

Now there was a circle of armed teeners close around him. Two were standing almost between him and the steps. The helicopter still buzzed in the distance, circling the blocks. George knew if he shouted, or even spoke clearly, and asked for help the copter pilot would bring the plane over in a count of seconds.

The blond kid did not move, still lounging, flashing his teeth in a small smile as he studied George up and down with the expression of a scientist at a zoo studying an odd specimen of gorilla.

"I got something important to tell you," George said to him. But they didn't listen.

"It's a kind of a shame," the blond kid said to the others. "He's so stupid already. I mean if we just bashed out his brains he wouldn't even notice they were gone."

George faced the leader and sidled another small step in the direction of the steps and the door, and heard the shuffle of feet closing in behind him. He stopped moving and they stopped moving. For sure that door was hiding something. They wanted to keep strangers away from it! "Look, if you found my watch I lost, and if you give it to me, I'll tell you about a thing you ought to know."

If he talked long and confusingly enough, every member of the gang would come out on the surface to hear what he was trying to say. They would all be out in the open. The helicopter was armed for riots, it could spray sleep gas and get every one of them.

He didn't even feel the blow. Suddenly he was on his knees, a purple haze before his eyes. He tried to get up and fell over sideways still in the curled-up position. He realized he wasn't breathing.

Could a back of the neck karate chop knock out your

136

breathing centers? What had the teacher said? His lungs contracted, wheezing out more air, unable to let air in. It must have been a solar plexus jab with a stick. But then how come he hadn't seen the stick? The purple haze was turning into spinning black spots. He couldn't see.

"What was it he wanted to tell us?"

"Ask him."

"He can't answer, dummy. He can't even grunt. You'll have to wait."

"I don't mind waiting," said the voice of the one carrying a chain. George heard the chain whistle and slap into something, and wondered if it had hit him. Nothing in his body registered anything but a red burning need for air.

"You don't want to trespass on our territory," said a voice. "We're just trying to teach you respect. You stay on the free public sidewalks and you don't go inside other people's Kingdoms. Not unless they ask you." The chain whistled and slapped again.

George tried to breathe, but the effort to inhale knotted his chest tighter, forcing breath out instead of in.

It is a desperate thing having your lungs working against you. The knot tightening the lungs held for another second and then loosened. He drew in a rasping breath of cool air, and another. Air came in like waves of light, dispelling the blindness and bringing back awareness of arms and legs. He straightened out from the curled up knot and lay on his back breathing deeply and listening to the sounds around him.

The helicopter motor hummed in the distance. *The copter pilot is listening,* he thought; *but he doesn't know I'm in trouble.*

He heard a clink and a hiss of breath like someone making an effort. He rolled suddenly over to one side and covered his face. The chain hit where he had been. He rolled to a crouch with both feet under him, and for the first time looked at the circle of faces of the teeners who had beaten and made fun of him when he was pretending to be drunk and making believe to be Carl Hodges, and had stumbled into this forbidden territory. He had been retracing Carl Hodges's actions, but he had not been sure it was working. He had been near Carl Hodges here, but he had no proof, no reason to protest when they punished him for violating their boundaries. The faces

137

were the same. Young but cold, some faces were uncertain about punishing an adult, but gaining courage from the others. All sizes of teeners in costumes from many communes, but the fellowship and good nature he was used to seeing in groups was missing.

"I used to be in a gang like yours once," he said sharply to inform the radio listener. "I thought you wouldn't jump me. I didn't come here to get stomped. I just want my antique watch and to tell you something."

He finished the sentence with a quick leap to one side, but the swinging chain swung up and followed, slapped into his skin and curled a line of dents around ribs, chest, and arms. The magnet on the end clanked and clung against a loop of chain. The owner of the chain yanked hard on his handle and the metal lumps turned to teeth and bit in and the chain tightened like rope. George staggered and straightened and stood wrapped up in biting steel chain.

He stood very still. "Hey," he said softly. "That ain't nice."

"Tell us about your news." The circle of teeners and juvs around him were curious about the message he wanted to deliver to them.

George said, "A friend of mine was figuring from my lumps that I got here last time that you've got something important you want me to keep away from. He figures you got the missing computerman. The one who blew up Brooklyn Dome. There's a reward out for him."

A ripple of shock ran through the group surrounding him but the blond kid did not need time to assimilate the threat. Without change of expression he made a gesture of command. "Three of you check the streets. Maybe he brought somebody with him." Three ran silently in different directions.

"I'm just doing you a favor telling you what people say," George said in stupid tones. "Now you gotta do me a favor and help me get my watch back."

"Favor?" screamed the tall, misproportioned one with the chain. "Favor? You stupid fink, you should have kept your stupid mouth shut." He yanked hard on the chain to make its teeth extend more sharply.

An outraged force had been expanding in George's chest. He stood still looking meek and confused one more second, watching his captors snarl and hate him for having "told his friend." Then he bent forward and butted the chain holder down, rolled over his form to the cement and rolled rapidly down three small cement steps, unrolling the chain behind him. He came up on one knee reaching for the chain as a weapon. It was a seven-foot chain with a handle at each end. A heavy chain is a terrible weapon in the hands of a strong man. If it had been behind him at the moment of impulse, he would have swept it around and forward and cut them down like grass. He gathered it looped into his hands, eyeing the crowd of oddly dressed teeners that was his target. His speed was too fast to intercept, his motions too smooth to look fast. He threw the chain up into the air behind him then arched back with every muscle tight and bent forward with a grunt of effort, ignoring two clubs that bounced off his shoulders, bringing the chain forward with a tremendous released surge of force that was rage. The teen gang scattered and fled and the chain swung its cutting deadly circle through the air where they had been.

"Dumb punks." George breathed noisily with the effort. "Whyncha act like brothers? Can't let anybody be your friend. Trying to be smart not knowing . . ."

He stopped and let the swinging chain drag along the ground, slowing. He rippled it in and let it wrap around his arm, with a short murderous loop of it in his hand. The sun had set and it was growing darker in the corners and harder to see. George fended off a flung stick by deflecting it with the chain, then grabbed a club for his other hand. Something whistled by and clanged against a wall. Probably a knife. The teener leader would see that George knew too much, and instruct the gang to kill him. The boy was logical and ruthless and would decide a stranger's life was less important to him than the million he hoped to gain from selling the computerman's answers.

"Carl Hodges," George bellowed. "Ally ally infree. I need help. Computerman Carl Hodges, come out." The police riot control man in the circling copter would at last hear a request for help, and bring his plane in fast. The teeners would only hear him yelling Carl Hodges's name and still not be sure the police were near.

The cellar door gave two thumps and a crash and fell forward off its rusty hinges across the steps. A man fell out

139

on top of it and scrambled across the door and up the steps without bothering to straighten from all fours.

At the top he straightened and looked at George. The other man was thin and balding, wiry and a little under average in size, totally unlike George in either shape or face, but the impression of lifetime familiarity was overwhelming. His own eyes looked out of the strange face.

George handed him a club from the ground. "Guard my back. They are going to try to take you alive, I think, but not me." He spun slowly looking and listening, but all was quiet. Teeners lurked in a distance along the routes George would use if he tried to escape.

George looked back at Carl Hodges and saw the thin computerman inspecting George's appearance with a knot of puzzlement between his brows. Looking at him was like looking into a mirror.

"Hello, me over there," George said.

"Hello, me over there," the man said. "Are you a computerman? When I get back on the job do you want to come play City Chess with me? Maybe you could get a job in my department."

"No, buddy, we are us, but I don't play City Chess. I'm not like you."

"Then why . . ." Carl Hodges ducked a flung club and it clattered against the cement. *Then why do I have this impression of two people being the same person?* he meant.

"We have an empathy link in our guts," George said. "I don't think like you. I just feel what you feel."

"God help anyone who feels the way I feel," Hodges said. "I see some kids advancing on my side."

"Hold them off. Back to back. All we need is a little time." George turned away from him again, and searched the corners with his eyes, ready for a rush. "About the way you feel. It's not all that bad. I'll get over it."

"I did it," Carl Hodges said. "How do I get over it. I feel . . . I mean, I have a reason, for feeling . . . I got drunk and the egg hit the fan. How do I get over *that*?" His voice was broken by grunts of effort and things clattered by, deflected, missing them and hitting walls and cement flooring.

They stood back to back and fended off bricks, sticks, and glittering objects that he hoped were not knives. "We can get killed if we don't watch it. That's one way," George said. A stick came through the air and rapped George's ear as he fended it off with his stick. The attackers advanced, silhouettes against the dimming view of stone walls. Another attacker shadow picked up the clattering stick from the ground and threw it back as he advanced.

"Ouch," said Carl Hodges. "Duck." They both ducked and a flung net went by. "We fight well together, we must get together and fight another teen gang sometime. Right?" said his brisk voice. "Ouch, damn."

George received a rush by the tallest of the gang, caught at the outstretched staff and yanked the enemy past. He tried to trip the teener as he hurtled by, but missed and turned to see him neatly tripped by a stick between the ankles by Carl. The teener went face forward to the ground, and rolled, getting out of range.

"Good pass!" Several new and heavy blows on head and shoulders reminded George to watch his own side. Dizzied, he spun, bracing the staff for a pushing blow with both hands, and felt it strike twice against blurred forms. He reversed it and struck down at an attacker with a contented growl.

With a heavy thrumming and a push of air the police helicopter came over a wall swooping low, like an owl settling over a nest of mice, and released a white cloud of gas over them all.

George took a deep breath of the clear air before the cloud reached him. Beside him Carl Hodges took a deep startled breath of the white cloud and went down as suddenly as if a club blow had hit.

Still holding his breath George straddled him, and stood alert peering through the fog at shapes that seemed to be upright and moving. Most of the teeners had run away, or gone down flat on the ground. What were these shapes? Eighteen seconds of holding his breath. Not hard. He could make two minutes usually. He held his breath and tried to see through the white clouds around him. The sound of the helicopter circled, in a wider and wider spiral, laying a cloud of gas to catch all the running mice from the center of the area to its edges.

The shapes suddenly appeared beside him, running, and struck with a double push, flinging him back ten feet and skidding on his back on the sandy concrete. He remembered

141

to hold his breath after one snort of surprise and silently rolled to his feet and charged back.

Carl Hodges's unconscious form was missing. George saw movement through the white fog ahead, heard feet scuffing cement and across hollow wood, and he charged in pursuit of the sounds. He half fell, half slid down the cement steps, across the wooden door on the ground and into a corridor, and glimpsed motion ahead, and heard a closet door shutting. Holding his breath, groping, he opened the door, saw broken wall with an opening, smelled the wet smell of cement and underground drafts, and leaped over a pile of ancient trash brooms into the opening.

Safe to breathe here. As he took a deep breath a brilliant flashlight suddenly came on, shining blindingly in his face from only two feet away. "I have a gun pointed at you," said the precise voice of the blond short teener. "Turn left and walk ahead in the directions I tell you. I could kill you here, and no one would find your body, so try to keep my good will."

"Where is Carl Hodges?" George asked, walking with his hands up. The flashlight threw his shadow ahead of him big and wavering across the narrow walls.

"We're all going to be holing down together. Turn left here." The voice was odd.

As he turned George looked back and saw that the short teener was wearing a gas mask. As he took a breath to ask why, the white fog rolled down from a night-sky crevice above them. It smelled damp and slightly alcoholic.

"Keep moving," said the teener, gesturing with his gun. George turned left, wondering what happened next when you breathed that fog. A busy day, a busy night. An experience of symbolic insight was often reported by people who had been flattened by police anti-riot gas. What had the day meant? Why were such things happening?

Floating in white mist, George floated free of his body over the city and saw a vast spirit being of complex and bitter logic who brooded over the city and lived also in its future. George spoke to it, in thoughts that were not words. "Ahmed uses the world view of his grandmother, the gypsy. He believes that you are Fate. He believes you have intentions and plans."

It laughed and thought. *The wheels of time grind tight. No room between gear and gear for change. Future exists, logi-cal and unchangeable. No room for change in logic. When it adds up, it must arrive at the same concluding scene. The city is necessity. The future is built. The gears move us toward it. I am Fate.*

George made a strange objecting thought. "The past can change. So everything that adds up from the past can change."

There was a wail from the atmosphere. The vast spirit that brooded over the city vanished, destroyed, dwindling to no-where, uncreated, never true, like the Wicked Witch of the West when Dorothy poured a bucket of water over her, leaving behind the same dwindling wail, "But all my beauti-ful disasters, the logic, the logic . . ."

"No arithmetic," George said firmly. "If you can see the future, you can change it. If you can't see the past, it can change by itself and be anything. It won't add up the same twice."

All the crystallized visions of the city of the future shat-tered and dissolved into white fog, a creative fog that could be shaped to anything by thought. George stood at the center of creation and felt stubborn. They were tempting him again, trying to get him into the bureaucratic game of rules and unfreedom. "No," he said. "I won't fence anyone in with my idea. Let them choose their own past."

He came to consciousness lying on the floor in a small tight room with the blond kid sitting on a bed pointing a gun at him.

"They got Carl Hodges back," the kid said. "You ruined everything. Maybe you are a cop. I don't know. Maybe I should kill you."

"I just had a wild dream," George said, lifting his head, but not moving because he did not want to be shot. "I dreamed I talked to the Fate of New York City. And I told Fate that the future can change anytime, and the past can change anytime. In the beginning was the middle, I said. And Fate started crying and boo-hooing and vanished. I mean no more Fate. Vanished."

There was a long pause while the short blond kid held the pistol pointed at George's face and stared at him over the top of it. The kid tried several tough faces, and then curiosity got the better of him. He was basically an intellectual, even

143

though a young one, and curiosity meant more to him than love or hate. "What do you mean? The past is variable? You can change it?"

"I mean, we don't know what happened in the past exactly. It's gone anyhow. It's not real anymore. So we can say anything happened we want to have happened. If one past is going to make trouble, we can change it just by being dumb, and everything will straighten out. Like, for example, we just met, right now, right here, we just met. Nothing else happened."

"Oh." The kid put away his gun, thinking about that. "Glad to meet you. My name's Larry."

"My name's George." He arranged himself more comfortably on the floor, not making any sudden moves.

They had a long philosophical discussion, while Larry waited for the police outside to finish searching and go away. Sometimes Larry took the gun out and pointed it again, but usually they discussed things and exchanged stories without accepting any past.

Larry was serious and persuasive in trying to convince George that the world had too many technicians. "They don't know how to be human beings. They like to read about being Tarzan, or see old movies and imagine they are Humphrey Bogart and James Bond, but actually all they have the guts to do is read and study. They make money that way, and they make more gadgets and they run computers that do all the thinking and take all the challenge and conquest out of life. And they give a pension to all the people who want to go out into the woods, or surf, instead of staying indoors pushing buttons, and they call the surfers and islanders the forest-farmers Free Loaders, and make sure they are sterilized and don't have children. That's genocide. They are killing off the real people. The race will be descended from those compulsive button pushers, and forget how to live."

It was a good speech. George was uneasy, because it sounded right, and he was sure no man was smart enough to refute the killer, but he tried.

"Couldn't a guy who really wanted children earn enough money to get a breeding permit for himself and an operation for his wife?"

"There aren't that many jobs anymore. The jobs that are

144

left are button-pusher jobs, and you have to study for twenty years to learn to push the right button. They're planning to sterilize everyone but button-pushers.''

George had nothing to say. It made sense, but his own experience did not fit. "I'm not sterilized, Larry, and I'm a real dope. I didn't get past the sixth grade."

"When did your childhood support run out?"

"Last year."

"No more free food and housing. How about your family, they support you?"

"No family. Orphan. I got lots of good friends, but they all took their pensions and shipped out. Except one. He got a job."

"You didn't apply for the unemployable youth pension yet?"

"No. I wanted to stay around the city. I didn't want to be shipped out. I figured I could get a job."

"That's a laugh. Lots of luck in getting a job, George. How are you planning to eat?"

"Sometimes I help out around communes and share meals. Everyone usually likes me in the Brotherhood communes." George shifted positions uneasily on the floor and sat up. This was almost lying. He had a job now, but he wasn't going to talk about Rescue Squad, because Larry might call him a cop and try to shoot him. "But I don't bum meals."

"When's the longest you've gone without meals?"

"I don't feel hungry much. I went two days without food once. I'm healthy."

The kid sat cross-legged on the bed and laughed. "Really healthy! You got muscles all over. You've got muscles from ear to ear. So you're trying to beat the system! It was built just to wipe out muscleheads like you. If you apply for welfare, they sterilize you. If you take you unemployable support pension, they sterilize you. If you are caught begging, they sterilize you. Money gets all you muscleheads sooner or later. It's going to get you, too. I'll bet when you are hungry you think of the bottle of wine and the big free meal at the sterility clinic. You think of the chance of winning the million sweepstakes if the operation gives you the right tattoo number, don't you?"

George didn't answer.

"Maybe you don't know it, but your unemployable pension is piling up, half saved for every week you don't claim it. You've been avoiding it a year almost? When it piles high enough, you'll go in and claim your money and let them sterilize you and ship you out to the boondocks, like everyone else."

"Not me."

"Why not?"

George didn't answer. After a while he said, "Are you going to let them sterilize you?"

Larry laughed again. He had a fox face and big ears. "Not likely. There are lots of ways for a smart guy to beat the system. My descendants are going to be there the year the sun runs down and we hook drives to Earth and cruise away looking for a new sun. My descendants are going to surf light-waves in space. Nobody's going to wipe me out, and nobody's going to make them into button-pushers."

"O.K., I see it." George got up and paced, two steps one way, two steps the other way in the narrow room. "Who are you working for, Larry? Who are you crying over? People who let themselves be bribed into cutting off their descendants? They're different from you. Do they have guts enough to bother with? Are they worth getting your brain wiped in a court of law? You're right about history I guess. I'm the kind of guy the techs are trying to get rid of. You're a tech type of guy yourself. Why don't you be a tech and forget about making trouble?"

At the end of the room, faced away from Larry, George stopped and stared at the wall. His fists clenched. "Kid, do you know what kind of trouble you make?"

"I see it on television," Larry said.

"Those are real people you killed." George still stared at the wall. "This afternoon I was giving artificial respiration to a girl. She was bleeding from the eyes." His voice knotted up. Big muscles bulged on his arms and his fists whitened as he tried to talk. "She was dead, they told me. She looked all right, except for her eyes. I guess because I'm stupid." He turned and his eyes glittered with tears and with a kind of madness. He glanced around the small room looking for a thing to use for a weapon.

Larry took out his gun and pointed it at George, hastily getting off the bed. "Oh oh, the past is real again. Time for me to leave!" Holding the gun pointed steadily and carefully at George's face he used his other hand to put on black goggles and slung the gas mask around his neck. "Hold still, George, you don't want a hole through your face. If you fight me, who are you working for? Not your kind of people. Think, man." He backed to the door. George turned, still facing him, his big hands away from his sides and ready, his eyes glittering with a mindless alertness.

Larry backed into the dark hall. "Don't follow. You don't want to follow me. This gun has infrasights, shoots in the dark. If you stick your head out the door, I might shoot it off. Just stand there for ten minutes and don't make any trouble. The gun is silenced. If I have to shoot you, you don't get any medal for being a dead hero. No one would know."

The short teener backed down the dark corridor and was gone.

George still stood crouched, but he shook his head, like a man trying to shake off something that had fallen over his eyes.

He heard Larry bump into something a long way down the corridor.

"I would know," a voice said from the ceiling. Ahmed let himself down from a hole in the ceiling, hung by both long arms and then dropped, landing catlike and silent. He was tall and sooty and filthy and covered with cobwebs. He grinned and his teeth were white in a very dark face. "You just missed a medal for being a dead hero. I thought you were going to try to kill him."

He twiddled the dial of his wrist radio, plugged an earphone into one ear and spoke into the wrist radio. "Flushed one. He's heading west on a cellar corridor from the center, wearing a gas mask and infragoggles, armed and dangerous. He's the kingpin, so try hard, buddies."

George sat down on the edge of the bunk, sweating. "I get too mad sometimes. I almost did try to kill him. What he said was probably right. What he said."

Ahmed unplugged the speaker from his ear. "I was mostly listening to you, good buddy. Very interesting philosophical discussion you were putting out. I kept wanting to sneeze. How come you get into philosophical arguments today and I just get beat up? Everything is backward."

"You're the smart one, Ahmed," said George slowly, accepting the fact that he had been protected. "Thanks for watching." He looked at his own hands, still worrying slowly on an idea. "How come everything the kid said made sense?"

"It didn't," Ahmed said impatiently. "*You* made sense."

"But Larry said that techs are wiping out non-techs."

"Maybe they are, but they aren't killing anybody. The kid kills."

George pushed his hands together, felt them wet with sweat and wiped them on his shirt. "I almost killed the kid. But it felt right, what he was saying. He was talking for the way things are and for the way they're going to be, like Fate."

"Killing is unphilosophical," Ahmed said. "You're tired, George, take it easy, we've had a long day."

They heard a police siren wail and then distant shots. Ahmed plugged the earphone into his ear. "They just dropped somebody in goggles, gas didn't work on him. They had to drop him with hypo bullets. Probably Larry. Let's try to get out of here."

They put a wad of blankets out into the corridor, head high. No shots, so they went out cautiously and started groping down the long black hall, looking for an exit.

Ahmed said, "So you think Larry was the fickle finger of Fate on the groping hand of the future. No power on Earth can resist the force of an idea whose time has come, said somebody once. But, Good-buddy, when I was listening to you whilst lying in the ceiling with the spiders crawling on me, I thought I heard you invent a new metaphysics. Didn't you just abolish Fate?"

The corridor widened, and George felt a draft of fresh air without dust, and saw a glimmer of light through a hole. They climbed through and saw a doorway, and a broken door. "I don't know, Ahmed," he said vaguely. "Did I?"

They climbed up the broken door and a flight of stone steps and found themselves in a deserted yard at the center of the ruin. It was quiet there. In the distance around the edges of the block police copters buzzed, landed in the streets.

"Sure you did," Ahmed said. "You abolished Fate. I heard you."

George looked up at the moon. It was bright and it shone across the entire city, like the evil Fate in his dream, but it was only the moon, and the city was quiet. Suddenly George leaped into the air and clicked his heels. "I did. I did." He bellowed. "Hey everybody! Hey, I did it! I abolished Fate!"

148

He landed and stopped leaping, and stood panting. The red glow in the sky over New York blinked on and off, on and off from the giant sign they could not see.

"Congratulations," said Ahmed and rested an arm briefly across his shoulders. "May I offer you a tranquilizer?"

"No, you may offer me a meal," George said. "No, cancel that, too. Judd gave me money yesterday. Steaks, hot showers, hotel room. *Wow*. I've got a job." He turned abruptly and walked away. "See you tomorrow. *Wow*."

Left alone, tall and tired, smeared with dirt and itchy with cobwebs, Ahmed stared after him, feeling betrayed. Where was all the respect George used to give him? George was a short fat kid, once, and treated Ahmed like a boss. Now he was beginning to loom like a Kodiak bear, and he walked away without permission.

Ahmed looked up at the lopsided moon. "Mirror, Mirror on the wall, who's the smartest guy of all? Don't answer that, lady. It's been a long day. I'm tired."

149

THE MOVEMENT

Gregory Benford

Ragan lay in the mud and heat and strained forward, trying to penetrate the night ahead of him. A drop of sweat traced a cool finger down his brow and was flicked off into the darkness by his breath when it reached his nostrils. Insects were hovering overhead with a low buzz, and every moment or two something would move nearby, diverting his attention.

Let them go. Some of them—particularly the night hunters, out on the prowl—had the weight to set off trip wires, so the guards couldn't use booby traps this far out from the perimeter.

"How's the time?"

He looked over at the big Negro lying beside him. Jake was only a few feet away, but he was almost invisible in this light. Ragan glanced down at his wristwatch.

"A few more minutes. See anything?"

"No. They don't like to light up the area around the fence, do they?" A slow, deep voice.

"That's standard Army practice, lately. They need to check for what the manuals call perimeter integrity, and nobody likes to do it under arc lights when there might be snipers in the bush fifty yards away."

Clouds were boiling in from the ocean, blotching out the hint of starlight that made the sky a hard blue. The lights of the buildings in the compound ahead danced in the warm air rising from the ground, still cooling.

"Been a long time since I went in on one of these," Jake whispered. "Two years. I'm tired of throwing a Molotov cocktail and running for it. We didn't try to hit this one, though, because of the fence."

"If your description of it is accurate, we shouldn't have any trouble." Off to the right at the edge of the forest a bird sang a tropical song to itself.

"It's okay. I got right up to it last week to make those sketches, and one of the men who has his crops near the other side says they haven't made any changes since near him. But they don't let Brazilians walk up and get a good look at it, so that's all we know."

Ragan shifted uncomfortably in the mud to redistribute the weight of the pack he carried. "I hadn't expected it to be this hard. Just luck that I brought all the gear when I left the States. The Army seems to be using high-powered equipment for such a small base."

Jake grinned in the darkness. "They're getting scared. After a few places in the States caught it, they took us seriously. They know as well as we do that NASA can't take a breakdown in its network."

Ragan motioned him to be silent. He'd known Jake only two weeks, while the men trained for this mission, and he liked him. But the other man had been out in the back country too long. All he had had to take on were district policemen who might get suspicious about a big Negro with an American accent, whose papers said he was from Haiti. Dealing with a trained military force was something else, and apparently Jake knew it. He talked too much, a sure sign of nervousness.

Ragan checked his watch and took one last semicircular sweep of the area, keeping his eyes fixed to use his peripheral vision. The only lights were those of the living quarters on the base, a good half mile away. The defensive zone, a raw field cleared of vegetation, lay between them and the buildings.

His mouth had a sour taste in it, part anxiety, he knew—and part fear.

He gave a signal and crawled forward, breathing the hot, moist air and inching up the incline. Jake followed behind and slightly to the left. The weight of the pack was beginning to make itself felt and the mud, starting to harden with the coming of night, pulled with liquid fingers.

151

Every few minutes they stopped and listened. The small animal rustlings around them were enough to blot out the quiet murmur of the ocean a mile away, and they caught no other sound.

They moved directly toward the lights. The barbs of small bushes plucked at Ragan's black coveralls and slowed his progress.

What do you mean you're interested in politics? Running around with a sign and never touching a book, never learning how to make an honest dollar, that's what you mean by politics. Didn't send you to school to shoot off your mouth, and don't talk back, you . . .

He didn't see the fence until it was two feet from his face, looming up suddenly like a spider web in the darkness. They turned and crawled parallel to it until he spotted one of the supporting posts.

Ragan rolled over onto his back and leaned against the pillow his pack made. In the dim light from the base the field of dead trees and scrub they had crossed was a primitive brown sea lapping futilely at the rigid logic of the fence.

The other man moved a few feet away to keep watch. There was barely enough light to see the threads of brown wrapped around the heavy wires of the fence.

This was the heart of the perimeter defense. The brown threads were superconducting filaments. They were the latest antipersonnel gimmick to come out of the federal government's pet laboratories; Ragan had seen them once before in the States. The natives here had mentioned unusual activity around the fence several weeks ago, and he had guessed the troops were stringing a new sensor system.

The threads were especially effective because they were superconductors even at tropical temperatures. A decade ago the only known superconductors had been unusual alloys that had to be chilled to near absolute zero before they suddenly lost their electrical resistance. Somehow the physicists had found a way to raise the superconducting temperature. As far as Ragan knew, the process was still a secret.

A superconductor has literally no resistance to current. This made the fence a very good detector. Cut a thread and it ceased conducting. Cut several and a technician could deduce from the complex pattern of the threads just where the break had occurred.

Superconducting elements made such a system practical and cheap. A computer cross-correlated small variations in the system due to the daily cycle in temperature and humidity, just to keep the chance of error low.

It was a formidable obstacle. Ragan didn't have the time to be suitably impressed, though, and anyway he had come prepared.

He rolled back a few feet, looked quickly around and opened the equipment pouch at his side. He reeled out a spool of the same brown threads and clasped the ends between two fingers.

He took out a small wire cutter and spliced his superconducting wires into the ones in the fences, starting near the earth and rising three feet in a vertical line. He did the same thing a few feet further away. The wires were long enough to trail down to the ground, along the fence and up to the same height again.

It took a few more moments to splice another reel into the superconducting network above and below the two vertical lines, forming a rectangle. Now the fence currents were running through the wires he had placed as well as through the usual fence circuits. When the fence was cut current would then flow through his wires alone. The electrical resistance would not vary so much as a flicker.

With ordinary copper conductors this bypassing would have been impossible. The computers would have noticed the drop in total resistance when he put the new wires in parallel with the old.

Ragan had guessed he'd need superconducting wire and he'd waited until some could be smuggled in from the States. The Movement wasn't supposed to have any, of course—it was still classified hardware—but they had friends everywhere and it wasn't hard to get anything they really needed.

A little spool of the same wire could be used to nullify the effects of several hundred thousand dollars worth of equipment. It was always like that—a base commander this far out would think he was dealing with guerrillas from the local peasants, so he wouldn't take precautions.

153

Now that the sensor network was bypassed the heavy cable that gave the fence mechanical strength could be cut without worry. He tried to avoid shaking the fence, but they were tough and thick and he had taken too long already.

He cut the last line and threw it behind him into the mud. Now there was a hole in the fence, three feet on a side.

He rolled over to Jake.

"In this light you can't spot it from more than a few yards away," he whispered. "When we come back out remember it's just to the left of this supporting post."

Jake nodded slightly, intently studying the surrounding night. "My move next, then."

They hit him once and when he started to get up they hit him again, hard, slamming him against a tree and cuffing him across the face so his head snapped back and forth rhythmically as each one of the thin-faced men stepped up for his turn. "These people okay down here without you, you don't understand what it's like . . ." They burned the car and he had to walk back the five miles to town, helping along the others who had gotten it worse. "What's behind all you people? Who told you to do this?"

He pushed some of Ragan's equipment further up the slope and scrambled up to the hole. The earth gave off a deep organic smell and exertion made the air seem thicker, but action was better than waiting.

Jake crouched beside the hole, testing the mud for good footing. He slid a heavy glove from under his shirt and took out a thick slab of meat. He fitted the glove over his left hand and wrapped the meat around it, holding the ends together with fingers and thumb. With his right hand he slipped a knife out of its sheath and leaned forward, blocking the empty square in the fence with his left arm. Sweat had collected under his arms and he thought he could hear his own pulse in the stillness.

Maybe it was only a precaution. Maybe they hadn't been detected and all this was a waste of time.

But he had only a moment to wait and then there was the scrabbling of soft nails on soft earth and a black form slipped out of the shadows near the fence. He lost sight of it for an instant and suddenly something struck his outstretched hand a powerful blow.

Everything had depended on the dog being well trained, not just hastily taught to seek and kill. If it had made a noise, let out a small bark when it picked up his scent, someone else would hear and find him. The government needed a lot of dogs now, and a lot of guards. The Movement had seen to that.

They had switched from the usual watchdog, who warns but will not attack. Alerted, intruders would fade back into the jungle here before guards arrived, and the scent could be lost in any of the swamps of the area. And more often than not they ambushed the guards just outside the base and escaped anyway.

So it was just good tactics to try to pin down an intruder near the base, with the dogs if necessary, and deal with him there. Jake had to count on the dogs being killers, and good ones.

The bite had taken him just above the edge of the glove, smashing his arm back against his chest and toppling him over. The dog, diverted at the last instant by the smell of the fresh meat, had hit slightly off target.

As Jake rolled onto his back he breathed in the musty odor of damp fur and almost choked. He brought the knife up quickly, smoothly, and it caught. He could tell by the feel that it was in the throat.

He pivoted to one side, using the momentum of the dog's rush to rip the knife across its throat and then throw the body on down the incline.

There was a soft thud as it hit the ground, rolled and lay still. Ragan gave it a kick, and nodded up at him. He breathed out slowly, letting the silence settle once more. It was a German Shepherd, about a hundred pounds of muscle, teeth and black hair, and all of it quite dead. They smiled at each other.

It would have worked on most people. Even trained fighting men don't like the idea of wrestling with a large dog in the dark, without being able to see the teeth or gauge the point of impact when it springs. Any man is a match for a dog in good light, but the first few seconds of the attack can kill before you realize what you're dealing with.

They collected their gear. If there were other dogs they would probably be far enough away to give the men time to penetrate beyond the fence. There would be at least one guard nearby, but he wouldn't be able to see the dog's body.

Ragan gestured at his watch, stepped through the hole and padded quietly toward the lights ahead, Jake following.

Now the factor of the dogs was on their side. With animals like that roving the base, guards wouldn't stay alert very long, and no people would be out for a casual stroll on the edge of the compound. Jake had to remind himself that for the people inside this was still just an ordinary night in the tropics, and there was no reason for them to be on the alert.

"I think, Mr. Ragan, it would be a good idea for you to apply somewhere else for graduate work."

"Why? I like the department here, and my record is good. There's no better place to study political science in the country."

The older man hesitated. "It's true you've done good course work. But the other members of the department feel your attitude isn't scholarly—the amount of time you spend on outside, ah, interests could be overlooked when you were an undergraduate, but . . ."

They moved swiftly, angling for the nearest of the buildings.

In the distance the snapping sound of rifle fire broke out, followed by a short angry burst from a machine gun. Malley was coming in ahead of time, off schedule. They ran faster. The rifle spoke again. The pneumatic *chung* of a trip flare came a second later from behind them and off to the left.

At the same instant Ragan turned. Jake was scrambling to his feet.

"Freeze!" he said.

"What . . ." Orange light burst on the muddy plain. Ragan turned casually and pointed in the direction of the rifle fire, looking back over his shoulder at Jake as though giving an order. Someone shouted behind them, back toward the fence.

Ragan looked in the direction of the shout and made the sign to take cover, then dropped himself. Jake followed.

"This was the first flare to go off," Ragan said, twisting around to look back at the fence. "They were alerted by the rifle fire, so they didn't expect the first one here."

He gestured and Jake made out the figure of a soldier lying a hundred yards away. "If they think fast enough they'll search this area, but probably the noise and confusion will distract them." He gave a short laugh. "They probably think I'm a Sergeant."

As if in reply other flares went off down the fence, and spotlights mounted on the tops of buildings snapped on and focused outward. Random shots broke out, the result of surprise and over-imagination from the guards.

"Malley's putting on a big show down there," Jake said. The tempo of firing rose at the other end of the base.

"We've got to move," Ragan said. The flare was sputtering down, lengthening the shadows on the field. "We should be okay. If anybody thought we weren't we'd be drawing fire by now."

They rose quickly and ran for the nearest building, bent over at the waist, half expecting a warning shout behind them. No shout came; they ducked into a shadowed doorway and watched the field for anyone approaching.

"Mac boy! Here old fella! Mac!" someone called out.

Jake laughed softly. "Old Mac isn't operating a watchdog business any more."

There was a small paved road beyond the concrete building, and a squad of troops was double-timing down it in the direction of Malley's attack. The two men waited for them to pass.

Ragan sucked in the cool dank air of the tropical night and looked over at the black man as sweat glistened on his face. He could count on Jake. He was slightly thinner than was usual for a man his size; the look of hunger clung to him. He'd come in through civil rights, like most of them, and went over to the Movement immediately when the Days of Liberation started.

They began slowly, gathering momentum with each blow that fell on America. Martin Luther King fell, and then Kennedy, and in the months that followed the slow filtration processes of a creaking, aged political system pulled and tugged at the old alignments. New ones began to form, but there was no time.

The solution in Viet Nam was the best possible one, consid-

157

ering the circumstances. But it gave ammunition to the Right and fed the growing bitterness on the Left.

University strikes increased. The slums festered; police went there only in pairs, then in squads. Black Power forgot about butter and concentrated on guns. It became a faith with a growing number of converts. In a year of desperation they had a program, they could organize when everyone else was running for cover. The list of names was long: Malcolm X, Muhammad Ali, Huey Newton, Eldridge Cleaver.

Summer came. Heat and disgust roiled through the streets and spoke of action. The mood was ready. It hung in the air, everywhere, and one night it crystallized about the crack of a rifle.

Confusion. Panic. Take a telephone system, cut it in a few vital places, and you have a mass of useless wire. It can be repaired in a few hours. But then cut it again.

Hit the water reservoirs. It's easy.

Use those beautiful freeways. Steal a car and go out to the suburbs. The police are all in the center of the city, where they think you'll strike next.

It was a curious coincidence of forces and ideas, just the right touch of isolation, long hours of boredom, dirt and noise.

Underneath, for months before, there was: "Hell with it. We pass all the damn laws they want and now they're getting mixed up with this left wing radical business and who knows what next. Naw, I sure haven't got jobs for one of them."

In a week the riots had gone beyond control in five major cities, partly reaction and part an accident of timing. Efforts to stop it created more problems than they solved as Uncle Toms used the opportunity to move up, to assume a leadership that didn't exist any longer. And as often as not, were cut down in the attempt.

There was: "We're sure we could solve this problem, too. After all, we did in the past. But now, if we had more time. . ." All this spoken by men who should've been a degree more aggressive, or kinder, or wiser. But weren't.

So more buildings burned and the Guard moved in against resistance that, this time, didn't slacken and die. The generals learned that to really police an area meant matching the community man for man. In the cities there were thousands, then almost millions, to match.

158

Numbers demand organization, so the Movement—the same word as Martin Luther King's, but with a different meaning now, a meaning that made a man stand up, the heart pump, breathing quicken—the Movement grew.

And finally:

"I'm afraid we can't wait any longer, gentlemen. Holding down this many troops just to keep the lid on endangers the national security elsewhere. You evidently can't control your own people. Who is it that's behind this? The President feels there is a conscious design here . . ."

For once—the first time—they were right.

Jake's training was good. According to the records Ragan saw before he left the States for this mission, Jake had shown an instinctive ability to make effective plans and lead men in the chaos that followed, and he moved quickly up into the national organization that was forming then, most of it underground. Within weeks he was traveling from one city to another to help plan operations, coordinating the militant and trying to keep the fiction of the "spontaneous revolution" going for a while longer.

When the lid blew off Jake didn't have to think about which way to go. Neither did Ragan. Be an Uncle Tom and play games with the power structure, or be a man. But even then, keep clean.

Jake didn't. The FBI pinned some of the assassinations on him and he barely got across the Mexican border in time. Now he was stuck in Brazil, lying low most of the time, organizing the peasants and waiting. Waiting for operations like this.

The large arc lights stabbed out a white ring around the center of the compound, and a siren wailed briefly.

Malley was probably sweating it out now, Ragan decided, trying to judge how long it would be before things got too hot. His men wouldn't back out until he gave the order, but rifles were no competition against what the Army had. They were only dirt farmers, some recruited from the Marxist parties that flourished in the rural regions, and they didn't have the internal discipline that only experience can give.

Someone ran by the corner near them, feet crunching on gravel.

"Better get the stuff ready," Jake said. The big Negro reached around to his pack and broke the seal with one hand. Timing and ignition switches were exposed, but the charge itself couldn't be reached without tearing away the canvas knapsack. Ragan did the same.

"If they keep coming down this street we're going to have to move anyway," Ragan said.

"I'll check," Jake replied, and before Ragan could stop him he was sliding along the wall to the corner that met the street. He looked quickly around and called back, "Clear."

Ragan followed him across the street, pack bouncing slightly on his back where it had been freed. The area smelled of new concrete; some of the base was still being built.

They slowed to a trot in the shadow of a building, glanced around and went on to the next.

"The residential section starts in the next block, beyond this," Jake whispered. They stopped, looking at the next street. "Most of the streets are still dirt—only the work areas have been paved yet."

Ragan nodded, leaning against the rough wall. The map he had studied was remarkably accurate, so far.

"The transmission tower is just beyond these houses, then," he said. "There aren't any more targets of opportunity now, we're too far behind schedule. It's the tower or nothing."

The growl of an engine had been growing louder, and now headlights abruptly rounded a corner and a jeep whined down the street. Two soldiers with carbines rode in back, watching both sides of the road.

The two men hit the dirt next to the wall, heads down. Ragan took advantage of the time to see if there was any other course he could follow.

The only reason the plan could work was that every part of the base was equally vulnerable. If the computers were destroyed, months could be consumed replacing them. Or the tracking antennas. Or power facilities. The loss of anything, this far off the normal shipping lanes, would hurt. If men were killed it would be hard to find the technicians and scientists to take their places—especially after the word got around that it was a dangerous job.

A shot to the moon or Mars demands that stations be set up around the world, capable of handling sophisticated transmissions and carrying out rescues, if necessary. Satellite communication networks like the Syncom system just couldn't handle the heavy signal flux. If only a few of the stations were put out of action, there wouldn't be any shot.

The jeep came down the block, grinding along in low gear.

Ragan grinned in the darkness. If he had anything to do with it, the Brazilian base would be out of the money for months. And if there were no shots, after a while the Congress might get tired of this waste and cut the NASA budget. Put it into helping people instead of pushing men back and forth to a dried-up ball of rock hundreds of thousands of miles away.

But even better, failure would turn one bureaucracy on another. If enough of them went for each others' throats, maybe the people would have a chance again.

He lifted his head, watching the troopers go by, eyes unseeing.

That's why *he* was in the Movement. The Negro problem was a symptom, not the disease. American democracy was a sham—rights were second to privileges, people less important than advertisements. The only way to stop it was by hitting the leaders themselves, disarming or making impotent the only thing they understood—the top-heavy structures that fed on the people. Assassinate the small administrators, or a big one if you could reach him. Destroy bases. Disrupt communications. Someday, the country would be given back to the people who lived in it.

Jake nudged him. "Okay."

The jeep rounded the curve of the street and they sprinted across behind it, bent into a crouch. They dodged among the shadows, making their way through the low cinder-block homes. A few dejected-looking flowers occasionally witnessed to an attempt at landscaping. Jake stopped at the next corner.

"Tower one more block." He gestured at the red aircraft warning lights blinking overhead. Ragan studied what he could see of the structure ahead, then glanced down the street of copper-colored dirt.

"When the shooting starts the civilians pull their holes in after them," he said. All windows were shaded, and as they watched two porch lights winked out.

They set out at an even pace, keeping close to the shadows

near the houses and watching the corner toward the transmission tower. Jake leading, they circled partway around the last home in the block and stopped near a patio wall, shielded from view of the occupants.

Parabolic antennas dominated a complex configuration on top of what looked like a truncated radio tower. The control booths halfway up were dark, so the big dish wasn't tracking. The adjacent concrete buildings had few offices lit.

"Hey!" Jake pointed to the right. A soldier rounded the corner and slowly walked down the street, rifle at the ready. There was no one else in sight.

"That's not very smart," Ragan whispered.

Jake leaned closer, panting slightly from the run. "They probably plan on stopping us at the edge of the base, before we get into the buildings. If our head count is right they haven't got the men to do that and patrol the streets too."

"But if anybody does get through the perimeter, one man alone won't stop them."

Ragan rolled onto his stomach and unbuttoned the holster at his side. He took the pistol out, removed a stubby tube from his belt and started screwing it onto the barrel. There were a number of small holes drilled into the surface of the tube.

"You're going to try a shot from here?" Jake whispered. Ragan nodded.

"That a silencer?"

"Yeah. Homemade. It'll hold for about three shots, but after that you've got to repack the steel wool inside. They have to be packed just so or there'll be enough back pressure to jam the action of the gun."

"I guess you can make anything if you have to. Even . . ."

"Quiet." Ragan checked the action of the pistol and moved forward. Bracing one arm against the wall and holding the pistol with both hands, he aimed at the sentry. The man walked slowly near a street lamp, looking from side to side.

His image seemed to float in front of the sights and Ragan squinted with concentration. His finger began to tighten on the trigger.

"No," he said, and looked up. "It's too far for a pistol shot."

Jake glanced at him, then back at the man. "I'd say chances are about even you can get him on the first try."

"But if I miss he might get off a shot and then half the base will be here."

In the stillness the rattling of smallarms fire from Malley's group was like a long, ragged drum roll.

"Look," Jake said. "When he gets to the end of the block he'll probably turn, make a complete circuit around the tower." He gestured at a small building on the corner. "That'll block his view. He won't see this part of the street for about twenty seconds, if we're lucky."

Ragan wiped his brow, trying to think. "Okay," he said.

The soldier was almost at the end of the block. He looked back once, turned the corner and Ragan was running swiftly across the street, holding the pistol at an angle in front of him. With a bound he cleared the sidewalk and flitted among the shadows underneath the tower.

He stopped suddenly and went into the kneeling position for the shot, waiting. Now his breathing was slow and regular.

The soldier appeared from behind the building. He tried to keep away from the light as much as possible and his eyes, partially shadowed by the helmet, flicked nervously back and forth. He was a middle-sized man in his late twenties, with a slow shuffling walk.

This isn't a war, it's slaughter, and anyone who goes along with the bureaucrats, the militarists, is an enemy of his own people. It's up to us, now, to preserve what is left of the American conscience.

There was a sound like a discreet cough and the soldier spun lightly, lazily around and fell solidly on the sidewalk. His rifle gave a sharp clatter as it hit. Ragan sprinted over to the body and lifted it partially off the cement by the arms. He dragged it quickly back into the shadows and dumped it without checking to see if the guard was still alive. Going back for the rifle, he noticed a scarlet smear of blood on the concrete.

He dropped the rifle near the body and looked around. No one yelled, no alarm sounded. Jake trotted up through the dark splotches cast by the tower and stopped beside him.

"He probably had a sight check with the sentry on the next beat every circuit. Not much time."

Ragan glanced impatiently down at his watch. "Malley's

got to get out now. Any more time and they'll outflank him for sure.''

They raced for the other end of the tower base, away from the guard's body. Jake swung the pack off his back, still running, and made for the furthest tower leg, his boots spitting the gravel aside as he ran.

Ragan stopped abruptly at the first major leg, almost losing his balance. He flipped the last lock off the arming switches.

Two large girders met at the base of the leg and the charge fitted neatly into the joint. The knapsack provided some tamping, but there was enough explosive to do the job unassisted.

He raised his arm for Jake to see, then dropped it as a signal when he started the timer. The blast would probably take the whole leg, but only the girders were necessary if both charges went.

As Jake came back Ragan studied the effect. Two legs on one side would be at least badly damaged, and the weight of the tower could be depended on to buckle them, toppling the whole structure. It would fall full length on the buildings next to it.

He nodded in satisfaction. Now to get back home.

They could run faster now, without the packs. They crossed the street quickly. In a few moments they were lost among the shadows, heading toward the fence once more.

Behind them the night sounds settled, broken only by occasional gunfire in the distance. The charges were ticking.

To Work Supervisor #49:

This account of a South American guerrilla action in the early history of the famous Last Phase of the Revolution was found recently in some otherwise unimportant papers. In that it describes the courageous struggle by non-Party elements against the reactionary monopolies known to have governed the United States at that time, it is unique.

This non-Party faction was destroyed in subsequent stages of the Last Phase, but they proved most useful in the struggle and this particular stage, being somewhat out of the ordinary, probably deserves some mention in the Official History of that time, currently being compiled in Nanking.

It has been stated by several historians that without these alienated groups who were systematically excluded from the

164

political workings of the reactionary cliques, there is some doubt that the Last Phase would have succeeded at all.

I commend the document to your inspection.

(signed)
Ling Chen.

THE WIND FROM A BURNING WOMAN

Greg Bear

Five years later, the glass bubbles were intact, the wires and pipes were taut, and the city—strung across Psyche's surface like a dewy spider's web wrapped around a thrown rock—was still breathtaking. It was also empty. Hexamon investigators had swept out the final dried husks and bones. The asteroid was clean again. The plague was over.

Giani Turco turned her eyes away from the port and looked at the displays. Satisfied by the approach, she ordered a meal and put her work schedule through the processor for tightening and trimming. She had six tanks of air, enough to last her three days. There was no time to spare. The robot guards in orbit around Psyche hadn't been operating for at least a year and wouldn't offer any resistance, but four small pursuit bugs had been planted in the bubbles. They turned themselves off whenever possible, but her presence would activate them. Time spent in avoiding and finally destroying them: one hour forty minutes, the processor said. The final schedule was projected in front of her by a pen hooked around her ear. She happened to be staring at Psyche when the readout began; the effect—red numerals and letters over gray rock and black space—was pleasingly graphic, like a film in training.

Turco had dropped out of training six weeks early. She had no need for a final certificate, approval from the Hexamon, or any other nicety. Her craft was stolen from Earth orbit, her

166

papers and cards forged, and her intentions entirely opposed to those of the sixteen Corporeal Desks. On Earth, some hours hence, she would be hated and reviled.

The impulse to sneer was strong in her—pure theatrics, since she was alone—but she didn't allow it to break her concentration. (Worse than sheep, the seekers after security, the cowardly citizens who tacitly supported the forces that had driven her father to suicide and murdered her grandfather; the seekers after security who lived by technology, but believed in the just influences: Star, Logos, Fate and Pneuma . . .)

To calm her nerves, she sang a short song while she selected her landing site.

The ship, a small orbital tug, touched the asteroid like a mote settling on a boulder and made itself fast. She stuck her arms and legs into the suit receptacles and the limb covers automatically hooked themselves to the thorax. The cabin was too cramped to get into a suit any other way. She reached up and brought down the helmet, pushed until all the semifluid seals seized and beeped, and began the evacuation of the cabin's atmosphere. Then the cabin parted down the middle and she floated slowly, fell more slowly still, to Psyche's surface.

She turned once to watch the cabin clamp together, and to see if the propulsion pods behind the tanks had been damaged by the unusually long journey. They'd held up well.

She took hold of a guide wire after a flight of twenty or twenty-five meters and pulled for the nearest glass bubble. Five years before, the milky spheres had been filled with the families of workers setting the charges which would form Psyche's seven internal chambers. Holes had been bored from the Vlasseg and Janacki poles, on the narrow ends of the huge rock, through the center. After the formation of the chambers, materials necessary for atmosphere would have been pumped into Psyche through the bore holes, while motors increased her natural spin to create artificial gravity inside.

In twenty years, Psyche would have been green and beautiful, filled with hope—and passengers. But now ignorance was Queen, fear King, and propaganda the jester.

The control bubble hatches had been sealed by the last of the investigators. Since Psyche was not easily accessible, even in its lunar orbit, the seals hadn't been applied thoroughly. But it took her an hour to break in. The glass ball towered above her, a hundred feet in diameter, translucent walls mottled by the shadows of rooms and equipment. Psyche rotated once every three hours, and light from the sun was beginning to flush the top of the bubbles in the local cluster. Moonlight illuminated the shadows. She pushed the cement shreds away, watching them float lazily to the pocked ground. Then she checked the airlock to see if it were still functioning. She wanted to keep the atmosphere inside the bubble, to check it for psychotropic chemicals; she would not leave her suit at any rate.

The lock door opened with a few jerks and closed behind her. She brushed crystals of frost off her faceplate and the inner lock door's port. Then she pushed the button for the inner door, but nothing happened. The external doors were on a different power supply, which was no longer functioning—or, she hoped, had only been turned off.

From her backpack she removed a half-meter pry bar. The break-in took another fifteen minutes. She was now five minutes ahead of schedule.

Across the valley, the fusion power plants which supplied power to the Geshel populations of Tijuana and Chula Vista sat like squat mountains of concrete. By Naderite law, all nuclear facilities were surrounded by multiple domes and pyramids, whether they posed any danger or not. The symbolism was two-fold—it showed the distaste of the ruling Naderites for energy sources which were not nature kinetic, and it carried on the separation of Naderites-Geshels. Farmer Kollert, advisor to the North American Hexamon and Ecumentalist to the California Corporeal Desk, watched the Sun set behind the false peak and wondered vaguely if there was any symbolism in the act. Was not fusion the source of power for the Sun? He smiled. Such things seldom occurred to him; perhaps it would amuse a Geshel technician.

His team of five Geshel scientists would tour the plants two days from now and make their report to him. He would then pass on *his* report to the Desk, acting as interface for the invariably clumsy, elitist language the Geshel scientists used. In this way, through the medium of advisors across the globe, the Naderites oversaw the production of Geshel power. By their grants and control of capital, his people had once plucked the world from technological overkill, and the battle was on-going still—a war against some of mankind's darker tendencies.

He finished his evening juice and took a package of writing utensils from the drawer in the veranda desk. The reports from last month's energy consumption balancing needed to be edited and revised, based on new estimates—and he enjoyed doing the work himself, rather than giving it to the literary computer personna. It relaxed him to do things by hand. He wrote on a positive feedback slate, his scrawly letters adjusting automatically into script, with his tongue between his lips and a pleased frown creasing his brow.

"Excuse me, Farmer." His ur-wife, Gestina, stood in the French doors leading to the veranda. She was as slender as when he'd married her, despite fifteen years and two children.

"Yes, *cara,* what is it?" He withdrew his tongue and told the slate to store what he'd written.

"Josef Krupkin."

Kollert stood up quickly, knocking the metal chair over. He hurried past his wife into the dining room, dropped his bulk into a chair and drew up the crystalline cube on the alabaster table top. The cube adjusted its picture to meet the angle of his eyes and Krupkin appeared.

"Josef! This is unexpected."

"Very," Krupkin said. He was a small man with narrow eyes and very curly black hair. Compared to Kollert's bulk, he was dapper—but thirty years behind a desk had given him the usual physique of a Hexamon side-roomer. "Have you ever heard of Giani Turco?"

Kollert thought for a moment. "No, I haven't. Wait—Turco. Related to Kimon Turco?"

"Daughter. California should keep better track of its radical Geshels, shouldn't it?"

"Kimon Turco lived on the Moon."

"But she lived in your district."

"Yes, fine. What about her?" Kollert was beginning to be perturbed. Krupkin enjoyed roundabouts even in important situations—and for him to call at this address, at such a time, meant something important had happened.

"She's calling for you. She'll only talk to you, none of the rest. She won't even accept President Praetori."

"Yes. Who is she? What has she done?"

"She's managed to start up Psyche. There was enough

reaction mass left in the Beckmann motors to alter it into an Earth-intersect orbit.'' The left side of the cube was flashing bright red, indicating the call was being scrambled.

Kollert sat very still for a few seconds. There was no need acting incredulous. Krupkin was in no position to joke. But the enormity of what he said—and the impulse to disbelieve, despite the bearer of the news—froze Kollert for an unusually long time. He ran his hand through lank blond hair.

"Kollert," Krupkin said. "You look like you've been pole-axed."

"Is she telling the truth?"

Krupkin shook his head. "No, Kollert, you don't understand. She hasn't *claimed* these accomplishments. She hasn't said anything about them yet. She just wants to speak to you. But our tracking stations say there's no doubt. I've spoken with the officer who commanded the last inspection. He says there was enough mass left in the Beckmann drive positioning motors to push the asteroid—"

"This is incredible! No precautions were taken? The mass wasn't drained, or something?"

"I'm no Geshel, Farmer. My technicians tell me the mass was left on Psyche because it would have cost several hundred million—"

"That's behind us now. Let the journalists worry about that, if they ever hear of it." He looked up and saw Gestina still standing in the French doors. He held up his hand to tell her to stay where she was. She was going to have to keep to the house, incommunicado, for as long as it took to straighten this out.

"You're coming?"

"Which center?"

"Does it matter? She's not being discreet. Her message is hitting an entire hemisphere, and there are hundreds of listening stations to pick it up. Several aren't under our control. Once anyone pinpoints the source, the story is going to be clear. For your convenience, go to Baja Station. Mexico is signatory to all the necessary pacts."

"I'm leaving now," Kollert said. Krupkin nodded and the cube went blank.

"What was he talking about?" Gestina asked. "What's *Psyche*?"

"A chunk of rock, dear," he said. Her talents lay in other

170

directions—she wasn't stupid. Even for a Naderite, however, she was unknowledgeable about things beyond the Earth.

He started to plan the rules for her movements, then thought better of it and said nothing. If Krupkin was right—and he would be—there was no need. The political consideration, if everything turned out right, would be enormous. He could run as Governor of the Desk, even President of the Hexamon . . .

And if everything didn't turn out right, it wouldn't matter where anybody was.

Turco sat in the middle of her grandfather's control center and cried. She was tired and sick at heart. Things were moving rapidly now, and she wondered just how sane she was. In a few hours, she would be the worst menace the Earth had ever known, and for what cause? Truth, justice? They had murdered her grandfather, discredited her father and driven him to suicide—but all seven billion of them, Geshels and Naderites alike?

She didn't know whether she was bluffing or not. Psyche's fall was still controllable, and she was bargaining it would never hit the Earth. Even if she lost and everything was hopeless, she might divert it, causing a few tidal disruptions, minor earthquakes perhaps, but still passing over four thousand kilometers from the Earth's surface. There was enough reaction mass in the positioning motors to allow a broad margin of safety.

Resting lightly on the table in front of her, its ends not clamped, was a chart which showed the basic plan of the asteroid. The positioning motors surrounded a crater at one end of the egg-shaped chunk of nickel-iron and rock. Catapults loaded with huge barrels of reaction mass had just a few hours earlier launched a salvo to rendezvous above the crater's center. Beckmann drive beams had then surrounded the mass with a halo of energy, releasing its atoms from the bonds of nature's weak force. The blast had bounced off the crater floor, directed by the geometric patterns of heat-resistant slag. At the opposite end, a smaller guidance engine was in position, but it was no longer functional and didn't figure in her plans. The two tunnels which reached from the poles to the center of Psyche opened into seven blast chambers, each containing a shaped fusion charge. She hadn't checked to see if the charges were still armed. There were so many things to do.

She sat with her head bowed, still suited up. Though the bubbles contained enough atmosphere to support her, she had no intention of unsuiting. In one gloved hand she clutched a small ampul with a nozzle for attachment to air and water systems piping. The Hexamon Nexus' trumped-up excuse of madness caused by near-weightless conditions was now a shattered, horrible lie. Turco didn't know why, but the Psyche project had been deliberately sabotaged, and the psychotropic drugs still lingered.

Her grandfather hadn't gone mad contemplating the stars. The asteroid crew hadn't mutinied out of misguided Geshel zeal and spacesickness.

Her anger rose again and the tears stopped. "You deserve whoever governs you," she said quietly. "Everyone is responsible for the actions of their leaders."

The computer display cross-haired the point of impact. It was ironic—the buildings of the Hexamom Nexus were only sixty kilometers from the zero point. She had no control over such niceties, but nature and fate seemed to be as angry as she was.

"Moving an asteroid is like carving a diamond," the Geshel advisor said. Kollert nodded his head, not very interested. "The charges for initial orbit change—moving it out of the asteroid belt—have to be placed very carefully or the mass will break up and be useless. When the asteroid is close enough to the Earth-Moon system to meet the major crew vessels, the work has only begun. Positioning motors have to be built—"

"Madness," Kollert's secretary said, not pausing from his monitoring of communications between associate committees.

"And charge tunnels drilled. All of this was completed on the asteroid ten years ago."

"Are the changes still in place?" Kollert asked.

"So far as I know," the Geshel said.

"Can they be set off now?"

"I don't know. Whoever oversaw dismantling should have disarmed to protect his crew—but then, the reaction mass should have been jettisoned, too. So who can say. The report hasn't cleared top secrecy yet."

And not likely to, either, Kollert thought. "If they haven't been disarmed, can they be set off now? What would happen if they were?"

"Each charge has a complex communications system. They were designed to be set off by coded signals and could probably be set off now, yes, if we had the codes. Of course, those are top-secret, too."

"What would happen?" Kollert was becoming impatient with the Geshel.

"I don't think the charges were ever given a final adjustment. It all depends on how well the initial alignment was performed. If they're out of true, or the final geological studies weren't taken into account, they could blow Psyche to pieces. If they are true, they'll do what they were intended to do—form chambers inside the rock. Each chamber would be about fifteen kilometers long, ten kilometers in diameter—"

"If the asteroid were blown apart, how would that affect our situation?"

"Instead of having one mass hit, we'd have a cloud, with debris twenty to thirty kilometers across and smaller."

"Would that be any better?" Kollert asked.

"Sir?"

"Would it be better to be hit by such a cloud than one chunk?"

"I don't think so. The difference is pretty moot—either way, the surface of the Earth would be radically altered, and few life forms would survive."

Kollert turned to his secretary. "Tell them to put a transmission through to Giani Turco."

The communications were arranged. In the meantime, Kollert tried to make some sense out of the Geshel advisor's figures. He was very good at mathematics, but in the past sixty years many physics and chemistry symbols had diverged from those used in biology and psychology. To Kollert, the Geshel mathematics was irritatingly dense and obtuse.

He put the paper aside when Turco appeared on the cube in front of him. A few background beeps and noise were eliminated and her image cleared. "Ser Turco," he said.

"Ser Farmer Kollert," she replied several seconds later. A beep signaled end of one side's transmission. She sounded tired.

"You're doing a very foolish thing."

"I have a list of demands," she said.

Kollert laughed. "You sound like the Good Man himself, Ser Turco. The tactic of direct confrontation. Well, it didn't work all the time, even for him."

"I want the public—Geshels and Naderites both—to know why the Psyche project was sabotaged."

"It was not sabotaged," Kollert said calmly. "It was unfortunate proof that humans cannot live in conditions so far removed from the Earth."

"Ask those on the Moon!" Turco said bitterly.

"The Moon has a much stronger gravitational pull than Psyche. But I'm not briefed to discuss all the reasons why the Psyche project failed."

"I have found psychotropic drugs—traces of drugs and containers—in the air and water the crew breathed and drank. That's why I'm maintaining my suit integrity."

"No such traces were found by our investigating teams. But Ser Turco, neither of us is here to discuss something long past. Speak your demands—your price—and we'll begin negotiations." Kollert knew he was walking a loose rope. Several Hexamon terrorist team officers were listening to everything he said, waiting to splice in a timely splash of static. Conversely, there was no way to stop Turco's words from reaching open stations on the Earth. He was sweating heavily under his arms. Stations on the Moon—the bastards there would probably be sympathetic to her—could pick up his messages and relay them back to the Earth. A drop of perspiration trickled from armpit to sleeve and he shivered involuntarily.

"That's my only demand," Turco said. "No money, not even amnesty. I want nothing for myself. I simply want the people to know the truth."

"Ser Turco, you have an ideal platform to tell them all you want them to hear."

"The Hexamons control most major reception centers. Everything else—except for a few ham and radio-astronomy amateurs—is cabled and controlled. To reach the most people, the Hexamon Nexus will have to reveal its part in the matter."

Before speaking to her again, Kollert asked if there were any way she could be fooled into believing her requests were being carried out. The answer was ambiguous—a few hundred people were thinking it over.

"I've conferred with my staff, Ser Turco, and I can assure you, so far as the most privy of us can tell, nothing so villainous was ever done to the Psyche project." At a later time, his script suggested, he might indicate that some tests had been overlooked, and that a junior officer had suggested Lunar sabotage on Psyche. That might shift the heat. But for the moment, any admission that drugs existed in the asteroid's human environments could backfire.

"I'm not arguing," she said. "There's no question that the Hexamon Nexus had somebody sabotage Psyche."

Kollert held his tongue between his lips and punched key words into his script processor. The desired statements formed over Turco's image. He looked at the camera earnestly. "If we had done anything so heinous, surely we would have protected ourselves against an eventuality like this—drained the reaction mass in the positioning motors—" One of the terrorist team officers was waving at him frantically and scowling. The screen's words showed red where they were being covered by static. There was to be no mention of how Turco had gained control of Psyche. The issue was too sensitive and blame hadn't been placed yet. Besides, there was still the option of informing the public that Turco had never gained control of Psyche at all. If everything worked out, the issue would have been solved without costly admissions.

"Excuse me," Turco said a few seconds later. The time lag between communications was wearing on her nerves, if Kollert was any judge. "Something was lost there."

"Ser Turco, your grandfather's death on Psyche was accidental, and your actions now are ridiculous. Destroying the Hexamon Nexus—" much better than saying "Earth"—"won't mean a thing." He leaned back in the seat, chewing on the edge of his index finger. The gesture had been approved an hour before the talks began, but it was nearly genuine. His usual elegance of speech seemed to be wearing thin in this encounter. He'd already made several embarrassing misjudgments.

"I'm not doing this for logical reasons," Turco finally said. "I'm doing it out of hatred for you and all the people who support you. What happened on Psyche was purely evil—useless, motivated by the worst intentions, resulting in the death of a beautiful dream, not to mention people I loved. No talk can change my mind about those things.''

"Then why talk to me at all? I'm hardly the highest official in the Nexus.''

"No, but you're in an ideal position to know who the higher officials involved were. You're a respected politician. And I suspect you had a great deal to do with suggesting the plot. I just want the truth. I'm tired. I'm going to rest for a few hours now.''

"Wait a moment,'' Kollert said sharply. "We haven't discussed the most important things yet.''

"I'm signing off. Until later.''

The team leader made a cutting motion across his throat which almost made Kollert choke. The young bastard and his indiscreet symbols were positively obscene in the current situation. Kollert shook his head and held his fingertips to his temples. "We didn't even have time to begin,'' he said.

The team leader stood and stretched his arms.

"You're doing quite well so far, Ser Kollert,'' he said. "It's best to ease into these things.''

"I'm Advisor Kollert to you, and I don't see how we have much time to take it easy.''

"Yes, sir. Sorry.''

She needed the rest, but there was far too much to do. She pushed off from the seat and floated gently for a few moments before drifting down. The relaxation of weightlessness would have been welcome, and Psyche's pull was very weak, but just enough to remind her there was no time for rest.

One of the things she had hoped she could do—checking the charges deep inside the asteroid to see if they were armed—was impossible. The main computer and the systems board indicated the transport system through the bore holes was no longer operative. It would take her days to crawl or float the distance down the shafts, and she wasn't about to take the small tug through a tunnel barely fifty meters wide. She wasn't that well-trained a pilot.

So she had a weak spot. The bombs couldn't be disarmed from where she was. They could be set off by a ship positioned along the axis of the tunnels, but so far none had shown up. That would take another twelve hours or so, and by then time would be running out. Hopefully all negotiations would be completed.

She desperately wanted out of the suit. The catheters and cups were itching fiercely, and she felt like a ball of tacky glue wrapped in wool. Her eyes were stinging from strain and sweat buildup on the lids. If she had a moment of bad irritation when something crucial was happening, she could be in trouble. One way or another, she had to clean up a bit—and there was no way to do that unless she risked exposure to the residue of drugs. She stood unsteadily for several minutes, vacillating, and finally groaned, slapping her thigh with a gloved palm. "I'm *tired*," something kept saying through her lips. "Not thinking straight."

She looked at the computer. There was a solution, but she couldn't make it clear in her head. "Come on, girl. So simple. But what?"

The drug would probably have a limited effective life, in case the Nexus wanted to do something with Psyche later. But how limited? Ten years? She chuckled grimly. She had the ampul and its cryptic chemical label. Would a Physician's Desk Reference be programmed into the computers?

She hooked herself into the console again. "PDR," she said. The screen was blank for a few seconds. Then it said, "Ready."

"Iropentaphonate," she said. "Two-seven diboltene."

The screen printed out the relevant data. She searched through the technical maze for a full minute before finding what she wanted. "Effective shelflife, four months two days from date of manufacture." There it was.

She tested the air again—it was stale but breathable—and unhooked her helmet. It was worth any risk. A bare knuckle against her eye felt so good.

The small lounge in the Baja Station was well-furnished and comfortable, but suited more for Geshels than Naderites—bright rather than natural colors, abstract paintings of mechanistic tendency, modernist furniture. To Kollert it was faintly oppressive. The man sitting across from him had been silent for the past five minutes, reading through a sheaf of papers.

"Who authorized this?" the man asked.

"Hexamon Nexus, Mr. President."

"But who proposed it?"

177

Kollert hesitated. "The Advisory Committee."

"Who proposed it to the committee?"

"I did."

"Under what authority?"

"It was strictly legal," Kollert said defensively. "Such activities have been covered under Emergency Code, classified section fourteen."

The president nodded. "She came to the right man when she asked for you, then. I wonder where she got her information. None of this can be broadcast—why was it done?"

"There were a number of reasons, among them financial—"

"What kind? This was mostly financed by lunar agencies. Earth had perhaps a five percent share, so no controlling interest—and there was no connection with radical Geshel groups, therefore no connection with section fourteen on revolutionary deterrence. I read the codes, too, Farmer."

"Yes, sir."

"What were you afraid of? Some irrational desire to pin the butterflies down? Jesus God, Farmer, the Naderite beliefs don't allow anything like this. But you and your committee took it upon yourselves to covertly destroy the biggest project in the history of mankind. You think this follows in the tracks of the Good Man?"

"You're aware of lunar plans to build particle guidance guns. They're cancelled now, because Psyche is dead. They were to be used to push asteroids like Psyche into deep space, so advanced Beckmann drives could be used."

"I'm not technically minded, Farmer."

"Nor am I. But such particle guns could have been used as weapons—considering lunar sympathies, probably would have been used. They could cook whole cities on Earth. The development of potential weapons *is* a matter of concern for Naderites, sir. And there are many studies showing that human behavior changes in space. It becomes less Earth-centered, less communal. Man can't live in space and remain human. We were trying to preserve humanity's right to a secure future. Even now, the Moon is a potent political force, and war has been suggested by our strategists . . . it's a dire possibility. That was because of the separation of a group of humans from the parent body, from wise government and safe creed."

The president shook his head and looked away. "I am

ashamed such a thing could happen in my government. Very well, Kollert, this remains your ballgame until she asks to speak to someone else. But my advisors are going to go over everything you say. I doubt you'll have the chance to botch anything. We're already acting with the Moon to stop this before it gets any worse. And you can thank God—for your life, not your career, which is already dead—that our Geshels have come up with a way out.''

Kollert was outwardly submissive, but inside he was fuming. Not even the President of the Hexamon had the right to treat him like a child or, worse, a criminal. He was an independent advisor, of a separate Desk, elected by Naderites of high standing. The Ecumentalist Creed was apparently much tighter than the president's. "I acted in the best interests of my constituency," he said.

"You no longer have a constituency, you no longer have a career. Nor do any of the people who planned this operation with you, or those who carried it out. Up and down the line. A purge.''

Turco woke up before the blinking light and moved her lips in a silent curse. How long had she been asleep? She panicked briefly—a dozen hours would be crucial—but then saw the digital clock. Two hours. The light was demanding her attention to an incoming radio signal.

There was no video image. Kollert's voice returned, less certain, almost cowed. "I'm here," she said, switching off her camera as well. The delay was a fraction shorter than when they'd first started talking.

"Have you made any decisions?" Kollert asked.

"I should be asking that question. My course is fixed. When are you and your people going to admit to sabotage?"

"We'd—I'd almost be willing to admit, just to—'' He stopped. She was about to speak when he continued. "We could do that, you know. Broadcast a world-wide admission of guilt. A cheap price to pay for saving all life on Earth. Do you really understand what you're up to? What satisfaction, what revenge could you possibly get out of this? My God, Turco, you—'' There was a burst of static. It sounded suspiciously like the burst she had heard some time ago.

"You're editing him," she said. Her voice was level and calm. "I don't want anyone editing anything between us, whoever you are. Is that understood? One more burst of static like that and I'll . . ." She had already threatened the ultimate. "I'll be less tractable. Remember—I'm already a fanatic. Want me to be a hardened fanatic? Repeat what you were saying, Ser Kollert."

The digital readout indicated one way delay-time of 1.496 seconds. She would soon be closer to the Earth than the Moon was.

"I was saying," Kollert repeated, something like triumph in his tone, "that you are a very young woman, with very young ideas—like a child leveling a loaded pistol at her parents. You may not even be a fanatic. But you aren't seeing things clearly. We have no evidence here on Earth that you've found anything, and we won't have evidence—nothing will be solved—if the asteroid collides with us. That's obvious. But if it veers aside, goes into an Earth orbit perhaps, then an—"

"That's not one of my options," Turco said.

"—investigating team could reexamine the crew quarters," Kollert continued, not to be interrupted for a few seconds, "do a more detailed search. Your charges could be verified."

"I can't go into Earth orbit without turning around, and this is a one-way rock, remember that. My only other option is to swing around the Earth, be deflected a couple of degrees, and go into a solar orbit. By the time any investigating team reached me, I'm be on the other side of the Sun, and dead. I'm the daughter of a Geshel, Ser Kollert—don't forget that. I have a good technical education, and my training under Hexamon auspices makes me a competent pilot and spacefarer. Too bad there's so little long-range work for my type—just Earth-Moon runs. But don't try to fool me or kid me. I'm far more expert than you are. Though I'm sure you have Geshel people on your staff." She paused. "Geshels! I can't call you traitors—you in the background—because you might be thinking I'm crazy, out to destroy all of you. But do you understand what these men have done to our hopes and dreams? I've never seen a finished asteroid starship, of course—Psyche was to have been the first. But I've seen good simulations. It's like seven Shangri-las inside, hollowed out of solid rock and metal, seven valleys separated by walls four kilometers high, each self-contained, connected with the others by tube-trains. The valley floors reach up to the sky, like magic, everything wonderfully topsy-turvy. And quiet—so much insulation none of the engine sounds reach inside." She was crying again.

"Psyche would consume herself on the way to the stars. By the time she arrived, there's be little left besides a cylinder thirty kilometers wide, and two hundred ninety long. Like the core of an apple, and the passengers would be luxurious worms—star travelers. Now ask why, *why* did these men sabotage such a marvelous thing? Because they are blind unto pure evil—blind, ugly-minded, weak men who hate big ideas . . ." She paused. "I don't know what you think of all this, but remember, they took something away from you. I know. I've seen the evidence here. Sabotage and murder." She pressed the button and waited wearily for a reply.

"Ser Turco," Kollert said, "you have ten hours to make an effective course correction. We estimate you have enough reaction mass left to extend your orbit and miss the Earth by about four thousand kilometers. There is nothing we can do here but try to convince you—"

She stopped listening, trying to figure out what was happening behind the scenes. Earth wouldn't take such a threat without exploring a large number of alternatives. Kollert's voice droned on as she tried to think of the most likely action, and the most effective.

She picked up her helmet and placed a short message, paying no attention to the transmission from Earth. "I'm going outside for a few minutes."

The acceleration had been steady for two hours, but now the weightlessness was just as oppressive. The large cargo handler was fully loaded with extra fuel and a bulk William Porter was reluctant to think about. With the ship turned around for course correction, he could see the Moon glowing with Earthshine, and a bright crescent so thin it was almost a hair.

He had about half an hour to relax before the real work began, and he was using it to read an excerpt from a novel by Anthony Burgess. He'd been a heavy reader all his memorable life, and now he allowed himself a possible last taste of pleasure.

Like most inhabitants of the Moon, Porter was a Geshel, with a physicist father and a geneticist mother. He'd chosen a career as a pilot rather than a researcher out of romantic predilictions established long before he was ten years old. There was something immediately effective and satisfying about piloting, and he'd turned out to be well suited to the work. He'd never expected to take on a mission like this. But then, he'd never paid much attention to politics, either. Even if he had, the disputes between Geshels and Naderites would have been hard to spot—they'd been settled, most experts believed, fifty years before, with the Naderites emerging as a ruling class. Outside of grumbling at restrictions, few Geshels complained. Responsibility had been lifted from their shoulders. Most of the population of both Earth and Moon was now involved in technical and scientific work, yet the mistakes they made would be blamed on Naderite policies—and the disasters would likewise be absorbed by the leadership. It wasn't a hard situation to get used to.

William Porter wasn't so sure, now, that it was the ideal. He had two options to save Earth, and one of them meant he would die.

He'd listened to the Psyche-Earth transmissions during acceleration, trying to make sense out of Turco's positions, to form an opinion of her character and sanity, but he was more confused than ever. If she was right—and not a raving lunatic, which didn't seem to fit the facts—then the Hexamon Nexus had a lot of explaining to do, and probably wouldn't do it under the gun. The size of Turco's gun was far too imposing to be rational—the destruction of the human race, the wiping of a planet's surface.

He played back the computer diagram of what would happen if Psyche hit the Earth. At the angle it would strike, it would speed the rotation of the Earth's crust and mantle by an appreciable fraction. The asteroid would cut a gouge from Maine to England, several thousand kilometers long and at least a hundred kilometers deep. The impact would vault hundreds of millions of tons of surface material into space, and that would partially counteract the speedup of rotation. The effect would be a monumental jerk, with the energy finally being released as heat. The continents would fracture in several directions, forming new faults, even new plate orientations, which would generate earthquakes on a scale never before seen. The impact basin would be a hell of molten crust and mantle, with water on the perimeter bursting violently into steam, altering weather patterns around the world. It would take decades to cool and achieve some sort of stability.

Turco may not have been raving, but she was coldly suggesting a cataclysm to swat what amounted to a historical fly. That made her a lunatic in anyone's book, Geshel or Naderite. And his life was well worth the effort to thwart her.

That didn't stop him from being angry, though.

Kollert impatiently let the physician check him over and give him a few injections. He talked to his wife briefly, which left him more nervous than before, then listened to the team leader's theories on how Turco's behavior would change in the next few hours. He nodded at only one statement: "She's going to see she'll be dead, too, and that's a major shock for even the most die-hard terrorist."

Then Turco was back on the air and he was on stage again.

"I've seen your ship," she said. "I went outside and looked around in the direction where I thought it would be. There it was—treachery all around. Goddamned hypocrites! Talk friendly to the little girl, but shiv her in the back! Public face cool, private face snarl! Well, just remember, before he can kill me, I can destroy all controls to the positioning engines. It would take a week to rewire them. You don't have the time!" The beep followed.

"Giani, we have only one option left, and that's to do as you say. We'll admit we played a part in the sabotage of Psyche. It's confession under pressure, but we'll do it." Kollert pressed his button and waited, holding his full chin with one hand.

"No way it's so simple, Kollert. No public admission and then public denial after the danger is over—you'd all come across as heroes. No. There has to be some record-keeping, payrolls if nothing else. I want full disclosure of all records, and I want them transmitted around the world—facsimile, authenticated. I want uninvolved government officials to see them and sign that they've seen them. And I want the actual documents put on display where anyone can look at them—memos, plans, letters, whatever. All of it that's still available."

"That would take weeks," Kollert said, "if they existed."

"Not in this age of electronic wizardry. I want you to take a lie-detector test, authenticated by half a dozen experts with their careers on the line—and while you're at it, have the other officials take tests, too.''

"That's not only impractical, it won't hold up in a court of law.''

"I'm not interested in formal courts. I'm not a vengeful person, no matter what I may seem now. I just want the truth. And if I still see that goddamn ship up there in an hour, I'm going to stop negotiations right now and blow myself to pieces.''

Kollert looked at the team leader, but the man's face was blank.

"Let me talk to her, then,'' Porter suggested. "Direct person-to-person. Let me explain the plans. She really can't change them any, can she? She has no way of making them worse. If she fires her engines or does any positive action, she simply stops the threat. So I'm the one who holds the key to the situation.''

"We're not sure that's advisable, Bill,'' Lunar Guidance said.

"I can transmit to her without permission, you know,'' he said testily.

"Against direct orders, that's not like you.''

"Like me, hell,'' he said, chuckling. "Listen, just get me permission. Nobody else seems to be doing anything effective.'' There was a few minutes' silence, then Lunar Guidance returned.

"Okay, Bill. You have permission. But be very careful what you say. Terrorist team officers on Earth think she's close to the pit.''

With that obstacle cleared away, he wondered how wise the idea was in the first place. Still, they were both Geshels— they had something in common compared to the elite Naderites running things on Earth.

Far away, Earth concurred and transmissions were cleared. They couldn't censor his direct signal, so Baja Station was unwillingly cut from the circuit.

"Who's talking to me now?'' Turco asked when the link was made.

"This is Lieutenant William Porter, from the Moon. I'm a pilot—not a defense pilot usually, either. I understand you've had pilot's training.''

184

"Just enough to get by." The lag was less than a hundredth of a second, not noticeable.

"You know I'm up here to stop you, one way or another. I've got two options. The one I think more highly of is to get in line-of-sight of your bore-holes and relay the proper coded signals to the charges in your interior."

"Killing me won't do you any good."

"That's not the plan. The fore end of your rock is bored with a smaller hole by thirty meters. It'll release the blast wastes more slowly than the aft end. The total explosive force should give the rock enough added velocity to get it clear of the Earth by at least sixty kilometers. The damage would be negligible. Spectacular view from Greenland, too, I understand. But if we've miscalculated, or if one or more charges doesn't go, then I'll have to impact with your aft crater and release the charge in my cargo hold. I'm one floating megaboom now, enough to boost the rock up and out by a few additional kilometers. But that means I'll be dead, and not enough left of me to memorialize or pin a medal on. Not too good, hm?"

"None of my sweat."

"No, I suppose not. But listen, sister—"

"No sister to a lackey."

Porter started to snap a retort, but stopped himself. "Listen, they tell me to be soft on you, but I'm under pressure, too, so please reciprocate. I don't see the sense in all of it. If you get your way, you've set back your cause by God knows how many decades—because once you're out of range and blown your trump, they'll deny it all, say it was manufactured evidence and testimony under pressure—all that sort of thing. And if they decide to hard-line it, force me to do my dirty work, or God forbid let you do yours—we've lost our home world. You've lost Psyche, which can still be salvaged and finished. Everything will be lost, just because a few men may or may not have done a very wicked thing. Come on, honey. That isn't the Geshel creed and you know it."

"What is our creed? To let men rule our lives who aren't competent to read a thermometer? Under the Naderites, most of the leaders on Earth haven't got the technical expertise to . . . to . . . I don't know what. To tie their goddamn shoes! They're blind, dedicated to some half-wit belief that progress is the most dangerous thing conceived by man. But they can't live without technology, so we provide it for them. And

185

when they won't touch our filthy nuclear energy, we get stuck with it—because otherwise we all have to go back four hundred years, and sacrifice half the population. Is that good planning, sound policy? And if they do what I say, Psyche won't be damaged. All they'll have to do is fetch it back from orbit around the Sun.''

"I'm not going to argue on their behalf, sister. I'm a Geshel, too, and a Moonman besides. I never have paid attention to Earth politics because it never made much sense to me. But now I'm talking to you on a one-to-one basis. And you're trying to tell me that revenging someone's irrational system is worth wiping away a planet?''

"I'm willing to take that risk.''

"I don't think you are. I hope you aren't. I hope it's all bluff and I won't have to smear myself against your backside.''

"I hope you won't, either. I hope they've got enough sense down there to do what I want.''

"I don't think they have, sister. I don't put much faith in them, myself. They probably don't even know what would happen if you hit the Earth with your rock. Think about that. You're talking about scientific innocents—flat-Earthers almost, naive. Words fail me. But think on it. They may not even know what's going on.''

"They know. And remind them that if they set off the charges, it'll probably break up Psyche and give them a thousand rocks to contend with instead of one. That plan may backfire on them.''

"What if they—we—don't have any choice?''

"I don't give a damn what choice you have,'' Turco said. "I'm not talking for a while. I've got more work to do.''

Porter listened to the final click with a sinking feeling. She was a tough one. How would he psych her? He smiled grimly at his *chutzpah* for even thinking he could. She'd committed herself all the way—and now, perhaps, she was feeling the power of her position. One lonely woman, holding the key to a world's existence. He wondered what it felt like.

Then he shivered and the sweat in his suit felt very, very cold. If he would have a grave for someone to walk over . . .

For the first time, she realized they wouldn't accede to her demands. They were more traitorous than even she could have imagined. Or—the thought was too horrible to accept—

she'd misinterpreted the evidence and they weren't at fault. Perhaps a madman in the Psyche crew had sought revenge and caused the whole mess. But that didn't fit the facts. It would have taken at least a dozen people to set all the psychotropic vials and release them at once—a concerted, preplanned effort. She shook her head. Besides, she had the confidential reports a friend had accidentally plugged into while troubleshooting a Hexamon computer plex. There was no doubt about who was responsible, just uncertainty about the exact procedure. Her evidence for Farmer Kollert's guilt was circumstantial, but not baseless.

She sealed her suit and helmet and went outside the bubble again, just to watch the stars for a few minutes. The lead-gray rock under her feet was pitted by eons of micrometeoroids. Rills several kilometers across attested to the rolling impacts of other asteroids, any one of which would have caused a major disaster on Earth. Earth had been hit before, not often by pieces as big as Psyche, but several times at least, and had survived. Earth would survive Psyche's impact and life would start anew. Those plants and animals—even humans—which survived would eventually build back to the present level, and perhaps it would be a better world, more daunted by the power of past evil. She might be a force for positive regeneration.

The string of bubbles across Psyche's surface was coldly pretty in the starlight. The illumination brightened slowly as Earth rose above the Vlasseg pole, larger than the Moon now. She had a few more hours to make the optimum correction. Just above the Earth was a tiny moving point of light—Porter in his cargo vessel. He was lining up with the smaller bore hole to send signals, if he had to.

She wanted to cry again. She felt like a little child, full of hatred and frustration, but caught now in something so immense and inexorable that all passion was dwarfed. She couldn't believe she was the controlling factor, that she held so much power. Surely something was behind her, some impersonal, objective force. Alone she was nothing, and her crime would be unbelievable—just as Porter had said. But with a cosmic justification, the agreeing nod of some vast, all-seeing God, she was just a tool, bereft of responsibility.

She grasped the guide wires strung between the bubbles and pulled herself back to the airlock hatch. With one gloved hand she pressed the button. Under her palm she felt the metal vibrate for a second, then stop. The hatch was still closed. She pressed again and nothing happened.

Porter listened carefully for a full minute, trying to pick up the weak signal. It had cut off abruptly a few minutes before, during his final lineup with the bore-hole through the Vlasseg pole. He called his director and asked if any signals had been received from Turco. Since he was out of line-of-sight now, the Moon had to act as a relay.

"Nothing," Lunar Guidance said. "She's been silent for an hour."

"That's not right. We've only got an hour and a half left. She should be playing the situation for all it's worth. Listen, LG, I received a weak signal from Psyche several minutes ago. It could have been a freak, but I don't think so. I'm going to move back to where I picked it up."

"Negative, Porter. You'll need all your reaction mass in case plan A doesn't go off properly."

"I've got plenty to spare, LG. I have a bad feeling about this. Something's gone wrong on Psyche." It was clear to him the instant he said it. "Jesus Christ, LG, the signal must have come from Turco's area on Psyche! I lost it just when I passed out of line-of-sight from her bubble."

Lunar Guidance was silent for a long moment. "Okay, Porter, we've got clearance for you to regain that signal."

"Thank you, LG." He pushed the ship out of its rough alignment and coasted slowly away from Psyche until he could see the equatorial ring of domes and bubbles. Abruptly, his receiver picked up the weak signal again. He locked his tracking antenna to it, boosted it, and cut in the communications processor to interpolate through the hash.

"This is Turco. William Porter, listen to me! This is Turco. I'm locked out. Something has malfunctioned in the control bubble. I'm locked out . . ."

"I'm getting you, Turco," he said. "Look at my spot above the Vlasseg pole. I'm in line-of-sight again." If her suit was a standard model, her transmissions would strengthen in the direction she was facing.

"God bless you, Porter. I see you. Everything's gone wrong down here. I can't get back in."

"Try again, Turco. Do you have any tools with you?"

"That's what started all this, breaking in with a chisel and a pry bar. It must have weakened something and now the whole mechanism is frozen. No, I left the bar inside. No tools. Jesus, this is awful."

"Calm down. Keep trying to get in. I'm relaying your signal to Lunar Guidance and Earth." That settled it. There was no time to waste now. If she didn't turn on the positioning motors soon, any miss would be too close for comfort. He had to set off the internal charges within an hour and a half for the best effect.

"She's outside?" Lunar Guidance asked when the transmissions were relayed. "Can't get back in?"

"That's it," Porter said.

"That cocks it, Porter. Ignore her and get back into position. Don't bother lining up with the Vlasseg pole, however. Circle around to the Janacki pole bore-hole and line up for code broadcast there. You'll have a better chance of getting the code through, and you can prepare for any further action."

"I'll be cooked, LG."

"Negative—you're to relay code from an additional thousand kilometers, and boost yourself out of the path just before detonation. That will occur—let's see—about four point three seconds after the charges receive the code. Program your computer for sequencing; you'll be too busy."

"I'm moving, LG." He returned to Turco's wavelength. "It's out of your hands now," he said. "We're blowing the charges. They may not be enough, so I'm preparing to detonate myself against the Janacki pole crater. Congratulations, Turco."

"I still can't get back in, Porter."

"I said, congratulations. You've killed both of us, and ruined Psyche for any future projects. You know that she'll go to pieces when she drops below Roche's limit? Even if she misses, she'll be too close to survive. You know, they might have gotten it all straightened out in a few administrations. Politicos die, or get booted out of office—even Naderites. I say you've cooked it good. Be happy, Turco." He flipped the switch viciously and concentrated on his approach program display.

Farmer Kollert was slumped in his chair, eyes closed but still awake, half-listening to the murmurs in the control room.

Someone tapped him on the shoulder and he started, jerking up in his seat.

"I had to be with you, Farmer." Gestina stood over him, a nervous smile making her dimples obvious. "They brought me here to be with you."

"Why?" he asked.

Her voice shook. "Because our house was destroyed. I got out just in time. What's happening, Farmer? Why do they want to kill me? What did I do?"

The team officer standing beside her held out a piece of paper and Kollert took it. Violence had broken out in half a dozen Hexamon centers, and numerous officials had had to be evacuated. Geshels weren't the only ones involved—Naderites of all classes seemed to share indignation and rage at what was happening. The outbreaks weren't organized—and that was even more disturbing. Wherever transmissions had reached the unofficial grapevines, people were reacting.

Gestina's large eyes regarded him without comprehension, much less sympathy. "I had to be with you, Farmer," she repeated. "They wouldn't let me stay."

"Quiet, please," another officer said. "More transmissions coming in."

"Yes," Kollert said softly. "Quiet. That's what we wanted. Quiet and peace and sanity. Safety for our children to come."

"I think something big is happening," Gestina said. "What is it?"

Porter checked the alignment again, put up his visual shields and instructed the processor to broadcast the coded signal. With no distinguishable pause, the ship's engines started to move him out of the particle blast.

Giana Turco worked at the hatch edge with a bit of metal bracing she had broken off her suitpack. The sharp edge just barely fit into the crevice, and by gouging and prying she had managed to force the door up half a centimeter. The evacuation mechanism hadn't been activated, so frosted air hissed from the crack, making the work doubly difficult. The Moon was rising above the Janacki pole.

Deep below her, seven prebalanced but unchecked charges, mounted on massive fittings in their chambers, began to whir.

Four processors checked the timing, concurred, and released safety shields.

Six of the charges went off at once. The seventh was late by ten thousandths of a second, and its blast was muted as the casing melted prematurely. The particle shockwaves streamed out through the bore-holes, now pressure release valves, and formed a long neck and tail of flame and ionized particles which grew steadily for a thousand kilometers, then faded. The neck from the Vlasseg pole was thinner and shorter, but no less spectacular. The asteroid shuddered, vibrations rising from deep inside to pull the ground away from Turco's boots, then swing it back to kick her away from the bubble and hatch. She floated in space, disoriented, ripped free of the guide wires, her back to the asteroid, faceplate aimed at peaceful stars, turning slowly as she reached the top of her arc.

Her leisurely descent gave her plenty of time to see the secondary plume of purple and white and red forming around the Janacki pole. The stars were blanked out by its brilliance. She closed her eyes. When she opened them again, she was nearer the ground, and her faceplate had polarized against the sudden brightness. She saw the bubble still intact, and the hatch wide open now. It had been jarred free. Everything was vibrating . . . and with shock she realized the asteroid was slowly moving out from beneath her. Her fall became a drawn-out curve, taking her away from the bubble, toward a ridge of lead-gray rock, without guide wires, where she would bounce and continue on unchecked. To her left, one dome ruptured and sent a feathery wipe of debris into space. Pieces of rock and dust floated past her, shaken from Psyche's weak surface grip. Then her hand was only a few meters from a guide wire torn free and swinging outward. It came closer like a dancing snake, hesitated, rippled again, and came within reach. She grabbed it and pulled herself down.

"Porter, this is Lunar Guidance. Earth says the charges weren't enough. Something went wrong."

"She held together, LG," Porter said in disbelief. "She didn't break up. I've got a fireworks show like you've never seen before."

"Porter, listen. She isn't moving fast enough. She'll still impact."

"I *heard* you, LG," Porter shouted. "I heard! Leave me alone to get things done." And nothing more was said between them.

Turco reached the hatch and crawled into the airlock, exhausted. She closed the outer door and waited for equalization before opening the inner. Her helmet was off and floating behind as she walked and bounced and guided herself into the control room. If the motors were still functional, she'd fire them. She had no second thoughts now. Something had gone wrong, and the situation was completely different.

In the middle of the kilometers-wide crater at the Janacki pole, the bore hole was still spewing debris and ionized particles. But around the perimeter, other forces were at work. Canisters of reaction mass were flying to a point three kilometers above the crater floor. The Beckmann drive engines rotated on their mountings, aiming their nodes at the canisters' rendezvous point.

Porter's ship was following the tail of debris down to the crater floor. He could make out geometric patterns of insulating material. His computers told him something was approaching a few hundred meters below. There wasn't time for any second guessing. He primed his main cargo and sat back in the seat, lips moving, not in prayer, but repeating some stray, elegant line from the Burgess novel, a final piece of pleasure.

One of the canisters struck the side of the cargo ship just as the blast began. A brilliant flare spread out above the crater, merging with and twisting the tail of the internal charges. Four canisters were knocked from their course and sent plummeting into space. The remaining six met at the assigned point and were hit by beams from the Beckmann drive nodes. Their matter was stripped down to pure energy.

All of this, in its lopsided, incomplete way, bounced against the crater floor and drove the asteroid slightly faster.

When the shaking subsided, Turco let go of a grip bar and asked the computers questions. No answers came back. Everything except minimal life support was out of commission. She thought briefly of returning to her tug, if it was still in place, but there was no place to go. So she walked and crawled and floated to a broad view-window in the bubble's dining room. Earth was rising over the Vlasseg pole again, filling half her view, knots of storm and streaks of brown continent twisting slowly before her. She wondered if it had been enough—it hadn't felt right. There was no way of knowing for sure, but the Earth looked much too close.

"It's too close to judge," the president said, deliberately standing wth his back to Kollert. "She'll pass over Greenland, hopefully just hit the upper atmosphere, perhaps lose bits of herself."

The terrorist team officers were packing their valises and talking to each other in subdued whispers. Three of the president's security men were looking at the screen with dazed expressions. The screen was blank except for a display of seconds until accession of picture. Gestina was asleep in the chair next to Kollert, her face peaceful, hands wrapped together in her lap.

"We'll have relay pictures from Iceland in a few minutes," the president said. "Should be quite a sight." Kollert frowned. The man was almost cocky, knowing he would come through it untouched. Even with survival uncertain, his government would be preparing explanations. Kollert could predict the story: a band of lunar terrorists, loosely tied with Giani Turco's father and his rabid spacefarers, were responsible for the whole thing. It would mean a few months of ill-feeling on the Moon, but at least the Nexus would have found its scapegoats.

A communicator beeped in the room and Kollert looked around for its source. One of the security men reached into a pocket and pulled out a small earplug, which he inserted. He listened for a few seconds, frowned, then nodded. The other two gathered close and they whispered.

Then, quietly, they left the room. The president didn't notice they were gone, but to Kollert their absence spoke volumes.

Six Nexus police entered a minute later. One stood by Kollert's chair, not looking at him. Four waited by the door. Another approached the president and tapped him on the shoulder. The president turned.

"Sir, fourteen Desks have requested your impeachment. We're instructed to put you under custody, for your own safety."

"May we stay to watch?" the president asked. No one objected.

Before the screen was switched on, Kollert asked, "Is anyone going to get Turco, if it misses?"

The terrorists team leader shrugged when no one else answered. "She may not even be alive."

Then, like a crowd of children looking at a horror movie, the men and women in the communications center grouped around the large screen and watched the dark shadow of Psyche blotting out stars.

From the bubble window, Turco saw the sudden aurorae, the spray of ionized gases from the Earth's atmosphere, the awesomely rapid passage of the ocean below, and the blur of white as Greenland flashed past. The structure rocked and jerked as the Earth exerted enormous tidal strains on Psyche.

Sitting in the plastic chair, numb, tightly gripping the arms, Giani looked up—down—at the bright stars, feeling Psyche die beneath her.

Inside, the still-molten hollows formed by the charges began to collapse. Cracks shot outward to the surface, where they became gaping chasms. Sparks and rays of smoke jumped from the chasms. In minutes the passage was over. Looking closely, she saw roiling storms forming over Earth's seas, and the spreading shockwave of the asteroid's sudden atmospheric compression. Big winds were blowing, but they'd survive.

It shouldn't have gone this far. They should have listened reasonably, admitted their guilt—

Absolved, girl, she wanted her father to say. She felt him very near. *You've destroyed everything we worked for—a fine architect of Pyrrhic victories.* And now he was at a great distance, receding.

The room was cold and her skin tingled.

One huge chunk rose to block out the Sun. The cabin screamed and the bubble was filled with sudden flakes of air.

HOW IT WAS WHEN THE PAST WENT AWAY

Robert Silverberg

The day that an antisocial fiend dumped an amnesifacient drug into the city water supply was one of the finest that San Francisco had had in a long while. The damp cloud that had been hovering over everything for three weeks finally drifted across the bay into Berkeley that Wednesday, and the sun emerged, bright and warm, to give the old town its warmest day so far in 2003. The temperature climbed into the high twenties, and even those oldsters who hadn't managed to learn to convert to the centigrade thermometer knew it was hot. Air-conditioners hummed from the Golden Gate to the Embarcadero. Pacific Gas & Electric recorded its highest one-hour load in history between two and three in the afternoon. The parks were crowded. People drank a lot of water, some a good deal more than others. Toward nightfall, the thirstiest ones were already beginning to forget things. By the next morning, everybody in the city was in trouble, with a few exceptions. It had really been an ideal day for committing a monstrous crime.

On the day before the past went away, Paul Mueller had been thinking seriously about leaving the state and claiming refuge in one of the debtor sanctuaries—Reno, maybe, or Caracas. It wasn't altogether his fault, but he was close to a million in the red, and his creditors were getting unruly. It had reached the point where they were sending their robot bill collectors around to harass him in person, just about every three hours.

"Mr. Mueller? I am requested to notify you that the sum of $8,005.97 is overdue in your account with Modern Age Recreators, Inc. We have applied to your financial representative and have discovered your state of insolvency, and therefore, unless a payment of $395.61 is made by the eleventh of this month, we may find it necessary to begin confiscation procedures against your person. Thus I advise you—"

"—the amount of $11,554.97, payable on the ninth of August, 2002, has not yet been received by Luna Tours, Ltd. Under the Credit Laws of 1995 we have applied for injunctive relief against you and anticipate receiving a decree of personal service due, if no payment is received by—"

"—interest on the unpaid balance is accruing, as specified in your contract, at a rate of four percent per month—"

"—balloon payment now coming due, requiring the immediate payment of—"

Mueller was growing accustomed to the routine. The robots couldn't call him—Pacific Tel & Tel had cut him out of their data net months ago—and so they came around, polite blank-faced machines stenciled with corporate emblems, and in soft purring voices told him precisely how deep in the mire he was at the moment, how fast the penalty charges were piling up, and what they planned to do to him unless he settled his debts instantly. If he tried to duck them, they'd simply track him down in the streets like indefatigable process servers, and announce his shame to the whole city. So he didn't duck them. But fairly soon their threats would begin to materialize.

They could do awful things to him. The decree of personal service, for example, would turn him into a slave; he'd become an employee of his creditor, at a court-stipulated salary, but every cent he earned would be applied against his debt, while the creditor provided him with minimal food, shelter, and clothing. He might find himself compelled to do menial jobs that a robot would spit at, for two or three years, just to clear that one debt. Personal confiscation procedures were even worse; under that deal he might well end up as the actual servant of one of the executives of a creditor company, shining shoes and folding shirts. They might also get an open-ended garnishment on him, under which he and his

196

descendants, if any, would pay a stated percentage of their annual income down through the ages until the debt, and the compounding interest thereon, was finally satisfied. There were other techniques for dealing with delinquents, too.

He had no recourse to bankruptcy. The states and the federal government had tossed out the bankruptcy laws in 1995, after the so-called Credit Epidemic of the 1980s, when for a while it was actually fashionable to go irretrievably into debt and throw yourself on the mercy of the courts. The haven of easy bankruptcy was no more; if you became insolvent, your creditors had you in their grip. The only way out was to jump to a debtor sanctuary, a place where local laws barred any extradition for a credit offense. There were about a dozen such sanctuaries, and you could live well there, provided you have some special skill that you could sell at a high price. You needed to make a good living, because in a debtor sanctuary everything was on a strictly cash basis—cash in advance, at that, even for a haircut. Mueller had a skill that he thought would see him through: he was an artist, a maker of sonic sculptures, and his work was always in good demand. All he needed was a few thousand dollars to purchase the basic tools of his trade—his last set of sculpting equipment had been repossessed a few weeks ago—and he could set up a studio in one of the sanctuaries, beyond the reach of the robot hounds. He imagined he could still find a friend who would lend him a few thousand dollars. In the name of art, so to speak. In a good cause.

If he stayed within the sanctuary area for ten consecutive years, he would be absolved of his debts and could come forth a free man. There was only one catch, not a small one. Once a man had taken the sanctuary route, he was forever barred from all credit channels when he returned to the outside world. He couldn't even get a post office credit card, let alone a bank loan. Mueller wasn't sure he could live that way, paying cash for everything all the rest of his life. It would be terribly cumbersome and dreary. Worse: it would be barbaric.

He made a note on his memo pad: *Call Freddy Munson in morning and borrow three bigs. Buy ticket to Caracas. Buy sculpting stuff.*

The die was cast—unless he changed his mind in the morning.

He peered moodily out at the row of glistening white-washed just-post-Earthquake houses descending the steeply inclined street that ran down Telegraph Hill toward Fisherman's Wharf. They sparkled in the unfamiliar sunlight. A beautiful day, Mueller thought. A beautiful day to drown yourself in the bay. Damn. Damn. Damn. He was going to be forty years old soon. He had come into the world on the same black day that President John Kennedy had left it. Born in an evil hour, doomed to a dark fate. Mueller scowled. He went to the tap and got a glass of water. It was the only thing he could afford to drink, just now. He asked himself how he had ever managed to get into such a mess. Nearly a million in debt!

He lay down dismally to take a nap.

When he woke, toward midnight, he felt better than he had felt for a long time. Some great cloud seemed to have lifted from him, even as it had lifted from the city that day. Mueller was actually in a cheerful mood. He couldn't imagine why.

In an elegant townhouse on Marina Boulevard, The Amazing Montini was rehearsing his act. The Amazing Montini was a professional mnemonist: a small, dapper man of sixty, who never forgot a thing. Deeply tanned, his dark hair slicked back at a sharp angle, his small black eyes glistening with confidence, his thin lips fastidiously pursed. He drew a book from a shelf and let it drop open at random. It was an old one-volume edition of Shakespeare, a familiar prop in his nightclub act. He skimmed the page, nodded, looked briefly at another, then another, and smiled his inward smile. Life was kind to The Amazing Montini. He earned a comfortable $30,000 a week on tour, having converted a freakish gift into a profitable enterprise. Tomorrow night he'd open for a week at Vegas; then on to Manila, Tokyo, Bangkok, Cairo, on around the globe. In twelve weeks he'd earn his year's take; then he'd relax once more.

It was all so easy. He knew so many good tricks. Let them scream out a twenty-digit number, he'd scream it right back. Let them bombard him with long strings of nonsense syllables; he'd repeat the gibberish flawlessly. Let them draw intricate mathematical formulas on the computer screen; he'd reproduce them down to the last exponent. His memory was perfect, both for visuals and auditories, and for the other registers as well.

The Shakespeare thing, which was one of the simplest routines he had, always awed the impressionable. It seemed so fantastic to most people that a man could memorize the complete works, page by page. He liked to use it as an opener.

He handed the book to Nadia, his assistant. Also his mistress; Montini liked to keep his circle of intimates close. She was twenty years old, taller than he was, with wide frost-gleamed eyes and a torrent of glowing, artificially radiant azure hair: up to the minute in every fashion. She wore a glass bodice, a nice container for the things contained. She was not very bright, but she did the things Montini expected her to do, and did them quite well. She would be replaced, he estimated, in about eighteen more months. He grew bored quickly with his women. His memory was too good.

"Let's start," he said.

She opened the book. "Page 537, left-hand column."

Instantly the page floated before Montini's eyes. "Henry VI, Part Two," he said. "King Henry: Say, man, were these thy words? Horner: An't shall please your majesty, I never said nor thought any such matter: God is my witness, I am falsely accused by the villain. Peter: By these ten bones, my lords, he did speak them to me in the garret one night, as we were scouring my Lord of York's armour. York: Base dung-hill villain, and—"

"Page 778, right-hand column," Nadia said.

"Romeo and Juliet. Mercutio is speaking: . . . an eye would spy out such a quarrel? Thy head is as full of quarrels as an egg is full of meat, and yet thy head hath been beaten as addle as an egg for quarreling. Thou hast quarreled with a man for coughing in the street, because he hath wakened thy dog that hath lain asleep in the sun. Didst thou not—"

"Page 307, starting fourteen lines down on the right side."

Montini smiled. He liked the passage. A screen would show it to his audience at the performance.

"Twelfth Night," he said. "The Duke speaks: Too old, by heaven. Let still the woman take an elder than herself, so wears she to him, so sways she level in her husband's heart: For, boy, however we do praise ourselves, our fancies are more giddy and unfirm—"

"Page 495, left-hand column."

"Wait a minute," Montini said. He poured himself a tall

glass of water and drank it in three quick gulps. "This work always makes me thirsty."

Taylor Braskett, Lt. Comdr., Ret., U.S. Space Service, strode with springy stride into his Oak Street home, just outside Golden Gate Park. At 71, Commander Braskett still managed to move in a jaunty way, and he was ready to step back into uniform at once if his country needed him. He believed his country did need him, more than ever, now that socialism was running like wildfire through half the nations of Europe. Guard the home front, at least. Protect what's left of traditional American liberty. What we ought to have, Commander Braskett believed, is a network of C-bombs in orbit, ready to rain hellish death on the enemies of democracy. No matter what the treaty says, we must be prepared to defend ourselves.

Commander Braskett's theories were not widely accepted. People respected him for having been one of the first Americans to land on Mars, of course, but he knew that they quietly regarded him as a crank, a crackpot, an antiquated Minute Man still fretting about the Redcoats. He had enough of a sense of humor to realize that he did cut an absurd figure to these young people. But he was sincere in his determination to help keep America free—to protect the youngsters from the lash of totalitarianism, whether they laughed at him or not. All this glorious sunny day he had been walking through the park, trying to talk to the young ones, attempting to explain his position. He was courteous, attentive, eager to find someone who would ask him questions. The trouble was that no one listened. And the young ones—stripped to the waist in the sunshine, girls as well as boys, taking drugs out in the open, using the foulest obscenities in casual speech—at times, Commander Braskett almost came to think that the battle for America had already been lost. Yet he never gave up all hope.

He had been in the park for hours. Now, at home, he walked past the trophy room, into the kitchen, opened the refrigerator, drew out a bottle of water. Commander Braskett had three bottles of mountain spring water delivered to his home every two days; it was a habit he had begun fifty years ago, when they had first started talking about putting fluorides in the water. He was not unaware of the little smiles they

200

gave him when he admitted that he drank only bottle spring water, but he didn't mind; he had outlived many of the smilers already, and attributed his perfect health to his refusal to touch the polluted, contaminated water that most other people drank. First chlorine, then fluorides—probably they were putting in some other things by now, Commander Braskett thought.

He drank deeply.

You have no way of telling what sort of dangerous chemicals they might be putting in the municipal water system these days, he told himself. Am I a crank? Then I'm a crank. But a sane man drinks only water he can trust.

Fetally curled, knees pressed almost to chin, trembling, sweating, Nate Haldersen closed his eyes and tried to ease himself of the pain of existence. Another day. A sweet, sunny day. Happy people playing in the park. Fathers and children. Husbands and wives. He bit his lip, hard, just short of laceration intensity. He was an expert at punishing himself.

Sensors mounted in his bed in the Psychotrauma Ward of Fletcher Memorial Hospital scanned him continuously, sending a constant flow of reports to Dr. Bryce and his team of shrinks. Nate Haldersen knew he was a man without secrets. His hormone count, enzyme ratios, respiration, circulation, even the taste of bile in his mouth—it all became instantaneously known to hospital personnel. When the sensors discovered him slipping below the depression line, ultrasonic snouts came nosing up from the recesses of the mattress, proximity nozzles that sought him out in the bed, found the proper veins, squirted him full of dynajuice to cheer him up. Modern science was wonderful. It could do everything for Haldersen except give him back his family.

The door slid open. Dr. Bryce came in. The head shrink looked his part: tall, solemn yet charming, gray at the temples, clearly a wielder of power and an initiate of mysteries. He sat down beside Haldersen's bed. As usual, he made a big point of not looking at the row of computer outputs next to the bed that gave the latest details on Haldersen's condition.

"Nate?" he said. "How goes?"

"It goes," Haldersen muttered.

"Feel like talking a while?"

"Not specially. Get me a drink of water?"

"Sure," the shrink said. He fetched it and said, "It's a gorgeous day. How about a walk in the park?"

"I haven't left this room in two and a half years, Doctor. You know that."

"Always a time to break loose. There's nothing physically wrong with you, you know."

"I just don't feel like seeing people," Haldersen said. He handed back the empty glass. "More?"

"Want something stronger to drink?"

"Water's fine." Haldersen closed his eyes. Unwanted images danced behind the lids: the rocket liner blowing open over the pole, the passengers spilling out like autumn seeds erupting from a pod, Emily tumbling down, down, falling eighty thousand feet, her golden hair swept up by the thin cold wind, her short skirt flapping at her hips, her long lovely legs clawing at the sky for a place to stand. And the children falling beside her, angels dropping from heaven, down, down, down, toward the white soothing fleece of the polar ice. They sleep in peace, Haldersen thought, and I missed the plane, and I alone remain. And Job spake, and said, Let the day perish wherein I was born, and the night in which it was said, There is a man child conceived.

"It was eleven years ago," Dr. Bryce told him. "Won't you let go of it?"

"Stupid talk coming from a shrink. Why won't it let go of *me?*"

"You don't want it to. You're too fond of playing your role."

"Today is talking-tough day, eh? Get me some more water."

"Get up and get it yourself," said the shrink.

Haldersen smiled bitterly. He left the bed, crossing the room a little unsteadily, and filled his glass. He had had all sorts of therapy—sympathy therapy, antagonism therapy, drugs, shock, orthodox freuding, the works. They did nothing for him. He was left with the image of an opening pod, and falling figures against the iron-blue sky. The Lord gave, and the Lord hath taken away; blessed be the name of the Lord. My soul is weary of my life. He put the glass to his lips. Eleven years. I missed the plane. I sinned with Marie, and Emily died, and John, and Beth. What did it feel like to fall so far? Was it like flying? Was there ecstasy in it? Haldersen filled the glass again.

"Thirsty today, eh?"

"Yes," Haldersen said.

"Sure you don't want to take a little walk?"

"You know I don't." Haldersen shivered. He turned and caught the psychiatrist by the forearm. "When does it end, Tim? How long do I have to carry this thing around?"

"Until you're willing to put it down."

"How can I make a conscious effort to forget something? Tim, Tim, isn't there some drug I can take, something to wash away a memory that's killing me?"

"Nothing effective."

"You're lying," Haldersen murmured. "I've read about the amnesifacients. The enzymes that eat memory-RNA. The experiments with di-isopropyl fluorophoshate. Puromycin. The—"

Dr. Bryce said, "We have no control over their operations. We can't simply go after a single block of traumatic memories while leaving the rest of your mind unharmed. We'd have to bash about at random, hoping we got the trouble spot, but never knowing what else we were blotting out. You'd wake up without your trauma, but maybe without remembering anything else that happened to you between, say, the ages of 14 and 40. Maybe in fifty years we'll know enough to be able to direct the dosage at a specific—"

"I can't wait fifty years."

"I'm sorry, Nate."

"Give me the drugs anyway. I'll take my chances on what I lose."

"We'll talk about that some other time, all right? The drugs are experimental. There'd be months of red tape before I could get authorization to try them on a human subject. You have to realize—"

Haldersen turned him off. He saw only with his inner eye, saw the tumbling bodies, reliving his bereavement for the billionth time, slipping easily back into his self-assumed role of Job. I am a brother to dragons, and a companion to owls. My skin is black upon me, and my bones are burned with heat. He hath destroyed me on every side, and I am gone; and mine hope hath he removed like a tree.

The shrink continued to speak. Haldersen continued not to listen. He poured himself one more glass of water with a shaky hand.

*   *   *

It was close to midnight on Wednesday before Pierre Gerard, his wife, their two sons, and their daughter had a chance to have dinner. They were the proprietors, chefs, and total staff of the Petit Pois Restaurant on Sansome Street, and business had been extraordinary, exhaustingly good all evening. Usually they were able to eat about half past five, before the dinner rush began, but today people had begun coming in early—made more expansive by the good weather, no doubt—and there hadn't been a free moment for anybody since the cocktail hour. The Gerards were accustomed to brisk trade, for theirs was perhaps the most popular family-run bistro in the city, with a passionately devoted clientele. Still, a night like this was too much!

They dined modestly on the evening's miscalculations: an overdone rack of lamb, some faintly corky Château Beychevelle '97, a fallen soufflé, and such. They were thrifty people. Their one extravagance was the Évian water that they imported from France. Pierre Gerard had not set foot in his native Lyons for thirty years, but he preserved many of the customs of the motherland, including the traditional attitude toward water. A Frenchman does not drink much water; but what he does drink comes always from the bottle, never from the tap. To do otherwise is to risk a diseased liver. One must guard one's liver.

That night Freddy Munson picked up Helene at her flat on Geary and drove across the bridge to Sausalito for dinner, as usual, at Ondine's. Ondine's was one of only four restaurants, all of them famous ones, at which Munson ate in fixed rotation. He was a man of firm habits. He awakened religiously at six each morning, and was at his desk in the brokerage house by seven, plugging himself into the data channels to learn what had happened in the European finance markets while he slept. At half past seven local time the New York exchanges opened and the real day's work began. By half past eleven, New York was through for the day, and Munson went around the corner for lunch, always at the Petit Pois, whose proprietor he had helped to make a millionaire by putting him into Consolidated Nucleonics' several components two and a half years before the big merger. At half past one, Munson was back in the office to transact business for

204

his own account on the Pacific Coast exchange; three days a week he left at three, but on Tuesdays and Thursdays he stayed as late as five in order to catch some deals on the Honolulu and Tokyo exchanges. Afterwards, dinner, a play or concert, always a handsome female companion. He tried to get to sleep, or at least to bed, by midnight.

A man in Freddy Munson's position *had* to be orderly. At any given time, his thefts from his clients ranged from six to nine million dollars, and he kept all the details of his jugglings in his head. He couldn't trust putting them on paper, because there were scanner eyes everywhere; and he certainly didn't dare employ the data net, since it was well known that anything you confided to one computer was bound to be accessible to some other computer somewhere, no matter how tight a privacy seal you slapped on it. So Munson had to remember the intricacies of fifty or more illicit transactions, a constantly changing chain of embezzlements, and a man who practices such necessary disciplines of memory soon gets into the habit of extending discipline to every phase of his life.

Helene snuggled close. Her faintly psychedelic perfume drifted toward his nostrils. He locked the car into the Sausalito circuit and leaned back comfortably as the traffic-control computer took over the steering. Helene said, "At the Bryce place last night I saw two sculptures by your bankrupt friend."

"Paul Mueller?"

"That's the one. They were very good sculptures. One of them buzzed at me."

"What were you doing at the Bryces?"

"I went to college with Lisa Bryce. She invited me over with Marty."

"I didn't realize you were that old," Munson said.

Helene giggled. "Lisa's a lot younger than her husband, dear. How much does a Paul Mueller sculpture cost?"

"Fifteen, twenty thousand, generally. More for specials."

"And he's broke, even so?"

"Paul has a rare talent for self-destruction," Munson said. "He simply doesn't comprehend money. But it's his artistic salvation, in a way. The more desperately in debt he is, the finer his work becomes. He creates out of his despair, so to speak. Though he seems to have overdone the latest crisis. He's stopped working altogether. It's a sin against humanity when the artist doesn't work."

205

"You can be so eloquent, Freddy," Helene said softly.

When The Amazing Montini woke Thursday morning, he did not at once realize that anything had changed. His memory, like a good servant, was always there when he needed to call on it, but the array of perfectly fixed facts he carried in his mind remained submerged until required. A librarian might scan shelves and see books missing; Montini could not detect similar vacancies of his synapses. He had been up for half an hour, had stepped under the molecular bath and had punched for his breakfast and had awakened Nadia to tell her to confirm the pod reservations to Vegas, and finally, like a concert pianist running off a few arpeggios to limber his fingers for the day's chores, Montini reached into his memory bank for a little Shakespeare and no Shakespeare came.

He stood quite still, gripping the astrolabe that ornamented his picture window, and peered out at the bridge in sudden bewilderment. It had never been necessary for him to make a conscious effort to recover data. He merely looked and it was there; but where was Shakespeare? Where was the left-hand column of page 136, and the right-hand column of page 654, and the right-hand column of page 806, sixteen lines down? Gone? He drew blanks. The screen of his mind showed him only empty pages.

Easy. This is unusual, but it isn't catastrophic. You must be tense, for some reason, and you're forcing it, that's all. Relax, pull something else out of storage—

The New York *Times,* Wednesday, October 3, 1973. Yes, there it was, the front page, beautifully clear, the story on the baseball game down in the lower right-hand corner, the headline about the jet accident big and black, even the photo credit visible. Fine. Now let's try—

The St. Louis *Post-Dispatch,* Sunday, April 19, 1987. Montini shivered. He saw the top four inches of the page, nothing else. Wiped clean.

He ran through the files of other newspapers he had memorized for his act. Some were there. Some were not. Some, like the *Post-Dispatch,* were obliterated in part. Color rose to his cheeks. Who had tampered with his memory?

He tried Shakespeare again. Nothing.

He tried the 1997 Chicago data-net directory. It was there.

He tried his third-grade geography textbook. It was there, the big red book with smeary print.

He tried last Friday's five-o'clock xerofax bulletin. Gone.

He stumbled and sank down on a divan he had purchased in Istanbul, he recalled, on the nineteenth of May, 1985, for 4,200 Turkish pounds. "Nadia!" he cried. "Nadia!" His voice was little more than a croak. She came running, her eyes only half frosted, her morning face askew.

"How do I look?" he demanded. "My mouth—is my mouth right? My eyes?"

"Your face is all flushed."

"Aside from that!"

"I don't know," she gasped. "You seem all upset, but—"

"Half my mind is gone," Montini said. "I must have had a stroke. Is there any facial paralysis? That's a symptom. Call my doctor, Nadia! A stroke, a stroke! It's the end for Montini!"

Paul Mueller, awakening at midnight on Wednesday and feeling strangely refreshed, attempted to get his bearings. Why was he fully dressed, and why had he been asleep? A nap, perhaps, that had stretched on too long? He tried to remember what he had been doing earlier in the day, but he was unable to find a clue. He was baffled but not disturbed; mainly he felt a tremendous urge to get to work. The images of five sculptures, fully planned and begging to be constructed, jostled in his mind. Might as well start right now, he thought. Work through 'til morning. That small twittering silvery one—that's a good one to start with. I'll block out the schematics, maybe even do some of the armature—

"Carole?" he called. "Carole, are you around?"

His voice echoed through the oddly empty apartment.

For the first time Mueller noticed how little furniture there was. A bed—a cot, really, not their double bed—and a table, and a tiny insulator unit for food, and a few dishes. No carpeting. Where were his sculptures, his private collection of his own best work? He walked into his studio and found it bare from wall to wall, all of his tools mysteriously swept away, just a few discarded sketches on the floor. And his wife? "Carole? *Carole?*"

He could not understand any of this. While he dozed, it seemed, someone had cleaned the place out, stolen his furniture, his sculptures, even the carpet. Mueller had heard of such thefts. They came with a van, brazenly, posing as moving men. Perhaps they had given him some sort of drug while they worked. He could not bear the thought that they had taken his sculptures; the rest didn't matter, but he had cherished those dozen pieces dearly. I'd better call the police, he decided, and rushed toward the handset of the data unit, but it wasn't there either. Would burglars take *that* too?

Searching for some answers, he scurried from wall to wall, and saw a note in his own handwriting. *Call Freddy Munson in morning and borrow three bigs. Buy ticket to Caracas. Buy sculpting stuff.*

Caracas? A vacation, maybe? And why buy sculpting stuff? Obviously the tools had been gone before he fell asleep, then. Why? And where was his wife? What was going on? He wondered if he ought to call Freddy right now, instead of waiting until morning. Freddy might know. Freddy was always home by midnight, too. He'd have one of his damned girls with him and wouldn't want to be interrupted, but to hell with that; what good was having friends if you couldn't bother them in a time of crisis?

Heading for the nearest public communicator booth, he rushed out of his apartment and nearly collided with a sleek dunning robot in the hallway. The things show no mercy, Mueller thought. They plague you at all hours. No doubt this one was on its way to bother the deadbeat Nicholson family down the hall.

The robot said, "Mr. Paul Mueller? I am a properly qualified representative of International Fabrication Cartel, Amalgamated. I am here to serve notice that there is an unpaid balance in your account to the extent of $9,150.55, which as of 0900 hours tomorrow morning will accrue compounded penalty interest at the rate of 5 percent per month, since you have not responded to our three previous requests for payment. I must further inform you—"

"You're off your neutrinos," Mueller snapped. "I don't owe a dime to I.F.C.! For once in my life I'm in the black, and don't try to make me believe otherwise."

The robot replied patiently, "Shall I give you a printout of the transactions? On the fifth of January, 2003, you ordered the follwing metal products from us: three 4-meter tubes of antiqued iridium, six 10-centimeter spheres of—"

"The fifth of January, 2003, happens to be three months

from now," Mueller said, "and I don't have time to listen to crazy robots. I've got an important call to make. Can I trust you to patch me into the data net without garbling things?"

"I'm not authorized to permit you to make use of my facilities."

"Emergency override," said Mueller. "Human being in trouble. Go argue with that one!"

The robot's conditioning was sound. It yielded at once to his assertion of an emergency and set up a relay to the main communications net. Mueller supplied Freddy Munson's number. "I can provide audio only," the robot said, putting the call through. Nearly a minute passed. Then Freddy Munson's familiar deep voice snarled from the speaker grille in the robot's chest, "Who is it and what do you want?"

"It's Paul. I'm sorry to bust in on you, Freddy, but I'm in big trouble. I think I'm losing my mind, or else everybody else is."

"Maybe everybody else is. What's the problem?"

"All my furniture's gone. A dunning robot is trying to shake me down for nine bigs. I don't know where Carole is. I can't remember what I was doing earlier today. I've got a note here about getting tickets to Caracas that I wrote myself, and I don't know why. And—"

"Skip the rest," Munson said. "I can't do anything for you. I've got problems of my own."

"Can I come over, at least and talk?"

"Absolutely not!" In a softer voice Munson said, "Listen, Paul, I didn't mean to yell, but something's come up here, something very distressing—"

"You don't need to pretend. You've got Helene with you and you wish I'd leave you alone. Okay."

"No. Honestly," Munson said. "I've got problems, suddenly. I'm in a totally ungood position to give you any help at all. I need help myself."

"What sort? Anything I can do for you?"

"I'm afraid not. And if you'll excuse me, Paul—"

"Just tell me one thing, at least. Where am I likely to find Carole? Do you have any idea?"

"At her husband's place, I'd say."

"*I'm* her husband."

There was a long pause. Munson said finally, "Paul, she divorced you last January and married Pete Castine in April."

"No," Mueller said.

"What, no?"

"No, it isn't possible."

"Have you been popping pills, Paul? Sniffing something? Smoking weed? Look, I'm sorry, but I can't take time now to—"

"At least tell me what day today is."

"Wednesday."

"Which Wednesday?"

"Wednesday the eighth of May. Thursday the ninth, actually, by this time of night."

"And the year?"

"For Christ's sake, Paul—"

"The *year?*"

"2003."

Mueller sagged. "Freddy, I've lost half a year somewhere! For me it's last October. 2002. I've got some weird kind of amnesia. It's the only explanation."

"Amnesia," Munson said. The edge of tension left his voice. "Is that what you've got? Amnesia? Can there be such a thing as an epidemic of amnesia? Is it contagious? Maybe you better come over here after all. Because amnesia's my problem too."

Thursday, May 9, promised to be as beautiful as the previous day had been. The sun once again beamed on San Francisco; the sky was clear, the air warm and tender. Commander Braskett awoke early as always, punched for his usual spartan breakfast, studied the morning xerofax news, spent an hour dictating his memoirs, and, about nine, went out for a walk. The streets were strangely crowded, he found, when he got down to the shopping district along Haight Street. People were wandering aimlessly, dazedly, as though they were sleepwalkers. Were they drunk? Drugged? Three times in five minutes Commander Braskett was stopped by young men who wanted to know the date. Not the time, the *date*. He told them, crisply, disdainfully; he tried to be tolerant, but it was difficult for him not to despise people who were so weak that they were unable to refrain from poisoning their minds with stimulants and narcotics and psychedelics and similar trash. At the corner of Haight and Masonic a forlorn-looking pretty girl of about seventeen, with wide blank blue eyes, halted him and said, "Sir, this city is San Francisco, isn't it? I mean, I was supposed to move here from Pittsburgh in May, and if this is May, this is San Francisco, right?" Commander Braskett nodded brusquely and turned away, pained. He was relieved to see an old friend, Lou Sandler, the manager of the Bank of America office across the way. Sandler was standing outside the bank door. Commander Braskett crossed to him and said, "Isn't it a disgrace, Lou, the way this whole street is filled with addicts this morning? What is it, some historical pageant of the 1960's?" And Sandler gave him an empty smile and said, "Is that my name? Lou? You wouldn't happen to know the last name too, would you? Somehow it's slipped my mind." In that moment Commander Braskett realized that something terrible had happened to his city and perhaps to his country, and that the leftist takeover he had long dreaded must now be at hand, and that it was time for him to don his old uniform again and do what he could to strike back at the enemy.

In joy and confusion, Nate Haldersen awoke that morning realizing that he had been transformed in some strange and wonderful way. His head was throbbing, but not painfully. It seemed to him that a terrible weight had been lifted from his shoulders, that the fierce dead hand about his throat had at last relinquished its grip.

He sprang from bed, full of questions.

Where am I? What kind of place is this? Why am I not at home? Where are my books? Why do I feel so happy?

This seemed to be a hospital room.

There was a veil across his mind. He pierced its filmy folds and realized that he had committed himself to—to Fletcher Memorial—last—August—no, the August before last—suffering with a severe emotional disturbance brought on by—brought on by—

He had never felt happier than at this moment.

He saw a mirror. In it was the reflected upper half of Nathaniel Haldersen, Ph.D. Nate Haldersen smiled at himself. Tall, stringy, long-nosed man, absurdly straw-colored hair, absurd blue eyes, thin lips, smiling. Bony body. He undid his pajama top. Pale, hairless chest; bump of bone like an epaulet on each shoulder. I have been sick a long time,

211

Haldersen thought. Now I must get out of here, back to my classroom. End of leave of absence. Where are my clothes?

"Nurse? Doctor?" He pressed his call button three times. "Hello? Anyone here?"

No one came. Odd; they always came. Shrugging, Haldersen moved out into the hall. He saw three orderlies, heads together, buzzing at the far end. They ignored him. A robot servitor carrying breakfast trays glided past. A moment later one of the younger doctors came running through the hall, and would not stop when Haldersen called to him. Annoyed, he went back into his room and looked about for clothing. He found none, only a little stack of magazines on the closet floor. He thumbed the call button three more times. Finally one of the robots entered the room.

"I am sorry," it said, "but the human hospital personnel is busy at present. May I serve you, Dr. Haldersen?"

"I want a suit of clothing. I'm leaving the hospital."

"I am sorry, but there is no record of your discharge. Without authorization from Dr. Bryce, Dr. Reynolds, or Dr. Kamakura, I am not permitted to allow your departure."

Haldersen sighed. He knew better than to argue with a robot. "Where are those three gentlemen right now?"

"They are occupied, sir. As you may know, there is a medical emergency in the city this morning, and Dr. Bryce and Dr. Kamakura are helping to organize the committee of public safety. Dr. Reynolds did not report for duty today and we are unable to trace him. It is believed that he is a victim of the current difficulty."

"*What* current difficulty?"

"Mass loss of memory on the part of the human population," the robot said.

"An epidemic of amnesia?"

"That is one interpretation of the problem."

"How can such a thing—" Haldersen stopped. He understood now the source of his own joy this morning. Only yesterday afternoon he had discussed with Tim Bryce the application of memory-destroying drugs to his own trauma, and Bryce had said—

Haldersen no longer knew the nature of his own trauma.

"Wait," he said, as the robot began to leave the room. "I need information. Why have I been under treatment here?"

"You have been suffering from social displacements and

212

dysfunctions whose origin, Dr. Bryce feels, lies in a situation of traumatic personal loss."

"Loss of what?"

"Your family, Dr. Haldersen."

"Yes. That's right. I recall, now—I had a wife and two children. Emily. And a little girl—Margaret, Elizabeth, something like that. And a boy named John. What happened to them?"

"They were passengers aboard Intercontinental Airways Flight 103, Copenhagen to San Francisco, September 5, 1991. The plane underwent explosive compression over the Arctic Ocean and there were no survivors."

Haldersen absorbed the information as calmly as though he were hearing of the assassination of Julius Caesar.

"Where was I when the accident occurred?"

"In Copenhagen," the robot replied. "You had intended to return to San Francisco with your family on Flight 103; however, according to your data file here, you became involved in an emotional relationship with a woman named Marie Rasmussen, whom you had met in Copenhagen, and failed to return to your hotel in time to go to the airport. Your wife, evidently aware of the situation, chose not to wait for you. Her subsequent death, and that of your children, produced a traumatic guilt reaction in which you came to regard yourself as responsible for their terminations."

"I *would* take that attitude, wouldn't I?" Haldersen said. "Sin and retribution. Mea culpa, mea maxima culpa. I always had a harsh view of sin, even when I was sinning. I should have been an Old Testament prophet."

"Shall I provide more information, sir?"

"Is there more?"

"We have in the files Dr. Bryce's report headed, *The Job Complex: A Study in the Paralysis of Guilt*."

"Spare me that," Haldersen said. "All right, go."

He was alone. The Job Complex, he thought. Not really appropriate, was it? Job was a man without sin, and yet he was punished grievously to satisfy a whim of the Almighty. A little presumptuous, I'd say, to identify myself with him. Cain would have been a better choice. Cain said unto the Lord, My punishment is greater than I can bear. But Cain was a sinner. I was a sinner. I sinned and Emily died for it. When, eleven, eleven-and-a-half years ago? And now I know

213

nothing at all about it except what the machine just told me. Redemption through oblivion, I'd call it. I have expiated my sin and now I'm free. I have no business staying in this hospital any longer. Strait is the gate, and narrow is the way, which leadeth unto life, and few there be that find it. I've got to get out of here. Maybe I can be of some help to others.

He belted his bathrobe, took a drink of water, and went out of the room. No one stopped him. The elevator did not seem to be running, but he found the stairs, and walked down, a little creakily. He had not been this far from his room in more than a year. The lower floors of the hospital were in chaos—doctors, orderlies, robots, patients, all milling around excitedly. The robots were trying to calm people and get them back to their proper places. "Excuse me," Haldersen said serenely. "Excuse me. Excuse me." He left the hospital, unmolested, by the front door. The air outside was as fresh as young wine; he felt like weeping when it hit his nostrils. He was free. Redemption through oblivion. The disaster high above the Arctic no longer dominated his thoughts. He looked upon it precisely as if it had happened to the family of some other man, long ago. Haldersen began to walk briskly down Van Ness, feeling vigor returning to his legs with every stride. A young woman, sobbing wildly, erupted from a building and collided with him. He caught her, steadied her, was surprised at his own strength as he kept her from toppling. She trembled and pressed her head against his chest. "Can I do anything for you?" he asked. "Can I be of any help?"

Panic had begun to enfold Freddy Munson during dinner at Ondine's Wednesday night. He had begun to be annoyed with Helene in the midst of the truffled chicken breasts, and so he had started to think about the details of business; and to his amazement he did not seem to have the details quite right in his mind; and so he felt the early twinges of terror.

The trouble was that Helene was going on and on about the art of sonic sculpture in general and Paul Mueller in particular. Her interest was enough to arouse faint jealousies in Munson. Was she getting ready to leap from his bed to Paul's? Was she thinking of abandoning the wealthy, glamorous, but essentially prosaic stockbroker for the irresponsible, impecunious, fascinatingly gifted sculptor? Of course, Helene kept company with a number of other men, but Munson knew them and discounted them as rivals; they were nonentities,

214

escorts to fill her idle nights when he was too busy for her. Paul Mueller, however, was another case. Munson could not bear the thought that Helene might leave him for Paul. So he shifted his concentration to the day's maneuvers. He had extracted a thousand shares of the $5.87 convertible preferred of Lunar Transit from the Schaeffer account, pledging it as collateral to cover his shortage in the matter of the Comsat debentures, and then, tapping the Howard account for five thousand Southeast Energy Corporation warrants, he had—or had those warrants come out of the Brewster account? Brewster was big on utilities. So was Howard, but that account was heavy on Mid-Atlantic Power, so would it also be loaded with Southeast Energy? In any case, had he put those warrants up against the Zurich uranium features, or were they riding as his markets in the Antarctic oil-lease thing? He could not remember.

He could not remember.

He could not remember.

Each transaction had been in its own compartment. The partitions were down, suddenly. Numbers were spilling about in his mind as though his brain were in free fall. All of today's deals were tumbling. It frightened him. He began to gobble his food, wanting now to get out of here, to get rid of Helene, to get home and try to reconstruct his activities of the afternoon. Oddly, he could remember quite clearly all that he had done yesterday—the Xerox switch, the straddle on Steel—but today was washing away minute by minute.

"Are you all right?" Helene asked.

"No, I'm not," he said. "I'm coming down with something."

"The Venus Virus. Everybody's getting it."

"Yes, that must be it. The Venus Virus. You'd better keep clear of me tonight."

They skipped dessert and cleared out fast. He dropped Helene off at her flat; she hardly seemed disappointed, which bothered him, but not nearly so much as what was happening to his mind. Alone, finally, he tried to jot down an outline of his day, but even more had left him now. In the restaurant he had known which stocks he had handled, though he wasn't sure what he had done with them. Now, he couldn't even recall the specific securities. He was out on the limb for millions of dollars of other people's money, and every detail was in his mind, and his mind was falling apart. By the time Paul Mueller called, a little after midnight, Munson was growing desperate. He was relieved, but not exactly cheered, to learn that whatever strange thing had affected his mind had hit Mueller a lot harder. Mueller had forgotten everything since last October.

"You went bankrupt," Munson had to explain to him. "You had this wild scheme for setting up a central clearing house for works of art, a kind of stock exchange—the sort of thing only an artist would try to start. You wouldn't let me discourage you. Then you began signing notes, and taking on contingent liabilities, and before the project was six weeks old you were hit with half a dozen lawsuits and it all began to go sour."

"When did this happen, precisely?"

"You conceived the idea at the beginning of November. By Christmas you were in severe trouble. You already had a bunch of personal debts that had gone unpaid from before, and your assets melted away, and you hit a terrible bind in your work and couldn't produce a thing. You really don't remember a thing of this, Paul?"

"Nothing."

"After the first of the year the fastest-moving creditors started getting decrees against you. They impounded everything you owned except the furniture, and then they took the furniture. You borrowed from all of your friends, but they couldn't give you nearly enough, because you were borrowing thousands and you owed hundreds of thousands."

"How much did I hit you for?"

"Eleven bigs," Munson said. "But don't worry about that now."

"I'm not. I'm not worrying about a thing. I was in a bind in my work, you say?" Mueller chuckled. "That's all gone. I'm itching to start making things. All I need are the tools—I mean, money to buy the tools."

"What would they cost?"

"Two-and-a-half bigs," Mueller said.

Munson coughed. "All right. I can't transfer the money to your account, because your creditors would lien it right away. I'll get some cash at the bank. You'll have three bigs tomorrow, and welcome to it."

"Bless you, Freddy." Mueller said, "This kind of amnesia

216

is a good thing, eh? I was so worried about money that I couldn't work. Now I'm not worried at all. I guess I'm still in debt, but I'm not fretting. Tell me what happened to my marriage, now.''

"Carole got fed up and turned off,'' said Munson. "She opposed your business venture from the start. When it began to devour you, she did what she could to untangle you from it, but you insisted on trying to patch things together with more loans, and she filed for a decree. When she was free, Pete Castine moved in and grabbed her.''

"That's the hardest part to believe. That she'd marry an art dealer, a totally noncreative person, a—a parasite, really—''

"They were always good friends,'' Munson said. "I won't say they were lovers, because I don't know, but they were close. And Pete's not that horrible. He's got taste, intelligence, everything an artist needs except the gift. I think Carole may have been weary of gifted men, anyway.''

"How did I take it?'' Meuller asked.

"You hardly seemed to notice, Paul. You were so busy with your financial shenanigans.''

Mueller nodded. He sauntered to one of his own works, a three-meter-high arrangement of oscillating rods that ran the whole sound spectrum into the high kilohertzes, and passed two fingers over the activator eye. The sculpture began to murmur. After a few moments Mueller said, "You sounded awfully upset when I called, Freddy. You say you have some kind of amnesia too?''

Trying to be casual about it, Munson said, "I find I can't remember some important transactions I carried out today. Unfortunately, my only record of them is in my head. But maybe the information will come back to me when I've slept on it.''

"There's no way I can help you with that.''

"No. There isn't.''

"Freddy, where is this amnesia coming from?''

Munson shrugged. "Maybe somebody put a drug in the water supply, or spiked the food, or something. These days, you never can tell. Look, I've got to do some work, Paul. If you'd like to sleep here tonight—''

"I'm wide awake, thanks. I'll drop by again in the morning.''

When the sculptor was gone, Munson struggled for a feverish hour to reconstruct his data, and failed. Shortly before two he took a four-hour-sleep pill. When he awakened, he realized in dismay that he had no memories whatever for the period from April 1 to noon yesterday. During those five weeks he had engaged in countless securities transactions, using other people's property as his collateral, and counting on his ability to get each marker in his game back into its proper place before anyone was likely to go looking for it. He had always been able to remember everything. Now he could remember nothing. He reached his office at seven in the morning, as always, and out of habit plugged himself into the data channels to study the Zurich and London quotes, but the prices on the screen were strange to him, and he knew that he was undone.

At the same moment of Thursday morning Dr. Timothy Bryce's house computer triggered an impulse and the alarm voice in his pillow said quietly but firmly, "It's time to wake up, Dr. Bryce." He stirred but lay still. After the prescribed ten-second interval the voice said, a little more sharply, "It's time to wake up, Dr. Bryce." Bryce sat up, just in time; the lifting of his head from the pillow cut off the third, much sterner, repetition, which would have been followed by the opening chords of the *Jupiter* Symphony. The psychiatrist opened his eyes.

He was surprised to find himself sharing his bed with a strikingly attractive girl.

She was a honey blonde, deeply tanned, with light-brown eyes, full pale lips, and a sleek, elegant body. She looked to be fairly young, a good twenty years younger than he was—perhaps twenty-five, twenty-eight. She wore nothing, and she was in a deep sleep, her lower lip sagging in a sort of involuntary pout. Neither her youth nor her beauty nor her nudity surprised him; he was puzzled simply because he had no notion who she was or how she had come to be in bed with him. He felt as though he had never seen her before. Certainly he didn't know her name. Had he picked her up at some party last night? He couldn't seem to remember where he had been last night. Gently he nudged her elbow.

She woke quickly, fluttering her eyelids, shaking her head.

"Oh," she said, as she saw him, and clutched the sheet up to her throat. Then, smiling, she dropped it again. "That's foolish. No need to be modest *now*, I guess."

"I guess. Hello."

"Hello," she said. She looked as confused as he was.

"This is going to sound stupid," he said, "but someone must have slipped me a weird weed last night, because I'm afraid I'm not sure how I happened to bring you home. Or what your name is."

"Lisa," she said. "Lisa—Falk." She stumbled over the second name. "And you're—"

"Tim Bryce."

"You don't remember where we met?"

"No," he said.

"Neither do I."

He got out of bed, feeling a little hesitant about his own nakedness, and fighting the inhibition off. "They must have given us both the same thing to smoke, then. You know"—he grinned shyly—"I can't even remember if we had a good time together last night. I hope we did."

"I think we did," she said. "I can't remember it either. But I feel good inside—the way I usually do after I've—" She paused. "We couldn't have met only just last night, Tim."

"How can you tell?"

"I've got the feeling that I've known you longer than that."

Bryce shrugged. "I don't see how. I mean, without being too coarse about it, obviously we were both high last night, really floating, and we met and came here and—"

"No. I feel at home here. As if I moved in with you weeks and weeks ago."

"A lovely idea. But I'm sure you didn't."

"Why do I feel so much at home here, then?"

"In what way?"

"In every way." She walked to the bedroom closet and let her hand rest on the touchplate. The door slid open; evidently he had keyed the house computer to her fingerprints. He had done that last night too? She reached in. "My clothing," she said. "Look. All these dresses, coats, shoes. A whole wardrobe. There can't be any doubt. We've been living together and don't remember it!"

A chill swept through him. "What have they done to us? Listen, Lisa, let's get dressed and eat and go down to the hospital together for a checkup. We—"

219

"Hospital?"

"Fletcher Memorial. I'm in the neurological department. Whatever they slipped us last night has hit us both with a lacunary retrograde amnesia—a gap in our memories—and it could be serious. If it's caused brain damage, perhaps it's not irreversible yet, but we can't fool around."

She put her hand to her lips in fear. Bryce felt a sudden warm urge to protect this lovely stranger, to guard and comfort her, and he realized he must be in love with her, even though he couldn't remember who she was. He crossed the room to her and seized her in a brief, tight embrace; she responded eagerly, shivering a little. By a quarter to eight they were out of the house and heading for the hospital through unusually light traffic. Bryce led the girl quickly to the staff lounge. Ted Kamakura was there already, in uniform. The little Japanese psychiatrist nodded curtly and said, "Morning, Tim." Then he blinked. "Good morning, Lisa. How come *you're* here?"

"You know her?" Bryce asked.

"What kind of question is that?"

"A deadly serious one."

"Of course I know her," Kamakura said, and his smile of greeting abruptly faded. "Why? Is something wrong about that?"

"You may know her, but I don't," said Bryce.

"Oh, God. Not you too!"

"Tell me who she is, Ted."

"She's your wife, Tim. You married her five years ago."

By half past eleven Thursday morning the Gerards had everything set up and going smoothly for the lunch rush at the Petit Pois. The soup caldron was bubbling, the escargot trays were ready to be popped in the oven, the sauces were taking form. Pierre Gerard was a bit surprised when most of the lunchtime regulars failed to show up. Even Mr. Munson, always punctual at half past eleven, did not arrive. Some of these men had not missed weekday lunch at the Petit Pois in fifteen years. Something terrible must have happened on the stock market, Pierre thought, to have kept all these financial men at their desks, and they were too busy to call him and cancel their usual tables. That must be the answer. It was impossible that any of the regulars would forget to call him.

The stock market must be exploding. Pierre made a mental note to call his broker after lunch and find out what was going on.

About two Thursday afternoon, Paul Mueller stopped into Metchknikoff's Art Supplies in North Beach to try to get a welding pen, some raw metal, loudspeaker paint, and the rest of the things he needed for the rebirth of his sculpting career. Metchnikoff greeted him sourly with, "No credit at all, Mr. Mueller, not even a nickel!"

"It's all right. I'm a cash customer this time."

The dealer brightened. "In that case it's all right, maybe. You finished with your troubles?"

"I hope so," Mueller said.

He gave the order. It came to about $2,300; when the time came to pay, he explained that he simply had to run down to Montgomery Street to pick up the cash from his friend Freddy Munson, who was holding three bigs for him. Metchnikoff began to glower again. "Five minutes!" Mueller called. "I'll be back in five minutes!" But when he got to Munson's office, he found the place in confusion, and Munson wasn't there. "Did he leave an envelope for a Mr. Mueller?" he asked a distraught secretary. "I was supposed to pick something important up here this afternoon. Would you please check?" The girl simply ran away from him. So did the next girl. A burly broker told him to get out of the office. "We're closed, fellow," he shouted. Baffled, Mueller left.

Not daring to return to Metchnikoff's with the news that he hadn't been able to raise the cash after all, Mueller simply went home. Three dunning robots were camped outside his door, and each one began to croak its cry of doom as he approached. "Sorry," Mueller said, "I can't remember a thing about any of this stuff," and he went inside and sat down on the bare floor, angry, thinking of the brilliant pieces he could be turning out if he could only get his hands on the tools of his trade. He made sketches instead. At least the ghouls had left him with pencil and paper. Not as efficient as a computer screen and a light-pen maybe, but Michelangelo and Benvenuto Cellini had managed to make out all right without computer screens and light-pens.

At four o'clock the doorbell rang.

"Go *away*," Mueller said through the speaker. "See my

accountant! I don't want to hear any more dunnings, and the next time I catch one of you idiot robots by my door I'm going to—"

"It's me Paul," a nonmechanical voice said.

Carole.

He rushed to the door. There were seven robots out there, surrounding her, and they tried to get in; but he pushed them back so she could enter. A robot didn't dare lay a paw on a human being. He slammed the door in their metal faces and locked it.

Carole looked fine. Her hair was longer than he remembered it, and she had gained about eight pounds in all the right places, and she wore an iridescent peekaboo wrap that he had never seen before, and which was really inappropriate for afternoon wear, but which looked splendid on her. She seemed at least five years younger than she really was; evidently a month and a half of marriage to Pete Castine had done more for her than nine years of marriage to Paul Mueller. She glowed. She also looked strained and tense, but that seemed superficial, the product of some distress of the last few hours.

"I seem to have lost my key," she said.

"What are you doing here?"

"I don't understand you, Paul."

"I mean, why'd you come here?"

"I *live* here."

"Do you?" He laughed harshly. "Very funny."

"You always did have a weird sense of humor, Paul." She stepped past him. "Only this isn't any joke. Where *is* everything? The furniture, Paul. My things." Suddenly she was crying. "I must be breaking up. I wake up this morning in a completely strange apartment, all alone, and I spend the whole day wandering in a sort of daze that I don't understand at all, and now I finally come home and I find that you've pawned every damn thing we own, or something, and—" She bit her knuckles. "Paul?"

She's got it, he thought. The amnesia epidemic.

He said quietly, "This is a funny thing to ask, Carole, but will you tell me what today's date is?"

"Why—the fourteenth of September—or is it the fifteenth—"

"2002?"

"What do you think? 1776?"

She's got it worse than I have, Mueller told himself. She's

222

lost a whole extra month. She doesn't remember my business venture. She doesn't remember my losing all the money. *She doesn't remember divorcing me.* She thinks she's still my wife.

"Come in here," he said, and led her to the bedroom. He pointed to the cot that stood where their bed had been. "Sit down, Carole. I'll try to explain. It won't make much sense, but I'll try to explain."

Under the circumstances, the concert by the visiting New York Philharmonic for Thursday evening was cancelled. Nevertheless the orchestra assembled for its rehearsal at half past two in the afternoon. The union required so many rehearsals— with pay—a week; therefore the orchestra rehearsed, regardless of external cataclysms. But there were problems. Maestro Alvarez, who used an electronic baton and proudly conducted without a score, thumbed the button for a downbeat and realized abruptly, with a sensation as of dropping through a trapdoor, that the Brahms Fourth was wholly gone from his mind. The orchestra responded raggedly to his faltering leadership; some of the musicians had no difficulties, but the concertmaster stared in horror at his left hand, wondering how to finger the strings for the notes his violin was supposed to be yielding, and the second oboe could not find the proper keys, and the first bassoon had not yet even managed to remember how to put his instrument together.

By nightfall, Tim Bryce had managed to assemble enough of the story so that he understood what had happened, not only to himself and to Lisa, but to the entire city. A drug, or drugs, almost certainly distributed through the municipal water supply, had leached away nearly everyone's memory. The trouble with modern life, Bryce thought, is that technology gives us the potential for newer and more intricate disasters every year, but doesn't seem to give us the ability to ward them off. Memory drugs were old stuff, going back thirty, forty years. He had studied several types of them himself. Memory is partly a chemical and partly an electrical process; some drugs went after the electrical end, jamming the synapses over which brain transmissions travel, and some went after the molecular substrata in which long-term memories are locked up. Bryce knew ways of destroying short-term memories by inhibiting synapse transmission, and he knew ways of destroying the deep long-term memories by washing out the complex chains of ribonucleic acid, brain-RNA, by which they are inscribed in the brain. But such drugs were experimental, tricky, unpredictable; he had hesitated to use them on human subjects; he certainly had never imagined that anyone would simply dump them into an aqueduct and give an entire city a simultaneous lobotomy.

His office at Fletcher Memorial had become an improvised center of operations for San Francisco. The mayor was there, pale and shrunken; the chief of police, exhausted and confused, periodically turned his back and popped a pill; a dazed-looking representative of the communications net hovered in a corner, nervously monitoring the hastily rigged system through which the committee of public safety that Bryce had summoned could make its orders known throughout the city.

The mayor was no use at all. He couldn't even remember having run for office. The chief of police was in even worse shape; he had been up all night because he had forgotten, among other things, his home address, and he had been afraid to query a computer about it for fear he'd lose his job for drunkenness. By now the chief of police was aware that he wasn't the only one in the city having memory problems today, and he had looked up his address in the files and even telephoned his wife, but he was close to collapse. Bryce had insisted that both men stay here as symbols of order; he wanted only their faces and their voices, not their fumble-headed official services.

A dozen or so miscellaneous citizens had accumulated in Bryce's office too. At five in the afternoon he had broadcast an all-media appeal, asking anyone whose memory of recent events was unimpaired to come to Fletcher Memorial. "If you haven't had any city water in the past twenty-four hours, you're probably all right. Come down here. We need you." He had drawn a curious assortment. There was a ramrod-straight old space hero, Taylor Braskett, a pure-foods nut who drank only mountain water. There was a family of French restaurateurs, mother, father, three grown children, who preferred mineral water flown in from their native land. There was a computer salesman named McBurney who had been in Los Angeles on business and hadn't had any of the drugged water. There was a retired cop named Adler who lived in

Oakland, where there were no memory problems; he had hurried across the bay as soon as he heard that San Francisco was in trouble. That was before all access to the city had been shut off at Bryce's orders. And there were some others, of doubtful value but of definitely intact memory.

The three screens that the communications man had mounted provided a relay of key points in the city. Right now one was monitoring the Fisherman's Wharf district from a camera atop Ghirardelli Square, one was viewing the financial district from a helicopter over the old Ferry Building Museum, and one was relaying a pickup from a mobile truck in Golden Gate Park. The scenes were similar everywhere: people milling about, asking questions, getting no answers. There wasn't any overt sign of looting yet. There were no fires. The police, those of them able to function, were out in force, and antiriot robots were cruising the bigger streets, just in case they might be needed to squirt their stifling blankets of foam at suddenly panicked mobs.

Bryce said to the mayor, "At half past six I want you to go on all media with an appeal for calm. We'll supply you with everything you have to say."

The mayor moaned.

Bryce said, "Don't worry. I'll feed you the whole speech by bone relay. Just concentrate on speaking clearly and looking straight into the camera. If you come across a terrified man, it can be the end for all of us. If you look cool, we may be able to pull through."

The mayor put his face in his hands.

Ted Kamakura whispered, "You can't put him on the channels, Tim! He's a wreck, and everyone will see it!"

"The city's mayor has to show himself," Bryce insisted. "Give him a double jolt of bracers. Let him make this one speech and then we can put him to pasture."

"Who'll be the spokesman, then?" Kamakura asked. "You? Me? Police Chief Dennison?"

"I don't know," Bryce muttered. "We need an authority-image to make announcements every half hour or so, and I'm damned if I'll have time. Or you. And Dennison—"

"Gentlemen, may I make a suggestion?" It was the old spaceman, Braskett. "I wish to volunteer as spokesman. You must admit I have a certain look of authority. And I'm accustomed to speaking to the public."

Bryce rejected the idea instantly. That right-wing crackpot, that author of passionate nut letters to every news medium in the state, that latter-day Paul Revere? Him, spokesman for the committee? But in the moment of rejection came acceptance. Nobody really paid attention to far-out political activities like that; probably nine people out of ten in San Francisco thought of Braskett, if at all, simply as the hero of the First Mars Expedition. He was a handsome old horse, too, elegantly upright and lean. Deep voice; unwavering eyes. A man of strength and presence.

Bryce said, "Commander Braskett, if we were to make you chairman of the committee of public safety—"

Ted Kamakura gasped.

"—would I have your assurance that such public announcements as you would make would be confined entirely to statements of the policies arrived at by the entire committee?"

Commander Braskett smiled glacially. "You want me to be a figurehead, is that it?"

"To be our spokesman, with the official title of chairman."

"As I said: to be a figurehead. Very well, I accept. I'll mouth my lines like an obedient puppet, and I won't attempt to inject any of my radical, extremist ideas into my statements. Is that what you wish?"

"I think we understand each other perfectly," Bryce said, and smiled, and got a surprisingly warm smile in return.

He jabbed now at his data board. Someone in the path lab eight stories below his office answered, and Bryce said, "Is there an up-to-date analysis yet?"

"I'll switch you to Dr. Madison."

Madison appeared on the screen. He ran the hospital's radioisotope department, normally: a beefy, red-faced man who looked as though he ought to be a beer salesman. He knew his subject. "It's definitely the water supply, Tim," he said at once. "We tentatively established that an hour and a half ago, of course, but now there's no doubt. I've isolated traces of two different memory-suppressant drugs, and there's the possibility of a third. Whoever it was was taking no chances."

"What are they?" Bryce asked.

"Well, we've got a good jolt of acetylcholine terminase," Madison said, "which will louse up the synapses and interfere with short-term memory fixation. Then there's something else, perhaps a puromycin-derivative protein dissolver, which is going to work on the brain-RNA and smashing up older memories. I suspect also that we've been getting one of the newer experimental amnesifacients, something that I haven't isolated yet, capable of working its way deep and cutting out really basic motor patterns. So they've hit us high, low, and middle."

"That explains a lot. The guys who can't remember what they did yesterday, the guys who've lost a chunk out of their adult memories, and the ones who don't even remember their names—this thing is working on people at all different levels."

"Depending on individual metabolism, age, brain structure, and how much water they had to drink yesterday, yes."

"Is the water supply still tainted?" Bryce asked.

"Tentatively, I'd say no. I've had water samples brought me from the upflow districts, and everything's okay there. The water department has been running its own check; they say the same. Evidently the stuff got into the system early yesterday, came down into the city, and is generally gone by now. Might be some residuals in the pipes; I'd be careful about drinking water even today."

"And what does the pharmacopoeia say about the effectiveness of these drugs?"

Madison shrugged. "Anybody's guess. You'd know that better than I. Do they wear off?"

"Not in the normal sense," said Bryce. "What happens is the brain cuts in a redundancy circuit and gets access to a duplicate set of the affected memories, eventually—shifts to another track, so to speak—provided a duplicate of the sector in question was there in the first place, and provided that the duplicate wasn't blotted out also. Some people are going to get chunks of their memories back, in a few days or a few weeks. Others won't."

"Wonderful," Madison said. "I'll keep you posted, Tim."

Bryce cut off the call and said to the communications man, "You have that bone relay? Get it behind His Honor's ear."

The mayor quivered. The little instrument was fastened in place.

Bryce said, "Mr. Mayor, I'm going to dictate a speech, and you're going to broadcast it on all media, and it's the last thing I'm going to ask of you until you've had a chance to pull yourself together. Okay? Listen carefully to what I'm saying, speak slowly, and pretend that tomorrow is election

227

day and your job depends on how well you come across now. You won't be going on live. There'll be a fifteen-second delay, and we have a wipe circuit so we can correct any stumbles, and there's absolutely no reason to be tense. Are you with me? Will you give it all you've got?''

"My mind is all foggy."

"Simply listen to me and repeat what I say into the camera's eye. Let your political reflexes take over. Here's your chance to make a hero of yourself. We're living history right now, Mr. Mayor. What we do here today will be studied the way the events of the 1906 fire were studied. Let's go, now. Follow me. *People of the wonderful city of San Francisco*—''

The words rolled easily from Bryce's lips, and, wonder of wonders, the mayor caught them and spoke them in a clear, beautifully resonant voice. As he spun out his speech, Bryce felt a surging flow of power going through himself, and he imagined for the moment that he were the elected leader of the city, not merely a self-appointed emergency dictator. It was an interesting, almost ecstatic feeling. Lisa, watching him in action, gave him a loving smile.

He smiled at her. In this moment of glory he was almost able to ignore the ache of knowing that he had lost his entire memory archive of his life with her. Nothing else gone, apparently. But, neatly, with idiot selectivity, the drug in the water supply had sliced away everything pertaining to his five years of marriage. Kamakura had told him, a few hours ago, that it was the happiest marriage of any he knew. Gone. At least Lisa had suffered an identical loss, against all probabilities. Somehow that made it easier to bear; it would have been awful to have one of them remember the good times and the other know nothing. He was almost able to ignore the torment of loss, while he kept busy. Almost.

"The mayor's going to be on in a minute," Nadia said. "Will you listen to him? He'll explain what's been going on."

"I don't care," said The Amazing Montini dully.

"It's some kind of epidemic of amnesia. When I was out before, I heard all about it. *Everyone's* got it. It isn't just you! And you thought it was a stroke, but it wasn't. You're all right."

"My mind is a ruin."

228

"It's only temporary." Her voice was shrill and unconvincing. "It's something in the air, maybe. Some drug they were testing that drifted in. We're all in this together. I can't remember last week at all."

"What do I care," Montini said. "Most of these people, they have no memories even when they are healthy. But me? Me? I am destroyed. Nadia, I should lie down in my grave now. There is no sense in continuing to walk around."

The voice from the loudspeaker said, "Ladies and gentlemen, His Honor Elliot Chase, the Mayor of San Francisco."

"Let's listen," Nadia said.

The mayor appeared on the wallscreen, wearing his solemn face, his we-face-a-grave-challenge-citizens face. Montini glanced at him, shrugged, looked away.

The mayor said, "People of the wonderful city of San Francisco, we have just come through the most difficult day in nearly a century, since the terrible catastrophe of April, 1906. The earth has not quaked today, nor have we been smitten by fire, yet we have been severely tested by sudden calamity.

"As all of you surely know, the people of San Francisco have been afflicted since last night by what can best be termed an epidemic of amnesia. There has been mass loss of memory, ranging from mild cases of forgetfulness to near-total obliteration of identity. Scientists working at Fletcher Memorial Hospital have succeeded in determining the cause of this unique and sudden disaster.

"It appears that criminal saboteurs contaminated the municipal water supply with certain restricted drugs that have the ability to dissolve memory structures. *The effect of these drugs is temporary*. There should be no cause for alarm. Even those who are most severely affected will find their memories gradually beginning to return, and there is every reason to expect full recovery in a matter of hours or days."

"He's lying," said Montini.

"The criminals responsible have not yet been apprehended, but we expect arrests momentarily. The San Francisco area is the only affected region, which means the drugs were introduced into the water system just beyond city limits. Everything is normal in Berkeley, in Oakland, in Marin County, and other outlying areas.

"In the name of public safety I have ordered the bridges to

San Francisco closed, as well as the Bay Area Rapid Transit and other means of access to the city. We expect to maintain these restrictions at least until tomorrow morning. The purpose of this is to prevent disorder and to avoid a possible influx of undesirable elements into the city while the trouble persists. We San Franciscans are self-sufficient and can look after our own needs without outside interference. However, I have been in contact with the President and with the Governor, and they both have assured me of all possible assistance.

"The water supply is at present free of the drug, and every precaution is being taken to prevent a recurrence of this crime against one million innocent people. However, I am told that some lingering contamination may remain in the pipes for a few hours. I recommend that you keep your consumption of water low until further notice, and that you boil any water you wish to use.

"Lastly. Police Chief Dennison, myself, and your other city officials will be devoting full time to the needs of the city so long as the crisis lasts. Probably we will not have the opportunity to go before the media for further reports. Therefore, I have taken the step of appointing a committee of public safety, consisting of distinguished laymen and scientists of San Francisco, as a coordinating body that will aid in governing the city and reporting to its citizens. The chairman of this committee is the well-known veteran of so many exploits in space, Commander Taylor Braskett. Announcements concerning the developments in the crisis will come from Commander Braskett for the remainder of the evening, and you may consider his words to be those of your city officials. Thank you."

Braskett came on the screen. Montini grunted. "Look at the man they find! A maniac patriot!"

"But the drug will wear off," Nadia said. "Your mind will be all right again."

"I know these drugs. There is no hope. I am destroyed." The Amazing Montini moved toward the door. "I need fresh air. I will go out. Good-bye, Nadia."

She tried to stop him. He pushed her aside. Entering Marina Park, he made his way to the yacht club; the doorman admitted him, and took no further notice. Montini walked out on the pier. The drug, they say, is temporary. It will wear off. My mind will clear. I doubt this very much. Montini peered at the dark, oily water, glistening with light reflected from the bridge. He explored his damaged mind, scanning for gaps. Whole sections of memory were gone. The walls had crumbled, slabs of plaster falling away to expose bare lath. He could not live this way. Carefully, grunting from the exertion, he lowered himself via a metal ladder into the water, and kicked himself away from the pier. The water was terribly cold. His shoes seemed immensely heavy. He floated toward the island of the old prison, but he doubted that he would remain afloat much longer. As he drifted, he ran through an inventory of his memory, seeing what remained to him and finding less than enough. To test whether even his gift had survived, he attempted to play back a recall of the mayor's speech, and found the words shifting and melting. It is just as well, then, he told himself, and drifted on, and went under.

Carole insisted on spending Thursday night with him.

"We aren't man and wife any more," he had to tell her. "You divorced me."

"Since when are you so conventional? We lived together before we were married, and now we can live together after we were married. Maybe we're inventing a new sin, Paul. Post-marital sex."

"That isn't the point. The point is that you came to hate me because of my financial mess, and you left me. If you try to come back to me now, you'll be going against your own rational and deliberate decision of last January."

"For me last January is still four months away," she said. "I don't hate you. I love you. I always have and always will. I can't imagine how I would ever have come to divorce you, but in any case I don't remember divorcing you, and you don't remember being divorced by me, and so why can't we just keep going from the point where our memories leave off?"

"Among other things, because you happen to be Pete Castine's wife now."

"That sounds completely unreal to me. Something you dreamed."

"Freddy Munson told me, though. It's true."

"If I went back to Pete now," Carole said, "I'd feel sinful. Simply because I supposedly married him, you want

231

me to jump into bed with him? I don't want him. I want you. Can't I stay here?''

"If Pete—''

"If Pete, if Pete, if Pete! In my mind I'm Mrs. Paul Mueller, and in your mind I am too, and to hell with Pete, and with whatever Freddy Munson told you, and everything else. This is a silly argument, Paul. Let's quit it. If you want me to get out, tell me so right now in that many words. Otherwise let me stay.''

He couldn't tell her to get out.

He had only the one small cot, but they managed to share it. It was uncomfortable, but in an amusing way. He felt twenty years old again for a while. In the morning they took a long shower together, and then Carole went out to buy some things for breakfast, since his service had been cut off and he couldn't punch for food. A dunning robot outside the door told him, as Carole was leaving, "The decree of personal service due has been requested, Mr. Mueller, and is now pending a court hearing.''

"I know you not,'' Mueller said. "Be gone!''

Today, he told himself, he would hunt up Freddy Munson somehow and get that cash from him, and buy the tools he needed, and start working again. Let the world outside go crazy; so long as he was working, all was well. If he couldn't find Freddy, maybe he could swing the purchase on Carole's credit. She was legally divorced from him and none of his credit taint would stain her; as Mrs. Peter Castine she should surely be able to get hold of a couple of bigs to pay Metchnikoff. Possibly the banks were closed on account of the memory crisis today, Mueller considered; but Metchnikoff surely wouldn't demand cash from Carole. He closed his eyes and imagined how good it would feel to be making things once more.

Carole was gone an hour. When she came back, carrying groceries, Pete Castine was with her.

"He followed me,'' Carole explained. "He wouldn't let me alone.''

He was a slim, poised, controlled man, quite athletic, several years older than Mueller—perhaps into his fifties already—but seemingly very young. Calmly he said, "I was sure that Carole had come here. It's perfectly understandable, Paul. She was here all night, I hope?''

232

"Does it matter?" Mueller asked.

"To some extent. I'd rather have had her spending the night with her former husband than with some third party entirely."

"She was here all night, yes," Mueller said wearily.

"I'd like her to come home with me now. She *is* my wife, after all."

"She had no recollection of that. Neither do I."

"I'm aware of that." Castine nodded amiably. "In my own case, I've forgotten everything that happened to me before the age of twenty-two. I couldn't tell you my father's first name. However, as a matter of objective reality, Carole's my wife, and her parting from you was rather bitter, and I feel she shouldn't stay here any longer."

"Why are you telling all this to me?" Mueller asked. "If you want your wife to go home with you, ask her to go home with you."

"So I did. She says she won't leave unless you direct her to go."

"That's right," Carole said. "I know whose wife I *think* I am. If Paul throws me out, I'll go with you. Not otherwise."

Mueller shrugged. "I'd be a fool to throw her out, Pete. I need her and I want her, and whatever breakup she and I had isn't real to us. I know it's tough on you, but I can't help that. I imagine you'll have no trouble getting an annulment once the courts work out some law to cover cases like this."

Castine was silent for a long moment.

At length he said, "How has your work been going, Paul?"

"I gather that I haven't turned out a thing all year."

"That's correct."

"I'm planning to start again. You might say that Carole has inspired me."

"Splendid," said Castine without intonation of any kind. "I trust that this little mixup over our—ah—shared wife won't interfere with the harmonious artist-dealer relationship we used to enjoy?"

"Not at all," Mueller said. "You'll still get my whole output. Why the hell should I resent anything you did? Carole was a free agent when you married her. There's only one little trouble."

"Yes?"

"I'm broke. I have no tools, and I can't work without tools, and I have no way of buying tools."

"How much do you need?"

"Two and a half bigs."

Castine said, "Where's your data pickup? I'll make a credit transfer."

"The phone company disconnected it a long time ago."

"Let me give you a check, then. Say, three thousand even? An advance against future sales." Castine fumbled for a while before locating a blank check. "First one of these I've written in five years, maybe. Odd how you get accustomed to spending by telephone. Here you are, and good luck. To both of you." He made a courtly, bitter bow. "I hope you'll be happy together. And call me up when you've finished a few pieces, Paul. I'll send the van. I suppose you'll have a phone again by then." He went out.

"There's a blessing in being able to forget," Nate Haldersen said. "The redemption of oblivion, I call it. What's happened to San Francisco this week isn't necessarily a disaster. For some of us, it's the finest thing in the world."

They were listening to him—at least fifty people, clustering near his feet. He stood on the stage of the bandstand in the park, just across from the De Young Museum. Shadows were gathering. Friday, the second full day of the memory crisis, was ending. Haldersen had slept in the park last night, and he planned to sleep there again tonight; he had realized after his escape from the hospital that his apartment had been shut down long ago and his possessions were in storage. It did not matter. He would live off the land and forage for food. The flame of prophecy was aglow in him.

"Let me tell you how it was with me," he cried. "Three days ago I was in a hospital for mental illness. Some of you are smiling, perhaps, telling me I ought to be back there now, but no! You don't understand. I was incapable of facing the world. Wherever I went, I saw happy families, parents and children, and it made me sick with envy and hatred, so that I couldn't function in society. Why? Why? Because my own wife and children were killed in an air disaster in 1991, that's why, and I missed the plane because I was committing sin that day, and for my sin they died, and I lived thereafter in unending torment! But now all that is flushed from my mind.

I have sinned, and I have suffered, and now I am redeemed through merciful oblivion!''

A voice in the crowd called, "If you've forgotten all about it, how come you're telling the story to us?"

"A good question! An excellent question!" Haldersen felt sweat bursting from his pores, adrenaline pumping in his veins. "I know the story only because a machine in the hospital told it to me, yesterday morning. But it came to me from the outside, a secondhand tale. The experience of it within me, the scars, all that has been washed away. The pain of it is gone. Oh, yes, I'm sad that my innocent family perished, but a healthy man learns to control his grief after eleven years, he accepts his loss and goes on. I was sick, sick right *here*, and I couldn't live with my grief, but now I can, I look on it objectively, do you see? And that's why I say there's a blessing in being able to forget. What about you, out there? There must be some of you who suffered painful losses too, and now can no longer remember them, now have been redeemed and released from anguish. Are there any? Are there? Raise your hands. Who's been bathed in holy oblivion? Who out there knows that he's been cleansed, even if he can't remember what it is he's been cleansed from?''

Hands were starting to go up.

They were weeping, now, they were cheering, they were waving at him. Haldersen felt a little like a charlatan. But only a little. He had always had the stuff of a prophet in him, even while he was posing as a harmless academic, a stuffy professor of philosophy. He had had what every prophet needs, a sharp sense of contrast between guilt and purity, an awareness of the existence of sin. It was that awareness that had crushed him for eleven years. It was that awareness that now drove him to celebrate his joy in public, to seek for companions in liberation—no, for disciples—to found the Church of Oblivion here in Golden Gate Park. The hospital could have given him these drugs years ago and spared him from agony. Bryce had refused, Kamakura, Reynolds, all the smooth-talking doctors; they were waiting for more tests, experiments on chimpanzees, God knows what. And God had said, Nathaniel Haldersen has suffered long enough for his sin, and so He had thrust a drug into the water supply of San Francisco, the same drug that the doctors had denied him, and

235

down the pipes from the mountains had come the sweet draught of oblivion.

"Drink with me!" Haldersen shouted. "All you who are in pain, you who live with sorrow! We'll get this drug ourselves! We'll purify our suffering souls! Drink the blessed water, and sing to the glory of God who gives us oblivion!"

Freddy Munson had spent Thursday afternoon, Thursday night, and all of Friday holed up in his apartment with every communications link to the outside turned off. He neither took nor made calls, ignored the telescreens, and had switched on the xerofax only three times in thirty-six hours.

He knew that he was finished, and he was trying to decide how to react to it.

His memory situation seemed to have stabilized. He was still missing only five weeks of market maneuvers. There wasn't any further decay—not that that mattered; he was in trouble enough—and, despite an optimistic statement last night by Mayor Chase, Munson hadn't seen any evidence that the memory loss was reversing itself. He was unable to reconstruct any of the vanished details.

There was no immediate peril, he knew. Most of the clients whose accounts he'd been juggling were wealthy old bats who wouldn't worry about their stocks until they got next month's account statements. They had given him discretionary powers, which was how he had been able to tap their resources for his own benefit in the first place. Up to now, Munson had always been able to complete each transaction within a single month, so the account balanced for every statement. He had dealt with the problem of the securities withdrawals that the statements ought to show by gimmicking the house computer to delete all such withdrawals provided there was no net effect from month to month; that way he could borrow 10,000 shares of United Spaceways or Comsat or IBM for two weeks, use the stock as collateral for a deal of his own, and get it back into the proper account in time with no one the wiser. Three weeks from now, though, the end-of-the-month statements were going to go out showing all of his accounts peppered by inexplicable withdrawals, and he was going to catch hell.

The trouble might even start earlier, and come from a different direction. Since the San Francisco trouble had begun, the market had gone down sharply, and he would probably be getting margin calls on Monday. The San Francisco exchange was closed, of course; it hadn't been able to open Thursday morning because so many of the brokers had been hit hard by amnesia. But New York's exchanges were open, and they had reacted badly to the news from San Francisco, probably out of fear that a conspiracy was afoot and the whole country might soon be pushed into chaos. When the local exchange opened again on Monday, if it opened, it would most likely open at the last New York prices, or near them, and keep on going down. Munson would be asked to put up cash or additional securities to cover his loans. He certainly didn't have the cash, and the only way he could get additional securities would be to dip into still more of his accounts, compounding his offense; on the other hand, if he didn't meet the margin calls they'd sell him out and he'd never be able to restore the stock to the proper accounts, even if he succeeded in remembering which shares went where.

He was trapped. He could stick around for a few weeks, waiting for the ax to fall, or he could get out right now. He preferred to get out right now.

And go where?

Caracas? Reno? São Paulo? No, debtor sanctuaries wouldn't do him any good, because he wasn't an ordinary debtor. He was a thief, and the sanctuaries didn't protect criminals, only bankrupts. He had to go farther, all the way to Luna Dome. There wasn't any extradition from the Moon. There'd be no hope of coming back, either.

Munson got on the phone, hoping to reach his travel agent. Two tickets to Luna, please. One for him, one for Helene; if she didn't feel like coming, he'd go alone. No, not round trip. But the agent didn't answer. Munson tried the number several times. Shrugging, he decided to order direct, and called United Spaceways next. He got a busy signal. "Shall we wait-list your call?" the data net asked. "It will be three days, at the present state of the backlog of calls, before we can put it through."

"Forget it," Munson said.

He had just realized that San Francisco was closed off, anyway. Unless he tried to swim for it, he couldn't get out of the city to go to the spaceport, even if he did manage to buy tickets to Luna. He was caught here until they opened the transit routes again. How long would that be? Monday, Tuesday, next Friday? They couldn't keep the city shut forever—could they?

What it came down to, Munson saw, was a contest of probabilities. Would someone discover the discrepancies in his accounts before he found a way of escaping to Luna, or would his escape access become available too late? Put on those terms, it became an interesting gamble instead of a panic situation. He would spend the weekend trying to find a way out of San Francisco, and if he failed, he would try to be a stoic about facing what was to come.

Calm, now, he remembered that he had promised to lend Paul Mueller a few thousand dollars, to help him equip his studio again. Munson was unhappy over having let that slip his mind. He liked to be helpful. And, even now, what were two or three bigs to him? He had plenty of recoverable assets. Might as well let Paul have a little of the money before the lawyers start grabbing it.

One problem. He had less than a hundred in cash on him—who bothered carrying cash?—and he couldn't telephone a transfer to funds to Mueller's account, because Paul didn't have an account with the data net any more, or even a phone. There wasn't any place to get that much cash, either, at this hour of evening, especially with the city paralyzed. And the weekend was coming. Munson had an idea, though. What if he went shopping with Mueller tomorrow, and simply charged whatever the sculptor needed to his own account? Fine. He reached for the phone to arrange the date, remembered that Mueller could not be called, and decided to tell Paul about it in person. Now. He could use some fresh air, anyway.

He half expected to find robot bailiffs outside, waiting to arrest him. But of course no one was after him yet. He walked to the garage. It was a fine night, cool, starry, with perhaps just a hint of fog in the east. Berkeley's lights glittered through the haze, though. The streets were quiet. In time of crisis people stay home, apparently. He drove quickly to Mueller's place. Four robots were in front of it. Munson eyed them edgily, with the wary look of the man who knows that the sheriff will be after him too, in a little while. But Mueller, when he came to the door, took no notice of the dunners.

Munson said, "I'm sorry I missed connections with you. The money I promised to lend you—"

"It's all right, Freddy. Pete Castine was here this morning and I borrowed the three bigs from him. I've already got my studio set up again. Come in and look?"

Munson entered. "Pete Castine?"

"A good investment for him. He makes money if he has work of mine to sell, right? It's in his best interest to help me get started again. Carole and I have been hooking things up all day."

"Carole?" Munson said. Mueller showed him into the studio. The paraphernalia of a sonic sculptor sat on the floor—a welding pen, a vacuum bell, a big texturing vat, some ingots and strands of wire, and such things. Carole was feeding discarded packing cases into the wall disposal unit. Looking up, she smiled uncertainly and ran her hand through her long dark hair.

"Hello, Freddy."

"Everybody good friends again?" he asked, baffled.

"Nobody remembers being enemies," she said. She laughed. "Isn't it wonderful to have your memory blotted out like this?"

"Wonderful," Munson said bleakly.

Commander Braskett said, "Can I offer you people any water?"

Tim Bryce smiled. Lisa Bryce smiled. Ted Kamakura smiled. Even Mayor Chase, that poor empty husk, smiled. Commander Braskett understood those smiles. Even now, after three days of close contact under pressure, they thought he was nuts.

He had a week's supply of bottled water brought from his home to the command post here at the hospital. Everybody kept telling him that the municipal water was safe to drink now, that the memory drugs were gone from it; but why couldn't they comprehend that his aversion to public water dated back to an era when memory drugs were unknown? There were plenty of other chemicals in the reservoir, after all.

He hoisted his glass in a jaunty toast and winked at them.

Tim Bryce said, "Commander, we'd like you to address the city again at half past ten this morning. Here's your text."

Braskett scanned the sheet. It dealt mostly with the relaxation of the order to boil water before drinking it. "You want me to go on all media," he said, "and tell the people of San Francisco that it's now safe for them to drink from the taps, eh? That's a bit awkward for me. Even a figurehead spokesman is entitled to some degree of personal integrity."

Bryce looked briefly puzzled. Then he laughed and took the text back. "You're absolutely right, Commander. I can't ask you to make this announcement, in view of—ah—your particular beliefs. Let's change the plan. You open the spot by introducing me, and *I'll* discuss the no-boiling thing. Will that be all right?"

Commander Braskett appreciated the tactful way they deferred to his special obsession. "I'm at your service, Doctor," he said gravely.

Bryce finished speaking and the camera lights left him. He said to Lisa, "What about lunch? Or breakfast, or whatever meal it is we're up to now."

"Everything's ready, Tim. Whenever you are."

They ate together in the holograph room, which had become the kitchen of the command post. Massive cameras and tanks of etching fluid surrounded them. The others thoughtfully left them alone. These brief shared meals were the only fragments of privacy he and Lisa had had, in the fifty-two hours since he had awakened to find her sleeping beside him.

He stared across the table in wonder at this delectable blond girl who they said was his wife. How beautiful her soft brown eyes were against that backdrop of golden hair! How perfect the line of her lips, the curve of her earlobes! Bryce knew that no one would object if he and Lisa went off and locked themselves into one of the private rooms for a few hours. He wasn't that indispensable; and there was so much he had to begin relearning about his wife. But he was unable to leave his post. He hadn't been out of the hospital or even off this floor for the duration of the crisis; he kept himself going by grabbing the sleep wire for half an hour every six hours. Perhaps it was an illusion born of too little sleep and too much data, but he had come to believe that the survival of the city depended on him. He had spent his career trying to heal individual sick minds; now he had a whole city to tend to.

240

"Tired?" Lisa asked.

"I'm in that tiredness beyond feeling tired. My mind is so clear that my skull wouldn't cast a shadow. I'm nearing nirvana."

"The worst is over, I think. The city's settling down."

"It's still bad, though. Have you seen the suicide figures?"

"Bad?"

"Hideous. The norm in San Francisco is 220 a year. We've had close to five hundred in the last two and a half days. And that's just the reported cases, the bodies discovered, and so on. Probably we can double the figure. Thirty suicides reported Wednesday night, about two hundred on Thursday, the same on Friday, and about fifty so far this morning. At least it seems as if the wave is past its peak."

"But *why*, Tim?"

"Some people react poorly to loss. Especially the loss of a segment of their memories. They're indignant—they're crushed—and they're scared—and they reach for the exit pill. Suicide's too easy now, anyway. In the old days you reacted to frustration by smashing the crockery; now you go a deadlier route. Of course, there are special cases. A man named Montini they fished out of the bay—a professional mnemonist, who did a trick act in nightclubs, total recall. I can hardly blame him for caving in. And I suppose there were a lot of others who kept their business in their heads—gamblers, stock-market operators, oral poets, musicians—who might decide to end it all rather than try to pick up the pieces."

"But if the effects of the drug wear off—"

"Do they?" Bryce asked.

"You said so yourself."

"I was making optimistic noises for the benefit of the citizens. We don't have any experimental history for these drugs and human subjects. Hell, Lisa, we don't even know the dosage that was administered; by the time we were able to get water samples most of the system had been flushed clean, and the automatic monitoring devices at the city pumping stations were rigged as part of the conspiracy so they didn't show a thing out of the ordinary. I've got no idea at all if there's going to be any measurable memory recovery."

"But there is, Tim. I've already started to get some things back."

"What?"

241

"Don't scream at me like that! You scared me."

He clung to the edge of the table. "Are you really recovering?"

"Around the edges. I remember a few things already. About us."

"Like what?"

"Applying for the marriage license. I'm standing stark naked inside a diagnostat machine and a voice on the loudspeaker is telling me to look straight into the scanners. And I remember the ceremony, a little. Just a small group of friends, a civil ceremony. Then we took the pod to Acapulco."

He stared grimly. "When did this start to come back?"

"About seven this morning, I guess."

"Is there more?"

"A bit. Our honeymoon. The robot bellhop who came blundering in on our wedding night. You don't—"

"Remember it? No. No. Nothing. Blank."

"That's all I remember, this early stuff."

"Yes, of course," he said. "The older memories are always the first to return in any form of amnesia. The last stuff in is the first to go." His hands were shaking, not entirely from fatigue. A strange desolation crept over him. Lisa remembered. He did not. Was it a function of her youth, or of the chemistry of her brain, or—?

He could not bear the thought that they no longer shared an oblivion. He didn't want the amnesia to become one-sided for them; it was humiliating not to remember his own marriage when she did. You're being irrational, he told himself. Physician, heal thyself!

"Let's go back inside," he said.

"You haven't finished your—"

"Later."

He went into the command room. Kamakura had phones in both hands and was braking data into a record. The screens were alive with morning scenes, Saturday in the city, crowds in Union Square. Kamakura hung up both calls and said, "I've got an interesting report from Dr. Klein at Letterman General. He says they're getting the first traces of memory recovery this morning. Women under thirty, only."

"Lisa says she's beginning to remember too," Bryce said.

"Women under thirty," said Kamakura. "Yes. Also the

242

suicide rate is definitely tapering. We may be starting to come out of it."

"Terrific," Bryce said hollowly.

Haldersen was living in a ten-foot-high bubble that one of his disciples had blown for him in the middle of Golden Gate Park, just west of the Arboretum. Fifteen similar bubbles had gone up around his, giving the region the look of an up-to-date Eskimo village in plastic igloos. The occupants of the camp, aside from Haldersen, were men and women who had so little memory left that they did not know who they were or where they lived. He had acquired a dozen of these lost ones on Friday, and by late afternoon on Saturday he had been joined by some forty more. The news somehow was moving through the city that those without moorings were welcome to take up temporary residence with the group in the park. It had happened that way during the 1906 disaster, too.

The police had been around a few times to check on them. The first time, a portly lieutenant had tried to persuade the whole group to move to Fletcher Memorial. "That's where most of the victims are getting treatment, you see. The doctors give them something, and then we try to identify them and find their next of kin—"

"Perhaps it's best for these people to remain away from their next of kin for a while," Haldersen suggested. "Some meditation in the park—an exploration of the pleasures of having forgotten—that's all we're doing here." He would not go to Fletcher Memorial himself except under duress. As for the others, he felt he could do more for them in the park than anyone in the hospital could.

The second time the police came, Saturday afternoon when his group was much larger, they brought a mobile communications system. "Dr. Bryce of Fletcher Memorial wants to talk to you," a different lieutenant said.

Haldersen watched the screen come alive. "Hello, Doctor. Worried about me?"

"I'm worried about everyone, Nate. What the hell are you doing in the park?"

"Founding a new religion, I think."

"You're a sick man. You ought to come back here."

"No, Doctor. I'm not sick any more. I've had my therapy

and I'm fine. It was a beautiful treatment: selective obliteration, just as I prayed for. The entire trauma is gone."

Bryce appeared fascinated by that; his frowning expression of official responsibility vanished a moment, giving place to a look of professional concern. "Interesting," he said. "We've got people who've forgotten only nouns, and people who've forgotten who they married, and people who've forgotten how to play the violin. But you're the first one who's forgotten a trauma. You still ought to come back here, though. You aren't the best judge of your fitness to face the outside environment."

"Oh, but I am," Haldersen said. "I'm doing fine. And my people need me."

"Your people?"

"Waifs. Strays. The total wipeouts."

"We want those people in the hospital, Nate. We want to get them back to their families."

"Is that necessarily a good deed? Maybe some of them can use a spell of isolation from their families. These people look happy, Dr. Bryce. I've heard there are a lot of suicides, but not here. We're practicing mutual supportive therapy. Looking for the joys to be found in oblivion. It seems to work."

Bryce stared silently out of the screen for a long moment. Then he said impatiently, "All right, have it your own way for now. But I wish you'd stop coming on like Jesus and Freud combined, and leave the park. You're still a sick man, Nate, and the people with you are in serious trouble. I'll talk to you later."

The contact broke. The police, stymied, left.

Haldersen spoke briefly to his people at five o'clock. Then he sent them out as missionaries to collect other victims. "Save as many as you can," he said. "Find those who are in complete despair and get them into the park before they can take their own lives. Explain that the loss of one's past is not the loss of all things."

The disciples went forth. And came back leading those less fortunate than themselves. The group grew to more than one hundred by nightfall. Someone found the extruder again and blew twenty more bubbles as shelters for the night. Haldersen preached his sermon of joy, looking out at the blank eyes, the slack faces of those whose identities had washed away on Wednesday. "Why give up?" he asked them. "Now is your chance to create new lives for yourself. The slate is clean! Choose the direction you will take, define your new selves through the exercise of free will—you are reborn in holy oblivion, all of you. Rest, now, those who have just come to us. And you others, go forth again, seek out the wanderers, the drifters, the lost ones hiding in the corners of the city—"

As he finished, he saw a knot of people bustling toward him from the direction of the South Drive. Fearing trouble, Haldersen went out to meet them; but as he drew close he saw half a dozen disciples, clutching a scruffy, unshaven, terrified little man. They hurled him at Haldersen's feet. The man quivered like a hare ringed by hounds. His eyes glistened; his wedge of a face, sharp-chinned, sharp of cheekbones, was pale.

"It's the one who poisoned the water supply!" someone called. "We found him in a rooming house on Judah Street. With a stack of drugs in his room, and the plans of the water system, and a bunch of computer programs. He admits it. He admits it!"

Haldersen looked down. "Is this true?" he asked. "Are you the one?"

The man nodded.

"What's your name?"

"Won't say. Want a lawyer."

"Kill him now!" a woman shrieked. "Pull his arms and legs off!"

"Kill him!" came an answering cry from the other side of the group. "Kill him!"

The congregation, Haldersen realized, might easily turn into a mob.

He said, "Tell me your name, and I'll protect you. Otherwise I can't be responsible."

"Skinner," the man muttered miserably.

"Skinner. And you contaminated the water supply."

Another nod.

"Why?"

"To get even."

"With whom?"

"Everyone. Everybody."

Classic paranoid. Haldersen felt pity. Not the others; they were calling out for blood.

A tall man bellowed, "Make the bastard drink his own drug!"

"No, kill him! Squash him!"

The voices became more menacing. The angry faces came closer.

"Listen to me," Haldersen called, and his voice cut through the murmurings. "There'll be no killing here tonight."

"What are you going to do, give him to the police?"

"No," said Haldersen. "We'll hold communion together. We'll teach this pitiful man the blessings of oblivion, and then we'll share new joys ourselves. We are human beings. We have the capacity to forgive even the worst of sinners. Where are the memory drugs? Did someone say you had found the memory drugs? Here. Here. Pass it up here. Yes. Brothers, sisters, let us show this dark and twisted soul the nature of redemption. Yes. Yes. Fetch some water, please. Thank you. Here, Skinner. Stand him up, will you? Hold his arms. Keep him from falling down. Wait a second, until I find the proper dose. Yes. Yes. Here, Skinner. Forgiveness. Sweet oblivion."

It was so good to be working again that Mueller didn't want to stop. By early afternoon on Saturday his studio was ready; he had long since worked out the sketches of the first piece; now it was just a matter of time and effort, and he'd have something to show Pete Castine. He worked on far into the evening, setting up his armature and running a few tests of the sound sequences that he proposed to build into the piece. He had some interesting new ideas about the sonic triggers, the devices that would set off the sound effects when the appreciator came within range. Carole had to tell him, finally, that dinner was ready. "I didn't want to interrupt you," she said, "but it looks like I have to, or you won't ever stop."

"Sorry. The creative ecstasy."

"Save some of that energy. There are other ecstasies. The ecstasy of dinner, first."

She had cooked everything herself. Beautiful. He went back to work again afterward, but at half past one in the morning Carole again interrupted him. He was willing to stop, now. He had done an honest day's work, and he was sweaty with the noble sweat of a job well done. Two minutes under the molecular cleanser and the sweat was gone, but the good ache of virtuous fatigue remained. He hadn't felt this way in years.

He woke to Sunday thoughts of unpaid debts.

"The robots are still there," he said. "They won't go away, will they? Even though the whole city's at a standstill, nobody's told the robots to quit."

"Ignore them," Carole said.

"That's what I've been doing. But I can't ignore the debts. Ultimately there'll be a reckoning."

"You're working again, though! You'll have an income coming in."

"Do you know what I owe?" he asked. "Almost a million. If I produced one piece a week for a year, and sold each piece for twenty bigs, I might pay everything off. But I can't work that fast, and the market can't possibly absorb that many Muellers, and Pete certainly can't buy them all for future sale."

He noticed the way Carole's face darkened at the mention of Pete Castine.

He said, "You know what I'll have to do? Go to Caracas, like I was planning before this memory thing started. I can work there, and ship my stuff to Pete. And maybe in two or three years I'll have paid off my debt, a hundred cents on the dollar, and I can start fresh back here. Do you know if that's possible? I mean, if you jump to a debtor sanctuary, are you blackballed for credit forever, even if you pay off what you owe?"

"I don't know," Carole said distantly.

"I'll find that out later. The important thing is that I'm working again, and I've got to go someplace where I can work without being hounded. And then I'll pay everybody off. You'll come with me to Caracas, won't you?"

"Maybe we won't have to go," Carole said.

"But how—"

"You should be working now, shouldn't you?"

He worked, and while he worked he made lists of creditors in his mind, dreaming of the day when every name on every list was crossed off. When he got hungry he emerged from the studio and found Carole sitting gloomily in the living room. Her eyes were red and puffy-lidded.

"What's wrong?" he asked. "You don't want to go to Caracas?"

"Please, Paul—let's not talk about it—"

"I've really got no alternative. I mean, unless we pick one of the other sanctuaries. São Paulo? Spalato?"

"It isn't that, Paul."

"What, then?"

"I'm starting to remember again."

The air went out of him. "Oh," he said.

"I remember November, December, January. The crazy things you were doing, the loans, the financial juggling. And the quarrels we had. They were terrible quarrels."

"Oh."

"The divorce. I remember, Paul. It started coming back last night, but you were so happy I didn't want to say anything. And this morning it's much clearer. You still don't remember any of it?"

"Not a thing past last October."

"I do," she said, shakily. "You hit me, do you know that? You cut my lip. You slammed me against that wall, right over there, and then you threw the Chinese vase at me and it broke."

"Oh. Oh."

She went on, "I remember how good Pete was to me, too. I think I can almost remember marrying him, being his wife. Paul, I'm scared. I feel everything fitting into place in my mind, and it's as scary as if my mind was breaking into pieces. It was so good, Paul, these last few days. It was like being a newlywed with you again. But now all the sour parts are coming back, the hate, the ugliness, it's all alive for me again. And I feel so bad about Pete. The two of us, Friday, shutting him out. He was a real gentleman about it. But the fact is that he saved me when I was going under, and I owe him something for that."

"What do you plan to do?" he asked quietly.

"I think I ought to go back to him. I'm his wife. I've got no right to stay here."

"But I'm not the same man you came to hate," Mueller protested. "I'm the old Paul, the one from last year and before. The man you loved. All the hateful stuff is gone from me."

"Not from me, though. Not now."

They were both silent.

"I think I should go back, Paul."

"Whatever you say."

"I think I should. I wish you all kinds of luck, but I can't stay here. Will it hurt your work if I leave again?"

"I won't know until you do."

She told him three or four more times that she felt she ought to go back to Castine, and then, politely, he suggested that she should go back right now, if that was how she felt, and she did. He spent half an hour wandering around the apartment, which seemed so awfully empty again. He nearly invited one of the dunning robots in for company. Instead, he went back to work. To his surprise, he worked quite well, and in an hour he had ceased thinking about Carole entirely.

Sunday afternoon, Freddy Munson set up a credit transfer and managed to get most of his liquid assets fed into an old account he kept at the Bank of Luna. Toward evening, he went down to the wharf and boarded a three-man hovercraft owned by a fisherman willing to take his chances with the law. They slipped out into the bay without running lights and crossed the bay on a big diagonal, landing some time later a few miles north of Berkeley. Munson found a cab to take him to the Oakland airport, and caught the midnight shuttle to L.A., where, after a lot of fancy talking, he was able to buy his way aboard the next Luna-bound rocket, lifting off at ten o'clock Monday morning. He spent the night in the spaceport terminal. He had taken with him nothing except the clothes he wore; his fine possessions, his paintings, his suits, his Mueller sculptures, and all the rest remained in his apartment, and ultimately would be sold to satisfy the judgments against him. Too bad. He knew that he wouldn't be coming back to Earth again, either, not with a larceny warrant or worse awaiting him. Also too bad. It had been so nice for so long, here, and who needed a memory drug in the water supply? Munson had only one consolation. It was an article of his philosophy that sooner or later, no matter how neatly you organized your life, fate opened a trapdoor underneath your feet and catapulted you into something unknown and unpleasant. Now he knew that it was true, even for him.

Too, too bad. He wondered what his chances were of starting over up here. Did they need stockbrokers on the Moon?

Addressing the citizenry on Monday night, Commander Braskett said, "The committee of public safety is pleased to report that we have come through the worst part of the crisis. As many of you have already discovered, memories are beginning to return. The process of recovery will be more swift for some than others, but great progress has been made. Effective at six A.M. tomorrow, access routes to and from San Francisco will reopen. There will be normal mail service and many businesses will return to normal. Fellow citizens, we have demonstrated once again the real fiber of the American spirit. The Founding Fathers must be smiling down upon us today! How superbly we avoided chaos, and how beautifully we pulled together to help one another in what could have been an hour of turmoil and despair!

"Dr. Bryce requests me to remind you that anyone still suffering severe impairment of memory—especially those experiencing loss of identity, confusion of vital functions, or other disability—should report to the emergency ward at Fletcher Memorial Hospital. Treatment is available there, and computer analysis is at the service of those unable to find their homes and loved ones. I repeat—"

Tim Bryce wished that the good commander hadn't slipped in that plug for the real fiber of the American spirit, especially in view of the necessity to invite the remaining victims to the hospital with his next words. But it would be uncharitable to object. The old spaceman had done a beautiful job all weekend as the Voice of the Crisis, and some patriotic embellishments now were harmless.

The crisis, of course, was nowhere near as close to being over as Commander Braskett's speech had suggested, but public confidence had to be buoyed.

Bryce had the latest figures. Suicides now totaled 900 since the start of trouble on Wednesday; Sunday had been an unexpectedly bad day. At least 40,000 people were still unaccounted for, although they were tracing 1,000 an hour and getting them back to their families or else into an intensive-care section. Probably 750,000 more continued to have memory difficulties. Most children had fully recovered, and many of the women were mending; but older people, and men in general, had experienced scarcely any memory recapture. Even those who were nearly healed had no recall of events of

Tuesday and Wednesday, and probably never would; for large numbers of people, though, big blocks of the past would have to be learned fom the outside, like history lessons.

Lisa was teaching him their marriage that way.

The trips they had taken—the good times, the bad—the parties, the friends, the shared dreams—she described everything, as vividly as she could, and he fastened on each anecdote, trying to make it a part of himself again. He knew it was hopeless, really. He'd know the outlines, never the substance. Yet it was probably the best he could hope for.

He was so horribly tired, suddenly.

He said to Kamakura, "Is there anything new from the park yet? That rumor that Haldersen's actually got a supply of the drug?"

"Seems to be true, Tim. The word is that he and his friends caught the character who spiked the water supply, and relieved him of a roomful of various amnesifacients."

"We've got to seize them," Bryce said.

Kamakura shook his head. "Not just yet. Police are afraid of any actions in the park. They say it's a volatile situation."

"But if those drugs are loose—"

"Let me worry about it, Tim. Look, why don't you and Lisa go home for a while? You've been here without a break since Thursday."

"So have—"

"No. Everybody else has had a breather. Go on, now. We're over the worst. Relax, get some real sleep, make some love. Get to know that gorgeous wife of yours again a little."

Bryce reddened. "I'd rather stay here until I feel I can afford to leave."

Scowling, Kamakura walked away from him to confer with Commander Braskett. Bryce scanned the screens, trying to figure out what was going on in the park. A moment later, Braskett walked over to him.

"Dr. Bryce?"

"What?"

"You're relieved of duty until sundown Tuesday."

"Wait a second—"

"That's an order, Doctor. I'm chairman of the committee of public safety, and I'm telling you to get yourself out of this hospital. You aren't going to disobey an order, are you?"

"Listen, Commander—"

"Out. No mutiny, Bryce. Out! Orders."

Bryce tried to protest, but he was too weary to put up much of a fight. By noon, he was on his way home, soupy-headed with fatigue. Lisa drove. He sat quite still, struggling to remember details of his marriage. Nothing came.

She put him to bed. He wasn't sure how long he slept; but then he felt her against him, warm, satin-smooth.

"Hello," she said. "Remember me?"

"Yes," he lied gratefully. "Oh, yes, yes, yes!"

Working right through the night, Mueller finished his armature by dawn on Monday. He slept a while, and in early afternoon began to paint the inner strips of loudspeakers on: a thousand speakers to the inch, no more than a few molecules thick, from which the sounds of his sculpture would issue in resonant fullness. When that was done, he paused to contemplate the needs of his sculpture's superstructure, and by seven that night was ready to move to the next phase. The demons of creativity possessed him; he saw no reason to eat and scarcely any to sleep.

At eight, just as he was getting up momentum for the long night's work, he heard a knock at the door. Carole's signal. He had disconnected the doorbell, and robots didn't have the sense to knock. Uneasily, he went to the door. She was there.

"So?" he said.

"So I came back. So it starts all over."

"What's going on?"

"Can I come in?" she asked.

"I suppose. I'm working, but come in."

She said, "I talked it all over with Pete. We both decided I ought to go back to you."

"You aren't much for consistency, are you?" he asked.

"I have to take things as they happen. When I lost my memory, I came to you. When I remembered things again, I felt I ought to leave. I didn't *want* to leave. I felt I *ought* to leave. There's a difference."

"Really," he said.

"Really. I went to Pete, but I didn't want to be with him. I wanted to be here."

"I hit you and made your lip bleed. I threw the Ming vase at you."

"It wasn't Ming, it was K'ang-hsi."

252

"Pardon me. My memory still isn't so good. Anyway, I did terrible things to you, and you hated me enough to want a divorce. So why come back?"

"You were right, yesterday. You aren't the man I came to hate. You're the old Paul."

"And if my memory of the past nine months returns?"

"Even so," she said. "People change. You've been through hell and come out the other side. You're working again. You aren't sullen and nasty and confused. We'll go to Caracas, or wherever you want, and you'll do your work and pay your debts, just as you said yesterday."

"And Pete?"

"He'll arrange an annulment. He's being swell about it."

"Good old Pete," Mueller said. He shook his head. "How long will the neat happy ending last, Carole? If you think there's a chance you'll be bouncing back in the other direction by Wednesday, say so now. I'd rather not get involved again, in that case."

"No chance. None."

"Unless I throw the Ch'ien-lung vase at you."

"K'ang-hsi," she said.

"Yes. K'ang-hsi." He managed to grin. Suddenly he felt the accumulated fatigue of these days register all at once. "I've been working too hard," he said. "An orgy of creativity to make up for lost time. Let's go for a walk."

"Fine," she said.

They went out, just as a dunning robot was arriving. "Top of the evening to you, sir," Mueller said.

"Mr. Mueller, I represent the accounts receivable department of the Acme Brass and—"

"See my attorney," he said.

Fog was rolling in off the sea now. There were no stars. The downtown lights were invisible. He and Carole walked west, toward the park. He felt strangely light-headed, not entirely from lack of sleep. Reality and dream had merged; these were unusual days. They entered the park from the Panhandle and strolled toward the museum area, arm in arm, saying nothing much to one another. As they passed the conservatory Mueller became aware of a crowd up ahead, thousands of people staring in the direction of the music shell. "What do you think is going on?" Carole asked. Mueller shrugged. They edged through the crowd.

Ten minutes later they were close enough to see the stage. A tall, thin, wild-looking man with unruly yellow hair was on the stage. Beside him was a small, scrawny man in ragged clothing, and there were a dozen others flanking them, carrying ceramic bowls.

"What's happening?" Mueller asked someone in the crowd.

"Religious ceremony."

"Eh?"

"New religion. Church of Oblivion. That's the head prophet up there. You haven't heard about it yet?"

"Not a thing."

"Started around Friday. You see that ratty-looking character next to the prophet?"

"Yes."

"He's the one that put the stuff in the water supply. He confessed and they made him drink his own drug. Now he doesn't remember a thing, and he's the assistant prophet. Craziest damn stuff!"

"And what are they doing up there?"

"They've got the drug in those bowls. They drink and forget some more. They drink and forget some more."

The gathering fog absorbed the sounds of those on the stage. Mueller strained to listen. He saw the bright eyes of fanaticism; the alleged contaminator of the water looked positively radiant. Words drifted out into the night.

"Brothers and sisters . . . the joy, the sweetness of forgetting . . . come up here with us, take communion with us . . . oblivion . . . redemption . . . even for the most wicked . . . forget . . . forget . . ."

They were passing the bowls around on stage, drinking, smiling. People were going up to receive the communion, taking a bowl, sipping, nodding happily. Toward the rear of the stage the bowls were being refilled by three sober-looking functionaries.

Mueller felt a chill. He suspected that what had been born in this park during this week would endure, somehow, long after the crisis of San Francisco had become part of history; and it seemed to him that something new and frightening had been loosed upon the land.

"Take . . . drink . . . forget . . ." the prophet cried.

And the worshippers cried, *"Take . . . drink . . . forget . . ."*

The bowls were passed.

"What's it all *about?*" Carole whispered.

"Take . . . drink . . . forget . . ."
"Take . . . drink . . . forget . . ."
"Blessed is sweet oblivion."
"Blessed is sweet oblivion."
"Sweet it is to lay down the burden of one's soul."
"Sweet it is to lay down the burden of one's soul."
"Joyous it is to begin anew."
"Joyous it is to begin anew."

The fog was deepening. Mueller could barely see the aquarium building just across the way. He clasped his hand tightly around Carole's and began to think about getting out of the park.

He had to admit, though, that these people might have hit on something true. Was he not better off for having taken a chemical into his bloodstream, and thereby shedding a portion of his past? Yes, of course. And yet—to mutilate one's mind this way, deliberately, happily, to drink deep of oblivion—

"Blessed are those who are able to forget," the prophet said.

"Blessed are those who are able to forget," the crowd roared in response.

"Blessed are those who are able to forget," Mueller heard his own voice cry. And he began to tremble. And he felt sudden fear: He sensed the power of this strange new movement, the gathering strength of the prophet's appeal to unreason. It was time for a new religion, maybe, a cult that offered emancipation from all inner burdens. They would synthesize this drug and turn it out by the ton, Mueller thought, and repeatedly dose cities with it, so that everyone could be converted, so that everyone might taste the joys of oblivion. No one will be able to stop them. After a while, no one will *want* to stop them. And so we'll go on, drinking deep, until we're washed clean of all pain and all sorrow, of all sad recollection, we'll sip a cup of kindness and part with auld lang syne, we'll give up the griefs we carry around, and we'll give up everything else, identity, soul, self, mind. We will drink sweet oblivion. Mueller shivered. Turning suddenly, tugging roughly at Carole's arm, he pushed through the joyful worshipping crowd, and hunted somberly in the fogwrapped night, trying to find some way out of the park.

ſAM HALL

Poul Anderſon

Click. Bzzz. Whrrrr.

Citizen Blank Blank, Anytown, Somewhere, U. S. A., approaches the hotel desk. "Single, with bath."

"Sorry, sir, our fuel ration doesn't permit individual baths. One can be drawn for you; that will be twenty-five dollars extra."

"Oh, is that all? O.K."

Citizen Blank reaches into his pocket with an automatic gesture and withdraws his punched card and gives it to the registry machine. Aluminum jaws close on it, copper teeth feel for the holes, electronic tongue tastes the life of Citizen Blank.

Place and date of birth. Parents. Race. Religion. Educational, military, and civilian-service record. Marital status. Occupations, up to and including current one. Affiliations. Physical measurements, fingerprints, retinals, blood type. Basic psychotype. Loyalty rating. Loyalty index as a function of time to moment of last checkup. *Click, click. Bzzz.*

"Why are you here, sir?"

"Salesman. I expect to be in New Pittsburgh tomorrow night."

The clerk—thirty-two years old, married, two children; N.B., confidential: Jewish; to be kept out of key occupations—punches the buttons.

Click, click. The machine returns the card. Citizen Blank puts it back in his wallet.

"Front!"

The bellboy—nineteen years old, unmarried; N.B., confidential: Catholic; to be kept out of key occupations—takes the guest's trunk. The elevator creaks upstairs. The clerk resumes his reading. The article is entitled "Has Britain Betrayed Us?" Other articles in the magazine include "New Indoctrination Program for the Armed Forces," "Labor Hunting on Mars," "I Was a Union Man for the Security Police," "New Plans for YOUR Future."

The machine talks to itself. *Click, click.* A tube winks at its neighbor as if they shared a private joke. The total signal goes out over the wires.

With a thousand other signals, it shoots down the last cable and into the sorter unit of Central Records. *Click, click. Bzzz. Whrrr.* Wink and glow. A scanner sweeps through the memory circuits. The distorted molecules of one spool show the pattern of Citizen Blank Blank and this is sent back. It enters the comparison unit, to which the incoming signal corresponding to Citizen Blank Blank has also been shunted. The two are perfectly in phase; nothing wrong. Citizen Blank Blank is staying in the town where, last night, he said he would, so he has not had to file a correction.

The new information is added to the record of Citizen Blank Blank. The whole of his life returns to the memory bank. It is wiped from the scanner and comparison units, so that these may be free for the next arriving signal.

The machine has swallowed and digested another day. It is content.

Thornberg came into his office at the usual time. His secretary glanced up to say, "Good morning," and looked closer. She had been with him for enough years to read the nuances in his carefully controlled face. "Anything wrong, chief?"

"No." He spoke it harshly, which was also peculiar. "No, nothing wrong. I feel a bit under the weather, maybe."

"Oh." The secretary nodded. You learned discretion in the government. "Well, I hope you get better soon."

"Thanks. It's nothing." Thornberg limped over to his desk, sat down, and took out a pack of cigarettes. He held one for a moment in nicotine-yellowed fingers before lighting it, and there was an emptiness in his eyes. Then he puffed ferociously and turned to his mail. As chief technician of Central Records, he got a generous tobacco ration, and used all of it.

The office was not large—a windowless cubicle, furnished with gaunt orderliness, it's only decoration a picture of his son and one of his late wife. Thornberg seemed too big for it. He was tall and lean, with thin straight features and neatly brushed graying hair. He wore a plain version of the Security uniform, with his insignia of Technical Division and major's rank but no other decoration, none of the ribbons to which he was entitled. The priesthood of Matilda the Machine were a pretty informal lot for these days.

He chain-smoked his way through the mail. Routine stuff, most of it having to do with the necessary change-overs for installing the new identification system. "Come on, June," he said to his secretary. Irrationally, he preferred dictating to her rather than a recorder. "Let's get this out of the way fast. I've got work to do."

He held one letter before him. "To Senator E. W. Harmison. S.O.B., New Washington. Dear Sir: In re your communication of the 14th inst., requesting my personal opinion of the new ID system, may I say that it is not a technician's business to express opinions. The directive ordering that every citizen shall have one number applying to all his papers and functions— birth certificate, education, rations, social security, service, et cetera—has obvious long-range advantages, but naturally entails a good deal of work in reconverting all our electronic records. The President having decided that the gain in the long run justifies the present difficulties, it behooves all citizens to obey. Yours, and so forth." He smiled with a certain coldness. "There, that'll fix *him!* I don't know what good Congress is anyway, except to plague honest bureaucrats."

Privately, June decided to modify the letter. Maybe a senator was only a rubber stamp, but you couldn't brush him off so curtly. It is part of a secretary's job to keep the boss out of trouble.

"O.K., let's get to the next," said Thornberg. "To Colonel M. R. Hubert, Director of Liaison Divison, Central Records Agency, Security Police, et cetera. Dear Sir: In re your memorandum of the 14th inst., requiring a definite date for completion of the ID conversion, may I respectfully state that it is impossible for me honestly to set one. It is necessary for us to develop a memory-modification unit which will make the change-over in all our records without our having to take out and alter each of the three hundred million or so spools in the machine. You realize that one cannot predict the exact time needed to complete such a project. However, research is progressing satisfactorily (refer him to my last report, will you?), and I can confidently say that conversion will be finished and all citizens notified of their numbers within two months at the latest. Respectfully, and so on. Put that in a nice form, June.''

She nodded. Thornberg went on through his mail, throwing most of it into the basket for her to answer alone. When he was done, he yawned and lit another cigarette. ''Praise Allah that's over. Now I can get down to the lab.''

''You have some afternoon appointments,'' she reminded him.

''I'll be back after lunch. See you.'' He got up and went out of the office.

Down an escalator to a still lower subterranean level, along a corridor, returning the salutes of passing technicians without thinking about it. His face was immobile, and perhaps only the stiff swinging of his arms said anything.

Jimmy, he thought. *Jimmy, kid.*

He entered the guard chamber, pressing hand and eye to the scanners in the farther door. Finger and retinal patterns were his pass; no alarm sounded; the door opened for him and he walked into the temple of Matilda.

She crouched hugely before him, tier upon tier of control panels, instruments, blinking lights, like an Aztec pyramid. The gods murmured within her and winked red eyes at the tiny men who crawled over her monstrous flanks. Thornberg stood for a moment regarding the spectacle. Then he smiled, a tired smile creasing his face along one side. A sardonic memory came back to him, bootlegged stuff from the '40s and '50s of the last century which he had read, French, German, British, Italian. The intellectuals had been all hot and bothered about the Americanization of Europe, the crumbling of old culture before the mechanized barbarism of soft drinks, advertising, chrome-plated automobiles—dollar grins, the Danes had called them—chewing gum, plastics. . . . None of them had protested the simultaneous Europeanization of America: government control, a military caste, light-years of bureaucratic records and red tape, censors, secret police, nationalism and racialism.

Oh, well.

But, Jimmy, boy, where are you now, what are they doing to you?

Thornberg went over to the bench where his best engineer, Rodney, was testing a unit. "How's it coming?" he asked.

"Pretty good, chief," said Rodney. He didn't bother to salute; Thornberg had, in fact, forbidden it in the labs as a waste of time. "A few bugs yet, but we're getting them out."

You had to have a gimmick which would change numbers without altering anything else. Not too easy a task, when the memory banks depended on individual magnetic domains. "O.K.," said Thornberg. "Look, I'm going up to the main controls. Going to run a few tests myself—some of the tubes have been acting funny over in Section Thirteen."

"Want an assistant?"

"No, thanks. I just want not to be bothered."

Thornberg resumed his way across the floor, its hardness echoed dully under his shoes. The main controls were in a special armored booth nestling against the great pyramid, and he had to be scanned again before the door opened for him. Not many were allowed in here. The complete archives of the nation were too valuable to take chances with.

Thornberg's loyalty rating was AAB-2—not absolutely perfect, but the best available among men of his professional caliber. His last drugged checkup had revealed certain doubts and reservations about government policy, but there was no question of disobedience. *Prima facie*, he was certainly bound to be loyal. He had served with distinction in the war against Brazil, losing a leg in action; his wife had been killed in the abortive Chinese rocket raids ten years ago; his son was a rising young Space Guard officer on Venus. He had read and listened to forbidden stuff, blacklisted books, underground and foreign propaganda, but then every intellectual dabbled with that; it was not a serious offense if your record was otherwise good and if you laughed off what the prohibited things said.

He sat for a moment regarding the control board inside the

booth. Its complexity would have baffled most engineers, but he had been with Matilda so long that he didn't even need the reference tables.

Well—

It took nerve, this. A hypnoquiz was sure to reveal what he was about to do. But such raids were, necessarily, in random pattern; it was unlikely that he would be called up again for years, especially with his rating. By the time he was found out, Jack should have risen far enough in the Guard ranks to be safe.

In the privacy of the booth, Thornberg permitted himself a harsh grin. "This," he murmured to the machine, "will hurt me worse than it does you."

He began punching buttons.

There were circuits installed which could alter the records—take an entire one out and write whatever was desired in the magnetic fields. Thornberg had done the job a few times for high officials. Now he was doing it for himself.

Jimmy Obrenowicz, son of his second cousin, hustled off at night by Security police on suspicion of treason. The records showed what no private citizen was supposed to know: Jimmy was in Camp Fieldstone. Those who returned from there were very quiet and said nothing about where they had been; sometimes they were incapable of speech.

It wouldn't do for the chief of Central Records to have a relative in Fieldstone. Thornberg punched buttons for half an hour, erasing, changing. It was a tough job—he had to go back several generations, altering lines of descent. But when he was through, Jimmy Obrenowicz was no relation whatsoever to the Thornbergs.

And I thought the world of that kid. But I'm not doing it for myself, Jimmy. It's for Jack. When the cops go through your file, later today no doubt, I can't let them find out you're related to Captain Thornberg on Venus and a friend of his father.

He slapped the switch which returned the spool to its place in the memory bank. *With this act do I disown thee.*

After that he sat for a while, relishing the quiet of the booth and clean impersonality of the instruments. He didn't even want to smoke.

So now they were going to give every citizen a number,

tattooed on him no doubt. One number for everything. Thornberg foresaw popular slang referring to the numbers as "brands," and Security cracking down on those who used the term. Disloyal language.

Well, the underground was dangerous. It was supported by foreign countries who didn't like an American-dominated world—at least, not one dominated by today's kind of America, though once U.S.A. had meant "Hope." The rebels were said to have their own base out in space somewhere, and to have honeycombed the country with their agents. It could be. Their propaganda was subtle—we don't want to overthrow the nation, we only want to liberate it, we want to restore the Bill of Rights. It could attract a lot of unstable souls. But Security's spy hunt was bound to drag in any number of citizens who had never meditated treason. Like Jimmy—or had Jimmy been an undergrounder after all? You never knew. Nobody ever told you.

There was a sour taste in Thornberg's mouth. He grimaced. A line of a song came back to him: "*I hate you one and all.*" How had it gone? They used to sing it in his college days. Something about a very bitter character who'd committed a murder.

Oh, yes. "Sam Hall." How did it go, now? You needed a gravelly bass to sing it properly.

> "*Oh, my name is Samuel Hall, Samuel Hall.*
> *Yes, my name is Samuel Hall, Samuel Hall.*
> *Oh, my name is Samuel Hall,*
> *And I hate you one and all,*
> *You're a gang of muckers all, damn your hide.*"

That was it. And Sam Hall was about to swing for murder. He remembered now. He felt like Sam Hall himself. He looked at the machine and wondered how many Sam Halls were in its memory banks.

Idly, postponing his return to work, he punched for the file—name, Samuel Hall, no other specifications. The machine mumbled to itself. Presently it spewed out a file of papers, microprinted on the spot from the memory banks. Complete dossier, on every Sam Hall, living and dead, from the time the records began to be kept. Thornberg chucked the papers down the incinerator slot.

"*Oh, I killed a man, they say, so they say—*"

262

The impulse was blinding in its savagery. They were dealing with Jimmy at this moment, probably pounding him over the kidneys, and he, Thornberg, sat here waiting for the cops to requisition Jimmy's file, and there was nothing he could do. His hands were empty.

No, he thought, *I'll give them Sam Hall!*

His fingers began to race, he lost his nausea in the intricate technical problem. Slipping a fake spool into Matilda—it wasn't easy. You couldn't duplicate numbers, and every citizen had a lot of them. You had to account for every day of his life.

Well, some of that could be simplified. The machine had only existed for twenty-five years, before then the files had been kept on paper in a dozen different offices. Let's make Sam Hall a resident of New York, his dossier there lost in the bombing thirty years ago—such of his papers as were on file in New Washington had also been lost, in the Chinese attack. That meant he simply reported as much detail as he could remember, which needn't be a lot.

Let's see. "Sam Hall" was an English song, so Sam Hall should be British himself. Came over with his parents, oh, thirty-eight years ago, when he was only three, and naturalized with them; that was before the total ban on immigration. Grew up on New York's lower East Side, a tough kid, a slum kid. School records lost in the bombing, but he claimed to have gone through the tenth grade. No living relatives. No family. No definite occupation, just a series of unskilled jobs. Loyalty rating BBA-O, which meant that purely routine questions showed him to have no political opinions at all that mattered.

Too colorless. Give him some violence in his background. Thornberg punched for information on New York Police stations and civilian-police officers destroyed in the last raids. He used them as the source of records that Sam Hall had been continually in trouble—drunkenness, disorderly conduct, brawls, a suspicion of holdups and burglary but not strong enough to warrant calling in Security's hypnotechnicians for quizzing him.

Hm-m-m. Better make him 4-F, no military service. Reason? Well, a slight drug addiction; men weren't so badly needed nowadays that hopheads had to be cured. Neocoke—that didn't impair the faculties too much, indeed the addict

263

was abnormally fast and strong under the influence, though there was a tough reaction afterwards.

Then he would have had to put in a term in civilian service. Let's see. He spent his three years as a common laborer on the Colorado Dam project; so many men had been involved there that no one would remember him, or at least it would be hard finding a supervisor who did.

Now to fill in. Thornberg used a number of automatic machines to help him. Every day had to be accounted for, in twenty-five years; but of course the majority would show no travel or change of residence. Thornberg punched for cheap hotels housing many at a time—no record would be kept there, everything being filed in Matilda, and no one would remember a shabby individual patron. Sam Hall's present address was given as the Triton, a glorified flophouse on the East Side, not far from the craters. At present unemployed, doubtless living off past savings. Oh, blast! It was necessary to file income tax returns. Thornberg did so.

Hm-m-m—physical ID. Make him of average height, stocky, black-haired and black-eyed, a bent nose and a scar on his forehead—tough-looking, but not enough so to make him especially memorable. Thornberg filled in the precise measurements. It wasn't hard to fake fingerprint and retinal patterns; he threw in a censor circuit so he wouldn't accidentally duplicate anyone else.

When he was done, Thornberg leaned back and sighed. There were plenty of holes yet in the record, but he could fill them at his leisure. It had been a couple of hours' hard, concentrated work—utterly pointless, except that he had blown off steam. He felt a lot better.

He glanced at his watch. *Time to get back on the job, son.* For a rebellious moment he wished no one had ever invented clocks. They had made possible the science he loved, but they had then proceeded to mechanize man. Oh, well, too late now. He got up and went out of the booth. The door closed itself behind him.

It was about a month later that Sam Hall committed his first murder.

The night before, Thornberg had been at home. His rank entitled him to good housing even if he did live alone—two rooms and bath on the ninety-eighth floor of a unit in town,

264

not far from the camouflaged entrance to Matilda's underground domain. The fact that he was in Security, even if he didn't belong to the manhunting branch, gave him so much added deference that he often felt lonely.

He had been looking through his bookshelves for something to read. The Literary Bureau had lately been trumpeting Whitman as an early example of Americanism, but though Thornberg had always liked the poet, his hands strayed perversely to the dog-eared volume of Marlowe. Was that escapism? The L.B. was very down on escapism. Oh, well, these were tough times. It wasn't easy to belong to the nation which was enforcing peace on a sullen world—you had to be realistic and energetic and all the rest, no doubt.

The phone buzzed. He went over and clicked the receiver on. Martha Obrenowicz's plain plump face showed in the screen; her gray hair was wild and her voice was a harsh croak.

"Uh . . . hello," he said uneasily. He hadn't called her since the news of her son's arrest. "How are you?"

"Jimmy is dead," she told him.

He stood for a long while. His skull felt hollow.

"I got word today that he died in camp," said Martha. "I thought you'd want to know."

Thornberg shook his head, back and forth, very slowly. "That isn't news I ever wanted, Martha," he said.

"It isn't *right!*" she shrieked. "Jimmy wasn't a traitor. I knew my own son. Who ought to know him better? He had some friends I was kind of doubtful of, but Jimmy, he wouldn't ever—"

Something cold formed in Thornberg's breast. You never knew when calls were being tapped.

"I'm sorry, Martha," he said without tone. "But the police are very careful about these things. They wouldn't act till they were sure. Justice is one of our traditions."

She looked at him for a long time. Her eyes held a hard glitter. "You, too," she said at last.

"Be careful, Martha," he warned her. "I know it's a blow to you, but don't say anything you might regret later. After all, Jimmy may have died accidentally. Those things happen."

"I . . . forgot," she said jerkily. "You . . . are . . . in Security . . . yourself."

"Be calm," he said. "Think of it as a sacrifice for the national interest."

She switched off on him. He knew she wouldn't call him again. And it wouldn't be safe to see her.

"Good-by, Martha," he said aloud. It was like a stranger speaking.

He turned back to the bookshelf. *Not for me*, he told himself thinly. *For Jack.* He touched the binding of "Leaves of Grass." *O Whitman, old rebel*, he thought, with a curious dry laughter in him, *are they calling you Whirling Walt now?*

That night he took an extra sleeping pill. His head still felt fuzzy when he reported for work, and after a while he gave up trying to answer the mail and went down to the lab.

While he was engaged with Rodney, and making a poor job of understanding the technical problem under discussion, his eyes strayed to Matilda. Suddenly he realized what he needed for a cathartic. He broke off as soon as possible and went into the main control booth.

For a moment he paused at the keyboard. The day-by-day creation of Sam Hall had been an odd experience. He, quiet and introverted, had shaped a rowdy life and painted a rugged personality. Sam Hall was more real to him than many of his associates. *Well, I'm a schizoid type myself. Maybe I should have been a writer.* No, that would have meant too many restrictions, too much fear of offending the censor. He had done exactly as he pleased with Sam Hall.

He drew a deep breath and punched for unsolved murders of Security officers, New York City area, within the last month. They were surprisingly common. Could it be that dissatisfaction was more general than the government admitted? But when the bulk of a nation harbors thoughts labeled treasonous, does the label still apply?

He found what he wanted. Sergeant Brady had incautiously entered the Crater district after dark on the twenty-seventh of last month, on a routine checkup mission; he had worn the black uniform, presumably to give himself the full weight of authority. The next morning he had been found in an alley with his head bashed in.

"Oh, I killed a man, 'tis said, 'tis said,
Yes, I killed a man, 'tis said, 'tis said.

266

I beat him on the head
  And I left him there for dead,
   Yes, I left him there for dead, damn his hide.''

Newspapers had, no doubt, deplored this brutality perpe-
trated by the traitorous agents of enemy powers. (*Oh, the
parson, he did come, he did come.*) A number of suspects had
been rounded up at once and given a stiff quizzing. (*And the
sheriff, he came too, he came too.*) There had been nothing
proven as yet, though one Andy Nikolsky—fifth generation
American, mechanic, married, four children, underground
pamphlets found in his room—had been arrested yesterday on
suspicion.

Thornberg sighed. He knew enough of Security methods to
be sure they would get somebody for such a killing. They
couldn't allow their reputation for infallibility to be smirched
by a lack of conclusive evidence. Maybe Nikolsky had done
the crime—he couldn't *prove* he had simply been out for a
walk that evening—and maybe he hadn't. But hell's fire, why
not give him a break? He had four kids.

Thornberg scratched his head. This had to be done carefully. Let's see. Brady's body would have been cremated by
now, but of course there had been a careful study first.
Thornberg withdrew the dead man's file from the machine
and microprinted a replica of the evidence—nothing. Erasing
that, he inserted the statement that a blurred thumbprint had
been found on the victim's collar and referred to ID labs for
reconstruction. In the ID file he inserted the report of such a
job, finished only yesterday due to a great press of work.
(True enough—they had been busy lately on material sent
from Mars, seized in a raid on a rebel meeting place.) The
probable pattern of the whorls was—and here he inserted Sam
Hall's right thumb.

He returned the spools and leaned back in his chair. It was
risky; if anyone thought to check with the ID lab, he was
done for. But that was unlikely, the chances were that New
York would accept the findings with a routine acknowledg-
ment which some clerk at the lab would file without studying.
The more obvious dangers were not too great either: a busy
police force would not stop to ask if any of their fingerprint
men had actually developed that smudge; and as for hypnoquizzing showing Nikolsky really was the murderer, well,

then the print would be assumed that of a passerby who had found the body without reporting it.

So now Sam Hall had killed a Security officer—grabbed him by the neck and smashed his skull with a weighted club. Thornberg felt a lot better.

New York Security shot a request to Central Records for any new material on the Brady case. An automaton received it, compared the codes, and saw that fresh information had been added. The message flashed back, together with the dossier on Sam Hall and two others—for the reconstruction could not be absolutely accurate.

The other two men were safe enough, as it turned out. Both had alibis. The squad that stormed into the Triton Hotel and demanded Sam Hall were met with blank stares. No such person was registered. No one of that description was known here. A thorough quizzing corroborated this. So—Sam Hall had managed to fake an address. He could have done that easily enough by punching the buttons on the hotel register when no one was looking. Sam Hall could be anywhere!

Andy Nikolsky, having been hypnoed and found harmless, was released. The fine for possessing subversive literature would put him in debt for the next few years, he had no influential friends to get it suspended, but he'd stay out of trouble if he watched his step. Security sent out an alarm for Sam Hall.

Thornberg derived a sardonic amusement from watching the progress of the hunt as it came to Matilda. No one with that ID card had bought tickets on any public transportation. That proved nothing. Of the hundreds who vanished every year, some at least must have been murdered for their ID cards, the bodies disposed of. Matilda was set to give the alarm when the ID of a disappeared person showed up somewhere. Thornberg faked a few such reports, just to give the police something to do.

He slept more poorly each night, and his work suffered. Once he met Martha Obrenowicz on the street—passed hastily by without greeting her—and couldn't sleep at all, even with maximum permissible drugging.

The new ID system was completed. Machines sent notices to every citizen, with orders to have their numbers tattooed on the right shoulder blade within six weeks. As each tattoo center reported that such-and-such a person had had the job done, Matilda's robots changed the record appropriately. Sam Hall, AX-428-399-075, did not report for his tattoo. Thornberg chuckled at the AX symbol.

Then the telecasts flashed a story that made the nation sit up and listen. Bandits had held up the First National Bank in Americatown, Idaho—formerly Moscow—making off with a good five million dollars in assorted bills. From their discipline and equipment it was assumed that they were rebel agents, possibly landing in a spaceship from their unknown interplantery base, and that the raid was intended to help finance their nefarious activities. Security was co-operating with the armed forces to track down the evildoers, and arrests were expected hourly, et cetera, et cetera, et cetera.

Thornberg went to Matilda for a complete account. It had been a bold job. The robbers had apparently worn plastic face-masks, and light body armor under ordinary clothes. In the scuffle of the getaway, one man's mask had slipped aside—only for a moment, but a clerk who happened to see it had, with the aid of hypnosis, given a fairly good description. A brown-haired, heavy-set fellow, Roman nose, thin lips, toothbrush mustache.

Thornberg hesitated. A joke was a joke; and helping poor Nikolsky was, perhaps, morally defensible, but aiding and abetting a felony which was, in all likelihood, an act of treason—

He grinned at himself, without much humor. Swiftly he changed the record. The crook had been of medium height, dark, scar-faced, broken-nosed— He sat for a while wondering how sane he was. How sane anybody was.

Security Central asked for the complete file on the holdup, with any correlations the machine could make. It was sent to them. The description given could have been that of many men, but the scanners eliminated all but one possibility. *Sam Hall*.

The hounds bayed forth again. That night Thornberg slept well.

Dear Dad,
    Sorry I haven't written before, but we've been kept pretty busy here. As you know, I've been with a patrol in Gorbuvashtar for the past several weeks—

269

desolate country, like all this blasted planet. Sometimes I wonder if I'll ever see the sun again. And lakes and forests and—who wrote that line about the green hills of Earth? We can't get much to read out here, and sometimes my mind feels rusty. Not that I'm complaining, of course. This is a necessary job, and somebody has to do it.

We'd hardly gotten back from the patrol when we were called out on special duty, bundled into rockets and tossed halfway around the planet through the worst gale I've ever seen, even on Venus. If I hadn't been an officer and therefore presumably a gentleman, I'd have upchucked. A lot of the boys did, and we were a pretty sorry crew when we landed. But we had to go into action right away. There was a strike in the thorium mines and the local men couldn't break it. We had to use guns before we could bring them to reason. Dad, I felt sorry for the poor devils, I don't mind admitting it. Rocks and hammers and sluice hoses against machine guns! And conditions in the mines are pretty rugged. They DELETED BY CENSOR someone has to do that job too, and if no one will volunteer for any kind of pay they have to assign civilian-service men arbitrarily. It's for the state.

Otherwise nothing new. Life is pretty monotonous. Don't believe the adventure stories—adventure is weeks of boredom punctuated by moments of being scared gutless. Sorry to be so brief, but I want to get this on the outbound rocket. Won't be another for a couple of months. Everything well, really. I hope the same for you and live for the day we'll meet again. Thanks a million for the cookies— you know you can't afford to pay the freight, you old spendthrift! Martha baked them, didn't she? I recognized the Obrenowicz touch. Say hello to her and Jim for me. And most of all, my kindest thoughts go to you.

As ever,
Jack

The telecasts carried "Wanted" messages for Sam Hall. No photographs of him were available, but an artist could draw an accurate likeness from Matilda's precise description, and his truculent face began to adorn public places. Not long thereafter, the Security offices in Denver were blown up by a grenade tossed from a speeding car which vanished into traffic. A witness said he had glimpsed the thrower, and the fragmentary picture given under hypnosis was not unlike Sam Hall's. Thornberg doctored the record a bit to make it still more similar. The tampering was risky, of course; if Security ever got suspicious, they could easily check back with their witnesses. But it was not too big a chance to take, for a scientifically quizzed man told everything germane to the subject which his memory, conscious, subconscious, and cellular, held. There was never any reason to repeat such an interrogation.

Thornberg often tried to analyze his own motives. Plainly enough, he disliked the government. He must have contained that hate all his life, carefully suppressed from awareness, and only recently had it been forced into his conscious mind; not even his subconscious could have formulated it earlier, or he would have been caught by the loyalty probes. The hate derived from a lifetime of doubts (Had there been any real reason to fight Brazil, other than to obtain those bases and mining concessions? Had the Chinese attack perhaps been provoked—or even faked, for their government had denied it?) and the million petty frustrations of the garrison state. Still—the strength of it! The violence!

By creating Sam Hall, he had struck back, but it was an ineffectual blow, a timid gesture. Most likely, his basic motive was simply to find a halfway safe release; in Sam Hall, he lived vicariously all the things that the beast within him wanted to do. Several times he had intended to discontinue his sabotage, but it was like a drug: Sam Hall was becoming necessary to his own stability.

The thought was alarming. He ought to see a psychiatrist—but no, the doctor would be bound to report his tale, he would go to camp and Jack, if not exactly ruined, would be under a cloud for the rest of his life. Thornberg had no desire to go to camp, anyway. His own existence had compensations—interesting work, a few good friends, art and music and literature, decent wine, sunsets and mountains, memories. He

271

had started this game on impulse, but now it was too late to stop it.

For Sam Hall had been promoted to Public Enemy Number One.

Winter came, and the slopes of the Rockies under which Matilda lay were white beneath a cold greenish sky. Air traffic around the nearby town was lost in that hugeness, brief hurtling meteors against infinity; ground traffic could not be seen at all from the Records entrance. Thornberg took the special tubeway to work every morning, but he often walked the five miles back, and his Sundays were usually spent in long hikes over the slippery trails. That was a foolish thing to do alone in winter, but he felt reckless.

He was working in his office shortly before Christmas when the intercom said: "Major Sorensen to see you, sir. From Investigation."

Thornberg felt his stomach tie itself into a cold knot. "All right," he answered in a voice whose levelness surprised him. "Cancel any other appointments." Security Investigation took priority over everything.

Sorensen walked in with a hard, military clack of boots. He was a big blond man, heavy-shouldered, his face expressionless and his eyes as pale and cold and remote as the winter sky. The black uniform fitted him like another skin, the lightning badge of his service glittered against it like a frosty star. He stood stiffly before the desk, and Thornberg rose to give him an awkward salute.

"Please sit down, Major Sorensen. What can I do for you?"

"Thanks." The cop's voice was crisp and harsh. He lowered his bulk into a chair and drilled Thornberg with his eyes. "I've come about the Sam Hall case."

"Oh—the rebel?" Thornberg's skin prickled. It was all he could do to meet those eyes.

"How do you know he's a rebel?" asked Sorensen. "It's never been proved officially."

"Why . . . I assumed . . . that bank raid . . . and then the posters say he's believed to be in the underground—"

Sorensen inclined his cropped head ever so slightly. When he spoke again, it was in a relaxed tone, almost casual: "Tell me, Major Thornberg, have you followed the Hall dossier in detail?"

272

Thornberg hesitated. He wasn't supposed to do so unless ordered; he only kept the machine running. A memory came back to him, something he had read once: "When suspected of a major sin, admit the minor ones frankly. It disarms suspicion." Something like that.

"As a matter of fact, I have," he said. "I know it's against regs, but I was interested and . . . well, I couldn't see any harm in it. I've not discussed it with anyone, of course."

"No matter." Sorensen waved a muscular hand. "If you hadn't done so, I'd have ordered you to. I want your opinion on this."

"Why . . . I'm not a detective—"

"You know more about Records, though, than anyone else. I'll be frank with you—under the rose, naturally." Sorensen seemed almost friendly now. *Was it a trick to put his prey off guard?* "You see, there are some puzzling features about this case."

Thornberg kept silent. He wondered if Sorensen could hear the thudding of his heart.

"Sam Hall is a shadow," said the cop. "The most careful checkups eliminate any chance of his being identical with anyone else of that name. In fact, we've learned that the name occurs in a violent old drinking song—is it coincidence, or did the song suggest crime to Sam Hall, or did he by some incredible process get that alias into his record instead of his real name? Whatever the answer there, we know that he's ostensibly without military training, yet he's pulled off some beautiful pieces of precision attack. His IQ is only 110, but he evades all our traps. He has no politics, yet he turns on Security without warning. We have not been able to find one person who remembers him, not one, and believe me, we have been thorough. Oh, there are a few subconscious memories which might be of him, but probably aren't—and so aggressive a personality should be remembered consciously. No undergrounder or foreign agent we've caught had any knowledge of him, which defies probability. The whole business seems impossible."

Thornberg licked his lips. Sorensen, the hunter of men, must know he was frightened; but would he assume it to be the normal nervousness of a man in the presence of a Security officer?

Sorensen's face broke in a hard smile. "As Sherlock Holmes once remarked," he said, "when you have eliminated every other hypothesis, then the one which remains, however improbable, must be the right one."

Despite himself, Thornberg was jolted. Sorensen hadn't struck him as a reader.

"Well," he asked slowly, "what is your remaining hypothesis?"

The other man watched him for a long time, it seemed forever, before replying: "The underground is more powerful and widespread than people realize. They've had some seventy years to prepare, and there are many good brains in their ranks. They carry on scientific research of their own. It's top secret, but we know they have perfected a type of weapon we cannot duplicate yet. It seems to be a hand gun throwing bolts of energy—a blaster, you might call it—of immense power. Sooner or later, they're going to wage open war against the government.

"Now, could they have done something comparable in psychology? Could they have found a way to erase or cover up, selectively, memories, even on the cellular level? Could they know how to fool a personality tester, how to disguise the mind itself. If so, there may be any number of Sam Halls in our very midst, undetectable until the moment comes for them to strike."

Thornberg felt almost boneless. He couldn't help gasping his relief, and hoped Sorensen would take it for a sign of alarm.

"The possibility is frightening, isn't it?" The blond man laughed harshly. "You can imagine what is being felt in high official circles. We've put all the psychological researchers we could get to work on the problem—bah! Fools! They go by the book, they're afraid to be original even when the state tells them to.

"It may just be a wild fancy, of course. I hope it is. But we have to *know*. That's why I approached you personally, instead of sending the usual requisition. I want you to make a search of the records—everything pertaining to the subject, every man, every discovery, every hypothesis. You have a broad technical background and, from your psychorecord, an unusual amount of creative imagination. I want you to do what you can to correlate all your data. Co-opt anybody you need. Submit to my office a report on the possibility—or should I say probability—of this notion and, if there is any likelihood of its being true, sketch out a research program which will enable us to duplicate the results and counteract them."

Thornberg fumbled for words. "I'll try," he said lamely. "I'll do my best."

"Good. It's for the state."

Sorensen had finished his official business, but he didn't go at once. "Rebel propaganda is subtle stuff," he said quietly, after a pause. "It's dangerous because it uses our own slogans, with a twisted meaning. Liberty, equality, justice, peace. Too many people can't appreciate that times have changed, and the meanings of words have necessarily changed with them."

"I suppose not," said Thornberg. He added the lie: "I never thought much about it."

"You should," said Sorensen. "Study your history. When we lost World War III, we had to militarize to win World War IV, and after that, for our own safety, we had to mount guard on the whole human race. The people demanded it at the time."

The people, thought Thornberg, *never appreciated freedom till they'd lost it. They were always willing to sell their birthright. Or was it merely that, being untrained in thinking, they couldn't see through demagoguery, couldn't visualize the ultimate consequences of their wishes?* He was vaguely shocked at the thought; wasn't he able to control his own mind any longer?

"The rebels," said Sorensen, "claim that conditions have changed, that militarization is no longer necessary—if it ever was—and that America would be safe enough in a union of free countries. It's devilishly clever propaganda, Major Thornberg. Watch out for it."

He got up and took his leave. Thornberg sat for a long time staring at the door. Sorensen's last words were—odd, to say the least. Was it a hint—or was it bait in a trap?

The next day Matilda received a news item whose details were carefully censored for the public channels. A rebel force had landed in the stockade of Camp Jackson, in Utah, gunned down the guards, and taken away the prisoners. The camp doctor had been spared, and related that the leader of the raid, a stocky man in a mask, had ironically said to him: "Tell your friends I'll call again. My name is Sam Hall."

Space Guard ship blown up on Mesa Verde Field. On a fragment of metal someone had scrawled: "Compliments of Sam Hall."

Army quartermaster depot robbed of a million dollars. Bandit chief says, before disappearing, that he is Sam Hall.

Squad of Security police, raiding a suspected underground hideout in New Pittsburgh, cut down by machine gun fire. Voice over hidden loudspeaker cries: "My name is Sam Hall!"

Dr. Matthew Thomson, chemist in Seattle, suspected of underground connections, is gone when his home is raided. Note left on desk says: "Off to visit Sam Hall. Back for liberation. M. T."

Defense plant producing important robomb parts blown up near Miami by pony atomic bomb, after being warned over the phone that the bomb has been planted and they have half an hour to get their workers out. The caller, masked, styles himself Sam Hall.

Army laboratory in Houston given similar warning by Sam Hall. A fake, but a day's valuable work is lost in the alarm and the search.

Scribbled on walls from New York to San Diego, from Duluth to El Paso, Sam Hall, Sam Hall, Sam Hall.

Obviously, thought Thornberg, the underground had seized on the invisible and invincible man of legend and turned him to their own purposes. Reports of him poured in from all over the country, hundreds every day—Sam Hall seen here, Sam Hall seen there. Ninety-nine per cent could be dismissed as hoaxes, hallucinations, mistakes; it was another national craze, fruit of a jittery time, like the sixteenth- and seventeenth-century witch hunts or the twentieth-century flying saucers. But Security and civilian police had to check on each one.

Thornberg planted a number of them himself.

Mostly, though, he was busy with his assignment. He could understand what it meant to the government. Life in the garrison state was inevitably founded on fear and mistrust, every man's eye on his neighbor; but at least psychotyping and hypnoquizzing had given a degree of surety. Now, with that staff knocked out from under them—

His preliminary studies indicated that a discovery such as Sorensen had hypothesized, while not impossible, was too far beyond the scope of modern science for the rebels to have perfected. Such research carried on nowadays would, from the standpoint of practicality if not of knowledge, be a waste of time and trained men.

He spent a good many sleepless hours, and used up a month's cigarette ration, before he could decide what to do. All right, he'd aided insurrection in a small way, and he shouldn't boggle at the next step. Still— Did he want to?

Jack—the boy had a career lined out for himself. He loved the big deeps beyond the sky as he would love a woman. If things changed, what then of Jack's career?

Well, what was it now? Stuck on a dreary planet as guardsman and executioner of homesick starvelings poisoned by radioactivity—never even seeing the sun. Come the day, Jack could surely wangle a berth on a real spacer; they'd need bold men to explore beyond Saturn. Jack was too honest to make a good rebel, but Thornberg felt that after the initial shock he would welcome a new government.

But treason! Oaths!

When in the course of human events—

It was a small thing which decided Thornberg. He passed a shop downtown and noticed a group of the Youth Guard smashing in its windows and spattering yellow paint over the goods. Once he had taken his path, a curious serenity possessed him. He stole a vial of prussic acid from a chemist friend and carried it in his pocket; and as for Jack, the boy would have to take his chances too.

The work was demanding and dangerous. He had to alter recorded facts which were available elsewhere, in books and journals and the minds of men. Nothing could be done with basic theory, of course, but quantitative results could be juggled a little so that the overall picture was subtly askew. He would co-opt carefully chosen experts, men whose psychotypes indicated they would take the easy course of relying on Matilda instead of checking the original sources. And the correlation and integration of innumerable data, the empirical equations and extrapolations thereof, they could be tampered with.

He turned his regular job over to Rodney and devoted himself entirely to the new one. He grew thin and testy; when

277

Sorensen called up trying to hurry him, he snapped back: "Do you want speed or quality?" and wasn't too surprised at himself afterward. He got little sleep, but his mind seemed unnaturally clear.

Winter faded into spring while Thornberg and his experts labored and while the nation shook, psychically and physically, with the growing violence of Sam Hall. The report Thornberg submitted in May was so voluminous and detailed that he didn't think the government researchers would bother referring to any other source. Its conclusion: Yes, given a brilliant man applying Belloni matrices to cybernetic formulas and using some unknown kind of colloidal probe, a psychological masking technique was plausible.

The government yanked every man it could find into research. Thornberg knew it was only a matter of time before they realized they had been had. How much time, he couldn't say. But when they were sure—

> *"Now up the rope I go, up I go.*
> *Now up the rope I go, up I go.*
> *And the devils down below,*
> *They say: 'Sam, we told you so.'*
> *They say: 'Sam, we told you so,'*
> *Damn their hide."*

REBELS ATTACK
SPACESHIPS LAND UNDERCOVER OF RAIN-
    STORM, SEIZE POINTS NEAR N. DETROIT
FLAME WEAPONS USED AGAINST ARMY BY
    REBELS

"The infamous legions of the traitors have taken key points throughout the nation, but already our gallant forces have hurled them back. They have come out in early summer like toadstools, and will wither as fast—WHEEEEEE-OOOOOO!" Silence.

"All citizens are directed to keep calm, remain loyal to their country and stay at their usual tasks until otherwise ordered. Civilians will report to their local defense commanders. All military reservists will report immediately for active duty."

278

"Hello, Hawaii! Are you there? Come in, Hawaii! Calling Hawaii!"

"CQ, Mars GHQ calling . . . *bzzz, wheeee* . . . seized Syrtis Major Colony and . . . whoooo . . . help needed—"

The Lunar rocket bases are assaulted and carried. The commander blows them up rather than surrender. A pinpoint flash on the Moon's face, a new crater, what will they name it?

"So they've got Seattle, have they? Send a robomb flight. Blow the place off the map. This is war!"

". . . In New York. Secretly drilled rebels emerged from the notorious Crater district and stormed—"

". . . Assassins were shot down. The new President has already been sworn in and—"

BRITAIN, CANADA, AUSTRALIA REFUSE ASSISTANCE TO GOV'T

". . . No, sir. The bombs reached Seattle all right. But they were all stopped before they hit—some kind of energy gun."

"COMECO to all Army commanders in Florida and Georgia: Enemy action has made Florida and the Keys temporarily untenable. Army units will withdraw as follows—"

"Today a rebel force engaging an Army convoy in Donner Pass was annihilated by a well-placed tactical atomic bomb. Though our own men suffered losses on this account—"

"COMWECO to all Army commanders in California: The mutiny of units stationed near San Francisco poses a grave problem—"

SP RAID REBEL HIDEOUT, BAG FIVE OFFICERS

"All right, so the enemy is about to capture Boston. We *can't* issue weapons to the citizens. They might turn them on us!"

SPACE GUARD UNITS EXPECTED FROM VENUS

Jack, Jack, Jack!

It was strange, living in the midst of a war. Thornberg had
never thought it would be like this. Drawn faces, furtive eyes,
utter confusion in the telecast news and the irregularly arriving papers, blackouts, civil-defense drills, shortages, occasional panic when a rebel jet whistled overhead—but nothing
else. No gunfire, no bombs, no battles at all except the unreal
ones you heard about. The only casualty lists here were due
to Security—people kept disappearing, and nobody spoke
about them.

But then, why should the enemy bother with this unimportant mountain town? The Army of Liberation, as it styled
itself, was grabbing key points of industry, transportation,
communication; was fighting military units, sabotaging buildings and machines, assassinating important men in the government. By its very purpose, it couldn't wage total war,
couldn't annihilate the folk it wanted to free. Rumor had it
that the defenders were not so finicky.

Most citizens were passive. They always are. It is doubtful
if more than one fourth of the population was ever near a
combat during the Third American Revolution. City dwellers
might see fire in the sky, hear the whistle and crash of
artillery, scramble out of the way of soldiers and armored
vehicles, cower in shelters when the rockets thundered
overhead—but the battle was fought outside town. If it came to
street fighting, the rebels wouldn't push in; they would either
withdraw and wait, or they would rely on agents inside the
city. Then one might hear the crack of rifles and grenades,
rattle of machine guns, sharp discharge of energy beams, and
see corpses in the street. But it ended with a return of official
military government or with the rebels marching in and setting up their own provisional councils. (They were rarely
greeted with cheers and flowers. Nobody knew how the war
would end. But there were words whispered to them, and
they usually got good service.) As nearly as possible, the
average American continued his average life.

Thornberg went on in his own ways. Matilda, as the information center, was working at full blast. If the rebels ever
learned where she was—

Or did they know?

He could not spare much time for his private sabotage, but
he planned it carefully and made every second tell when he

was alone in the control booth. Sam Hall reports, of course—Sam Hall here, Sam Hall there, pulling off this or that incredible stunt. But what did one man, even a superman, count for in these gigantic days? Something else was needed.

Radio and newspapers announced jubilantly that Venus had finally been contacted. The Moon and Mars had fallen, there was only silence from the Jovian satellites, but everything seemed in order on Venus, a few feeble uprisings had been quickly smashed. The powerful Guard units there would be on their way to Earth at once. Troops transports had to orbit most of the way, so it would take a good six weeks before they could arrive, but when they did they would be a powerful reinforcement.

"Looks like you might see your boy soon chief," said Rodney.

"Yes," said Thornberg. "I might."

"Tough fighting." Rodney shook his head. "I'd sure hate to be in it."

If Jack is killed by a rebel gun, when I have aided the rebels' cause—

Sam Hall, reflected Thornberg, had lived a hard life, all violence and enmity and suspicion. Even his wife hadn't trusted him.

*". . . And my Nellie dressed in blue
Says: 'Your trifling days are through.
Now I know that you'll be true. Damn your hide.' "*

Poor Sam Hall. It was no wonder he had killed a man.
Suspicion!

Thornberg stood for a taut moment while an eerie tingle went through him. The police state was founded on suspicion. Nobody could trust anyone else. And with the new fear of psychomasking, and research on that project suspended during the crisis—

Steady, boy, steady. Can't rush into this. Have to plan it out very carefully.

Thornberg punched for the dossiers of key men in the administration, in the military, in Security. He did it in the presence of two assistants, for he thought that his own frequent sessions alone in the control booth were beginning to look funny.

"This is top secret," he warned them, pleased with his own cool manner. He was becoming a regular Machiavelli. "You'll be skinned alive if you mention it to anyone."

Rodney gave him a shrewd glance. "So they're not even sure of their own top men now, are they?" he murmured.

"I've been told to make some checks," snapped Thornberg. "That's all you need to know."

He studied the files for many hours before coming to a decision. Secret observations were, of course, made of everyone from time to time. A cross-check with Matilda showed that the cop who had filed the last report on Lindahl had been killed the next day in a spontaneous and abortive uprising. The report was innocuous: Lindahl had stayed at home, studying some papers; he had been alone in the house except for a bodyguard who had been in another room and not seen him. And Lindahl was Undersecretary of Defense.

Thornberg changed the record. A masked man—stocky, black-haired—had come in and talked for three hours with Lindahl. They had spoken low, so that the cop's ears, outside the window, couldn't catch what was said. The visitor had gone away then, and Lindahl had retired. The cop went back in great excitement and made out his report and gave it to the signalman, who had sent it on to Matilda.

Tough on the signalman, thought Thornberg. *They'll want to know why he didn't tell this to his chief in New Washington, if the observer was killed before doing so. He'll deny every such report, and they'll hypnoquiz him—but they don't trust that method any more!*

His sympathy didn't last long. What counted was having the war over before Jack got here. He re-filed the altered spool and did a little backtracking, shifting the last report of Sam Hall from Salt Lake City to Philadelphia. Make it more plausible. Then, as opportunity permitted, he did some work on other men's records.

He had to wait two haggard days before the next requisition came from Security for a fresh cross-check on Sam Hall. The scanners swept in an intricate pattern, a cog turned over, a tube glowed. Circuits were activated elsewhere, the spool LINDAHL was unrolled before the microprinter inside the machine. Cross-references to that spool ramified in all directions. Thornberg sent the preliminary report back with a query: This matter looked interesting, did they want more information?

They did!

Next day the telecast announced a drastic shakeup in the Department of Defense. Lindahl was not heard from again.

And I, thought Thornberg grimly, *have grabbed a very large tiger by the tail. Now they'll have to check everybody—and I'm one man, trying to keep ahead of the whole Security Police!*

Lindahl is a traitor. How did his chief ever let him get on the board? Secretary Hoheimer was pretty good friends with Lindahl, too. Get Records to cross-check Hoheimer.

What's this? Hoheimer himself! Five years ago, yes, but even so—the records show that he lived in an apartment unit where *Sam Hall* was janitor! Grab Hoheimer! Who'll take his place? General Halliburton? That stupid old fool? Well, at least his dossier is clean. Can't trust those slick characters.

Hoheimer has a brother in Security, general's rank, good detection record. A blind? Who knows? Slap the brother in jail, at least, for the duration. Better check his staff— Central Records show that his chief field agent, Jones, has five days unaccounted for a year ago; he claimed Security secrecy at the time, but a double cross-check shows it wasn't so. Shoot Jones! He has a nephew in the Army, a captain. Pull that unit out of the firing line till we can study it man by man! We've had too many mutinies already.

Lindahl was also a close friend of Benson, in charge of the Tennessee Atomic Ordinance Works. Haul Benson in! Check every man connected with him! No trusting those scientists, they're always blabbling secrets.

The first Hoheimer's son is an industrialist, he owns a petroleum-synthesis plant in Texas. Nab him! His wife is a sister of Leslie, head of the War Production Co-ordination Board. Get Leslie, too. Sure, he's doing a good job, but he may be sending information to the enemy. Or he may just be waiting for the signal to sabotage the whole works. We can't trust *anybody*, I tell you!

What's this? Records relays an Intelligence report that the mayor of Tampa was in cohoots with the rebels. It's marked

"Unreliable, Rumor"—but Tampa *did* surrender without a fight. The mayor's business partner is Gale, who has a cousin in the Army, commanding a robomb base in New Mexico. Check both the Gales, Records— So the cousin was absent four days without filing his where-abouts, was he? Military privileges or not, arrest him and find out where he was!

Attention, Records, attention, Records, urgent. Brigadier John Harmsworth Gale, et cetera, et cetera, et cetera, refused to divulge information required by Security officers, claiming to have been at his base all the time. Can this be an error on your part?

Records to Security Central, ref: et cetera, et cetera. No possibility of error exists except in information received.

To Records, ref: et cetera, et cetera. Gale's story corroborated by three of his officers.

Put that whole base under arrest! Re-check those reports! Who sent them in, anyway?

To Records, ref: et cetera, et cetera. On attempt to arrest entire personnel, Robomb Base 37-J fired on Security detachment and repulsed it. At last reports, Gale was calling for rebel forces fifty miles off to assist him. Details will follow for the files as soon as possible.

So Gale was a traitor! Or was he driven to it by fear? Have Records find out who filed that information about him in the first place. *We can't trust anybody!*

Thornberg was not much surprised when his door was kicked open and the Security squad entered. He had been expecting it for days now. One man can't keep ahead of the game forever. No doubt the accumulated inconsistencies had finally drawn suspicion his way; or perhaps, ironically, the chains of accusation he had forged had by chance led to him; or perhaps Rodney or another person here had decided something was amiss with the chief and lodged a tip.

He felt no blame for whoever it was if that had been the case. The tragedy of civil war was that it turned brother against brother; millions of good and decent men were with the government because they had pledged themselves to be. Mostly, he felt tired.

He looked down the barrel of the gun and then raised

weary eyes to the hard face behind it. "I take it I'm under arrest?" he asked tonelessly.

"Get up!" The face was flat and brutal, there was sadism in the heavy mouth. A typical blackcoat.

June whimpered. The man who held her was twisting her arm behind her back. "Don't do that," said Thornberg. "She's innocent."

"Get up, I said!" The gun thrust closer.

"Don't come near me, either." Thornberg lifted his right hand. It was clenched around a little ball. "See this? It's a gimmick I made. No, not a bomb, just a small radio control. If my hand relaxes, the rubber will expand and pull a switch shut."

The men recoiled a little.

"Let the girl go, I said," repeated Thornberg patiently.

"You surrender first!"

June screamed as the cop twisted harder.

"No," said Thornberg. "This is more important than any one of us. I was prepared, you see. I expect to die. So if I let go of this ball, the radio signal closes a relay and a powerful magnetic field is generated in Matilda—in the records machine. Every record the government has will be wiped clean. I hate to think what your fellows will do to you if you let that happen."

Slowly, the cop released June. She slumped to the floor, crying.

"It's a bluff!" said the man with the gun. There was sweat on his face.

"Try it and find out." Thornberg forced a smile. "I don't care."

"You traitor!"

"And a very effective one, wasn't I? I've got the government turned end for end and upside down. The Army's in an uproar, officers deserting right and left for fear they'll be arrested next. Administration is hog-tied and trembling. Security is chasing its own tail around half a continent. Assassination and betrayal are daily occurrences. Men go over to the rebels in droves. The Army of Liberation is sweeping a demoralized and ineffectual resistance before it everywhere. I predict that New Washington will capitulate within a week."

"And your doing!" Finger tense on the trigger.

"Oh, no. No single man can change history. But I was a rather important factor, yes. Or let's say—Sam Hall was."

"What are you going to do?"

"That depends on you, my friend. If you shoot me, gas me, knock me out, or anything of that sort, my hand will naturally relax. Otherwise, we'll just wait till one side or the other gets tired."

"You're bluffing!" snapped the squad leader.

"You could, of course, have the technicians here check Matilda and see if I'm telling the truth," said Thornberg. "And if I am, you could have them disconnect my electromagnet. Only I warn you, at the first sign of any such operation on your part, I'll let go of this ball. Look in my mouth." He opened it. "A glass vial, full of poison. After I let the ball go, I'll close my teeth together hard. So you see, I have nothing to fear from you."

Bafflement and rage fitted over the faces that watched him. They weren't used to thinking, those men.

"Of course," said Thornberg, "there is one other possibility for you. At last reports, a rebel jet squadron was based not a hundred miles from here. We could call it and have them come and take this place over. That might be to your own advantage, too. There is going to be a day of reckoning with you blackcoats, and my influence could shield you however little you deserve it."

They stared at each other. After a very long while, the squad leader shook his head. "No!"

The man behind him pulled out a gun and shot him in the back.

Thornberg smiled.

"As a matter of fact," he told Sorensen, "I *was* bluffing. All I had was a tennis ball with a few small electrical parts glued on it. Not that it made much difference at that stage, except to me."

"Matilda will be handy for us in mopping up," said Sorensen. "Want to stay on?"

"Sure, at least till my son arrives. That'll be next week."

"You'll be glad to hear we've finally contacted the Guard in space: just a short radio message, but the commander has agreed to obey whatever government is in power when he arrives. That'll be us, so your boy won't have to do any fighting."

There were no words for that. Instead Thornberg said, with a hard-held casualness, "You know, I'm surprised that *you* should have been an undergrounder."

"There were a few of us even in Security," said Sorensen. "We were organized in small cells, spotted throughout the nation, and wangled things so we could hypnoquiz each other." He grimaced. "It wasn't a pleasant job, though. Some of the things I had to do— Well, that's over with now."

He leaned back in his chair, putting his booted feet on the desk. A Liberation uniform was usually pretty sloppy, they didn't worry about spit-and-polish, but he had managed to be immaculate. "There was a certain amount of suspicion about Sam Hall at first," he said. "The song, you know, and other items. My bosses weren't stupid. I got myself detailed to investigate you; a close check-up gave me grounds to suspect you of revolutionary thoughts, so naturally I gave you a clean bill of health. Later on I cooked up this fantasy of the psychological mask and got several high-ranking men worried about it. When you followed my lead on that, I was sure you were on our side." He grinned. "So naturally our army never attacked Matilda!"

"You must have joined your forces quite recently."

"Yeah, I had to scram out of Security during the uproar and witch hunt you started. You almost cost me my life, Thorny, know that? Well worth it, though, just to see those cockroaches busily stepping on each other."

Thornberg leaned gravely over his desk. "I always had to assume you rebels were sincere," he said. "I've never been sure. But now I can check up. Do you intend to destroy Matilda?"

Sorensen nodded. "After we've used her to help us find some people we want rather badly, and to get reorganized—of course. She's too powerful an instrument. It's time to loosen the strings of government."

"Thank you," said Thornberg.

He chuckled after a moment. "And that will be the end of Sam Hall," he said. "He'll go to whatever Valhalla is reserved for the great characters of fiction. I can see him squabbling with Sherlock Holmes and shocking King Arthur and striking up a beautiful friendship with Long John Silver. You know how the ballad ends?'' He sang softly: *''Now up in heaven I dwell, in heaven I dwell—''*

Unfortunately, the conclusion is pretty rugged. Sam Hall never was satisfied.

WATERCLAP

Isaac Asimov

I

Stephen Demerest gazed up at the textured sky. He found the blue opaque and revolting.

He had unwarily looked at the sun, for there was nothing to blank it out automatically, and had snatched his eyes away in panic. He had not been blinded, but his vision swam with after-images. Even the sun was washed out.

Involuntarily, he thought of Ajax's prayer in *Iliad: Make the sky clear, grant us to see with our eyes! Kill us in the light, since it is thy pleasure to kill us!*

Demerest thought: *Kill us in the light . . .*

Kill us in the clear light on the Moon, where the sky is black and soft, where the stars shine brightly, where the cleanliness and purity of vacuum sharpen the sight . . .

—Not in this low-clinging, fuzzy blue.

He shuddered. The shudder was physical and real—it shook his lanky body and he was annoyed. He was going to die. He was sure of it. And not under this blue sky but under black—and no sky.

It was as though in answer to that thought that the ferry pilot, short, swarthy, crisp-haired, came up to him and said, "Ready for the black, Mr. Demerest?"

Demerest nodded. He towered over the other as he did over most of the men of Earth. They were thick, all of them, and took their short, low steps with ease. He himself had to feel

289

his footsteps, guide them through the air—even the impalpable bond that held him to the ground was textured.

"I'm ready," he said. He took a deep breath and deliberately repeated his earlier glance at the sun. It stood low in the morning sky, washed out by dusty air, and he knew it wouldn't blind him. He didn't think he would ever see it again.

He had never seen a bathyscaphe before. He tended to think of it in terms of prototypes—an oblong balloon with a spherical gondola beneath. It was as though he persisted in thinking of spaceflight in terms of tons of fuel spewed backward in fire and an irregular module feeling its way, spiderlike, toward the Lunar surface.

The bathyscaphe was not like the image in his thoughts at all. Under its skin it might still be buoyant bag and gondola but it was all engineered sleekness now.

"My name is Javan," said the ferry pilot, "Omar Javan."

"Javan?"

"Queer name to you? I'm Iranian by descent—Earthman by persuasion. Once you get down there nationalities cease to matter." He grinned and his complexion grew darker against the even whiteness of his teeth. "If you don't mind, we'll be starting in a minute. You'll be my only passenger so I guess you carry weight."

"Yes," said Demerest, dryly. "At least a hundred pounds more than I'm used to."

"You're from the Moon? I thought you had a queer walk on you. I hope it's not uncomfortable."

"It's not exactly comfortable but I manage. We exercise for this."

"Well, come on board." He stood aside and let Demerest walk down the gangplank. "I wouldn't go to the Moon myself."

"You go to Ocean-Deep."

"About fifty times, so far. That's different."

Demerest got on board. The space was cramped but he didn't mind that. The 'scaphe's interior might be a space module's except that it was more—well, textured. There was that word again. The overriding feeling was that mass didn't matter. Mass was held up—it did not have to be hurled up.

* * *

They were still on the surface. The blue sky could be seen greenishly through the clear thick glass.

Javan said, "You don't have to be strapped in. There's no acceleration. Smooth as oil, the whole thing. It won't take long—just about an hour. You can't smoke."

"I don't smoke," said Demerest.

"I hope you don't have claustrophobia."

"Moonmen don't have claustrophobia."

"All that open—"

"Not in our cavern. We live in a—" he groped for the phrase—"Lunar-Deep, a hundred feet deep."

"A hundred feet?" The pilot seemed amused but he didn't smile. "We're slipping down now."

The interior of the gondola was fitted into angles but here and there a section of wall beyond the instruments seemed to be an extension of his arms—his eyes and hands moved over them lightly, almost lovingly.

"We're all checked out," he said, "but I like a last minute lookover—we'll be facing a thousand atmospheres down there." His finger touched a contact, and the round door closed massively inward and pressed against the beveled rim it met. "The higher the pressure, the tighter that will hold. Take your last look at sunlight, Mr. Demerest."

The light still shone through the thick glass of the window. It was wavering now; there was water between the Sun and themselves now.

"The last look?" said Demerest.

Javan snickered. "Not the last look. I mean for the trip. I suppose you've never been on a bathyscaphe before."

"No, I haven't. Have many?"

"Very few," admitted Javan. "But don't worry. It's just an underwater balloon. We've introduced a million improvements since the first bathyscaphe. We're nuclear-powered now and we can move freely by water jet up to certain limits—but cut it down to basics and it's still a spherical gondola under buoyancy tanks. And it's still towed out to sea by a mother ship because it needs what power it carries too badly to waste any on surface travel. Ready?"

The supporting cable of the mother ship flicked away and the bathyscaphe settled lower, then lower still, as seawater fed into the buoyancy tanks. For a few moments, caught in surface currents, it swayed, and then there was nothing. Neither sense of motion nor lack of it. The bathyscaphe sank slowly through a deepening green.

Javan relaxed.

He said, "John Bergen is head of Ocean-Deep. You're going to see him?"

"That's right."

"He's a nice guy. His wife's with him."

"She is?"

"Oh, sure. They have women down there. There's a bunch down there, fifty people. Some stay for months."

Demerest put his fingers on the narrow and nearly invisible seam where door met wall. He took it away and looked at it. He said, "It's oily."

"Silicony, really. The pressure squeezes some out. It's supposed to. Don't worry. Everything's automatic. Everything's fail safe. The first sign of malfunction, any malfunction at all, our ballast is released and up we go."

"You mean nothing's ever happened to these bathyscaphes?"

"What can happen?" The pilot looked sidewise at his passenger. "Once you get too deep for sperm whales, there's nothing that can go wrong."

"Sperm whales?" Demerest's thin face creased in a frown.

"Sure. They dive as deep as half a mile. If they hit a bathyscaphe—well, the walls of the buoyancy chambers aren't particularly strong. They don't have to be, you know. They're open to the sea and when the gasoline, which supplies the buoyancy, compresses, seawater enters."

Darkness became tangible. Demerest found his gaze fastened to the viewport. The inside of the gondola was lighted but it was dark in that window. And the darkness was not the darkness of space—it was thick, solid.

Demerest said sharply, "Let's get this straight, Mr. Javan. You are not equipped to withstand the attack of a sperm whale. Presumably, you are not equipped to withstand the attack of a giant squid. Have there been any actual incidents of that sort?"

"Well, it's like this—"

"No games, please, and don't try ragging the greenhorn. I am asking out of professional curiosity. I am head safety engineer at Luna City and I am asking what precautions this bathyscaphe can take against possible collision with large creatures."

Javan looked embarrassed. He muttered, "Actually there have been no incidents."

"Are any expected? Even as a remote possibility?"

"Anything is remotely possible. But actually sperm whales are too intelligent to monkey with us and giant squid are too shy."

"Can they see us?"

"Yes, of course. We're lit up."

"Do you have floodlights?"

"We're already past the large-animal range but we have them. I'll turn them on for you."

Beyond the black of the window suddenly appeared a snowstorm, inverted, upward-falling. The blackness had come alive with stars in three-dimensional array and all moving upward.

Demerest said, "What's that?"

"Just crud. Organic matter. Small creatures. They float, don't move much, and they catch the light. We're going down past them. They seem to be going up in consequence."

Demerest's sense of perspective adjusted itself and he said, "Aren't we dropping too quickly."

"No, we're not. If we were I could use the nuclear engines if I want to waste power—or I could drop some ballast. I'll be doing that later but for now everything is fine. Relax, Mr. Demerest. The snow thins as we drive and we're not likely to see much in the way of spectacular life forms. There are small angler fish and such but they avoid us."

Demerest said, "How many do you take down at a time?"

"I've had as many as four passengers in this gondola but that's crowded. We can put two bathyscaphes in tandem and carry ten but that's clumsy. What we really need are trains of gondolas, heavier on the nukes—the nuclear engines—and lighter on the buoyancy. Stuff like that is on the drawing board, they tell me. Of course, they've been telling me that for years."

"There are plans for large-scale expansion of Ocean-Deep, then?"

"Sure, why not? We've got cities on the continental shelves—why not on the deep-sea bottom? The way I look at it, Mr. Demerest, where man can go he will go and he should

293

go. The Earth is ours to populate and we will populate it. All we need to make the deep sea habitable are completely maneuverable 'scaphes. The buoyancy chambers slow us, weaken us and complicate the engineering.''

"But they also save you, don't they? If everything went wrong at once the gasoline on board would still float you to the surface. What would do that for you if your nuclear engines went wrong and you had no buoyancy?''

"If it comes to that—you can't expect to eliminate the chances of accident altogether, not even fatal ones.''

"I know that very well," said Demerest feelingly.

Javan stiffened. The tone of his voice changed. "Sorry. Didn't mean anything by that. Tough about that accident.''

Fifteen men and five women had died on the Moon. One of the individuals listed among the "men" had been fourteen years old. It had been pinned down to human failure. What could a head safety engineer say after that?

"Yes," he said.

A pall dropped between the two men, a pall as thick and as turgid as the pressurized sea water outside. How could one allow for panic, distraction and depression all at once? There were the Moon Blues—stupid name—but they struck men at inconvenient times. When the Moon Blues came was not always noticeable but it made men torpid and slow to react.

How many times had a meteorite come along and been averted or smothered or successfully absorbed? How many times had a Moonquake done damage and been held in check? How many times had human failure been backed up and compensated for? How many times had accidents not happened?

But you don't pay off on accidents not happening. Now twenty were dead.

II

Javan said—how many long minutes later?—''There are the lights of Ocean-Deep.''

Demerest could not make them out at first. He didn't know where to look. Luminescent creatures had flicked past the windows twice before—at a distance and with the floodlight

294

off again Demerest had thought them the first sign of Ocean-Deep. Now he saw nothing.

"Down there," said Javan, without pointing. He was busy now, slowing the drop and edging the 'scaphe sideways.

Demerest could hear the distant sighing of the water jets, steam-driven, the steam formed by the heat of momentary bursts of fusion power.

Demerest's thought had a filmy transparency. It did not distract him.

Deuterium is their fuel and it's all around them. Water is their exhaust and it's all around them . . .

Javan was dropping some of his ballast, too, and began a kind of distant chatter.

"The ballast used to be steel pellets and they were dropped by electromagnetic controls. Anywhere up to fifty tons of it were used in each trip. Conservationists worried about spreading rusting steel over the ocean floor—so we switched to metal nodules that are dredged up from the continental shelf. We put a thin layer of iron over them so they can still be electromagnetically handled and the ocean bottom gets nothing that wasn't subocean to begin with. Cheaper, too. But when we get our real nuclear 'scaphes, we won't need ballast at all."

Demerest scarcely heard him. Ocean-Deep could be seen now. Javan had turned on his floodlight and far below was the muddy floor of the Puerto Rican Trench. Resting on that floor like a cluster of equally muddy pearls was the spherical conglomerate of Ocean-Deep.

Each unit was a sphere such as the one in which Demerest was now sinking toward contact—but much larger. As Ocean-Deep expanded—expanded—expanded, new spheres were added.

They're only five and a half miles from home, not a quarter of a million . . .

"How are we going to get through?" asked Demerest.

The 'scaphe had made contact. Demerest had heard the dull sound of metal against metal but for minutes afterward the only sound had been a kind of occasional scrape as Javan bent over his instruments in rapt concentration.

"Don't worry about that," Javan said at last, in belated answer. "There's no problem. The delay now is caused by my having to make sure we fit tightly. An electromagnetic

295

joint holds at every point of a perfect circle—when the instruments read correctly we fit over the entrance door."

"Which then opens?"

"It would if there were air on the other side. But there isn't. There's sea-water and that has to be driven out. Then we enter."

Demerest did not miss this point. He had come here on this, the last day of his life, to give that same life meaning and he intended to miss nothing.

He said, "Why the added step? Why not keep the airlock—if that's what it is—a real airlock and have air in it at all times."

"They tell me it's a matter of safety," said Javan. "Your specialty. The interface has equal pressure on both sides at all times, except when men are moving across. This door is the weakest point of the whole system because it opens and closes—it has joints—it has seams. You know what I mean?"

"I do," murmured Demerest. He saw a logical flaw here and that meant there was a possible chink through which—but later.

He asked, "Why are we waiting now?"

"The lock is being emptied. The water is being forced out."

"By air."

"Hell, no. They can't afford to waste air like that. It would take a thousand atmospheres to empty the chamber of its water and filling the chamber with air at that density, even temporarily, takes more air than they can afford to expend. Steam is what does it."

"Of course. Yes."

Javan said cheerfully, "You heat the water. No pressure in the world can stop water from turning to steam at a temperature of less than 374°C. And the steam forces the sea-water out through a one-way valve."

"Another weak point," said Demerest.

"I suppose so. It's never failed yet. The water in the lock is being pushed out now. When hot steam starts bubbling out the valve the process automatically stops and the lock is full of overheated steam."

"And then?"

"And then we have a whole ocean to cool it with. The temperature drops and the steam condenses. Once that happens ordinary air can be let in at a pressure of one atmosphere. And then the door opens.''

"How long must we wait?"

"Not long. If anything were wrong sirens would be sounding. At least so they say. I never heard one in action.''

Silence held for a few minutes. Then came a sudden sharp clap and a simultaneous jerk.

Javan said, "Sorry, I should have warned you. I'm so used to it, I forgot. When the door opens a thousand atmospheres of pressure on the other side forces us hard against the metal of Ocean-Deep. No electromagnetic force can hold us hard enough to prevent that last hundredth-of-an-inch slam.''

Demerest unclenched his fist and released his breath.

He asked, "Is everything all right?"

"The walls didn't crack, if that's what you mean. It sounds like doom, though, doesn't it. It sounds even worse when I leave and the airlock fills up again. Be prepared for that.''

But Demerest was suddenly weary.

Let's get on with it—I don't want to drag it out.

He asked, "Do we go through now?"

"We go through."

The opening in the 'scaphe wall was round and small—even smaller than the one through which they had originally entered. Javan went through it sinuously, muttering that it always made him feel like a cork in a bottle.

Demerest had not smiled since he entered the 'scaphe. Nor did he really smile now but a corner of his mouth quirked at the thought that a skinny Moonman would have no trouble.

He went through also, feeling Javan's hands firmly at his waist, helping him through.

Javan said, "It's dark in here. No point in introducing an additional weakness by wiring for lighting. But that's why flashlights were invented.''

Demerest found himself on a perforated walk, its stainless metallic surface gleaming dully. And through the perforations he could make out the wavering surface of water.

He said, "The chamber hasn't been emptied."

"You can't do any better, Mr. Demerest. If you're going to use steam to empty it you're left with that steam. And to get the pressures necessary to do the emptying that steam must be compressed to about one third the density of liquid water. When it condenses the chamber remains one third full of water—but it's water at just one-atmosphere pressure. Come on, Mr. Demerest.''

John Bergen's face wasn't entirely unknown to Demerest. Recognition was immediate. Bergen, as head of Ocean-Deep for nearly a decade now, was a familiar face on the TV screens of Earth—just as the leaders of Luna City had become familiar.

Demerest had seen the head of Ocean-Deep both flat and in three-dimensions, in black-and-white and in color. Seeing him in life added little.

Like Javan, Bergen was short and thickset, opposite in structure in the traditional Lunar pattern of physiology. He was fairer than Javan by a good deal and his face was noticeably asymmetric, though his somewhat thick nose leaned a little to the right.

He was not handsome. No Moonman would think he was. But then Bergen smiled and a sunniness emanated from him as he held out a large hand.

Demerest extended his own thin one, steeling himself for a hard grip that did not come. Bergen shook hands and let go.

He said, ''I'm glad you're here. We don't have much in the way of luxury, nothing that will make our hospitality stand out. We can't even declare a holiday in your honor but the spirit is there. Welcome!''

''Thank you,'' said Demerest softly.

He remained unsmiling. He was facing the enemy and he knew it. Surely Bergen must know it also. His smile was hypocrisy.

And at that moment a clang like metal against metal sounded deafeningly and the chamber shuddered. Demerest leaped back and staggered against the wall.

Bergen did not budge.

He said quietly, ''That was the bathyscaphe unhitching and the waterclap of the airlock filing. Javan ought to have warned you.''

Demerest panted and tried to make his racing heart slow.

''Javan did warn me. But I was still caught by surprise.''

Bergen said, ''Well, it won't happen again for a while. We don't often have visitors, you know. We're not equipped for it and fight off all kinds of big wheels who think a trip down here would be good for their careers. Politicans and all kinds, chiefly. Your case is different, of course."

Is it?

Demerest wondered. It had been hard enough to get permission to make the trip down. His superiors back at Luna City had not approved in the first place and had scouted the idea that a diplomatic interchange would be of any use ("diplomatic interchange" was what they had called it). And when he had overridden them. he had run into Ocean-Deep's reluctance to receive him.

Persistence alone had made his present visit possible.

Bergen said, "I suppose you have your junketing problems on Luna City, too?"

Demerest said, "Your average politician isn't as anxious to make a half-million-mile roundtrip as he is to make a ten-mile one."

"I can see that," agreed Bergen, "and it's more expensive out to the Moon, of course. In a way, this is the first meeting of inner and outer space. No ocean man has ever gone to the Moon as far as I know and you're the first Moonman to visit a subsea station of any kind. No Moonman has even been to one of the settlements on the continental shelf."

"It's a historic meeting, then," said Demerest and tried to keep the sarcasm out of his voice.

If any leaked through, Bergen showed no sign.

He rolled up his sleeves as though to emphasize his attitude of informality (or the fact that they were very busy, so that there would be little time for visitors?) and asked, "Do you want coffee? I assume you've eaten. Would you like to rest before I show you around? Do you want to wash up, for that matter, as they say euphemistically?"

For a moment curiosity stirred in Demerest; yet not entirely aimless curiosity. Everything involving the interface of Ocean-Deep with the outside world could be of importance.

He spoke carefully.

"How are sanitary facilities handled here?"

"It's cycled mostly—as on the Moon, I imagine. We can eject if we want to or have to. Man has a bad record of fouling the environment but as the only deep-sea station, what we eject does no perceptible damage. Adds organic matter."

He laughed.

Demerest filed that away, too. Matter was ejected. Ejection

299

mechanisms existed. Their workings might be of interest and he, as a safety engineer, had a right to exhibit interest.

"Actually," he said, "I'm comfortable at the moment. If you're busy—"

"That's all right. We're always busy but I'm the least so—if you see what I mean. Suppose I show you around. We've got over fifty units here, each as big as this one, some bigger."

Demerest looked about. He saw angles everywhere but beyond the furnishings and equipment he detected signs of the inevitable spherical outer wall. Fifty units!

"Built up," went on Bergen, "over a generation of effort. The unit we're standing in is actually the oldest and there's been some talk of demolishing and replacing it. Some of the men say we're ready for second-generation units but I'm not sure. It would be expensive—everything's expensive down here—and getting money out of the Planetary Project Council is always a depressing experience."

Demerest felt his nostrils flare involuntarily and a spasm of anger shot through him. It was a thrust surely. Luna City's miserable record with the PPC must be well known to Bergen.

But Bergen went on, unnoticing.

"I'm a traditionalist, too—just a little bit. This is the first deep-sea unit ever constructed. The first two people to remain overnight on the floor of an ocean trench slept here with nothing except a miserable portable fusion unit to work the escape hatch. I mean the airlock—we called it the escape hatch to begin with—and just enough controls for the purpose. Reguera and Tremont—those were the men. They never made a second trip to the bottom, either; stayed topside forever after. Well, they served their purpose and both are dead now. And here we are with fifty people and with six months as the usual tour of duty. I've spent only two weeks topside in the last year and a half."

He motioned vigorously to Demerest to follow him, slid open a door that moved evenly into a recess to give access to the next unit. Demerest paused to examine the opening. He could detect no seams between the adjacent units.

Bergen took note and said, "When we add on units they're welded under pressure into the equivalent of a single piece of metal and then reinforced. We can't take chances as I'm sure you understand. I have been given to understand that you're the chief safe—''

Demerest cut him off.

"Yes," he said. "We on the Moon admire your safety record.''

Bergen shrugged.

"We've been lucky. Our sympathy, by the way, on the rotten break you fellows had. I mean that fatal—''

Demerest cut him off again.

"Yes.''

Bergen, the Moonman decided, was either a naturally voluble man or else was eager to drown him in words and get rid of him.

"The units," said Bergen, "are arranged in a highly branched chain—three dimensional actually. We have a map we can show you if you're interested. Most of the end units represent living-sleeping quarters. For privacy, you know. The working units tend to be corridors as well, which is one of the embarrassments of having to live down here." He gestured.

"This is our library, part of it, anyway. Not big. But it holds our records on carefully indexed and computed microfilm, so that for its kind it's not only the biggest in the world but the best and the only. And we have a special computer designed to handle the references to meet our needs exactly. It collects, selects, coordinates, weighs, then gives us the gist. We have another library, too, book films and even some printed volumes. But that's for amusement.''

A voice broke in on Bergen's cheerful flow of talk.

"John? May I interrupt?''

Demerest started—the voice had come from behind him.

Bergen said, "Annette—I was going to get you. This is Stephen Demerest of Luna City. Mr. Demerest, may I introduce my wife, Annette.''

Demerest had turned.

He said stiffly, a little mechanically, "I'm pleased to meet you, Mrs. Bergen.''

But he was staring at her waistline.

Annette Bergen seemed in her early thirties. Her brown hair was combed simply and she wore no makeup. Attractive, not beautiful, Demerest noted vaguely. But his eyes kept returning to that waistline.

She shrugged.

301

"Yes, I'm pregnant, Mr. Demerest. I'm due in about two months."

"Pardon me," Demerest muttered. "So rude of me—I did not—"

His voice faded. He felt as though the blow had been a physical one. He hadn't expected women, though he didn't know why. He knew there would have to be women in Ocean-Deep. And the ferry pilot had said Bergen's wife was with him.

Annette Bergen remained silent and Demerest stammered when he asked, "How many women are there in Ocean-Deep, Mr. Bergen?"

"Nine at the moment," said Bergen. "All wives. We look forward to a time when we can have the normal ratio of one to one, but we still need workers and researchers primarily and unless women have important qualifications of some sort—"

"They all have important qualifications of some sort, dear," said Mrs. Bergen. "You could keep the men for longer duty if—"

"My wife," said Bergen, laughing, "is a convinced feminist but is not above using sex as an excuse to enforce equality. I keep telling her that that is the feminine way of doing it and not the feminist way, and she keeps saying that's why she's pregnant. You think it's love, sex mania, yearning for motherhood? Nothing of the sort. She's going to have a baby down here to make a philosophical point."

Annette said coolly, "Why not? Either this is going to be home for humanity or it isn't going to be. If it is, we're going to have babies here, that's all. I want a baby born in Ocean-Deep. There are babies born in Luna City, aren't there, Mr. Demerest?"

Demerest took a deep breath. "I was born in Luna City, Mrs. Bergen."

"And well she knew it," muttered Bergen.

"And you are in your late twenties, I think?" she said.

"I am twenty-nine," said Demerest.

"And well she knew that, too," said Bergen with a short laugh. "You can bet she looked up all possible data on you when she heard you were coming."

"That is quite beside the point," said Annette. "The point

302

is that for twenty-nine years at least children have been born in Luna City and no children have been born in Ocean-Deep.''

"Luna City, my dear," said Bergen, "is longer established. It is over half a century old—we are not yet twenty.''

"Twenty years is quite enough. It takes a baby nine months.''

Demerest interposed. "Are there any children in Ocean-Deep?''

"No," said Berg. "No. Some day, though.''

"In two months, anyway," said Annette Bergen, positively.

III

The tension grew inside Demerest and when they returned to the unit in which he had first met Bergen he was glad to sit down and accept a cup of coffee.

"We'll eat soon," said Bergen matter-of-factly. "I hope you don't mind sitting here, meanwhile. As the prime unit this place isn't used for much except, of course, for the reception of vessels, an item I don't expect will interrupt us for a while. We can talk if you wish.''

"I do wish," said Demerest.

"I hope I'm welcome to join in," said Annette.

Demerest looked at her doubtfully but Bergen said to him, "You'll have to agree. She's fascinated by you and by Moonmen generally. She thinks they're—uh—you're a new breed. I think that when she's quite through being a Deepwoman she wants to be a Moonwoman.''

"I just want a word in edgewise, John, and when I get that in, I'd like to hear what Mr. Demerest has to say. What do you think of us, Mr. Demerest?''

Demerest said cautiously, "I've asked to come here, Mrs. Bergen, because I'm a safety engineer. Ocean-Deep has an enviable safety record.''

"Not one fatality in almost twenty years," said Bergen cheerfully. "Only one death by accident in the C-shelf settlements and none in transit by either sub or 'scaphe. I wish I could say, though, that this was the result of wisdom and care on our part. We do our best, of course, but the breaks have been with us—''

"John," said Annette, "I really wish you'd let Mr. Demerest speak."

"As a safety engineer," said Demerest, "I can't afford to believe in luck and breaks. We cannot stop Moonquakes or large meteorites out at Luna City but we are designed to minimize the effects even of those. There are no excuses or there should be none for human failure. We have not avoided failure on Luna City—our record recently has been—" his voice dropped—"bad. While humans are imperfect, as we all know, machinery should be designed to take that imperfection into account. We lost twenty men and women needlessly."

"I know. Still, Luna City has a population of nearly one thousand, doesn't it? Your survival isn't in danger."

"The people on Luna City number nine hundred and seventy-two, including myself—but our survival is in danger. We depend on Earth for essentials. That need not always be so. It wouldn't be so right now if the Planetary Project Council could resist the temptation toward pygmy economies—"

"There, at least, Mr. Demerest," said Bergen, "we see eye to eye. We are not self-supporting, either, and we could be. What's more, we can't grow much beyond our present level unless nuclear 'scaphes are built. As long as we are bound to the buoyancy principle we are limited. Transportation between Deep and Top is slow—slow for men, slower still for material and supplies. I've been pushing, Mr. Demerest, for—"

"Yes, and you'll be getting it now, Mr. Bergen, won't you?"

"I hope so. But what makes you so sure?"

"Mr. Bergen, let's not play around. You know very well that Earth is committed to spending a fixed amount of money on expansion projects—on programs designed to expand the human habitat—and that it is not a terribly large amount. Earth's population is not going to lavish resources in an effort to expand either outer space or inner space if it thinks this will cut into the comfort and convenience of the prime habitat of humans—the land surface of Earth."

Annette broke in.

"You make Earthmen sound callous, Mr. Demerest, and that's unfair. It's only human, isn't it, to want to be secure? Earth is overpopulated and is only slowly reversing the havoc inflicted on the planet by the mad Twentieth. Surely man's

304

original home must come first, ahead of either Luna City or Ocean-Deep. Heavens, Ocean-Deep is almost home to me— but I don't want to see it flourish at the expense of Earth's land.''

"It's not an either-or, Mrs. Bergen," said Demerest earnestly. "If the ocean and outer space are firmly, honestly and intelligently exploited, it can only rebound to Earth's benefit. A small investment will be lost but a large one will redeem itself with profit.''

Bergen held up his hand. "Yes, I know. You don't have to argue with me on that point. You'd be trying to convert the converted. Come, let's eat. I tell you what. We'll eat here. If you'll stay with us overnight, or several days for that matter— you're quite welcome—there will be ample time to meet everybody. Perhaps you'd rather take it easy for a while, though.''

"Much rather," said Demerest. "Actually, I want to stay here. I would like to ask, by the way, why I met so few people when we went through the units.''

"No mystery," said Bergen, genially. "At any given time, some fifteen of our men are asleep and perhaps fifteen more are watching films or playing chess, or, if their wives are with them—''

"Yes, John," said Annette.

"—and it's customary not to disturb them. The quarters are constricted and what privacy a man can have is cherished. A few are out at sea—three right now, I think. That leaves a dozen or so at work in here and you met them.''

"I'll get lunch," said Annette, rising.

She smiled and stepped through the door, which closed automatically behind her.

Bergen looked after her. "That's a concession. She's playing woman for your sake. Ordinarily, it would be just as likely for me to get the lunch. The choice is not defined by sex but by the striking of random lightning.''

Demerest said, "The doors between units, it seems to me, are of dangerously limited strength.''

"Are they?''

"If an accident happened and one unit were punctured—''

Bergen smiled.

"No meteorites down here.''

305

"Oh yes, wrong word. If there were a leak of any sort, for any reason, could a unit or a group of units be sealed off against the full pressure of the ocean?"

"You mean, the way Luna City can have its component units automatically sealed off in case of meteorite puncture in order to limit damage to a single unit."

"Yes," said Demerest, with a faint bitterness. "As did not happen recently."

"In theory we could do that—but the chances of accident are much less down here. As I said, there are no meteorites and, what's more, there are no currents to speak of. Even an earthquake centered immediately below us would not be damaging since we make no fixed or solid contact with the ground beneath and are cushioned by the ocean itself against the shocks. So we can afford to gamble on no massive influx."

"Yet if one happened?"

"We could be helpless. You see, it is not so easy to seal off component units here. On the Moon there is a pressure differential of just one atmosphere—one atmosphere inside and the zero atmosphere of vacuum outside. A thin seal is enough. Here at Ocean-Deep the pressure differential is roughly a thousand atmospheres. To secure absolute safety against that differential would take a great deal of money and you know what you said about getting money out of PPC. So we gamble. And so far we've been lucky."

"And we haven't," said Demerest.

Bergen looked uncomfortable but Annette distracted both men by coming in with lunch at this moment.

She said, "I hope, Mr. Demerest, that you're prepared for Spartan fare. All our food in Ocean-Deep is prepackaged and requires only heating. We specialize in blandness and nonsurprise and the nonsurprise of the day is a bland chicken a la king, with carrots, boiled potatoes, a piece of something that looks like a brownie for dessert and, of course, all the coffee you can drink."

Demerest rose to take his tray and tried to smile.

"It sounds very like Moon fare, Mrs. Bergen, and I was brought up on that. We grow our own microorganismic food. It is patriotic to eat it but not particularly enjoyable. We hope to keep improving it, though."

"I'm sure you will improve it."

Demerest said, as he ate with a slow and methodical chewing, "I hate to ride my specialty but how secure are you against mishaps in your airlock entry?"

"It is the weakest point of Ocean-Deep," said Bergen. He had finished eating and was nearly through with his first cup of coffee. "But there's got to be an interface, right? The entry is as automatic as we can make it and as fail safe. Number one: there has to be contact at every point about the outer lock before the fusion generator begins to heat the water within the lock. What's more, the contact has to be metallic and of a metal with just the magnetic permeability we use on our 'scaphes. Presumably, a rock or some mythical deep-sea monster might drop down and make contact at just the right places—but if so, nothing happens. Then, too, the outer door doesn't open until the steam has pushed the water out and then condensed—in other words, not till both pressure and temperature have dropped below a certain point. At the moment the outer door begins to open a relatively slight increase in internal press, as by water entry, will close it again."

Demerest said, "But once men have passed through the lock, the inner door closes behind them and sea-water must be allowed into the lock again. Can you do that gradually against the full pressure of the ocean outside?"

"No." Bergen smiled. "It doesn't pay to fight the ocean too hard. You have to roll with the punch. We slow it down to about one tenth of free entry but even so it comes in like a rifle shot—louder, a thunderclap—or waterclap, if you prefer. The inner door can hold it, though, and it is not subjected to the strain very often. You heard the waterclap when we first met—when Javan's 'scaphe took off again. Remember?"

"I remember," said Demerest. "But here is something I don't understand. You keep the lock filled with ocean at high pressure at all times to keep the outer door without strain. But that keeps the inner door at full strain. Somewhere there has to be strain."

"Yes, indeed. But if the outer door, with a thousand-atmosphere differential on its two sides, breaks down, the full ocean in all its millions of cubic miles tries to enter and that would be the end of all. If the inner door is the one under strain and it gives, then it will be messy indeed—but the only water that enters Ocean-Deep will be the limited quantity in the lock and its pressure will drop at once. We will have plenty of time for repair—the outer door will certainly hold a long time."

"But if both go at once?"

"We are through." Bergen shrugged. "I need not tell you that neither absolute certainty nor absolute safety exist. You have to live with some risk and the chance of double and simultaneous failure is so microscopically small that it can be lived with easily."

"If all your mechanical contrivances fail—"

"They fail safe," said Bergen stubbornly.

Demerest nodded. He finished the last of his chicken. Mrs. Bergen was already beginning to clean up.

"You'll pardon my questions, Mr. Bergen, I hope."

"You're welcome to ask. I wasn't informed, actually, as to the precise nature of your mission here. 'Fact-finding' is a weasel phrase. However, I assume there is keen distress on the Moon over the recent disaster and as safety engineer you rightly feel the responsibility of correcting whatever short-comings exist and would be interesting in learning, if possible, from the system used in Ocean-Deep."

"Exactly. But, see here, if all your automatic contrivances fail safe for some reason, for any reason, you would be alive but all your escape mechanisms would be sealed permanently shut. You would be trapped inside Ocean-Deep and would exchange a slow death for a fast one, that's all."

"It's not likely to happen but we'd hope we could make repairs before our air supply gave out. Besides we do have a manual backup system."

"Oh?"

"Certainly. When Ocean-Deep was first established and this was the only unit—the one we're sitting in now—manual controls were all we had. That was unsafe, if you like. There they are, right behind you—covered with friable plastic."

"In emergency, break glass," muttered Demerest, inspecting the covered setup.

"Pardon me?"

"Just a phrase commonly used in ancient fire-fighting systems. Well, do the manuals still work or has the system been covered with your friable plastic for twenty years to the point where it has all decayed into uselessness with no one noticing."

"Not at all. It's periodically checked—as all our equipment

308

is. That's not my job but I know it is done. If any electrical or electronic circuit is out of its normal working condition, lights flash, signals sound, everything happens but a nuclear blast. You know, Mr. Demerest, we are as curious about Luna City as you are about Ocean-Deep. I presume you would be willing to invite one of our young men—"

"How about a young woman?" interposed Annette at once.

"I am sure you mean yourself, dear," said Bergen. "And I can only answer that you are determined to have a baby here and to keep it here for a period of time after birth—and that effectively eliminates you from consideration."

Demerest said stiffly, "We hope you will send men to Luna City. We are anxious to have you understand our problems."

"Yes, a mutual exchange of problems and of weeping on each other's shoulders might be of great comfort to all. For instance, you have one advantage on Luna City that I wish we could have. With low gravity and a low pressure-differential you can make your caverns take on any irregular and angular fashion that appeals to your esthetic sense or is required for convenience. Down here we're restricted to the sphere—at least for the foreseeable future—and our designers develop a hatred for the spherical that surpasses belief. Actually it isn't funny. It breaks them down. They eventually resign rather than continue to work spherically." Bergen shook his head and leaned his chair back against a microfilm cabinet. "You know, when William Beebe built the first deep-sea chamber in history in the nineteen-thirties—it was just a gondola suspended from a mother ship by a half-mile cable. It had no buoyancy chambers and no engines—and if the cable broke, good night. Only it never did. Anyway, what was I saying? Oh, when Beebe built his first deep-sea chamber he was going to make it cylindrical; you know, so a man would fit in it comfortably. After all, a man is essentially a tall, skinny cylinder. However, a friend of his argued him out of that and into a sphere on the very sensible grounds that a sphere would resist pressure more efficiently than any other possible shape."

Demerest considered that briefly but made no comment. He returned to the earlier topic.

"We would particularly like someone from Ocean-Deep," he said, "to visit Luna City because it might lead to a great enough understanding of the need, on Ocean-Deep's part, for a course of action that might involve considering self-sacrifice."

309

"Oh?" Bergen's chair came down on all four legs. "How's that?"

"Ocean-Deep is a marvelous achievement—I wish to detract nothing from that. I can see where it will become greater still, a wonder of the world. Still—"

"Still?"

"Still the oceans are only a part of the Earth—a major part but only a part. The deep sea is only part of the ocean. It is inner space indeed—it works inward, narrowing constantly to a point."

"I think," broke in Annette, looking rather grim, "that you're about to make a comparison with Luna City."

"Indeed I am," said Demerest. "Luna City represents outer space, widening to infinity. There is nowhere to go down here in the long run—everywhere to go out there."

"We don't judge by size and volume alone, Mr. Demerest," said Bergen. "The ocean is only a small part of Earth, true, but for that very reason it is intimately connected with over five billion human beings. Ocean-Deep is experimental but the settlements on the Continental Shelf already deserve the name of cities. Ocean-Deep offers mankind the chance of exploiting the whole planet—"

"Of polluting the whole planet," broke in Demerest, excitedly. "Of raping it, of ending it. The concentration of human effort to Earth itself is unhealthy and even fatal if it isn't balanced by a turning outward to the frontier."

"There is nothing at the frontier," said Annette, snapping out the words. "The Moon is dead. All the other worlds out there are dead. If there are live worlds among the stars, light-years away, they can't be reached. The ocean is living."

"The Moon is living, too, Mrs. Bergen. And if Ocean-Deep allows it, the Moon will become an independent world. We Moonmen will then see to it that other worlds are reached and made alive and, if mankind has the patience, we will reach the stars. We! We! It is only Moonmen, used to space, used to a world in a cavern, used to an engineered environment, who could endure life in a spaceship that may have to travel centuries to reach the stars."

"Wait, wait, Demerest," said Bergen, holding up his hand. "Back up. What do you mean—if Ocean-Deep allows it? What have we to do with it?"

"You're competing with us, Mr. Bergen. The Planetary Project Commission will swing your way, give you more, give us less, because in the short term, as your wife says, the ocean is alive and the Moon, except for a thousand men, is not—because you are a half-dozen miles away and we a quarter of a million—because you can be reached in an hour and we only in three days. And because you have an ideal safety record and we have had—misfortunes."

"The last, surely, is trivial. Accidents can happen at any time, anywhere."

"But the trivial can be used," said Demerest angrily. "It can be made to manipulate emotions. To people who don't see the purpose and the importance of space exploration the death of Moonmen in accidents is proof enough that the Moon is dangerous, that its colonization is a useless fantasy. Why not? It's their excuse for saving money and they can then salve their conscience by investing part of it in Ocean-Deep instead. That's why I said the accident on the Moon had threatened the survival of Luna City even though it killed only twenty people out of nearly a thousand."

"I don't accept your argument. There has been enough money for both for a score of years."

"Not enough money. That's exactly it. Not enough to make the Moon self-supporting in all these years—and then they use that lack of self-support against us. Not enough to make Ocean-Deep self-supporting either—but now they can give you enough if they cut us out altogether."

"Do you think that will happen?"

"I'm almost sure it will—unless Ocean-Deep shows a statesmanlike concern for man's future."

"How?"

"By refusing to accept additional funds. By not competing with Luna City. By putting the good of the whole race ahead of self-interest."

"Surely you don't expect us to dismantle—"

"You won't have to. Don't you see? Join us in explaining that Luna City is essential, that space exploration is the hope of mankind—that you will wait, retrench if necessary."

Bergen looked at his wife and raised his eyebrows. She shook her head angrily.

Bergen said, "You have a rather romantic view of the PPC, I think. Even if I made noble, self-sacrificing speeches,

311

who's to say they would listen. There's a great deal more involved in the matter of Ocean-Deep than my opinion and my statements. There are economic considerations and public feeling. Why don't you relax, Mr. Demerest? Luna City won't come to an end. You'll receive funds. I'm sure of it. I tell you I'm sure of it. Now let's break this up—''

"No, I've got to convince you one way or another that I'm serious. If necessary, Ocean-Deep must come to a halt unless the PPC can supply ample funds for both.''

Bergen said, "Is this some sort of official mission, Mr. Demerest? Are you speaking for Luna City officially or just for yourself?''

"Just for myself—but maybe that's enough, Mr. Bergen,'' said Demerest.

"I don't think it is. I'm sorry, but this is turning out to be unpleasant. I suggest that after all you had better return topside on the first available 'scaphe.''

"Not yet! Not yet!'' Demerest looked about wildly, then rose unsteadily and put his back against the wall. He was a little too tall for the room and he became conscious of life receding. One more step and he would have gone too far to back out.

IV

He had told them back on the Moon that there would be no use talking, no use negotiating. It was dog-eat-dog for the available funds and Luna City's destiny must not be aborted—not for Ocean-Deep, not for Earth—no, not for all of Earth, since mankind and the Universe came even before the Earth. Man must outgrow his womb.

Demerest could hear his own ragged breathing and the inner turmoil of his whirling thoughts. The other two were looking at him with what seemed concern.

Annette rose and said, "Are you ill, Mr. Demerest?''

"I am not ill. Sit down. I'm a safety engineer and I want to teach you about safety. Sit down, Mrs. Bergen.''

"Sit down, Annette,'' said Bergen. "I'll take care of him.''

He rose and took a step forward.

312

But Demerest said, "No. Don't you move either. I have something right here. You're too naive concerning human dangers, Mr. Bergen. You guard against the sea and against mechanical failure and you don't search your human visitors, do you? I have a weapon, Bergen."

Now that it was out and he had taken the final step from which there was no returning—for he was now dead, whatever he did—he was quite calm.

Annette said, "Oh, John," and grasped her husband's arm. Bergen stepped in front of her.

"A weapon? Is that what that thing is? Now slowly, Demerest, slowly. There's nothing to get hot over. If you want to talk we'll talk. What is that?"

"Nothing dramatic. A portable laser beam."

"But what do you want to do with it?"

"Destroy Ocean-Deep."

"But you can't, Demerest. You know you can't. You can pack only so much energy into your fist and any laser you can hold can't pump enough heat to penetrate the walls."

"I know that. This packs more kick than you think. It's Moonmade and there are some advantages to manufacturing an energy unit in a vacuum—but you're right. Even so it's designed only for small jobs and requires frequent recharging. So I don't intend to try to cut through a foot-plus of alloy steel. But it will do the job indirectly. For one thing it will keep you two quiet. There's enough energy in my fist to kill two people."

"You wouldn't kill us," said Bergen evenly. "You have no reason."

"If by that," said Demerest, "you imply that I am an unreasoning being to be somehow made to understand my madness, forget it. I have every reason to kill you and I will kill you. By laser beam if I have to, though I would rather not."

"What good will killing us do you? Make me understand. Is it that I have refused to sacrifice Ocean-Deep funds? I couldn't do anything else. I'm not really the one to make the decision. And your killing me won't help force the decision in your direction, will it? In fact, quite the contrary. If a Moonman is a murderer, how will that reflect on Luna City? Consider human emotions on Earth."

An edge of shrillness was in Annette's voice as she joined

in: "Don't you see there will be people who will say that solar radiation on the Moon has dangerous effects? That the genetic engineering which has reorganized your bones and muscles has affected mental stability? Consider the word 'lunatic,' Mr. Demerest. Men once believed the Moon brought madness."

"I am not mad, Mrs. Bergen."

"It doesn't matter," said Bergen, following his wife's lead smoothly. "Men will say that you were—that all Moonmen are—and Luna City will be closed down and the Moon itself closed to all further exploration, perhaps forever. Is that what you want?"

"That might happen if they thought I killed you—but they won't. It will be an accident."

With his left elbow, Demerest broke the plastic that covered the manual controls.

"I know units of this sort," he said. "I know exactly how they work. Logically, breaking that plastic should set up a warning flash—after all, it might be broken by accident—and then someone would be here to investigate or, better yet, the controls should lock until deliberately released to make sure the break was not merely accidental." He paused, then said, "But I'm sure no one will come, that no warning has taken place. Your manual system is not fail safe because in your heart you were sure it would never be used."

"What do you plan to do?" said Bergen.

He was tense and Demerest watched his knees carefully.

He said, "If you try to jump toward me I'll shoot at once—and then keep right on with what I'm doing."

"I think maybe you're giving me nothing to lose."

"You'll lose time. Let me go right on without interference and you'll have some minutes to keep on talking. You may even be able to talk me out of it. There's my proposal. Don't interfere with me and I will give you your chance to argue."

"But what do you plan to do?"

"This," said Demerest. He did not have to look. His left hand snaked out and closed a contact. "The fusion unit will now pump heat into the airlock and the steam will empty it. It will take a few minutes. When it's done, I'm sure one of those little red-glass buttons will light."

"Are you going to—"

314

Demerest said, "Why do you ask? You know that I must be intending, having gone this far, to flood Ocean-Deep?"

"But why? Damn it, why?"

"Because it will be marked down as an accident. Because your safety record will be spoiled. Because it will be a complete catastrophe and will wipe you out. The PPC will then turn from you and the glamor of Ocean-Deep will be gone. We will get the funds. We will continue. If I could bring this to pass in some other way I would—but the needs of Luna City are the needs of mankind and those are paramount."

"You will die, too," Annette managed to say.

"Of course. Once I am forced to do something like this— would I want to live? I'm not a murderer."

"But you will be. If you flood this unit you will flood all of Ocean Deep and kill everyone in it—and doom those who are out in their subs to slower death. Fifty men and women—an unborn child—"

"That is not my fault," said Demerest, in clear pain. "I did not expect to find a pregnant woman here but now that I have—I can't stop because of it."

"But you must stop," said Bergen. "Your plan won't work unless what happens can be shown to be an accident. They'll find you with a beam-emitter in your hand and with the manual controls clearly tampered with. Do you think they won't deduce the truth?"

Demerest was feeling very tired.

"Mr. Bergen, you sound desperate. Listen—when the outer door opens, water under a thousand atmospheres of pressure will enter. It will be a massive battering ram that will destroy and mangle everything in its path. The walls of the Ocean-Deep units will remain but everything inside will be twisted beyond recognition. Human beings will be mangled into shredded tissue and splintered bone and death will be instantaneous and unfelt. Even if I were to burn you to death with the laser there'd be nothing left to show it had been done, so I won't hesitate, you see. This manual unit will be smashed anyway— anything I can do will be erased by the water."

"But the beam-emitter; the laser gun. Even damaged, it will be recognizable," said Annette.

"We use such things on the Moon, Mrs. Bergen. It is a common tool; it is the optical analog of a jackknife. I could

315

kill you with a jackknife, you know, but one would not deduce that a man carrying a jackknife—or even holding one with the blade open—was necessarily planning murder. He might be whittling. Besides, a Moon-made laser is not a projectile gun. It doesn't have to withstand an internal explosion. It is made of thin metal, mechanically weak. After it is smashed by the waterclap I doubt that it will make much sense as an object.''

Demerest did not have to think to make these statements. He had worked them out within himself through months of self-debate.

"In fact," he went on, "how will the investigators ever know what happened in here? They will send 'scaphes down to inspect what is left of Ocean-Deep but how can they get inside without first pumping out the water. They will, in effect, have to build a new Ocean-Deep and that would take—how long? Perhaps, given public reluctance to throw good money after bad, they might never do it at all and content themselves with dropping a laurel wreath on the dead walls of the dead Ocean-Deep.''

Bergen said, "The men on Luna City will know what you have done. Surely one of them will have a conscience. The truth will be known.''

"One truth," said Demerest, "is that I am not a fool. No one on Luna City knows what I planned to do or will suspect what I have done. They sent me down here to negotiate cooperation on the matter of financial grants. I was to argue and nothing more. There's not even a laser beam-emitter missing up there. I put this one together myself out of scrapped parts. And it works. I've tested it.''

Annette said slowly, "You haven't thought it through. Do you know what you're doing?''

"I've thought it through. I know what I'm doing. And I know also that you are both conscious of the lit signal. I'm aware of it. The airlock is empty and time's up, I'm afraid.''

Rapidly, holding his weapon tensely high, he closed another contact. A circular part of the unit wall cracked into a thin crescent and rolled smoothly away.

Out of the corner of his eye Demerest saw the gaping darkness, but he did not look. A dank salt vapor issued from it—a queer odor of dead steam. He even imagined he could

316

hear the flopping sound of the gathered water at the bottom of the lock.

He said, "The outer door ought to be frozen shut now if the manual unit had been rationally designed. With the inner door open, nothing ought to make the outer door budge. I suspect, though, that the manuals were put together too quickly at first for proper precautions to have been taken. And if I need further evidence that I'm guessing correctly you wouldn't be sitting there so tensely. The outer door will open. I need to touch one more contact and the waterclap will come. We will feel nothing."

Annette said, "Don't push it just yet. I have one more thing to say. You said we would have time to persuade you."

"While the water was being pushed out."

"Just let me say this. A minute. A minute. I said you didn't know what you were doing. You don't. You're destroying the space program, the space program. There's more to space than space."

Her voice had grown shrill.

"What are you talking about? Make sense or I'll end it all. I'm tired. I'm frightened. I want it over."

Annette said, "You're not in the inner councils of the PPC. Neither is my husband. But I am. Do you think because I am a woman that I'm secondary here. I'm not. You, Mr. Demerest, have your eyes fixed on Luna City only. My husband has his fixed on Ocean-Deep. Neither of you know anything. Where do you expect to go, Mr. Demerest, if you had all the money you wanted? Mars? The asteroids? The satellites of the gas giants? These are all small worlds—all dry surfaces under a blank sky. It may be generations before we are ready to try for the stars and till then we'd have only pygmy real estate. Is that your ambition? My husband's is no better. He dreams of pushing man's habitat over the ocean floor, a surface not much larger in the last analysis than the surface of the Moon and the other pygmy worlds. We of the PPC, on the other hand, want more than either of you—and if you push that button, mankind's greatest dream will come to nothing."

Demerest found himself interested despite himself but he said, "You're just babbling."

It was possible, he knew, that somehow they had warned others in Ocean-Deep, that any moment someone would come to interrupt, someone would try to shoot him down. He was,

317

however, staring at the only opening and he had only to close one contact without even looking—a second's movement.

Annette said, "I'm not babbling. You know it took more than rocket ships to colonize the Moon. To make a successful colony possible men had to be altered genetically and adjusted to low-gravity. You are a product of such genetic engineering."

"Well?"

"And might not genetic engineering also help adjust men to greater gravitational pull? What is the largest solar planet?"

"Jupiter."

"Yes, Jupiter. Eleven times the diameter of the Earth—forty times the diameter of the Moon. A surface a hundred and twenty times that of the Earth in area—sixteen hundred times that of the Moon. Conditions so different from anything we can encounter anywhere on the worlds the size of Earth or less that any scientist of any persuasion would give half his life to observe them at close range."

"But Jupiter is an impossible target."

"Indeed?" said Annette and even managed a faint smile. "As impossible as the Moon? As impossible as flying? Why is it impossible? Genetic engineering could design men with stronger and denser bones, stronger and more compact muscles. The same principles that enclose Luna City against the vacuum and Ocean-Deep against the sea can also enclose the future Jupiter-Deep against its ammoniated surroundings."

"The gravitational field—"

"Can be negotiated by nuclear ships now on the drawing board. You don't know that but I do."

"We're not even sure about the depth of the atmosphere. The pressures—"

"The pressures! Mr. Demerest, look about you. Why do you suppose Ocean-Deep was really built? To exploit the ocean? The settlements on the Continental Shelf are doing that quite adequately. To gain knowledge of the deep-sea bottom? We could do that by 'scaphe easily and we could then have spared the hundred billion dollars invested in Ocean-Deep.

"Don't you see, Mr. Demerest, that Ocean-Deep must mean something more than that? The purpose of Ocean-Deep is to devise the ultimate vessels and mechanisms that will explore and colonize Jupiter. Look about you and see the

318

beginnings of a Jovian environment—the closest approach to it we can achieve on Earth. It is only a faint image—but it's a beginning. Destroy this, Mr. Demerest, and you destroy any hope for Jupiter. On the other hand, let us live and we will, together, penetrate and settle the brightest jewel of the solar system. And long before we can reach the limits of Jupiter we'll be ready for the stars, for the Earth-type planets circling them—and the Jupiter-type planets, too. Luna City won't be abandoned because both are necessary for this ultimate aim."

For the moment Demerest had altogether forgotten about that last button.

He said, "Nobody on Luna City has heard of this."

"You haven't. There are those on Luna City who know. If you had told them of your plan of destruction they would have stopped you. Naturally, we can't make this common knowledge and only a few people anywhere can know. The public supports only with difficulty the planetary projects now in progress. If the PPC is parsimonious it is because public opinion limits its generosity. What do you suppose public opinion would say if they thought we were aiming toward Jupiter? What a super-boondoggle that would be in their eyes. But we continue and whatever money we can save and make use of we place in the various facets of Project Big World."

"Project Big World?"

"Yes," said Annette. "You know now and I have committed a serious security breach. But it doesn't matter, does it? Since we're all dead and since the project is, too."

"Wait now, Mrs. Bergen."

"If you change your mind now—don't think you can ever talk about Project Big World. That would end the project just as effectively as destruction here would. And it would end both your career and mine. It might end Luna City and Ocean-Deep, too—so now that you know, maybe it makes no difference anyway. You might just as well push that button."

Demerest's brow was furrowed and his eyes burned with anguish.

"I don't know—"

Bergen gathered for the sudden jump as Demerest's tense alertness wavered into uncertain introspection but Annette grasped her husband's sleeve.

A timeless interval that might have been ten seconds long followed and then Demerest held out his laser.

"Take it," he said. "I'll consider myself under arrest."

"You can't be arrested," said Annette, "without the whole story coming out." She took the laser and gave it to Bergen. "It will be enough that you return to Luna City and keep silent. Till then we will keep you under guard."

Bergen was at the manual controls. The inner door slid shut and after that came the thunderous waterclap of the water returning into the lock.

Husband and wife were alone again. They had not dared to say a word until Demerest was safely put to sleep under the watchful eyes of two men detailed for the purpose. The unexpected waterclap had aroused everybody and a sharply bowdlerized account of the incident had been given out.

The manual controls were now locked off and Bergen said, "From this moment on the manuals will have to be adjusted to fail safe. Visitors will have to be searched."

"Oh, John," said Annette. "I think people are insane. There we were, facing death for us and for Ocean-Deep, just the end of everything. And I kept thinking—I must keep calm, I mustn't have a miscarriage."

"You kept calm all right. You were magnificent. I mean, Project Big Planet! I never conceived of such a thing but, by Jove, it's an attractive thought. Wonderful!"

"I'm sorry I had to say all that, John. It was all a fake, of course. I made it up. Demerest wanted me to make something up, really. He wasn't a killer or destroyer—he was, according to his own overheated lights, a patriot. And I suppose he was telling himself he must destroy in order to save—a common enough view among the small-minded. But he said he would give us time to talk him out of it and I think he was praying we would manage to do so. He wanted us to think of something that would give him the excuse and I gave it to him. I'm sorry I had to fool you, John."

"You didn't fool me."

"I didn't?"

"How could you? I knew you weren't a member of PPC."

"What made you so sure of that? Because I'm a woman?"

"Not at all. Because I'm a member, Annette, and that's confidential. And, if you don't mind, I will begin a move to initiate exactly what you suggested—Project Big World."

"Well!" Annette considered that and, slowly, smiled. "Well! Women do have their uses."

"Something," said Bergen, smiling also, "I have never denied."

VERY PROPER CHARLIES

Dean Ing

". . . I found fear a mean, overrated motive; no
deterrent and, though a stimulant, a poisonous stimulant whose every injection served to consume more
of the system . . ."
　　　—T. E. Lawrence, *Seven Pillars Of Wisdom*

At the first buzz of the phone, Everett decided to ignore it.
He'd planned his selfish Saturday for weeks, determined that
official business would positively not deflect him from one
last autumn day in the high country. Born a hundred and fifty
years too late to be a mountain man, Maurice Everett lived
his fantasy whenever he could—briefly by necessity, alone by
choice. It wasn't until the third buzz, as he struggled into a
turtleneck, that he recognized the buzzer tone of his unlisted
number. Only his informants, and probably the FBI, had
access to this tenuous link between newsmen and the federal
government.

Everett spoke briefly, listened long, and promptly forgot
the Rockies that lay in sere majesty on his horizon in Colorado Springs. "You're already en route, then," he said,
thrusting the earpiece between head and shoulder as he tugged
on heavy socks. "But why the Shoshone-Beardsley intersection? Doesn't the parade go through the center of Pueblo?" A

pause. "Sure; handy for you and me, and the tactical squads too. Those mothers must be awfully confident." A final pause. "Maybe fifty minutes if I drive the superskate, but I haven't a CB rig in it. My problem anyhow; and thanks, Leo. Really."

Once before he hit U.S. route eighty-seven and twice after, Everett was noticed by Colorado Highway Patrol cruisers. He kept the tiny Mini-Cooper in racing tune though he rarely had time for his infatuation with the little freeway raptor. The big cruisers invariably saw his honorary highway patrol decals, fell back to check his plates, then let him continue fleeing south at nearly three kilometers a minute. A Federal Communications Commissioner was supposed to be circumspect, and Maurice Everett had been criticized for his maverick ways; but he used special privilege only in the line of duty. Mavericks had settled the West, and they might yet settle the electromagnetic spectrum.

Everett took the second offramp at Pueblo as if the curve were a personal affront, then eased off as he entered boulevard traffic. According to the newsman's tip, he would be at the intersection in time for the terrorist demonstration. Briefly, Everett was reminded of Charlie George, who had sat near him at—what was it, the Associated Press convention? The comedian had opined, in his laconic drawl, "TV will still play whore to any pimp with a machine pistol. We're the tush of terrorism." Everett had laughed at the remedy Charlie had proposed. But then, you were supposed to laugh at Charlie.

Everett spotted vehicles of two different networks as he neared the target area, and forgot about TV comedians. The van, he overtook; the big Honda bike overtook them both, more by maneuverability than speed. *The van gets you status, the bike gets you there first,* he mused. Electronic newsgathering equipment was so compact, newspeople could do ENG with two-wheeled vehicles though the Honda was too small to carry powerful transmisson equipment.

Everett kept the van in his rearview and when it stopped, he found a niche for the Mini. From that point on, he was in enemy country.

He hesitated a moment in choosing decoy emblems. His was a camouflage problem: he wanted to avoid a make by newsmen, and a few knew Maury Everett on sight. But he also wanted to avoid getting himself killed. He donned wrap-around dark glasses for the first criterion, and an armband over his rough leather jacket to meet the second. Terrorists knew who their friends were; the armband said simply, PRESS.

Following a National Broadcasting Network cameraman on foot, Everett wished he too had a lightweight videotape rig—even a dummy Micam would do. It had been years since a terrorist had deliberately downed a media man, and while Everett's informant could not predict details of the demonstration, it was prudent to suspect gunfire.

The boulevard was lined with spectators enjoying that foolish marvel of autumn anachronism, a homecoming parade. Everett could not pause to enjoy the brassy polychrome of assembled high school bands which high-stepped, a bit wearily by now, between wheeled floats. He focused instead on the newsmen. One, a bulky Portacam slung over his back, clambered atop a marquee for a better view. Two others from competing stations took up positions nearer the intersection, almost a block from Everett. The comforting mass of a stone pillar drew Maury Everett into its shadow. He could see a thousand carefree people laughing, pointing, children darting at stray float decorations, cheering the discordances in the music of these devoted amateurs. Was the tip a false alarm? If not, Everett thought, this happy ambiance might be shattered within minutes. And he, one of the famed FCC Seven Dwarfs, was powerless.

Watching nubile majorettes cavort despite a chill breeze on naked thighs, Maurice Everett faced his personal dilemma for the hundredth time since his appointment. Newsmen dubbed their solution "disinvolvement." You have a job and you assume its risks. If you are government, you stay in your bureau and off the toes of other bureaucrats. If you are business, and most explicitly media newsgathering, you rise or fall chiefly on informal contacts and you do not interfere with news. You do not divulge sources for two reasons. The legal reason is backed by the Supreme Court, and the selfish reason is that fingering a contact is professional suicide. If Everett somehow interrupted the impending show after its careful leakage to TV newsmen by some unknown malcontent, his sources would evaporate instantly, permanently. And his primary utility lay in knowing the actual nuts and bolts of ENG, newsgathering by compact electronic gear. Freedom of reportage, even when irresponsible, was a fundamental func-

324

tion of media. Theorists called it surveillance: Maurice Everett called it hellish.

The Portacam man had shifted position to a second-landing fire escape next to the synagogue. A thorough pro, he was taking shots of the parade so that whatever happened, some sort of story might be salvaged. Everett saw that all the floats featured the same general theme: athletics. Lumbering beyond him was a float honoring the 1980 Olympics winners, a crudely animated statue labeled "Uri" waving three gold medals. That would be Yossuf Uri, Israel's surprise middle-distance winner. The hulking mannikin beside it represented the Soviet weights man, whose heart had later failed under the demands placed upon it by too many kilos of steroid-induced muscle tissue.

The casual connection of death with the display goaded Everett's mind toward a causal inference, but he froze for too many seconds. A synagogue on the corner, an Israeli hero approaching it, and a vague tipoff by a terrorist. No matter how little the newsman knew, Maurice Everett clawed his way to a terrible conclusion.

Later, he could regain an uneasy sleep whenever he awoke streaming with the perspiration of guilt; for he *had* vaulted the horns of his dilemma. "Stop," he bawled, and knew his voice was hopelessly lost in the general clamor. Everett sprinted between bystanders, knocked a beldame sprawling, caromed into the side of another float. He was still on his feet, still shouting for attention, when the great torso of Yossuf Uri came abreast of the synagogue and disappeared in a blinding flash.

How Jewish can you get? The stable manager fingered the crisp twenty-dollar bill, smiling down at the signature. "I've saddled up a perty spirited mare, Mr. Rabbinowitz," he said, taking in the wistful smile, the olive skin, the dark hypnotic eyes. "Sure that's what you want?"

"Precisely," the little man pronounced his favorite word, and paced out to the corral. He mounted the mare quickly, gracefully, and cantered her out along the rim of the arroyo. The stableman watched him, puzzled, certain that he had seen Rabbinowitz before. Suddenly, as the figure dipped below his horizon in the afternoon sun, the stableman laughed. Meticulous silken dress and manner made the illusion even better, a youthful cosmetic version of a man more character than actor. "George Raft," he murmured, satisfied.

The mare was no filly, but she had Arabian lines. The rider held her at a gallop, imagining that he was in Iraq and not California. He savored the earthy scents and rhythms of this, a small pleasure he could justify in terms of security. No one, he felt, would bug a bridle trail. Presently he came in view of San Jose rooftops and at that moment—precisely—knew that he was being watched.

He made an elaborate show of patting the mare's neck, leaning first to one side and then the other, scanning—without seeming to—every mass of shrub cover within reasonable pistol-shot. Nothing. His heels pressured the mare. She was already plunging ahead when he heard the girl cry out behind him. He had passed her before sensing her? Most disturbing.

He wheeled the mare and returned, erasing his frownlines for the girl. She was clapping now, a jet-haired comely thing. "Ayyy, *que guapo*," she laughed aloud, showing a pink tongue between dazzling teeth. The gold cross at her throat, the peasant blouse: a latina.

He misjudged her in two ways: "You like the horse?"

"The combination," she answered, growing more serious. Her hands were clearly in sight, fingernails trimmed close, and he did not see how she could hide a significant weapon while showing so much youthful flesh. But still— Now she stroked the mare's nose, looking up at him. He liked that. "Like music," she said, and waited.

The formula should not have surprised him so. "Music by Sedaka?"

"Imsh'Allah," she said. How convenient that a popular composer's name should also, in several related tongues, mean *gift*. Well, this one would give.

He complimented her on the deception, dismounting, walking with her to a tree-shaded declivity. The mare tethered, they sat. "Curious," he began, "how my appetites are whetted by a job well done." They spoke English and then Arabic, softly, warmly, and when he remounted it was not on the mare. Presently they drew apart.

The girl combed her hair with impatient fingers. "You have seen videotapes of the morning's work?"

"Very early morning," he yawned. "I nearly missed my

flight to San Jose. But no, I only heard a bulletin. Did we get suitable coverage?''

She nodded gravely. ''Hakim will be pleased.''

''Of that, I am certain.'' Their great bituminous eyes locked for a moment before, toying with her, he continued. ''But Hakim must have a media center. You are prepared?''

''Prepared? When I hailed you,'' she riposted, ''did you or did you not think I was a local chicana?''

Echoes of repugnance clashed like scimitars behind his quiet words. ''You are clever, you are nubile. I speak of greater things than—'' and paused after using a grossly sexist Bedouin term for their recent communion. He saw her corneas expand. Pleasure or pain? ''I must know whether you have the site, the men, and the equipment I required.''

''I cannot say. My instructions are to provide only for the leader himself. He may not arrive. Or he may.'' She shrugged.

''You *are* clever. But you are prepared for Hakim Arif?''

She said simply, ''We are Fat'ah.''

''And who am I?'' He removed his left small finger at the last joint, replaced the prosthetic tip while she regained her composure. ''I signed your instructions, 'Rabbinowitz.' ''

''I—sire, you are Hakim Arif,'' she murmured, seeming to grow smaller.

''So I am. And angry at continued small talk, and impatient for my media. We have another demonstration to plan, depending on the results we see from today's work.''

She quickly explained the route to the site she had prepared, naming each landmark three times. He did not remind her of his long familiarity with travel in the United States, but listened with critical approval. It was best to arrive after sunset, she said, which also gave her time to alert the others.

''Two of the three knew you before,'' she added, and named them. The third had been recruited in Damascus after Hakim Arif's last sojourn there, but Arif had read impressive reports.

''They will serve,'' he said, rising to collect the somnolent mare some distance away. He flung over his shoulder, ''Better perhaps than a woman who deflects my questions.'' She could not see him smile. He turned the mare and trotted her back to the girl. Again he stared down from a commanding height, stern, refractory: the visage of Fat'ah. ''Soon, then,'' he said, eyeing the sun.

"Sire," she stammered. Her body was controlled; only her voice trembled. "I did not know you. Your face is known to few in Fat'ah."

"Or out of it, as Allah is merciful," he rejoined. "Perhaps I shall be merciful too."

"If God wills," she said in Arabic.

"Or perhaps—" he waited until she met his eyes again, "I shall beat you."

"Perhaps you will," she said, not flinching.

Hakim Arif flogged the mare mercilessly up the trail, enjoying the experience, enjoying the memory of the girl's eyes. They had dilated again at his threat. Under a westering sun he sped back to the stable. He was thinking: *spawn of pain. We Fat'ah are the children of El Aurans after all . . .*

Two hours later he found the Fat'ah site, temporary as it must be but better situated than he expected. The bungalow commanded a clear view of the San Jose skyline and, on three sides, open pastures beyond carbine range. On the fourth side a swath of scrub oak followed a brook so near the house that he could almost leap from its porch into thick cover. Two men patrolled the greenery, protecting Hakim Arif's escape route. Hakim was pleased. He let his distant smiles and nods say so. Let those idiots in the PLO show all the ersatz egalitarianism they liked: Fat'ah, born of Fat'h, born of Al Fat'h, born of injustice, was effective because he, Hakim Arif, was so.

But despite himself: "Ah," he breathed jubilantly, surveying the media center the girl had assembled. Four small TV sets half-encircled a desk which also faced an expanse of window. Four multiband radios were ranged to one side. All sets had earplugs. Three telephones were within reach. Note pads, blank card files, colored pens, a typewriter, a minivid recorder and two audio cassette machines filled most of the working space. The squat table underfoot was almost hidden by stacks of directories; Bay Area numbers, Los Angeles numbers, Washington numbers precisely as he had specified. Hakim knew the danger of heavy dependence on help supplied by telephone companies. There were ways to trace one from his patterns of inquiry. Unless, of course, one mastered the system.

The girl stood near, gnawing a full underlip, watching him

328

assess the media center. "Rashid and Moh'med," he rapped suddenly. "Are they prepared to spend the night as pickets?"

"Each after his way," she murmured.

"And the husky one, the Panamanian?"

"En route to Santa Cruz. A powerful parafoil requires skill. He knows his work; when he secures telephones he will call." She hesitated, then went on. "Yet he does not know how to address you in person." Her inflection said that she shared the man's concern.

The Fat'ah leader had not risen this far by allowing cynicism to show in his voice. "Do we fight for democracy? Is my name Hakim? Then Hakim it is!"

He began to play with his new equipment, not waiting for the latino's call. It was nearly an hour before the news shows, but the girl flicked a finger toward the minivid. He fumbled it into operation and saw that she had edited earlier newscasts into a videotape festival of the Pueblo horror. Hakim Arif settled back into a chair, notepad ready, and watched his favorite show.

Like a dry bearing in his head, a thin pure tone pierced Everett's awareness. "When will I quit hearing that whistle," he demanded.

The white smock shrugged. "It goes with the injury," the doctor replied. "With luck, another day or so. No, don't try to sit up, you'll disturb the tubes. Follow orders and you'll be up in a few days, Mr. Everett. You're a big healthy animal; give your system a chance."

Everett glanced out the window of the Denver hospital. The fine cloudless day was lost to him, and he to the Rockies. "Hell of a day to be down."

"But a very good day to be alive," the doctor insisted. "Eleven others weren't so lucky, including a whole handful of TV people. You have no idea what an outcry the networks are making over those five particular fatalities."

Thanks to the drugs, Everett did not feel the bruised kidney, hairline fracture, and other modest rearrangements of his middle-aged anatomy. During his thirty-six hours of coma, the Denver people had done very well by him. But there were things they could not do. Curbing impatience he said, "Let's assume I stay put, don't hassle my nurse, and take lunch in

329

approved fashion,'' glancing at the intravenous feeding apparatus.

The surgeon folded his arms. "If," he prompted.

"If I can trade the nurse for a staff member in here to—"

"Contraindicated. We're trying to excite regrowth around that flap torn in your tympanum, Mr. Everett. At your age, a blown eardrum is tough to repair. The nurse stays, the FCC goes."

"My left ear's okay, though. And even a felon gets *one* phone call."

After a judicious pause: "You've got it." He spoke to the nurse for a moment, stopped with his hand on the door. "We're starting you on solid foods, provided you make that one call and no more. *We* can haggle too. Agreed?"

"Agreed." Maury Everett watched the door swing shut, thinking of channels. FCC staff to network honchos? A mutual friend? Both too slow, and always loss of fidelity when the message was indirect. The hell with it. "Nurse, I want you to call NBN Hollywood and get one man on the line. I want nobody else, I want him with all possible dispatch, and it might help if you tell him Commissioner Everett is ready to lay the tush of terrorism."

She waited starchily, receiver in hand. "You're to avoid excitement. Is this an obscene call?"

"Everybody's a comedian," he grunted. "But the one I want is Charlie George."

Everett never knew exactly when the whistle died in his cranium. It was gone when he donned street clothes five days later, and that was enough. He was shaky, and wore an earplug on the right side, but he was functioning again. A staff member packed his bag because there was no wife to do it, and brought the taxi because he wasn't going home. The office would simply have to improvise until he had recuperated in Palm Springs—a tender negotiation with militant medics, based on his promise to relax with friends at the California resort city. He did not tell them it would be his first visit, nor that he had met only one of those friends.

Everett did not feel the Boeing clear the runway, so deep was he into a sheaf of clippings collated by his staff. A dozen dissident groups claimed so called credit for the Pueblo blast, each carefully outlining its reasons, each hopeful that its motive would be touted. As usual, the commissioner noted with a shake of the massive head, our media system accommodated them all.

Only one group was armed with guilty knowledge: Fat'ah, led by the wraithlike Iraqi, Hakim Arif. Shortly after the blast, a United Press International office took a singular call from Pueblo, Colorado. It spoke in softly accented English of a microwave transmitter hidden in a tennis ball on a synagogue roof, and of galvanized nails embedded in the explosive. These details were easily checked by UPI. They were chillingly authentic. The caller went on to demand that Fat'ah, the only true believers in Palestinian justice, be given a base of operations for its glorious fight against Jewish tyranny. Ousted from Jordan, then ostensibly from Syria, Fat'ah was simply too militant even for its friends. It had nowhere to go. It chose, therefore, to go to the American people. Its channel of choice was a hideous explosion which left nearly a dozen dead and three dozen injured, half a world away from its avowed enemy.

When the caller began to repeat his spiel, police were already tracing the call. The message was on its fourth rerun when a breathless assault team stormed a Pueblo motel room. Not quite abandoned, the room contained a modified telephone answering device which, upon receiving a coded incoming call, had made its own prearranged call with an endless tape cartridge. The device was quite cunning: when an officer disgustedly jerked the telephone receiver away, it blew his arm off.

According to the *Newsweek* bio, Fat'ah's leader was a meticulous planner. When Hakim Arif was twelve, U.S. and Israeli agencies had only recently aided Iran in designing its secret police organ, SAVAK. SAVAK was still naive and Hakim already subtle when, during a visit to Iran by the youth and his father, security elements paid a lethal call on the elder Arif. The boy evaporated at the first hint of trouble, taking with him most of the emeralds his father had earmarked for bribes in Iran. SAVAK knew a good joke when it was played on them, and praised the boy's foresight. They would have preferred their praise to be posthumous; in the Middle East, drollery tends to be obscure.

Hakim took his secondary schooling in English-speaking private academies under the benevolent gaze of relatives in Syria, who never did discover where the jewels were. He also came under sporadic crossfires between Arab guerrillas and their Israeli counterparts, and knew where his sympathies lay. The magazine hinted that young Arif may have taken additional coursework in a school of socialist persuasion near Leningrad. How he got into an Ivy League school was anybody's guess, but a thumbnail-sized emerald was one of the better suppositions.

Trained in finance, media, and pragmatism, Hakim Arif again disappeared into the Near East—but not before leaving indelible memories with a few acquaintances. He quoted the Koran and T. E. Lawrence. He was not exactly averse to carrying large amounts of cash on his person. He won a ridiculously small wager by chopping off the end of a finger. And he was preternaturally shy of cameras.

Arif and Fat'ah were mutually magnetized by desire and bitterness, but not even Interpol knew how Arif came to lead a guerrilla band who rarely saw their leader. Thwarted by security forces in Turkey, England, Syria, and Jordan, Fat'ah was evidently fingering the tassels at the end of its tether. Perhaps Arif had sold his last jewel; the fact was clear that the goals of Fat'ah, reachable by sufficient injections of cash into the proper systems, were elusive.

Everett paused in his reading to gaze wistfully at California's mighty Sierra range that stretched away below the Boeing. With the dusting of early snow on sawtooth massifs, it looked as cold and hard down there as the heart of Hakim Arif. What sort of egotist did it take to shorten his pinkie on an absurd wager, yet avoid photographers? A very special one, to say the least. Everett resumed reading.

The conservative Los Angeles *Times* devoted much space to a strained parallel between law enforcement agencies and Keystone Kops. The smash hit of the new TV season was a Saturday night talk show in which a battery of NBN hosts deigned to speak, live, only to callers who were already in the news. Soon after midnight on the Saturday of the Pueblo disaster, a caller identified himself as Hakim Arif. He demanded instant air time. A reigning cinema queen was discussing oral sex at 12:17:25; and found herself staring into a dead phone at 12:17:30. Arif was speaking.

Incredibly, the Iraqi responded to questions; prerecording was out of the question. While Arif launched into the plight of Palestinian Arabs and the need for funding to continue the

332

heroic struggle, network officials feverishly collaborated with police, the FBI, and the telephone company. Arif was obviously watching the show, to judge by his critique of one host's silent mugging.

Arif used no terms objectionable enough to require bleeping; he merely promised to repeat the Pueblo entertainment in larger and larger gatherings until, in its vast wisdom and power, the United States of America found a haven for Fat'ah. And oh, yes, there was one condition: the country of the haven must adjoin Israel.

While voiceprint experts established the identical patterns of the Pueblo and NBN show voices, a co-host asked if Arif realized that he was asking for World War Three. Arif, chuckling, replied that he trusted the superpowers to avoid over-response to Israeli banditry. As Arif chuckled, a Lockheed vehicle lifted vertically from Moffett Field in California for nearby Santa Cruz. Its hushed rotors carried four case-hardened gentlemen over the coast range in minutes to a parking lot two hundred yards from the Santa Cruz telephone booth which comprised one end of the telephone connection. Police cordoned the area and awaited the fight.

There was no fight. There was only another clever device in the booth, relaying the conversation by radio. Its sensors noted the approach of the bomb squad to the booth with the "out of order" sign, and suddenly there was no telephone, no device, and no booth; there was only concussion. The *Times* surmised that Arif could have been within thirty miles of the booth. No one, including Arif, knew that the Lockheed assault craft had passed directly over his bungalow in San Jose.

Arif's next call passed through another booth in Capitola, near Santa Cruz, to CBS. He was in good spirits. Government agencies were in overdrive. No one was in a position to corral even one arm of Fat'ah and when Arif was good and ready, he closed down his media center. By the time his bungalow had been discovered, Arif had a two-day start. That is, said the private report compiled for Everett, if it had been Arif. Fingerprint plants were common gambits in disinformation games. The Iraqi's MO varied, but he always knew how to use available channels, including the illegal importation of some of his devices from sources among the Quebecois. There was more, and Everett forced himself to read it. Behind the old-fashioned reading glasses, his eyes ached. Presently he closed them and tried to ignore the faintly resurgent whistle in his head.

Two flights and a limousine later, Maurice Everett declined help with his suitcase and carried its reassuring bulk in Palm Springs heat toward a vacant lot. At least it looked vacant, until he strode through a slot in the sloping grassy berm and realized that this comedian knew how to use money.

The berm surrounded a sunken terrace open to the sun. Around the terrace and below ground level lay the translucent walls of Charlie George's hideaway. It reminded Everett of a buried doughnut, its hole a glass-faced atrium yawning into the sky, slanted solar panels more attraction than excrescence. It was thoroughly unlike the monuments erected nearby: logical, insulated, understated. Already, Everett liked Charlie George better for making sense even when he was not compelled to.

The commissioner was nonplussed for an instant by the man who met him at the door like a sodbuster's valet. Denims tucked into beflapped, rundown boots; suspenders over an ancient cotton work shirt; a stubble of beard. Yet there was no mistaking the loosejointed frame or the shock of corntassel hair over bushy brows, familiar to anyone who watched prime time. Beneath the strong nose was a mouth legendary for its mobility, from slackjawed idiocy to prudish scorn. Everett realized with a start that it was speaking.

"You wanted it informal," said Charlie George, and ushered Everett to a guest room.

They talked easily while Everett changed into his scruffies. "I haven't sounded out the rest of the Commission," Everett admitted, wincing as he adjusted his pullover. "McConnell's a reasonable sort, though, and I'll lay it out for him so he'll know you're serious about separating TV from terrorism. These panel talks with the AP and UPI sure haven't excited him—or me. I like your scenario better."

The comedian kept his eyes sociably averted as Everett donned soft leather trousers. "We've been batting out details for an hour."

"Who's we?"

Charlie leaned his head toward the window facing the atrium. "No net veepees, just a couple of pivotal people I told you about.'' He led Everett through a kitchen saturated with musks of tortilla and taco sauce, into sunlight toward a buzz of voices in a hidden corner of the atrium.

They found two men seated, dividing their attention between sketch pads and bottles of Mexican beer. The smaller one made a point of rising; the taller, a show of not rising. ''This is our friend in the feds.'' Charlie placed a gentle hand on Everett's shoulder. ''Maury Everett: Rhone Althouse here, and Dahl D'Este there.''

Althouse wore faded jeans and Gucci loafers. Only the footgear and a stunning Hopi necklace belied his undergraduate appearance. He was closely-knit and tanned, and his handshake had the solidity of a park statue. It was hard to believe that this pup was a media theorist who had deserted academia for a meteoric rise in gag writing. ''I hope you guys move quicker separately than you do together,'' he said to Everett, with the barest suggestion of a wink.

Everett smiled at this threadbare gibe. FCC decisions never came quickly enough for the industry it regulated. ''Don't bet on it,'' he replied. ''I'm still pretty rickety today.''

D'Este, doodling furiously on a mammoth sketch pad, stopped to gaze at Everett with real interest. ''I forgot,'' he said in a caramel baritone, ''you were the star of the Pueblo thing. Perhaps you'll tell me about it.'' His tone implied, *some other time, just we two*.

Everett accepted a Moctezuma from Charlie George and eased his broad back into a lawn chair. ''All I know, literally, is what I've read since I woke up. I hope to learn a lot more from you three, in hopes it doesn't happen again.''

''Ah,'' said D'Este, beaming. His elegant slender height was covered by a one-piece burgundy velour jumpsuit which, Everett hazarded, might have been tailored expressly for this event. Dahl D'Este affected tight dark curls, his tan was by Max Factor. He hugged the sketch pad to him and stood to claim his audience. ''Well then, the story thus far—'' He paused as though for their host's permission and seemed gratified. ''Charlie has this—*wild* idea that he can ring in a new era of comedy. Instead of avoiding the issue of terrorism in comedy, and believe me, luv, we *do*, he wants to create a fabulous character.''

''A whole raft of 'em,'' the comedian put in. Everett

nodded; he knew the general idea but would not rob D'Este of his moment.

"Charlie has seduced the best talents he could find to plan graphics, that's me, and situations, that's Rhone. Of course, that's ironic, because Charlie is NBN, Rhone is an ABC captive, and for the nonce I'm doing CBS sets. I don't know how Charlie beguiled his old *enfant terrible*," he smirked at Althouse, "to cross traditional lines in this madness." Everett, who knew it had been the other way around, kept silent. "As for me, I couldn't resist the challenge."

"Or the retainer," Althouse drawled in a murmur designed to carry.

The splendid D'Este ignored him. "While Charlie and Rhone brainstormed their little skits, I've been inventing Charlie's logo for the new character. A cartoon of the sort of loser who—how did you put it, Rhone?"

"Rates no respect," the younger man supplied. "If he tried dial-a-prayer he'd get three minutes of raucous laughter."

"Well, my logo will peer out at the world from Charlie's backdrop like a malediction. I really ought to sign it. Behold, a very proper Charlie!" With this fanfare, Dahl D'Este spun the sketch pad around and awaited reactions.

Everett was thankful that he didn't need to surrogate approval. The sketch was, somehow, the face of Charlie George as an enraged Goya might have seen him. Yet the surface similarity was unimportant. Splashed across the paper in hard sunlight was a stylized symbol of repellence. The head and shoulders of a vicious imbecile faced them as it would glare out at untold millions of viewers. The face was vacuously grinning, and gripped a fused stick of dynamite in its teeth. The fuse was too short, and it was lit. In redundant arrogance, just exactly out of scale as though reaching toward the viewer, was a time-dishonored hand gesture: the stink-finger salute.

Laughter welled up from the group and geysered. Althouse raised his beer in obeisance.

"Ah—about the monodigital scorn," Charlie wavered, darting a look at Everett.

Althouse held his hands open, cradling an invisible medicine ball. "C'mon, Charlie, it's perfect." He took risked a sidelong glance at the FCC man. "And for its public use, our precedent was a recent vice president."

336

D'Este: "Of which net?"

"Of the United bloody States," cried Althouse in mock exasperation. "Yes it's naughty, and yes it's safe!"

"I'm inclined to agree," said Everett, "if it's done by a questionable character for a crucial effect."

D'Este leaned the sketch against the solar panels. "A proper Charlie," he repeated, then looked up quickly. "Did you know that British slang for a total loser is a veddy propah Chahlie?"

"Poor Dahl," sighed Althouse. "Did you know we picked the name 'Charlie George' in 1975 because semantic differential surveys told me they were the outstanding loser names in the English-speaking world? Bertie is good, Ollie is better; but Charlie George is the people's choice!"

"Thanks for nothing," Everett chortled. "I always wondered why citizens band jargon for the FCC was 'Uncle Charlie.'" Althouse affected surprise, but not chagrin.

Charlie looked out into the middle-distance of his past. "I wasn't too keen to change my name from Byron Krause to Charlie George," he mused, "until I thought about that poem."

Althouse saw curiosity in Everett's face and broke in. "I tacked it up on a soundstage bulletin board, and Charlie saw people react, and bingo: Charlie George." He squinted into the sun, then recited.

"Heroes all have lovely names,
    Like Lance, or Mantz, or Vance, or James;

But authors elevate my gorge
    By naming losers Charles and George.

There's no suspense on the late, late show;
    Big deal: the bad guy's Chas., or Geo.

Goof-offs, goons, schliemiels and schmucks:
    Georgies, every one—or Chucks.

Since the days of Big Jim Farley,
    Fiction's fiends have been George and Charlie;

No wonder heroes all seem crass
    To any guy named Geo., or Chas.

I think I'll change my name, by golly!
My last name's George.
The nickname's Cholly."

Everett grinned, but: "Obviously some of your earliest work," D'Este purred.

"Point is, Dahl, it fitted the image I was after. And it's been good to me," the comedian insisted. "Your logo is great, by the way; it *is* a proper Charlie." He paused. "I want you to release it to the public domain."

The ensuing moment held a silence so deep, Everett's ear hurt. D'Este broke it with a strangled, "Just—*give* it away? Like some *amateur?* No—" and there was horror in his husked voice, "—*residuals?*"

"Oh, I'll pay you a great lump. But I want the thing available with no restrictions, for any medium anywhere, anytime. PBS. *Mad* Magazine. The *National Enquirer* maybe."

"Madness. *Mad*ness," D'Este said again, aghast, his normal hyperbole unequal to this task. He reached for a beer.

When Rhone Althouse spoke again it was in almost fatherly tones. "I'm afraid you haven't been listening very closely, Dahl. It's no accident that Charlie and I are planning to spring this idea in different networks. Charlie's the rudder of several committees where the power is in some veepee. I have a little leverage in ABC and with any positive audience response we can slowly escalate the trend. *If* there's no problem in, ah, certain quarters." He raised an eyebrow toward Maurice Everett.

Everett traced a pattern on the label of his beer bottle, thinking aloud. "There shouldn't be any serious objection from us," he began. "It's in the public interest to pit media against terrorism—and if you find yourselves in jeopardy it won't be from the Commission." He could not keep an edge from his voice. "Personally I think you've waited too goddam long."

"They nearly bagged an FCC man, you mean," Charlie prodded.

"No. Yes! That too, I can't deny personal feelings; but I was thinking of ENG men from three networks, casually hashed like ants under a heel. That's why networks execs care. That's why your iron is hot. But so far I don't hear evidence of any broad scope in your plans."

The comedian bit off an angry reply and Everett realized, too late, that he teetered on the brink of a lecture that none of them needed. This group represented not problem, but solution.

Althouse rubbed his jaw to hide a twitch in it. "You came in late," he said softly. "You didn't hear us planning to expand this idea into news and commentary. If you've ever tried to apply a little torque to a network commentator, you know what howls of censorship sound like. Morning news and editorializing are more folksy, a good place to start."

"Start what? Boil it down to essentials."

"It boils down to two points: we turn every act of terrorism into a joke at the terrorist's expense; and we absolutely must refuse, ever again, to do a straight report on their motives."

Everett sat rigidly upright at the last phrase, ignoring the pain in his side. "Good God, Althouse, that really is censorship!"

"De facto, yes; I won't duck that one. But legally it's a case of each network freely choosing to go along with a policy in public interest. Wartime restrictions beyond what the government demands are a precedent, if we need one. And the National Association of Broadcasters could publish guidelines for independent stations. The NAB is an ideal go-between."

The issue lay open between them now like a doubly discovered chess game. Everett saw in Althouse a formidable player who had studied his moves and his opponent. "It's unworkable," Everett said. "What'll you do when some Quebec separatist gang tortures a prime minister? Sit on the news?"

"Maybe not, if it's that big a story. We *can* give coverage to the event, sympathetic to the victim—but we *must* deride the gang as proper charlies, and refuse to advertise their motives."

"While you let newspapers scoop you on those details?"

"Probably—until they get an attack of conscience."

Everett's snort implied the extravagance of that notion. "A couple of Southern Cal people did in-depth surveys that suggest there's no 'probably' to it. Editors print assassination attempts as front-page stuff even if they know it brings out more assassins. They admit it."

"Hey; the Allen-Piland study," Althouse breathed, new respect in his face. "You get around."

"I've been known to read hard research," Everett replied.

"And newsmen have been known to modify their ethics," Charlie George said. "If this becomes censorship, Maury, it'll be entirely self-imposed."

"I'm sure this sounds like an odd stance for me to take," Everett smiled sadly, "but I tend to balk at social control. Hell, Althouse, you've studied Shramm and his people."

"Right. And I remember something you don't, it seems. Most media philosophers claim that, between simple-minded total liberty to slander and hard-nosed total control over the message, there's something we always move toward when we confront a common enemy. It's called Social Responsibility Theory. We used it to advantage in 1917 and 1942. It's time we used it again."

That the issue would arise in the Commission seemed certain. It was equally certain that Everett must select a principle to override others sooner or later. He had a vivid flash of recollection: a willowy girl with gooseflesh and a baton, bravely smiling after an hour of parading, ten seconds before her obliteration. "I don't like it," he said slowly, measuring the words, "but I don't like wars on children either. You make God-damned sure this social responsibility doesn't go beyond the terrorism thing." His promise, and its limitation, were implicit.

"I don't like it either," D'Este spat. "I seem to be part of a media conspiracy I never asked for. Charlie, you didn't ask me here just for graphics. What, then?"

"Commitment," Charlie said evenly.

"I'm working on CBS specials! How I'm expected to collar newsmen, writers, and producers is beyond me, regular programming is out of my line."

"Nothing in television is out of your line," Rhone Althouse began, laying stress on each word. As he proceeded, Everett noted the upswing in tempo, the appeal to D'Este's vanity, the loaded phrases, and he was glad Althouse did not write speeches for politicians. "You're independent; you work for all the nets, you know everybody in key committees all over the industry, and when you lift an idea you pick a winner. Charlie can sweet-talk NBN news into using that logo when there's a place for it—we think—while he develops his satire.

"You know the old dictum in showbiz: if it succeeds, beat it to death. I'll start working the same shtick in ABC comedy—Christ, I'm doing three shows!—and I can drop the hint that this lovely logo is public domain. With any luck, the idea can sweep NBN and ABC both. News, commentary, comedy.

"And you, Dahl? Will CBS keep out of the fun for some asinine inscrutable reason? Or will one of its most active—" he paused, the word *homosexuals* hanging inaudibly in the air like an echo without an antecedent,—"free spirits, champion the idea from the inside? That's really the only question, Dahl. Not whether you can do it, but whether you *will*."

Intending support, Everett murmured, "It'll take guts, in a milieu that hasn't shown many," and immediately wished he hadn't.

"No one corporation owns me, Mr. E." D'Este flung the words like ice cubes. "I don't have to stroke your armor."

"That's not what I meant. None of you have considered asking the next question," Everett responded.

Charlie George misunderstood, too. "Ask yourself if it's worth some trouble to keep this industry from being a flack for maniacs, Dahl. If we don't start soon, ask yourself if you'd like to see the FCC license networks themselves when Congress considers tighter government control."

An even longer silence. "Madness," D'Este said at last, "but in this crazy business—I have misgivings, but I'll go along." He folded his arms challengingly and stared at Everett. "Licensing? Is that the sword you were brandishing, the next question you meant?"

Everett swigged his beer, then set it down. His smile was bleak. "That never crossed my mind; I think Charlie overstated. Here's what I meant: if this idea takes hold, the idea men could be spotlighted, and that means to people like Hakim Arif. I had a brush with their rhetoric, and they weren't even after me. See what it brought me." He peeled his shirt up to reveal the tape that bound the bandage to his right side. Angry stripes, the paths of debris in human flesh, marked his belly and pectorals beyond the tape.

He hauled the fabric down, regarded the sobered media men. "We have a lot of questions to thrash out, but none of you can afford to ignore the next one: if you take them *all* on—Palestinians, IRA, Chileans, Japanese extremists—what are the chances they'll come after you personally?" For once, he noted with satisfaction, Rhone Althouse sat unprepared, openmouthed.

*   *   *

341

Hakim's feet were light on the steps as he hurried from the bank. The sheer weight of banknotes in his attaché case tugged at his left arm but failed to slow his stride. Fourteen minutes to rendezvous; plenty of time unless he were followed. His quick pace was perfectly normal in metropolitan New York City. He checked his watch again before entering the cafeteria. No one followed or seemed to loiter outside the place. He bought a chocolate bar to tempt, but not to entertain, his empty stomach. Slipping the candy into a pocket of his silk shirt, away from the extended shoulder holster, he thought of the pleasures of self-denial. He salivated for the chocolate. Later he would watch the girl eat it. He surveyed the cafeteria's glass front through reflective sun glasses. Twelve minutes; time to burn. He left by a different exit, moving unobtrusively down the street.

It was sheerest luck that the antique store was placed just so, and boasted a mirror angled just so. Hakim spotted the glance from a stroller to the unmarked sedan, both moving behind him and in his direction. The stroller drifted into another shop. A tall blond man emerged from the sedan, and in a hurry. Hakim's body braced for action.

He continued his brisk pace. Instead of converging on him they had exchanged tails, which meant he was expected to lead them—whoever they were. Federals, probably, judging from the cut of their suits. He tested the notion of the Jewish Defense League, not so farfetched in Manhattan, and felt perspiration leap at his scalp. But their methods were more direct, and the tail he had picked up must have mooched around the bank for days. And that meant inefficiency, which implied government. He cursed the overcoat that impeded his legs in November cold, then saw the third-rate hotel.

The blond man entered the lobby as Hakim was leaving the stair onto the filthy mezzanine and wasted seconds on two other passages; seconds that saved him. Hakim found the fire exit, burst the door seal, and slithered past the metal grating to drop into the alley. He sprinted for the street, adjusted his breathing again as he slowed to a walk, then turned another corner and risked a peek over his shoulder. The sedan was following with its lone driver.

Hakim had nine minutes and needed seven. He wanted that rendezvous, not relishing the alternative risks of public transportation to Long Island. Nearing the next corner he noted the lack of pedestrians and made his decision. He broke into a run, turned sharply, ran a few steps, then turned back and melted into a doorway. He did not want the driver to pursue him afoot and knew this to be the next option of his pursuer.

A small girl sat on the stair in his doorway at Hakim's eye level, watching silently as he fumbled in his coat. He flashed her a smile and a wink. The sedan squalled around the corner. Hakim gauged his move to coincide with commitment to the turn, made five leaping paces, and fired as many times. The parabellum rounds pierced glass, cloth, flesh, bone, upholstery, and body panels in that order, each silenced round making no more noise than a great book suddenly closed. The sedan's inertia carried it into a forlornly stripped foreign coupe. Hakim held the sidearm in his coat and retraced his steps, winking again at the little girl just before he shot her. Then he reseated the pistol, careful to keep the hot silencer muzzled away from the expensive shirt.

Seven minutes later Hakim hurried up another alley, squirmed into a delivery van, and nodded at the sturdy Panamanian who lazed behind the wheel in coveralls as the engine idled.

The van's engine was mounted between front seats with an upholstered cover. Bernal Guerrero had built an extension just long enough to accommodate a small Iraqi and the makeshift upholstery would pass casual inspection. Kneeling with the extension cover up, reluctant to relinquish control to the latino, Hakim urged caution. "Drive south first; I was followed." He did not elaborate.

For a time, Guerrero attended strictly to driving. Soon the distant beeps of police vehicles were lost and Hakim directed his driver to the bridge approach. Once over the East River, in heavy traffic, Hakim began to relax but did not stir from his position. Guerrero adjusted the inside rearview. "The funds were on hand, then."

Hakim met his eyes in the mirror. "Was that a question?"

"Deduction, señor. The briefcase seems heavy—and you are smiling."

"A wise man smiles in adversity," Hakim quoted, reloading six rounds into the clip.

"I trust Moh'med was smiling at the last," Guerrero said obliquely. "I liked him."

"Moh'med was a fool. You cannot load down an underpowered aircraft and maneuver it, too."

"A fool, then," Guerrero said. "I agree that a satchel charge would have been simpler."

Hakim's irritation was balanced by the utility of the sinewy Guerrero. The Panamanian's suggestions were good and he did not press them. Yet his conversation always provoked broader answers than Hakim cared to give. "You agree with whom? Have you toured the Statue of Liberty, Guerrero? A satchel charge might disfigure the torch, nothing more. I planned to destroy the thing. Think of the coverage," he breathed, and chuckled.

They were past Queens, halfway to the site in Farmingdale, before Hakim spoke again. "The new funds," he said as if to himself, "will pour into accounts for Fat'ah exactly as long as our coverage is adequate. But our supporters may not enjoy last night's media sport at our expense."

Guerrero nodded, remembering. But to prattle is to reveal, and this time he said nothing. Amateur films had caught Moh'med, his handmade bomb shackles hopelessly jammed, as he veered away from his first pass at the great gray statue, the previous day. The canister weighed nearly three hundred kilos and as it dangled swaying from the little Piper, Moh'med must have known he could neither land, nor long maintain control. To his credit, he had fought the craft into a slow shallow turn and straightened again, kilometers from his target. With any luck he might have completed his run, barely off the surface of the harbor, and crashed directly into the Statue of Liberty. But the new fireboat hovercraft were very quick, faster under these circumstances than the Piper that careened along at all of ninety kilometers an hour.

Hakim sighed. What ignominy, to be downed by a stream of dirty salt water! Still, "The Charlie George show made Moh'med a martyr," he asserted.

"To what? Idiot liberation, they said. And," Guerrero reminded him, "NBN news did not carry the story well. 'A terrorist quenched with a water pistol,' indeed. It is—*la palabra,* ah, the word? Provocative."

"As you are," Hakim said shortly. "Let me worry about media, and let the Americans worry about our next demonstration."

"Our next demonstration," Guerrero echoed. It was not quite a question.

"Soon, Guerrero, soon! Be silent." Again Hakim felt

moisture at his temples, forcing him to acknowledge a sensation of pressure. Harassment was the guerrilla's tool; when he himself felt harassed, it was best to cancel the operation. But he dared not. Something in Guerrero's attitude, indeed in Hakim's own response to television's smug mockery, said that Hakim Arif must choke that dark laughter under a pall of smoke.

He shifted his cramped legs to sit atop the attaché case as they skirted Mineola. Soon they would roll into the garage at Farmingdale, soon he would bear the case inside with a show of indifference, reviewing the site again to assure its readiness for—for whatever; he did not know what.

Fat'ah must be ready with only four members now, and he could not easily muster more on short notice. The Damascus site and its people would again be secure for a time, now that Hakim could furnish bribes, but Damascus is not Farmingdale, New York and Hakim knew he was improvising. Fat'ah could not afford always to improvise. Nor could it afford to delay vengeance for the Moh'med fiasco.

The double-bind was adversity. Hakim forced himself to smile, thinking of smoke. Of black smoke and of media, and of the girl who would be warm against him in the chill Long Island night. He vowed to deny himself the third, which made his smile more genuine, and knew that he could now concentrate on the first two.

Rashid and the girl failed to hide their relief at the sight of the money, stacks of twenties and fifties, which Hakim revealed in due time. During supper their eyes kept wandering to the cash until Hakim wordlessly arose and dumped it all back into the case. "Now we will have sweet coffee," he sighed, the girl rising to obey, "and contemplate sweeter revenges. Even today I struck a small blow; the eleven o'clock news may bear fruit." He was gratified to see curiosity in their silent responses.

Hakim did not expect to occupy the ABC lead story, but grew restive as national, then local news passed. Had his escape gone unnoticed, then? It had not, for, "There was an evident postscript, today, to the blundering attempt on the Statue of Liberty," said the anchorlady. "If anyone can make sense of it, perhaps Richard can."

Her co-anchor gazed out at millions, his backdrop a leering idiot that was becoming familiar. He dropped a piece of

typescript as if it were defiled and related little more, factu-
ally, than the locale and the killing of Hakim's pursuer. He
went on: "What places this below the usual level of crime in
the Big Apple, according to one source, is that the gunman's
description matches that of a Fat'ah charlie, and his victim
was a Daoudist, another terrorist. The current guess is that the
victim was trying to make friendly contact, and the gunman
mistook him for someone who knew too much." A frosty
smile. "Or perhaps that's a charlie's way of handling a taxi."

Injected by his co-anchor lady: "About the little girl he
missed at point-blank range?"

"Maybe he thought she knew too much, too. And compared to these charlies, maybe she does. She's almost five
years old."

Hakim used great restraint to continue his televiewing. The
girl at his side began with, "But you said—" until Hakim's
hand sliced the air for silence.

The weather news endorsed the frigid gusts that scrabbled
at the windows, and Hakim's mood was like the wind. He
could not have missed the urchin—and his daring coup was
against domestic security forces, he was certain. Well, *almost*
certain. Was it even remotely possible that the coxcomb Abu
Daoudists had intended—? On the other hand, government
sources could have deliberately lied to the newsman with a
release designed to confuse Fat'ah.

The girl ghosted to the kitchenette to prepare fresh sweet
coffee which Hakim craved, and subsequently ignored, as he
lounged before blank television screens. The art of disinformation was but recently borrowed from the Near East, but the
Americans were learning. *But if they know I know that Daoud
could not know where I am,* his thoughts began, and balked
with, *where am I*?

He released a high-pitched giggle and the girl dropped her
cup. Hakim angrily erased the rictus from his face and pursued another notion. Daoudists could be behind this, seeking
to share the media coverage in their bungling fashion. He,
Fat'ah, would need to arrange more talks with his television
friends. Not exactly friends, he amended, so much as co-
opportunists who could always be relied upon to give accurate
and detailed coverage if it were available. *Except in wartime*,
whispered a wisp from a forgotten text. It was unthinkable

346

that American television networks could perceive themselves at war with Fat'ah.

Unthinkable, therefore Hakim thought about it.

The same grinning salacious fool was becoming the prominent image behind every news item on terrorism. On competing networks! He thought about it some more. While Fat'ah planned the attack that was to cost Moh'med his life, Ukrainian dissenters had made news by murdering three enemies in the Soviet Secretariat. A scrap of dialogue haunted Hakim from a subsequent skit on the Charlie George Show.

INT. SQUALID BASEMENT NIGHT

CHARLIE wears a Rasputin cloak and villainous mustache, leaning over a rickety table lit by a bent candle. He scowls at CRETINOV, who cleans a blunderbuss with a sagging barrel.

TWO-SHOT CHARLIE AND CRETINOV

CHARLIE

Comrade leader, I say we kidnap everyone who calls us fools!

CRETINOV
(bored)

Nyet; where would we keep four billion people?

This established the general tenor of a five-minute lampoon, redolent of impotent fools, on terrorism against the Kremlin. The Ukrainians had enjoyed the sympathy of the United States government. Perhaps they still did, but obviously television moguls thought differently.

When had Hakim last heard a sympathetic rendering of the justice, the demands, the motivations, of a terrorist group? For that matter, he persisted, any factual rendering at all? A harrowing suspicion helped a pattern coalesce in Hakim's mind as he absently reached for his coffee. Every datum he applied seemed to fit an undeclared war that he should have

347

suspected from this medium. A medium upon which Fat'ah was all too dependent; newspapers brought details, but TV brought showers of cash from Fat'ah well-wishers. Had the Americans at last conspired to rob him of his forum, his voice, his cash?

Hakim Arif retrieved his images of smoke and media, this time imagining a greasy black roil erupting from a picture tube. It should be simple enough to test this suspicion. If it proved to be accurate, Hakim vowed, he would bring war to this monster medium.

He sipped the tepid coffee, then realized that he had forbidden it to himself. Rage flung the cup for him, shattering it against a television set that squatted unharmed. The girl's gasp paced Guerrero's reaction, a sidelong roll from his chair from which the latino emerged, a crouching wolverine, his Browning sidearm drawn. Guerrero was not particularly quick, but his hand was steady. In the silent staring match with the latino, Hakim told himself, he dropped his own eyes first to atone for his rashness.

Hakim stood erect and exhaled deeply from his nose. "We need rest," he said.

"Yes, you do," Guerrero agreed, tucking the automatic away.

Hakim did not pause in his march to the far bedroom. He read the latino's implied criticism, but would absorb it for now. He could not afford to waste Guerrero. Yet.

As long as the National Association of Broadcasters wanted to hold a convention during Thanksgiving holidays, Everett admitted, it was nice to find that Reno was its choice. He wandered among the manufacturers' exhibits in the hotel foyer, grudgingly accepting some responsibility for the presence of so many new security devices. Say what you like about media men, their self-interest is intelligent. Cassette systems shared display space with microwave alarms. One import drew the commissioner's admiration: an outgrowth of an English medical thermovision system, it could display so small a mass of metal as coins in a pocket—unless they were at body heat, no more, no less.

A voice behind him said, "Neat. Any charlie who sneaks his forty-five past that rig will have to carry it as a suppository," and Everett wheeled to face Rhone Althouse.

348

Everett's delight was real, though brief. "Thank God for somebody I can ask questions of, instead of just answering 'em," he said.

"I heard your speech on porn," was the reply, "and I can't believe you have any answers. Seriously, I did want to—well, uh, actually Charlie George, um." He cocked his head to one side. "The fact is, our Palm Springs meeting has become the worst-kept secret since the Bay of Pigs. Dahl D'Este couldn't sit on such a juicy tidbit for long. For one thing, his lady-love is a gossip columnist."

"It's a little late, but thanks for the warning. Lady? D'Este makes both scenes?"

A one-beat pause. "Yeah, ob and epi—and thanks for the straight line. Charlie G. and I thought you should know that the word would be leaking. It should have a positive effect in the industry," Althouse added quickly. It had the sound of an excuse.

Everett nodded, hands thrust into pockets of his stylishly discomfiting jacket. "Well, you're answering my questions before I ask. I'll have to deny my part in it for the record; but between us, Rhone, I'm willing to let it live as a rumor. The commission is interested in this ethical epidemic, naturally. I've been asked how long you can keep it up." Raised eyebrows invited an answer.

"Hell, it's popular," the writer grinned. "With CBS taking it up, it's a trendy thing—oh," he amended. "You mean the reprisals?"

This time Everett's nod was quick. "Those Fat'ah pismires cost NBN a bundle when the net refused to air that videotape Arif sent them."

"Fortunes of war," Althouse shrugged. "Don't think our own Charlie isn't hurting, even if he doesn't flinch. He's got a piece of several stations, and those transmission towers Fat'ah destroyed didn't do the dividends any good. Insurance tripled."

"Didn't flush out any friendly envoys from the nets to pay anybody off, I suppose."

Althouse squinted in the subdued light. "I think I would've heard if that were in the mill. If that's the crux of your concern—officially, I mean—I can't answer for the whole industry. Maury, it's become a grass-roots movement, just as I hoped; doesn't have a single spokesman. That's where its strength lies. But it looks to me like a full-scale media war.'' He hesitated, glanced around them, bit his lip. For the first time, Everett saw something in the writer that was not young, something of the mature hunted animal. ''We haven't forgotten those scenarios you laid on us. Do you have—cancel that, I don't want to know. Do you think we should have around-the-clock protection when our names hit the newspapers?''

''Let me put it this way: you and I both know D'Este can put us on the list of endangered species. You think our names are due to hit news stands?''

''I *know* they are,'' said Althouse, with a sickly smile that told Everett this was why the writer had flown to Reno: face-to-face admission that Everett could expect the worst. There could be little pleasure in a print-media hero label when it was also a death warrant.

No point in asking how Althouse knew. His pallor said he knew. ''Tell Charlie George we are about to learn what it's like to be a popular politico,'' Everett remarked, fashioning a cross-hair X with his forefingers. As an effort at lightness, the gesture fell flat. ''How long before our oh-so-responsible press fingers us?''

''Tomorrow.''

Everett drew a long breath. ''Goddam the world's D'Estes, we ought to put out a contract on that guy ourselves. Well, can't say I didn't expect this sooner or later. I intended to stay and gamble 'til Sunday, but somebody just raised the stakes on us and I've decided to find some pressing business elsewhere. Luck, Rhone.'' He turned and moved away.

Althouse stood and watched the big man, wondering if Everett would hide, wondering if he should disappear himself as D'Este had already done. He took some comfort in Everett's refusal to blame him for the original idea. But the commissioner had known the danger, even while he lent tacit bureaucratic support. D'Este gone to ground, Everett forewarned: better than nothing, yet poor defense against the fury of terrorism which his own scripts had deflected against them all. An unfamiliar itch between his shoulders made Althouse aware that he was standing absolutely still, alone in a hotel, a perfect target. Rhone Althouse walked away quickly. He did not care who noticed that his path was a zigzag.

The news magazines made up in depth what they lacked in

immediacy. The articles was satisfyingly thorough under its head, "TV: No More Strange Bedfellows?" It began:

> For weeks, every pundit in the sprawling television medium had matched his favorite terrorism rumor against the rumors in the next studio. The scathing satire on terrorism, newly unleashed and widespread in TV, was said to originate in an oval office. Or, less likely, that it was a propaganda ploy jointly financed by Israel and England. One pollster claimed that the scripts merely reflect what the American viewer wants to see.
>
> The truth, as it filtered from CBS this week, was both likelier and stranger than whodunits. There had been no tugs at domestic political strings and no foreign influence. But in the persons of four highly regarded media men, there was definitely a plot. The top banana, to no one's great surprise, turned out to be NBN's answer to Jacques Tati, the protean Charlie George. Of considerably more interest was the reputed anchorman, anomalous FCC sachem Maurice D. Everett (*see box*). . . .

"All bedfellows are strange," murmured Hakim, patting the rump of the girl who slept as he scanned the stack of magazines. He read the four-page article carefully, marking some passages with flow pen, then concentrated on the thumbnail biography of Maurice Everett. The short piece commented on Everett's unpredictability, his sparse personal life, and his penchant for outdoor sport. Hakim did not find these details pleasant; the man could be trouble.

Presently Hakim riffled through other magazines, finding—as he had expected—invaluable information on his enemies. His sullen longing found its focus in names, faces, details which, given time, Hakim could fashion into targets.

Print media made one thing clear: no matter how successful his coup, the terrorist was still to be treated as a proper charlie. Hakim saw this dictum as a simple clash of wills. If the *fait accompli* carried no leverage, one could try the threat. No hollow promise, but one steeped in potency. The sort of threat one could employ when the enemy is isolated, immobilized, and at risk. Hakim wondered which of the four men he would take first and felt a lambent surge of rekindled strength. He turned off the light and nudged the girl. It had not once occurred to the Fat'ah leader that other charlies, less cautious than he, might react with a blinder savagery.

Everett urged his Mini-Cooper up the ice-slick highway out of Golden, Colorado, wishing he had accepted the company of a federal agent. He had refused that and a snub-nosed piece in a shoulder holster on the same grounds: they were both confining and might call attention to the user. The car was repainted and relicensed, though, and during his five days of new celebrity his Denver office had intercepted only a lone ceramic letterbomb. Perhaps he was exaggerating his importance, but he would feel safer spending his weekend at one of the rental cabins outside the little town of Empire. Even do a little winter stalking, who could say?

The three men who could say kept well to the rear. For a time the driver sweated to keep his BMW in sight of the Mini and settled for occasional glimpses of the tiny vehicle as the terrain permitted. There were few turnouts available after the new snow, and the further Maurice Everett isolated himself, the better they liked it.

Everett chose the roadhouse on impulse, backing the Mini in to assure easy return. He ordered coffee and began shucking the furlined coat before he realized that he was alone with the counterman. He slapped snow from the front of his winter hat, then saw the dark blue BMW ease off the highway. Everett took his coffee with hands that shook, watching through fogged windows as the sleek sedan began to emulate his parking manners. No, not quite; the BMW blocked his Mini, and only one of the car's three occupants emerged. Three coffees to go, or one commissioner?

Everett saw the raincoated man cradle his long, gaily-wrapped package, speak briefly to his driver; Everett noted the Vermont license plate and used his time wisely. He walked to one end of the roadhouse, far from the windows and counterman, and piled his coat high in the last booth, putting his hat atop it. The coffee steamed in the center of the booth table, untasted bait.

Everett stepped directly across the aisle from his end booth into the men's room, hoping that his circumstantial case was nothing more than that, hoping that the raincoated man would get his coffee and go to Empire, or Georgetown, or hell. He did not close the door or try the light switch.

There was nothing he could see in the gloom that would serve as a weapon and as he settled on the toilet, fully clothed and staring at his coffee three meters away, he felt the toilet seat move. One of its two attachment wingnuts was gone. Gently, silently, Everett set about removing the other. Early or late, he reasoned, the audacious bird gets the worm.

He heard the front door of the roadhouse sigh shut, heard a mumbled exchange—one voice had an odd lilt to it—at the counter ten meters from him, heard the counterman open a refrigerator. So Mr. Raincoat wanted more than coffee? Cheeseburgers, or diversion?

Under the clank and scrape of short-order cookery, Everett heard soft footfalls. He stood, breathing quickly and lightly through his mouth, gripping the toilet lid with no earthly thought of what he was doing with it. He felt like a fool: *oh, hello, I was just leaving, sorry about the lid, it didn't fit me anyhow* . . . and then Mr. Raincoat stepped to Everett's booth as if offering his package, one hand thrust into the false end of the package, and he must have seen that he was confronting an uninhabited hat and coat just as Everett swung the lid, edge on, against the base of his skull from behind and to one side.

Everett was appalled at himself for an instant. He had drygulched a harmless holiday drunk, he thought, as the man toppled soundlessly onto Everett's coat. The contents of the package slid backward onto the floor then, and Everett reflected that harmless drunks do not usually carry sawed-off automatic shotguns in Christmas packages with false ends.

Everett's snowshoes were in the Mini and without them he would be stupid to run out the back way. The counterman, incredibly, was busy incinerating three steaks and had seen nothing. Everett wrote the BMW license number on his table with catsup, though he could have used blood, and wrestled the raincoat from the unconscious man.

The only way out was past the BMW. He hoped it would flee at his first warning shot, then realized that the occupants were waiting to hear that shot. How would Mr. Raincoat exit? Backward, no doubt, holding the shotgun on the counterman. Everett's trousers were the wrong shade of gray but he could not afford to dwell on that.

He slid into the raincoat which pinched at the armpits, turned its collar up, retrieved the shotgun and checked the safety. Gripped in glacial calm, he reminded himself of Pueblo and quashed his fear with one thought: *my turn!* Everett had time to pity the counterman, but not to question his own sanity, as he moved past windows near the front door and turned his back on it.

The blast tore a fist-sized hole in the floor and sent a lance of pain through Everett's bad ear. The counterman ran without hesitation out the rear door into the snowdrift, screaming, and Everett backed out the front door fast. The BMW engine blipped lustily and a voice called, "In, in, ye fookin' twit," and Everett spun to see a man holding a rear door open with one hand, a machine pistol forgotten in the other. Everett did not forget the weapon and aimed for it. He missed, but blew out the windshield from the inside.

The driver accelerated to the highway, the left rear door of the car flapping open, and Everett fired twice more. The first shot sent pellets caroming off the inside of the sedan and the second was a clean miss. Everett flopped hard into the snow so that he only heard, but could not see, the shiny BMW slide off the highway. It was a long vertical roll to the river but neither of the occupants minded the cold water, being dead at the time.

Everett burst into the roadhouse to find that his first victim was still unconscious, and realized that he had things to set right. The counterman must be tamed, the telephone must be used; but first things first. He needed the toilet lid for a mundane purpose, and *right now*.

The NBN electrician learned from an honest bartender in Burbank that his wallet had turned up minus cash, but with papers intact. He verified that his licenses and the new NBN security pass were accounted for and vowed to forget it.

NBN officials assured Charlie George that the fenced backlot in the San Fernando Valley was secure, far better than a leased location and nearer Hollywood. They did not add that their own security chief disagreed, and avoided mentioning the obvious: backlots are cheap. The new passes, they said, employed dipoles for inexpensive electronic ID. Of course, Fat'ah employed them too.

It was midmorning before Charlie George and his writers were mollified with the script, a tepid takeoff on the attempt at Maurice Everett the previous Friday. The skit had two things going for it: Charlie's Irish accent was uproarious, and he could do pantomimic wonders as an IRA Provisional trying to pull a trigger and chew gum at the same time. They threw out the lines identifying the terrorist driver as French-Canadian. It was faithful to the new connection between separatist gangs, but it was also confusingly unfunny.

They managed a half-dozen takes before noon and, as lunch vans began their setups at unobtrusive distances from the exterior set, Charlie's nose directed his eyes toward the new van which advertised hot Mexican food. Charlie's mania for Mexican food had been duly noted by news magazines.

"Okay, it's a wrap," the unit director called. "Lunch!" Charlie threw off his prop raincoat, ignoring the free spread by NBN. He drifted instead toward the *menudo* and its vendor, Bernal Guerrero.

Only one side panel of the van was raised, for the excellent reason that one side was rigged for lunch, the other for Charlie. The comedian waited his turn. The compact latino appeared to recognize his patron only at second glance, bestowed a grave smile on Charlie and said, "For you, Señor Carlito, something special." Had Charlie not followed Guerrero to the hidden side of the van, Hakim could have fired the veterinarian's tranquilizer gun from inside the van, through his thin silvered mylar panel.

Charlie's smile was quizzical until he felt Guerrero's needle enter his side like a cold lightning bolt. He cried only, "Hey, that hurts," not convincingly, before Guerrero's gristly fingers numbed his diaphragm. Three other patrons on the innocent side of the van turned, then were rediverted as racks of warm lunch items began to spill onto the macadam—one of Hakim's deft touches.

Guerrero grasped Charlie by the thighs and lifted, hurling the limp NBN star against the featureless side panel. The panel swung inward, dumped Charlie at the feet of Hakim Arif, and swung shut again. Guerrero hurried back to see patrons catching the spill of food, made a gesture of hopelessness, said "Keep it," and dropped the open side panel. He found it difficult to avoid furious action before reaching the driver's seat because he could hear, a hundred meters away, screams from the script girl who had seen it all.

As the van howled between two hangarlike sound stages,

Guerrero bore far to the right to begin his left turn. He had thirty seconds on his pursuers but Hakim had made it clear that they must expect communication between the exterior sets and the guarded backlot gate. Guerrero smiled, hearing Hakim's curses as he struggled with a dead weight greater than his own, and sped toward the perimeter cyclone fencing. Outside the fence was an access road, deserted except for a small foreign sedan and a larger car towing an old mobile home. These vehicles were motionless.

Guerrero slapped the button in plenty of time but was not pleased. He slapped it again, then pressed it with a rocking motion as he tapped the brakes hard. Fifteen feet of cyclone fencing peeled back as the bangalore torpedo at last accepted his microwave signal, the Guerrero felt the pressure wave cuff the van. He angled through the hole, negotiating the shallow ditch with elan, and exulted in his choice of a vehicle with high ground clearance. As he made a gear change, accelerating toward escape, he could see Rashid in his outside rearview, dutifully towing the decrepit mobile home into position to block immediate pursuit along the access road.

The girl waited for Rashid in her smaller car, the only vehicle of their regular fleet that was not a van. Guerrero waited for nothing, but tossed quick glances to check the possibility of air surveillance. Van Nuys airport was soon sliding past on his right and they would be vulnerable until he reached the state university campus where their other vans waited.

Minutes later, Guerrero eased the van into a campus parking lot. Hakim was ready with the crate and together they wrestled it from their vehicle into the rear of a somewhat smaller van. As Hakim urged the smaller vehicle away, encouraging its cold engine with curses, Guerrero wheeled the kidnap van across the lot and abandoned it along with his vendor's uniform. It might be many hours before the kidnap van was noticed, among the hundreds of recreational vehicles on the campus. Guerrero knew what every student knew: a recreational vehicle was limited only by what one defined as recreation.

He moved then to his last vehicle change, flexing his hands in the thin gloves as he waited for the engine to warm, for the flow of adrenaline to subside, for the next item on his private agenda. He had carefully ascertained that Arif's fingerprints were on the abandoned kidnap vehicle, and that his own were not. On the other hand, Arif had given him only a public rendezvous some kilometers to the west in Moorpark and not the location of the new site which, Guerrero knew, might be in any direction. The latino grumbled to himself in irritation. Arif's monolithic insistence on sole control was a continuing problem, but Guerrero had to admit that little *palo blanco* was precise. He checked the time and grinned to himself; it wouldn't do to be late picking up Rashid and the girl. Guerrero's masters were precise, too.

By six PM, Hakim was so far out of patience that he fairly leaped from his seat in the Moorpark bus station at his first sight of Guerrero. The Panamanian bought a newspaper, saw Arif stand, then ambled out onto the street. It was too dark to read the fine print but, waiting for Hakim to catch up, Guerrero saw that they had again made the front page above the fold.

Though Guerrero walked slowly, Hakim sounded breathless. "I told *the girl* to make rendezvous," he said, as they paused for a stop light. "And you are four hours late!"

"The Americans had other ideas," Guerrero growled convincingly. "She and Rashid tried to run a blockade."

"Escape?"

"I was lucky to escape, myself. They were cut down, Hakim."

Hakim's voice was exceedingly soft. "This you saw?"

"I saw. It may be here," he lied again, brandishing the folded newspaper, ready to grapple with the Iraqi if he saw his cover blown. Hakim Arif only looked straight ahead, and fashioned for himself a terrible smile.

They walked another block, forcing themselves to study window displays, checking for surveillance as they went. "The comedian will be conscious soon," Hakim said as if to himself. "He will be noisy, no doubt." Then, as a new possibility struck him: "Was your van compromised?"

Guerrero gave a negative headshake, very much desiring to keep his own vehicle. "It is just ahead there," he indicated. "Do I abandon it now?" Always, he knew, Hakim was perversely biased against an underling's suggestion.

"We have expended twelve thousand dollars in vehicles, and two Fat'ah lives this day," Hakim snarled. "No more waste. Stay here, wait for my van, then follow."

Guerrero nodded and sauntered to his parked van as Arif hurried away. One cigarette later, the latino saw Arif's vehicle pass. He followed closely in traffic, then dropped back as they turned north onto Highway 23 toward the mountains. Well beyond the town of Fillmore, the lead van slowed abruptly, loitered along the highway until it was devoid of other traffic. Then Hakim swung onto a gravel road; Guerrero sensed that they were very near the new Fat'ah site and philosophically accepted his inability to share that suspicion.

After two kilometers they turned again, and Guerrero saw that the new site was a renovated farmhouse in a small orchard. He hurried to help Hakim unload the crate at the porch, ignoring the awful sounds from inside it. Only when the crate was opened inside did Guerrero learn why Charlie George, gagged and tightly bound, was such a noisy passenger.

The long legs had been taped flexed, so that muscle cramps would almost certainly result. More tape looped from neck to thighs, assuring that a tall man would make a smaller package. Heavy adhesive bands strapped his arms across his chest, the left hand heavily retaped over a crimson-and-rust bandage. Guerrero did a brief double-take, rolling the captive over to see the maimed left hand. Despite the gag, the prisoner moaned at the rough movement. From Guerrero, a sigh: "Will you rid the world of fingers, Hakim?"

The Fat'ah leader knelt to examine the bandage while Charlie tried to speak through the gag. "An ancient and honored custom, my friend," he said, and backhanded Charlie viciously to quell the interruption. "I mailed his small finger special delivery to the National Broadcasting Network people. I added a promise to forward more pieces until my demands are aired," he continued, staring into Charlie's face as he spoke. He wheeled to regard Guerrero. "I might have delivered it there myself while waiting for you!"

"Your demands, not Fat'ah's," Guerrero mused aloud.

"I am Fat'ah," almost inaudible.

"It is reducing itself to that," Guerrero agreed ambiguously, then adroitly blunted the goad. "What may I do now?"

Hakim retained a precarious control. "Familiarize yourself with the house, cook a meal, mend your tongue. I shall arrange for our guest to—entertain us."

* * *

The nearest lights, Guerrero found, were over a kilometer off, too far to carry the sounds of the interrogation of Charlie George. The latino took his time, kept away from the "guest" room, and waited for Arif to kill their captive in outlet for his frustration. When the screams subsided, Guerrero began to heat their stew.

The American was stronger than either of them had thought. He managed to walk, a tape-wrapped garrotte wire looped as leash about his throat, to the table but fell trying to sit in the folding chair. Hakim's smile was a beatitude, so well did his captive behave. Charlie's nose was a ruin, his right ear torn—"It will come off anyway," Hakim chuckled—but his mouth had been left equipped for conversation. He was not disposed to eat and his hands shook so badly that Hakim laughed; but Hakim needed say only once, "Eat it all," softly. Charlie George ate it all.

Hakim produced a huge chocolate bar for dessert and helped eat it. He felt no desire or need to deny the stuff, while the garrotte wire was in his hand. After the chocolate: "You maintain that this satire is too widespread to halt," he prodded the exhausted captive, "and I say you will halt it, piece by piece."

"You underestimate their greed," Charlie replied, scarcely above a whisper. From time to time he squeezed his left wrist hard. "Every nightclub schlepper in the Catskills is inventing stealable material—and the public loves it." He managed something that could have been a smile. "You're a smash, Arif."

Hakim looked at the wall a moment. "And the new series you mentioned? What is the investment?"

"One on ABC, one on CBS," Charlie said. "Buy 'em off if you can. Try ten million apiece. They'll laugh at you." With this unfortunate phrase he trailed off; exhaustion tugged at his eyelids. Hakim reached out with delicate precision and thumped the bloody bandage. "Ahhhhh . . . I don't see what you gain by torture," Charlie grunted. "I have no secrets."

Guerrero, taking notes, gestured at the captive with the butt of his pen. "Perhaps you do not *know* what you know."

"And perhaps you are being punished," Hakim murmured.

"What else is new," Charlie said, and was rewarded by a sudden tug on the wire. "Sorry," he managed to croak.

"Repeat after me: 'I beg forgiveness, Effendi,' " Hakim

smiled, and tugged again. Charlie did it. "Now tell us again how your network amassed those extra tapes to be aired in the event one of you was captured." Charlie did that, too. Eventually Hakim saw that the answers were more disjointed, less useful, and led the unprotesting Charlie to the torture room. Guerrero saw the captive trussed flat on a tabletop before Hakim was satisfied, and kept the butt of his ballpoint pen aimed at the doorway, putting away his gear as Hakim returned.

"I will set up the media center," Hakim said mildly. "You will install this lock on our guest's door." It was a heavy push-bolt affair.

Guerrero set about clearing the bowls away as Hakim brought media monitors in. "I saw lights of a village from the porch," Guerrero reported. "With only the two of us left, you might brief me to that extent."

"I might—when you need to know. Information is at a premium now, is it not? We have not even a telephone here. But no matter," he said, setting his small portable TV set up. "We can do what we must."

Guerrero paused, framed another guarded question, then thought better of it and went after tools for the door lock. From his van he saw that the windows of Charlie's room were boarded. Returning with the tools, he installed the simple lock, pausing to watch the monitors with Arif. There was no mention of a shootout between Rashid and police—naturally— but there was also absolute silence on the daring daylight abduction of Charlie George. Guerrero saw Arif's subliminal headshakes and was emboldened; the Iraqi might have doubted Guerrero's story if the kidnapping had received major coverage. As it was, Hakim Arif focused only on television as his source of dis-, mis-, and non-information.

When the last newscast was done, Hakim read and made notes on alternative courses of action. At last he replaced the notebook, ascertained that Charlie George was breathing heavily, and sought his own bedroll. Then, for the first time, he missed the girl until he thrust the image of her body from him. "We shall see, tomorrow," he said to the sleeping Guerrero, and fell into a sleep of confidence.

The next morning, there was still no news of the abduction on television. A National Public Radio newscast mentioned the fact that newspapers carried headlines on a reported kidnapping while television sources refused comment. Hakim forced their captive to eat a mighty breakfast and smiled fondly as Charlie complied. The comedian had bled more during the night but, Guerrero judged, not nearly enough. Hakim Arif seemed content to sit in their orchard site until their food ran out. The noon news was innocent of Fat'ah, but Hakim was ebullient.

Finally at supper Hakim hinted at his motive for optimism. "Your show goes on at eight," he said to Charlie. "If your people place any value on you, we shall have what we demand."

"The show was taped in pieces weeks ago, you know," Charlie replied, constant pain diluting his voice. "They don't have to worry about dead air."

"I shouldn't talk so casually about pieces or death, if I were you," Hakim rejoined. "I shall bet you one ear that we get coverage."

Charlie made no reply, but tried to read a paperback which Guerrero had discarded. Shortly after his own show began, the captive showed signs of distress. Hakim handed the leash wire to Guerrero who waited in the bathroom while Charlie lost his supper. The audio was up, the door nearly closed. Guerrero took a calculated risk. "You will not leave here alive, Carlito. If you hope, throw that up, too."

Charlie knelt, face in his hands, rocking fore and aft. Muffled by his bandaged hand: "Why d'you think I'm so puking scared? NBN won't cave in; we agreed on that tactic. I wish I could retract it but I can't. And if I did, *they* wouldn't." He looked up through streaming silent tears, his hands bloodily beseeching. "And if they would?"

"You would still die," Guerrero said, wondering if it were true.

"What can I do?" It was an agonized whisper.

"Die. Slowly, appeasing him, in a week; or quickly, avoiding pain, if you anger him enough." Their eyes met for a long moment of communion. Charlie retched again briefly, and the moment passed.

The Charlie George Show passed as well, without reference to the kidnapping until the end of the show. Charlie normally traded jokes with his live audience for a few moments but, instead of the piece Charlie had taped, his rotund second-banana comic appeared. Standing before the familiar logo, he mimicked a gossip columnist with barbed one-liners.

361

Finally, he said, there was no rumor in the truth—his tongue pointedly explored his cheek—that Charlie was in a plummet conference with stagestruck terrorists. They wanted a big hand, but Charlie only gave them the finger.

Hakim watched the credits roll, snapped off the set, and treated Charlie George to a malevolent smile. "You win," he said, "and you lose."

"You got coverage," Charlie husked, "and anyhow, you're going to do whatever you want to. NBN got your message, and you got theirs."

"I have other messages," Hakim said, and spat in Charlie's face.

Charlie saw cold rage in the zealot eyes and accepted, at last, that the network would not save him from consequences of events he had shaped. He spoke to Hakim, but looked at Guerrero. "Have it your way, you pile of pigshit. We did a sketch on that: we'll give you coverage in a pig's pratt, that's where you rate it—"

The garrotte cut off the sudden tirade. Without Hakim's tape over the wire it would have cut more than that, as Hakim used the wire leash to throw Charlie to the floor. Hakim held the leash tight, kicking expertly at elbows and knees until his victim lay silent and gray on the red-smeared floor. He squatted to loosen the wire and nodded with satisfaction as the unconscious man's breathing resumed in ragged spasms, the larynx bruised but not crushed. Guerrero kept his face blank as he helped drag their burden into the torture room, then laid his ballpoint pen on a shelf while Hakim trussed Charlie George to the table.

"Keep him alive awhile," Guerrero urged. To his dismay, he heard Hakim grumble assent.

"He must not cheat me of his awareness," the Fat'ah leader explained, "when I take more souvenirs." He paused, studying the inert hostage, then jerked his gaze to the Panamanian. "What was he really saying, Guerrero? *Damn you,* or *kill me*?"

"Does it matter what the tree says to the axe?"

"If only all your questions were so cogent," Hakim laughed. "That was worthy of El Aurans himself; he who understood pain so well— No, it does not matter. Tomorrow the comedian will be replenished. And wrung empty again."

* * *

Charlie was half-dragged to their morning meal; one arm useless, the other barely functional. He moaned softly as Guerrero and Hakim attacked their cereal. Then Hakim, using his own traditionally unclean left hand in private amusement, gravely took Charlie's spoon and began to feed him. Charlie knew better than to refuse, saying only, "You are one strange man."

"You must continue to function, and it is easy to be polite to an inferior. Another thing," he said, watching Charlie's difficulty in swallowing, "your schoolboy taunts will not compel me to kill you. Fat'ah is not compelled. It compels. And punishes."

"The monitors," Guerrero said, indicating his wristwatch.

"You will watch them when we have taken Charlie George to his room." Hakim had tired of his game with the spoon and, with the implacable Guerrero, conveyed Charlie to the room Charlie dreaded.

Hakim trussed Charlie to the table again as Guerrero faced the monitors in the next room, then hauled Charlie's torso to the table's edge. The captive lay face up, hanging half off the table, his head a foot from the spattered floor. He saw Hakim produce the knife, elastic bands, clear plastic tube and gossamer bag, and tried not to guess their uses. Hakim taped him firmly in place as blood gradually pounded louder in the ears of Charlie George.

Hakim brought the knife to Charlie's throat, smiling, and Charlie closed his eyes. Hakim tugged at the torn ear until Charlie opened his eyes again and then, in two quick sweeps, he severed the ear.

Charlie fought his own screams through clenched teeth, sobbing, straining against the bonds. His face a study in dispassionate interest, Hakim stanched the flow of blood and, holding Charlie by his hair, sprinkled a clotting agent over the gory mess before he applied a rough bandage.

It took Charlie George four tries to say, between gasps, "Why?"

"Questions, questions," Hakim sighed. "Your ear will go to the *Los Angeles Times* and its coverage may provoke your television people. This may even start a modest media war. And *this* is because I choose," he continued, quickly pulling the flimsy polyethylene bag over Charlie's head.

Hakim snapped the elastic bands around Charlie's neck and

stood back, watching the red stain spread past his bandage inside the bag. Charlie's eyes became huge with horror as his first breath sucked the bag against his nose and mouth. After twenty seconds, Hakim thrust the plastic tube under the elastic and into Charlie's mouth, then tugged the bag in place. The tube was short and not entirely flaccid, and Hakim pulled his chair near to hold the free end of the tube away from loose ends of the bag.

Hakim waited until the breathing steadied. Charlie's eyes were closed. "Open your eyes," Hakim said gently. No response. "Open them," he said, placing a fingertip lightly over the tube's end. Charlie's eyes flew open and Hakim's finger moved back.

"Have you heard of the dry submarine, my friend? You are wearing one. The wet submarine is favored in Chile; it features a variety of nasty liquids in the bag. Yours may soon qualify as wet," he added, seeing the runnel of crimson that painted the bag's interior in Charlie's feeble struggles.

"Why, you ask, and ask, and ask," Hakim continued, crooning near as though speaking to a valued confidante, a beloved. "Because you will perhaps return to your sumptuous life, if it pleases me. You will be my message to your medium, a man who knows he has been totally broken. El Aurans, the Lawrence of Arabia, broke after long torture and found ambition gone. Few were his equal but," the dark eyes held a soft luminosity as he quoted, " *'My will had gone and I feared to be alone, lest the winds of circumstance . . . blow my empty soul away.'* I do not think you can avoid carrying that message," Hakim added. "This is true Eastern martial art: corner the enemy, and leave him nothing. Your Machiavelli understood."

From the other room came Guerrero's call: "Coverage, Hakim!"

The little man turned in his chair, picked up the severed ear, and released the tube which lay nearly invisible against the bag. In three strides he was through the door, to loom at Guerrero's side.

The item was insignificant, merely an admission that an NBN star was a possible kidnap victim. Television was carrying the news, but obviously was not going to dwell on this event. "So I must contact another medium," Hakim said, and held up his ghastly trophy.

Guerrero blinked. "It has been quiet in there."

"He no longer complains," Hakim answered, deliberately vague.

"You are finished, then," Guerrero persisted.

It was Hakim's pleasure to joke, thinking of the abject terror in the eyes of Charlie George. "Say, rather, *he* is finished," he rejoined, and turned back toward the torture room.

Guerrero followed unbidden, his excitement mounting. He saw their captive hanging inert like some butchered animal, his head half-obscured in glistening red polymer. He could not know that Charlie George had spent the past moments desperately inhaling, exhaling, trying with an animal's simplicity to bathe his lungs in precious oxygen. Charlie's mind was not clear but it held fast to one notion: Guerrero was anxious for his death. Mouth and eyes open wide, Charlie George ceased to breathe as Guerrero came into view.

Guerrero's mistake was his haste to believe what he wanted to believe. He saw the plastic sucked against nostrils, the obscenely gaping mouth and staring eyes. He did not seek the thud of Charlie's heart under his twisted clothing and failed to notice the slender tube emergent from the plastic bag. "The poor *pendejo* is dead, then?" He rapped the question out carelessly.

Hakim's mistake was the indirect lie, his automatic response to questions asked in the tone Guerrero used now. "Truly, as you see," Hakim said, gesturing toward Charlie George, amused at Charlie's ploy.

His merriment was fleeting. From the tail of his eye he saw Guerrero's hand slide toward the Browning and in that instant, Hakim resolved many small inconsistencies. Still, he flung the knife too hastily. Guerrero dodged, rolling as he aimed, but could not avoid the chair that struck him as he fired. The Iraqi sprang past the doorway, slammed the door and flicked the bolt in place as chunks of wallboard peppered his face. He counted five shots from the Browning but knew the damned thing held nine more. Half blinded by debris from Guerrero's slugs, Hakim elected to run rather than retrieve his own automatic which lay at his media display in the path of Guerrero's fire against the door lock.

Hakim reached his van quickly, almost forgetting to snap the hidden toggle beneath the dash, and lurched toward the road with a dead-cold engine racing and spitting. He dropped low over the wheel, unable to see if Guerrero followed. He had cash and an exquisite Israeli submachinegun, Fat'ah's survival kit, behind him in the van.

Hakim considered stopping to make a stand on the gravel road but checked his rearviews in time to reconsider. Guerrero was there, twenty seconds behind. Hakim would need ten to stop, ten more to reach and feed the weapon. He would fare better if he could increase his lead, and guessed that Guerrero would withhold fire as they passed through the village of Piru. It was worth a try.

Slowing at the edge of the little town, Hakim saw his rearview fill with Guerrero's van. Whatever his motive, the Panamanian evidently had a hard contract to fulfill and might take insane chances. Hakim wrenched the wheel hard, whirling through a market parking lot. A grizzled pickup truck avoided him by centimeters and stalled directly in Guerrero's path, and then Hakim was turning north, unable to see how much time he had gained.

The road steepened as Hakim learned from a road sign that Lake Piru and Blue Point lay ahead. He searched his rearviews but the road was too serpentine for clear observation, and Hakim began to scan every meter of roadside for possible cover.

He took the second possible turnoff, a rutted affair with warnings against trespassers, flanked by brush and high grass. The van threw up a momentary flag of dust, a small thing but sufficient for Guerrero, who came thundering behind, alert for just such a possibility.

Hakim topped a low ridge and did not see Guerrero two turns back. Dropping toward a hollow, he tried to spin the van but succeeded only in halting it broadside to the road. He hurtled from his bucket seat, threw open the toolbox, and withdrew the stockless Uzi with flashing precision. Two forty-round clips went into his jacket and then he was scrambling from the cargo door which thunked shut behind him. If Guerrero were near, let him assault the empty van while Hakim, on his flank, would cut him down from cover.

But he had not reached cover when the van of Bernal Guerrero appeared, daylight showing under all four tires as it crested the rise before the mighty *whump* of contact. Hakim stopped in the open, taking a splayed automatic-weapons stance, and fitted a clip in the Uzi.

Almost.

It may have been dirt from the jouncing ride, or a whisker of tempered steel projecting like a worrisome hangnail; whatever it was, it altered many futures.

Hakim dropped the clip and snatched at its twin, missed his footing, and sprawled in the dust. The van of Guerrero impended, crashing around Hakim's wheeled roadblock into the grassy verge, a great beast rushing upon him. Guerrero set the handbrake and exited running as Hakim, his weapon hoary with dirt, essayed a multiple side roll. He was mystified when Guerrero merely kicked him in the head instead of triggering the automatic.

Hakim waited for death as he gazed into the dark nine-millimeter eye of the Browning. "Daoudist," he surmised bitterly.

"I am Fat'ah," Guerrero mimicked, breathing deeply. His face shone with sweat and elation. "And in Panama, a *Torrijista*, and everywhere, always, KGB." He wiped dust from his mouth, the gun muzzle absolutely unwavering and much too distant for a foot sweep by Hakim. "Rise, turn, hands on your head." Hakim obeyed.

The latino marched him back to his own van and forced him to lie prone in the pungent dust. While Guerrero ransacked the tool box, Hakim listened for distant engines, voices, a siren. In the primeval mountain stillness he could even hear ticks from his cooling engine, but nothing remotely suggested deliverance.

Presently, standing above the little Iraqi, Guerrero ordered his hands crossed behind him. Hakim recognized his garrotte wire by its bite and was briefly thankful it was not about his neck. At further orders, Hakim stalked to Guerrero's own vehicle and lay on his face beside it as he tried to identify a succession of odd sounds.

"Had you the wit to take a four-wheel-drive path," Guerrero mused pleasantly as he worked, "you might have escaped. Since the day before yesterday my front differential housing has been full of transceiver gear." Guerrero leaned into his van, arranged the controls, flicked the engine on and stood back. "You wanted coverage, Hakim? Well, turn and stand—and smile, you are live on Soviet television."

367

The camera in Guerrero's hand looked very like a ballpoint pen but, unlike the unit left in the torture room, it did not store audiovisual data. It merely fed its impressions to the transceiver equipment packed into the van's dummy differential case. Hakim considered the possibility of a hoax until he heard the fierce whine of a multikilowatt alternator over the whirr of the engine, and then saw the great inflated meter-broad balloon, spidery metallic film covering its lower segment, that sat on Guerrero's horizontal rear cargo door. Almost certainly a dish antenna, he marveled, for a Molniya satellite in clarkeian orbit.

Hakim did not show his relief but remained docile as Guerrero shoved him down at the base of a manzanita shrub. Such equipment was fiendishly expensive and tallied well with Guerrero's claim to be a KGB infiltrator, which meant Soviet control. Hakim was limp with gratification; at least his captor represented law and order, not capricious revenge by some gang of charlies.

"There was no American blockade," Hakim accused, and drew a hissing breath as the wire tugged at his wrists.

"What does it matter to whom I turned them? It was neatly done except for the girl, and a bent mount on the differential housing," Guerrero replied, slitting Hakim's sleeves, tearing away the fifty-dollar shirt. "Rashid is entertaining the KGB—as you would be, had we known your idiotic choice of sites in advance. We opted against a motorcade, and then I was unable to transmit our location." Pride forbade him to add that he had not been furnished with sophisticated receiving gear, so that feedback to Guerrero was by relatively primitive tonal signals.

"You are a fool; they could have homed in on your unit, had you only kept it going."

"And so might you, with the noise and microwave interference." Hakim took a stinging slap. "That was for the lecture." Another slap, with an effect that shocked Hakim. "And that was for making it necessary to interrogate you here; I dare not pass that village again before dark."

Hakim swallowed hard. It was not Guerrero's brawn that bred such terror with each small successive violence. Hakim and pain were dearer friends than that. Yet he felt a rising sense of dread, and of something else; a betrayal of faith.

368

And how could this be so, when Hakim's only faith was in Hakim?

Guerrero stepped away and laid the pencil-slim camera on an outcrop of weathered basalt. "You have seen these before," he chided. "A similar device recorded your last tender sessions with the comedian. Later I will retrieve the microcorder and feed those scenes to the Molniya."

As he spoke, he took a slender case from an inside pocket. Hakim feared the hypodermic but, far worse, dreaded the fact that he was bathed in sweat. He prepared to flail his body, hoping to destroy the injector or waste its unknown contents.

Guerrero was much too battle-wise. He chose a nearby stick of the iron-hard manzanita and, with a by-your-leave gesture to the camera, suddenly deluged Hakim with blows. It became a flood, a torrent, a sea of torment, and Hakim realized that the thin shrieking was his own. He, Hakim Arif, mewling like any craven berber? He invoked his paladin's wisdom: " . . . *no longer actor, but spectator, thought not to care how my body jerked and squealed.*" Jerking and squealing, Hakim cared too much to feel the prick of the needle in his hip.

Hakim rallied with great shuddering gasps, rolled onto his back, and fought down a horror he had expected never to meet. His emissary, pain, had turned against him.

Guerrero leaned easily against a boulder, tossing and catching a drycell battery of respectable voltage. "You have long been a subject of KGB study at Lubianka in Moscow," he glowered, "and I am impressed by our psychologists. You built a legend with your vain volunteer anguish, Hakim, and never knew that the operative word was *volunteer*." His face changed to something still uglier. "You will divulge two items. The first, Fat'ah accounts. The second is your new Damascus site." He raised the stick and Hakim cowered, but the things that touched his naked flesh were merely the drycell terminals.

Merely an onslaught of unbearable suffering. Hakim needed no verbal assurance to learn that the drug made each joint in his body a locus of gruesome response to even the mildest electrical stimulus. When his spasm had passed he had fouled himself, to the syncopation of Guerrero's laughter.

"Your funds," Guerrero said, extending the drycell, and Hakim bleated out a stream of information. Squinting into the overcast as if to confirm the satellite link over thirty-six thousand kilometers away, Guerrero grinned. "Coding, I am told, is automatic, and *gracias a Dios* for small favors. But it may take some minutes to check your figures. Perhaps in Los Angeles, perhaps Berne or at Lubianka. But if you lie, you must understand that I will quickly know it. Lie to me, Hakim. Please. It justifies me."

Raging at himself, Hakim hurriedly amended crucial figures. The pain in his joints did not linger but its memory overhung him like a cliff. Through it all, degrading, enervating, the sinuous path of Guerrero's amusement followed each of Hakim's capitulations.

When Hakim fell silent, the other pressed his demand. "You are learning, I see. Now: the Damascus site, the new one. The Americans would like to know it, too, but they tend to impose order slowly. We shall be more efficient even without pentothal." Hakim squeezed his eyes tight-shut, breathing quickly, wondering if it were really possible to swallow one's tongue—and then the drycell raked his bicep and jawline.

Hakim was transfixed, skewered on a billion lances that spun in his body, growing to fiery pinwheels that consumed him, drove all else from his being. Hakim was a synonym of appalling agony. Guerrero, who had previously laughed for the necessary effect, punished his lower lip between his teeth and looked away. He wished he were back soldiering under Torrijos, hauling garrison garbage, anything but this filthy duty.

Yet appearances were everything and, "Again? I hope you resist," he lied, and had to caution Hakim to answer more slowly. Under the torture, answers came in a fitful rhythm; a phrase, shallow breathing, another strangled phrase, a sob, and still another phrase. Hakim was finished so soon that Guerrero knew embarrassment. He had hurried, and now he needed only wait. The military, he shrugged to himself, must be the same everywhere.

Waiting for his van's radio speaker to verify or deny, Guerrero viewed his keening captive with glum distaste. "The girl was more man than you," he said in innocent chauvinism. "Rashid accepted capture, but not she. Another agent took her knife. She fought. When he pointed the knife against her belly she embraced him. I never heard the sound of a knife like that before, it . . ."

"Kill me," he heard Hakim plead.

"Before I know how truly you betray Fat'ah? For shame."

"Yes, for shame. Kill me."

"Because you are so quick to surrender? Because you are not your beloved Lawrence, but only a small puppeteer? Absurd, Hakim. Think yourself lucky to know what you are, at last: a primitive little executive, a controller—even of yourself as victim. Is it so much more glorious to be a masochist pure and simple, than what you really are?"

"Enough! End it," Hakim begged.

"As you ended it for the comedian, perhaps. I waited for days to record your disposal of that man. Without those orders, my work would have been simpler." Guerrero spat in irritation.

Hakim stared. The Soviet security organ had waited only to obtain a video record of Fat'ah killing the comedian? He fathomed the KGB logic gradually, concluding that they could use the evidence to justify reprisals if it suited them.

Another thought brought a measure of calm: he still had control over Guerrero's future. Hakim exercised it. "It was not my intent to kill Charlie George," he said distinctly. *"And we left him alive."*

Guerrero said nothing for ten seconds. "The video record will show that he died," he asserted, licking lips that were suddenly dry.

"It will show his breathing tube, and also what we both knew: that he is an actor." Their eyes met in angry silence.

Guerrero insisted, "The record will vindicate me," and Hakim knew that Guerrero too was posturing for the benefit of the camera pickups. His own effectiveness contaminated by haste, Guerrero would be forced to return and kill Charlie George himself.

Guerrero approached again with the drycell and locked his gaze to Hakim's for the last time. Torture would prove nothing more, and Guerrero feared what it might seem to prove. The crowning irony was that under further torture, Hakim might further compromise his torturer. Hakim trembled in tears, but did not drop his gaze. Guerrero laid the drycell on a stone.

Hakim did not recognize the coded sequence from the van but saw Guerrero register relief at a musical signal. In any case, Hakim in his weakness had spoken the truth. Guerrero was lashing Hakim's feet with wire at the time, and resumed the job until his prisoner was positioned feet spread, knees bent, face up. Enraged at Hakim's revelation, Guerrero had chosen a vengeance option. He enjoyed that choice but realized only half of its full expense as he stalked to his van and returned.

Guerrero tore a strip of tape, placed it dangling from a branch before Hakim's eyes, and stuck a capsule to the tape within range of Hakim's mouth. "Before I knew you, Arif, I would not do what I do now. Let us say it is for Moh'med, whom I hated to sacrifice. Did you think the bomb shackles jammed themselves?" He read the surge of anger that raced across Hakim's face. "So: no, I will not end your life—but *you will*. I wonder if you are devout, and if your followers are. In any event, the capsule acts quickly. Exercise your control, Hakim; take one last life on television," he finished, whisking Hakim's van keys away. He brought the drycell near Hakim's side and the Iraqi arched away as well as he might, lashed to bushes by lengths of his garrotte wire.

The drycell went beneath Hakim's naked back, centimeters from contact. Guerrero trotted away with one backward look and Hakim strained fitfully to hold his arch. Weeping, laughing, Hakim knew that Guerrero had left his own van to permit transmission of Hakim's option. But Guerrero did not know of the toggle beneath Hakim's dash panel, which reduced the Panamanian's own options to zero.

There was no sound of starter engagement, only the slam of a door before, a moment later, a heavy concusssion wave. The ground bucked and Hakim, muscles already past endurance, fell back. He cared nothing for the rain of metal and flesh that showered around him but, deafened and half stunned by the five kilos of explosive he had buried in the van, Hakim could still exult. The drycell had been turned on its side.

Hakim spent nearly ten minutes scrabbling at debris before he managed to grasp a stone that would abrade the garrotte wire. He kept enough tension on the wire to satisfy his hunger for torment, all the while glaring at the Soviet camera. He could perhaps make use of the van equipment. He might find most of the money in the wreckage of his own van.

And after that, what? His exploitation of media finally smothered, he had known for weeks that the enemy had found an offense that could destroy him. Even before ransacking by the KGB, his coffers were too empty to maintain Fat'ah. The Soviet videotapes would produce hatred and scorn in the people who had previously financed him as easily as they bought English country estates and ten-meter limousines. Hakim would find respect nowhere—not even within himself. There was no more Fat'ah and Hakim was Fat'ah. Therefore there could be no Hakim.

The wire parted silently and Hakim rolled away. Eventually he freed his feet, then sat squatting before the drycell. He had triumphed over Guerrero, but that triumph was his last. He could not bring himself to touch the drycell.

Hakim took the capsule from the tape with gentle fingers, smashed the camera. "Forgive, *El Aurans*," he whispered, and swallowed. It was minutes before he realized that the capsule was a harmless antihistamine, Guerrero's malignant joke, and an hour before he found that the injection, as Guerrero had known from the first, was the slow killer. But by that time Hakim had stumbled, twitching, into a stream far from the silent smouldering wreckage and was past caring. The body, a source of concern in some shadowy circles, was never found.

Maurice Everett did not attend the private cremation service for Charlie George in Pasadena, on advisement of his Government Issue companion. Rhone Althouse attended, then was driven with two vehicle changes to his rendezvous with Everett. Althouse gained entry to the building by way of a conduit tunnel with its own guarded entrance. The only identification procedure was handprint analysis but its brevity was deceptive. Gas chromatography assured that the whorls were not synthetic while standard optical matching assured that they belonged to Althouse. The writer dismissed his burly aide temporarily and found the waiting room alone.

"Somehow I never thought of you as a redhead," was Everett's first remark as Althouse entered the room.

"Welcome to the puttynose factory," Althouse returned, taking the hand he was offered. "They do very good work in this clinic; you think facelifts will improve our chances?"

"I couldn't afford the tab," Everett pointed out. "For those bent on nudging it, a free society gets awfully expensive. I'll make do with a bodyguard until we've slid off the back pages of the newspapers."

373

"That shouldn't take long, now that Charlie George is dead." Althouse smiled at the consternation that fled across Everett's face. "Hey, Maury, we must think of it that way. Charlie George is *dead!* Defunct, expired, cashed in his chips, a dear departed. But my old friend Byron Krause," he said, wagging a gleeful forefinger, "is still suckin' wind."

"I keep forgetting. Look, do we really have to wait for visiting hours?" They glanced together at the wall clock. "Let's jump the gun a few minutes."

"Don't say 'gun,' " Althouse grumbled, leading the way to the elevator. Moments later they submitted to another print-check outside the private room of one Barry Shaunessy, alias Byron Krause, no longer Charlie George. The attendant who accompanied them into the room never spoke, but he did a lot of watching. Everett thought it wise to make every gesture slow and cautious.

The face behind the bandages must have tried to smile, judging from the crinkles around the mouth and eyes. "Ow, dammit," said a familiar voice. "Maury, good to see you. Listen, Rhone: the first one-liner out of you, and my silent partner here will cut you down."

"Don't say 'cut,' " Althouse muttered, then slapped his own mouth.

Everett found a chair, Althouse another. They learned from the NBN star that federal agents had found him half alive, six hours after they began to backtrack from the explosion near Lake Piru. They were aided by tire tracks, reports of a high-speed chase, and fingerprints linking the destroyed van with the avowed kidnapper of Charlie George. "They had the good sense to keep me under wraps from the locals and the media too," added the comedian. "I spent a lot of time thinking before I passed out, and decided I'd rather be a live Krause than dead with all the other charlies. Funny thing is, that sadistic little shit Arif messed me up so much, cosmetic surgery would've been necessary anyhow."

"And that finger?"

"They tell me they can make me another real one, even though it may be stiff. The ear, too. You knew they took my goddam ear? Some agent stepped on it. Boy, some of the apologies I get," he finished, shaking the bandaged head ruefully.

Everett leaned back, folding his arms. The emotional sharing of close friendship came rarely to him and he detested what must be said. "You know, Char—Byron, I can't be allowed to know who you'll be, or what you'll look like. Not for a long, long time anyhow. Just in case . . ."

One eye winked in the bandage. "That's what I didn't want to tell *you*, Maury. Like you said: not for a long time. Though I gather from the news that Fat'ah was creamed by some other bunch in Syria—and Arif is feeding flies all over the Los Padres National Forest."

"No he isn't," Everett said, and shrugged into the silence he had created. "This is for your ears only, and God knows it's little enough but my contact wouldn't tell me more. It seems the Soviets get nervous when outsiders try to panic the American public. They were helpful enough—don't ask me why—to tell us that Arif turned his whole fanatical gang under interrogation. Probably the kind of interrogation we don't like to do; anyway, he got away into the mountains afoot after that explosion. They think he was dying."

"But they don't know," Althouse whispered. "Now I will damned sure get that facelift."

"Nothing's for sure. Disinformation at all levels," Everett replied. "It's inevitable."

"We're part of it," said Byron Krause. "Letting Charlie George die is really like dying, for me. But if my new face works as it should, and if they can alter my larynx to fool a voiceprint, there may be a retreaded top banana cavorting on your set one of these days. And if not—well, I don't have to work. Then in a few days, we'll have a reunion. Without D'unspeakable Este."

"I really want that," Everett said.

"Could happen sooner than we think," Althouse put in. "I keep my fingers into surveys at ABC. It'd be easy to include a few items to find out who the public sees as enemies of terrorism. If the names change quickly I could see that the data gets published, for every charlie on earth to see it's the idea, and not the man, they're up against. If I'm wrong and the same few names keep cropping up . . ." He spread his hands in a characteristic gesture.

"You'll falsify the names," Everett suggested.

"I will like hell," said Althouse quickly. "I have *some* ethics. Nope; but I wouldn't publish the data either."

"That's a relief," said Byron Krause. "Your media theories have cost us enough bits and pieces. Oh, quit looking at me that way, Rhone, I wasn't blaming you. You were right about the solution.''

"And Maury was right about the risk," Althouse sighed.

"All the same," gloomed the commissioner, "I'll miss the Charlie George show.''

"Just remind yourself it was all a lot of hype," Rhone Althouse said, grinning at the bandaged face for understanding. "When you think of the odds this guy beat, you realize he was never a very proper Charlie."